***They're raving about* Surrender to the Dawn!**

"A story of violence and passion, love and burning desire. Annee Cartier's *Surrender To The Dawn* will keep you breathlessly turning the pages."

—Kat Martin, bestselling author of *The Devil's Game*

"Murder and revenge, love and betrayal—this book has it all! Run, don't walk, to your nearest bookstore for *Surrender To The Dawn!* You won't be disappointed!"

—Kristina Wright, *The Literary Times*

"A compelling story, we couldn't put it down until the last page was turned. A delicious blend of passion and suspense—a definite keeper!"

—Romantic Readers Group

"With this book, Annee Cartier leaps to the forefront of gifted storytellers. Her London is so real you can feel the fog. In Gwendolen Marsh and Taylor Stafford, Ms. Cartier gives the reader a hero and a heroine to care about as they make their way through Victorian England in the tangled search for a serial killer. Though both carry scars from the past, it is the love they find in each other that heals their wounds and seals the promise of the future."

—Gail Link, author of *Wolf's Embrace* and *Encantadora*

Turn the page and see why!

He was a man she should never love . . .
He was a man she couldn't resist!

Taylor opened the book and began to read aloud to her.

"On Another's Sorrow, by William Blake," he pronounced.

Maybe this was *not* such a brilliant idea, Gwen decided, as the pain of her losses ran through her anew. "No," she blurted. "I don't think I'm going to enjoy this at all, my lord."

" 'Can I see another's woe, and not be in sorrow, too? Can I see another's grief, and not seek for kind relief?' "

"I asked you to stop."

He didn't listen. But he forced her to do just that. And try as she would to fight the attraction, to gaze out the window, to close her heart against him completely, she heard him. She heard each stanza read by that mesmerizing voice, rising and falling and pressing at her emotions as if the ghost of Blake himself had appeared to Taylor Stafford and infused him with the same anguish that the piece was conceived in—the same human yearning to reach out to another human being, even in their terrible grieving times. The same longing to say *I understand you . . . I understand your pain.*

Gwen's eyes flew open. Taylor's words resounded in her head with crystal-bell clarity. His lips moved through the last lines of the poem by heart. Then, most incredible of all, his gaze met hers and shared his true message:

I understand.

For a long moment, she sat and stared—and struggled to breathe. Then she asked him the question that had haunted her since the day she met him.

"What are you doing to me?"

"I have seen your grief, Miss Marsh," he said softly. "One day soon, I hope you'll let me ease it."

SURRENDER TO THE DAWN

ANNEE CARTIER

PINNACLE BOOKS
KENSINGTON PUBLISHING CORP.

PINNACLE BOOKS are published by

Kensington Publishing Corp.
850 Third Avenue
New York, NY 10022

First Pinnacle Books Printing: March, 1996

Printed in the United States of America
10 9 8 7 6 5 4 3 2 1

With thanks to a wonderful lady
who not only understands my stories,
but believes in them.
Rob Cohen, you truly are
the agent from heaven.

Special gratitude to
Laura Cifelli
for crying in all the right places.

You are both the best.

One

February 1891
The Saint Jerome's Home for Needing Orphans
London

"Miss Gwen? Miss Gwen, I'm sorry fer bargin' in so early, but—"

"Nonsense, Tessie," Gwendolen Marsh assured, turning from the rain-splattered window three floors over the empty East End street. "I'm awake. Come in."

She forced a smile to her lips for the dark-haired girl still fidgeting in the doorway—thankful the action also helped whittle the tearful lump swelling her throat.

One would think she'd learned by now, she reproached herself. As many times as she insisted on extending her volunteer's duties at Saint Jerome's for a fevered or needing child, so numbered the dawns she'd had to endure as this. Grey. Silent. Solitary. Nothing for company but her breath on that window's glass, and the fairyland of a life she envisioned in that haze again.

Yes, that world had once been hers. She had not just dreamt it, no matter how far away the fairyland seemed now. No matter how distant the ballroom where she'd met a dashing young charmer named Lloyd Alexander Waterston; no matter how fleeting the sweeping waltzes, balmy summer walks, and romantic hand squeezes of his courtship. No matter how much a stranger the laughing, flirting Gwen of those days seemed now.

She wiped the mist away, swallowing against the flood of pain, then left the window behind. "What is it, Tessie?" she asked. "What do you need?"

"Well, I—well, there—" The girl mercilessly twisted her index fingers together. "There be *visitors* here for ye, Miss Gwen."

"Visitors?" Gwen glanced at the clock on the wall. The early hour of seven-thirty didn't amaze her as much as the fact that she had guests. No one had formally called on her in more than two years. Not since the "incident," as Aunt Margaret tersely phrased it. Not at the townhouse Gwen shared with the somber woman on fashionably proper Devonshire Street, much less here at Saint Jerome's, where, Aunt Maggie further humphed, Gwen persisted in "consorting with who-knows-what-kind of rabble in the name of Christian charity."

"Aye, miss," Tess blurted on. "Visitors. Two gentlemen." A shy smile flitted across the girl's lips. "And one rather comely, if I may say so. He smiled at me, and bowed. Like I was a lady, I was. He bowed like this."

During Tess's demonstration, curious pricks alternated with tense knives down Gwen's arms and legs. Could it actually be . . . was it *Lloyd?*

Her right hand flew to her left, straightening the meticulously shined engagement ring there. For the first time in months, the emeralds looked to twinkle, not taunt. Gwen felt her lips curl upward of their own volition.

Her smile dropped at the same moment as her hope.

Two men. She suddenly realized Tess had said two. That eliminated Lloyd, leaving behind only one terrible conclusion.

Helson. It had to be Inspector Helson.

Her heart climbed to her throat again. Why couldn't he leave her alone? She'd told him—and what seemed half the Metropolitan Police—everything she could recall before her world had been changed in those black, blank hours on that cold, foggy night. And now she didn't want to remember any more. She wanted to forget the night of January 5, 1889, had happened at all.

In short, her heart retorted, *you want the impossible.*

A touch beneath the curls at her right temple served testimony to that fact well enough. Yes, she discovered with the usual jolt of dismay, it was still there. Almost as thin as the strands of hair hiding it, just over three inches long and hardly discernible to an eye not looking for it, but there. The reminder. The scar, and the event it represented, that might as well have been the spots of leprosy to the society she'd once called friends.

Gwen forced her hand to her side. She spread her fingers into the skirt of her burgundy house gown instead. Pausing a moment to check on Gertie, her now peacefully resting patient, she followed Tess down the main stairwell, commanding each step to restore her composure in place of the angered frustration. The bitterness only tangled her like iron shackles when trying to escape the torture of Inspector Helson's calls.

She stopped at the door to the parlor, fidgeting again in an effort to hoard a moment's more time. "Dear Lord," she murmured, running a nervous finger along her lace collar, "Dear Lord, help me through this ordeal . . . again."

She took one more deep breath and pushed the door open.

She almost laughed aloud when she saw the real ogre she'd been dreading to confront. With his top hat cocked a jaunty angle over his sandy hair and a mustard-yellow suit tailored well to his lean frame, Bryan Reginald Corstairs presented as opposite a picture from stuffy Inspector Helson as anyone on the earth could. His light-blue eyes sparkled when he saw Gwen; a lopsided grin formed beneath his mustache.

How many times had she turned to that smile for support and reassurance in the last two hellish years? Gwen had long since lost count. Yes, despite Aunt Maggie's scandalized declarations that "a reputable young lady is not just *friends* with a man," Bryan Corstairs was the best of the few remaining friends she had.

"Ah!" he exclaimed with a dramatic sweep of his hand. "What light through yonder doorway breaks? 'Tis certainly the east, and sweet Gwen the—"

"Bryan, you incorrigible fox." She approached him with a finger wagging in admonishment. "Did you know you nearly had me slinking down the drainpipe like a housebreaker? I feared I was doomed to Helson and more of his horrid quest . . ."

Her statement fizzled away as a form shifted just beyond the realm of the room's single gas light. The form emitted a cough, low and controlled. Gwen leaned and peered into the shadows.

She gasped and jerked a step back.

He was still dressed in his heavy black rain cloak, one unbuttoned flap pushed behind the crook of his right elbow. His other arm rested on the mantel, almost blocking the shelf completely. An errant swag of his dark-brown hair brushed at his shoulder. He studied her, his features still just a teasing inch from the light. Silently, steadily, he continued to appraise her.

Just as she stood in numb shock at the sight of him.

Her arms succumbed to the impact first. Her hands plummeted into the folds of her skirt. She felt the smile drain from her lips. The air whooshed from her lungs as she struggled to speak.

"Oh," she finally blurted. "Oh, Lloyd."

The relief, the utter victory of comprehending that he stood here waiting for her, filled her like the glory of a bower of roses on May Day. For a long moment, she didn't move. Then she laughed. She laughed long and freely and joyously.

"I knew it," she cried. "I knew you'd be back. I knew you were bigger than those ridiculous rumors, darling . . . I knew you wouldn't listen or care! We're going to show them, Lloyd; we're going to show them all what they can do with their gossip and their lies—"

"Gwen."

Bryan's interruption echoed his soft but insistent touch at her shoulder. And as distant thunder rumbled outside, she felt the May Day roses sagging.

"Gwen," Bryan continued, "I believe there are some introductions to be made."

"Introductions?"

Long booted legs stepped from the shadows.

Gwen looked up.

The peaceful lake-blue of Lloyd's eyes didn't meet her scrutiny. Instead, an explosion of color seared her: a riot of gold, green, copper, and even touches of black bordered by unblinking dark lashes. Where Lloyd's features made a noble, aquiline profile, this stranger's nose jutted out a prominent edge—too prominent. His jaw rose so rugged above a neck three shades too brown, even beneath a cravat the color of creamed coffee, Gwen wondered which dock Bryan yanked him from.

Indeed, the only trait Lloyd shared with this person was the thick dark-brown hair which had fooled her in the first place. Now Gwen perceived the differences. Her betrothed never missed his twice-monthly appointments with the barber; the shoulder-length waves before her now only deepened the conception that she confronted a half-blooded Celtic warrior . . . perhaps a full-blooded one.

With horror, she realized she still stared at the stranger just as he examined her: curiously, intently—brazenly. "Wh-what's going on?" she managed, ripping her gaze away and fixing it to the safety of the wall.

Even then, his scrutiny made her abnormally conscious of her less-than-tidy appearance. High heavens, one might even think the reprobate *liked* the way she looked.

Nonsense. How in the world could she think he'd ogle anything other than what everyone else gawked at? How could she think the long-haired infidel interested in anything but *that?*

She should be used to such scrutiny by now. She *was* used

to it, she corrected, even if she no longer chose to endure the perverted distraction she provided people at parties, the probing glances trying to violate the coiffed curls at her temple, struggling to distinguish the scar hidden in her natural hairline. Even if she no longer battled to ignore the pointed fingers, the arched eyebrows, the whispers and the gasps—some discreet, many not so discreet—all brandished as if on January 5, 1889, she'd been transformed from a human being into a circus sideshow freak.

"Gwen," Bryan interjected. "It's all right. I'm sorry we startled you. We were on our way back through this neighborhood, and I remembered your aunt telling me you were here tending one of the girls for the week—"

"On your way through?" She reclaimed her voice to aid her perturbed thoughts. "At seven in the morning? Just blocks from the most popular brothel in the East End?"

At *that,* the stranger's eyebrows shot up. Bryan cracked a knowing smile. "What did I tell you?" he said to the warrior. "Now do you think she's strong enough to do it?"

"Do what?" Gwen demanded—more than aware of her suspicious tone.

An uncomfortable pause stretched as her only reply. Gwen coiled her arms across her chest and threw a glare from the stranger to her friend.

"Bryan, if neither you nor your stone-faced lackey wishes to let me in on your dandy little secret, I've got a sick little girl upstairs who cares about what I do with my time." She set her sights toward the door, following quickly with her feet. "Good day, gentlemen."

Only a step more separated her from a clean escape when a voice stopped her. A gripping, yet caressing voice; power gleaned from conviction, not volume.

"The Lancer attacked his eighth victim last night, Miss Marsh."

Her knuckles went white around the doorknob. "God have mercy. Is she . . . ?"

"No. She didn't survive."

"Dear God."

She slowly turned around—to where the tall stranger's gaze awaited her. "Who?" she heard herself rasp.

"Lady Veronica Spencer, of Middleham," Bryan supplied. "I believe you knew her, Gwen."

She stumbled, watching her hand grasp for something—anything—to steady herself against the flood of pain. One of the room's spindly chairs reeled into view. She fell onto the seat with a shudder.

"We played together as girls," she murmured. Her voice echoed with memories long neglected. "We'd take turns pretending to be Queen Victoria. There was a medieval bench in her mother's garden. It was our throne. Oh, Nicky—" Her throat caught on the nickname. "Dear Nicky."

Out in the front hall, Saint Jerome's prized table clock called out eight o'clock. The last knell faded away into a heavier deluge of violent rain.

"Eight bells" came the stranger's voice again, a muted sound when set against the torrent outside. Gwen looked up and concluded the same softness didn't hold true for his profile. His eyes drove a hard glare out the rain-soaked window; his jawline grew even more harsh as he clenched and unclenched the muscles beneath. "Eight bells for eight victims. Eight women defiled by that damn bastard."

If Aunt Maggie were here, Gwen would have been dragged from the room at the first syllable of such language. But in this moment, she found herself silently thanking the man for the words she'd yearned to scream herself so many times in the last two years.

She supposed he sensed that, for he turned back then, straight eyebrows lowering in a more profound study of her. Every ounce of reason told Gwen to look away, to escape that disturbing, disconcerting, even crude scrutiny from across the room . . . She couldn't. In his gaze, she saw something she never thought she'd find in another human's eyes.

A pain as deep as her own.

"Eight victims, Miss Marsh," he repeated quietly. "And you, his third, still the only one of them who survived."

She didn't know how to respond to that. She gripped her hands together in her lap and watched the warrior stalk across the rug, shined leather boots reflecting the wan lamplight with each measured, steady step.

As she dreaded, he stopped beside her chair. Gwen closed her eyes, alarmed by the effect his nearness had upon her: the shivers from the scratch of his coal-colored trousers against her arm, the unfamiliar scent of spiced men's cologne mixed with early-morning rain.

But worst of all, dear Lord, the feeling, backed by not the smallest sense of logic, that despite his size and strength and strangeness, she . . . she trusted this man.

She knew she was in trouble. And she had no will to struggle away from the danger. When he took her right hand, pulling her to her feet, she went without thought or protest. His fingers surrounded hers, warm and large. Her left hand, and Lloyd's engagement ring, felt cold and far away.

"Miss Marsh," he told her then, "my name is Taylor Stafford. My wife, Constance, was victim number four."

Two

Taylor watched Gwendolen Marsh pull her hand from his and bolt away in a single movement.

He didn't try to stop her. He only looked on as she retreated to the window and pressed one shaking hand against the rain-soaked glass.

Damn, he mouthed to the old rug beneath his feet. Despite Bryan's contentions that Miss Marsh was "different, gloriously different," Taylor had prepared himself for this reaction when he told her who he was.

But his forethought didn't make her distress any easier to accept. Didn't make it a fraction less disturbing to meet the lush green world of her eyes, only to watch that life smothered by fear. Didn't loosen the pressure in his chest, increasing by the minute, as he observed her white-knuckled fingers coiling back tendrils of hair that glinted a gold-kissed copper with the movement.

Didn't relieve the disturbing, disconcerting vibrations working up his body from God knew where . . .

No. Taye sprang forward, angrily brushing at his trousers as if he could cast off the bewildering sensation as rapidly as dust specks . . . as if one stroke could sweep back the gut-wrenching memories.

His thoughts needed to be here, damn it. Here, directed on the now and why of this visit. Directed on his purpose.

Yes, the purpose. The familiar coldness returned to his body with the silent chant; Taylor inhaled a breath of welcome to the accompanying tension in his bones, the bitterness he now called friend. The purpose was all that mattered now.

I haven't forgotten, Connie, the deepest reaches of his soul proclaimed. *I'll never forget. I'll never rest, my lady, until I've found that murdering monster and avenged the spilling of your blood with the end of his worthless life.*

And right now, no matter how fragile she looked in the misty grey light filtering through the thin curtains, Miss Gwendolen Marsh personified his only hope of accomplishing that.

"I—I know who you are, Lord Stafford," the subject of his perusal managed. Then in a tone suggesting she already knew the answer, "Wh-what do you want with me?"

"Gwen." Bryan threw Taylor a swift but reassuring glance as he stepped toward the window. "Just hear him through," he murmured to her. "Just hear him through—for me."

With the good-natured chuckle Bryan couched the words in, some barrier inside her clearly crumbled. A brick-colored warmth suffused her pale cheeks. The hint of an awkward smile played havoc with her composure; Taylor found himself sympathizing with her discomfort. It appeared that, just like him, Gwendolen Marsh didn't smile much anymore.

He snapped his gaze away. What the hell was he doing, gaping at her like some untried whelp?

All right, so she was a handsome woman. The memory came easily of the London season almost three years ago when those thick-lashed eyes, angled cheekbones, and full lips turned more than a few heads among the elite's prime bachelor stock, much to the chagrin of London's remaining debutantes and their mothers. *"Only a shipping merchant's daughter, and he's dead at that!"* he recalled the shocked whispers around him and Constance on glittering dance floors. *"She wouldn't be here but for the kindness of her dear aunt, you know." "Look at them fawning all over her. Oh my, what is society coming to?"*

But something else shined about Miss Gwendolen Marsh, his memory clarified. Something that kept London's pups filling her dance card again and again. Something more than good cheekbones and captivating eyes.

Taylor, too, had noticed the ethereal draw of the lovely newcomer—but only briefly. He'd thrown a few silent "bravos" to Margaret Marsh's niece as the mob gathered around her.

Then thoughts of Gwendolen Marsh had turned to ashes from the fire consuming his blood and bones. Amazing, how vividly his soul re-created the hot satisfaction of parting that crowd with unswerving authority, the fierce pride when the onlookers' glares yielded at the first look Constance gave him . . . yes, *yes,* that magic midnight-blue gaze he thanked God their three-year-old son had inherited. Then came the vision of those sensual lips raising so gracefully to his cheek, branding him *husband,* branding her *his* . . .

Connie. Ah God, Connie.

He banished the grief with a force that shook every muscle in his body. Even then Taylor fought the heat behind his eyes as he looked again to the pair at the window.

"Just hear his story, Gwen," Bryan encouraged once more. "*I* believe you can do it. Don't you know that's all that matters?"

At that, the threatening smile broke past her lips. Gwendolen Marsh shook her head with a rueful chuckle. "Bryan Corstairs, what am I to do with you?"

"Give my friend Taylor ten little minutes?" he prodded. "Let him tell you what he's doing—all the work he's put into finding that beast—and how you can help him?"

She didn't answer. At least not in words. Taylor sensed how hard she wanted to nod yes to Bryan's challenge, to overcome some invisible, looming wall. But a ragged sigh drowned her smile; furrows of pain marred her forehead. "Bryan, I want to. But . . . but I can't." She shook her head. "Don't you see? I . . . *can't.*"

Taylor's heavy exhalation trailed Bryan's by seconds. He had known to expect this, he censured himself. *He had known.*

Yet hiding his clenched hands in his coat pockets didn't

cloak the anger and frustration from his spirit. She was his only remaining chance. His last spark of light on the black path toward finding the bastard who had ripped his life apart.

She had to help them. She had no choice.

He wasn't going to give her one.

He reached her side again in two steps, planted his feet to the carpet with the full intention of appearing a captain at the helm of his battleship. "You mean you can't," he snarled, "or you won't?"

Her eyes flew up and locked with his. The smoke Taylor previously witnessed in those forest-green depths now parted for the fire beneath, blazing at him, through him.

"How dare you," she accused. "You have no idea—*no idea* what it's like to wake up with bruises on your body and people staring at your face, and no memory of how you got there or why you're that way. No memory except the dreams you've lost and the friends who have become strangers!"

Her lips compressed. She released them on a trembling breath. "With all respect, my lord," she rasped, "it's hell."

"I know."

"Really, now?" Her eyebrows imitated her sardonic lilt.

"You'd be surprised."

"I don't want to be surprised, Lord Stafford! Now if you'll just leave—"

"Come come, you two!" Bryan dotted the admonishment with a wry version of his notorious chuckle. He caught her lace-trimmed elbow in one hand, Taylor's rigid shoulder in the other. "Let's discuss this like the reasonable people we are."

"No," Taye interrupted, pressing the back of his hand across his friend's chest. "It's all right, Bryan. Don't you see? The lady is correct. Compared to Miss Marsh, I'm a green-eared novice at this sort of thing. My life's only been destroyed for eighteen months, not the two years of her seasoned experience." He arched one brow. "Perhaps, madam, you'd be so kind as to take tea with me sometime and enlighten me of your vast knowledge on this great suffering."

"That won't be necessary." She jerked away from him. "I am sorry, my lord, for your loss and your grief. I realize how desperately you long to see the Lancer found and punished. But if you think I can help you any further than I have the police, then I'm afraid I can offer you no hope."

Bryan leaned forward again, his face and voice insistent. "Gwen—"

"You are my *only* hope," Taylor cut him off.

He gave her no quarter with the ultimatum, buttressing the words by tightening and squaring his shoulders.

She gave him no quarter with her response.

"Don't," Gwendolen Marsh threatened, chin shaking, but posture clinging to a stance as uncompromising as his. "Don't you dare do this to me."

"Gwen, he's not trying to do anything—"

"Stop it, Bryan. Please stop it!"

"I'm telling you the truth!"

For a long moment, only the steady cadence of the rain echoed his outburst.

Then, with just a blink of hesitation, she swung that dark-emerald stare from Bryan to him.

Taye's equilibrium keeled to a precarious angle. There was something different about Gwendolen Marsh's scrutiny now. Unnervingly different. Light flickered in the virescent depths, but not the angry fire she seared him with earlier. This was a . . . a force, like beacons set in the front windows to tell a man he was home on a cold winter's night.

Home. His senses listed harder. Bloody hell, where did a word like that come from? And why did his gut wrench this way at the mention? And *why* did he let that obstinate, impertinent green gaze expose every corner of his soul like God's own judgment?

He didn't need this. He didn't need *her.*

"I need you, Miss Marsh." *Damn damn bloody damn.* "I haven't come here to torment you. I've come because I'm at the end of my rope, because there's no more leads to follow and—I need you."

Unbelievably, her expression faltered. She swallowed and averted her gaze, appearing as fragile as the lace at her throat again.

"But why?" she asked. "Why me? Why now? You said it yourself, it's been over two years since my—" she expelled a harsh breath, "my incident. Certainly, my lord, the police have collected enough evidence by now to—"

"The police are a gaggle of fools."

Another uncertain silence downpoured between them. He knew he should apologize for the brusque rebuttal, but Taye locked both sides of his jaw against expressing any more of his more graphic opinions regarding this city's "esteemed" law enforcement.

"The police have nothing," he stated in a dead voice instead. "Nothing."

"It's true." Bryan inclined against the back of the room's aging sofa as he nodded agreement. "With each murder, the Lancer has made his path harder and harder to follow." Her friend gave an ironic laugh. "The *Chronicle* even called him a genius."

"Then the *Chronicle* is written by monsters," she retaliated.

"Yes, it is," Taylor agreed, and meant it. As he hoped, her features rumpled again—maybe as evidence she'd started to believe him.

He dared a step forward. Another. "But," he said softly, taking one of her hands into his own, "they're only going to get worse. Their exaggeration will stretch ever outward. The lies will get bigger." He pressed closer, making her feel his conviction through his grip. "And the Lancer will keep getting away with murder."

She tried to pull away. He pressed tighter on the long fingers between his, forcing himself to ignore her answering trembles. "You can help the insanity come to a stop, Miss Marsh. You can help me; you can help us all. You can remember again.

There are ways. The science of hypnotism has taken great strides in the last fifteen years. The tiniest detail you recall may be the deciding clue—"

"No," she protested. "I—I don't remember any more—"

"Yes, you do. You *can.*"

"I can't!" She finally wrenched free and stumbled back, trying to steady herself with shaking arms. "My Lord Stafford, I appreciate your dilemma, but I cannot help you with it. Not me. Not now!"

Taylor sucked in a leaden breath. "And that's it?"

"I said I'm sorry."

"You won't even try?"

Her shoulders rose with a labored breath. "As I already told you, I *have* tried. I tried for hours. For days. I tried until I thought my head would burst—" Her voice cracked and her eyes closed. "I have done my best."

"The hell you have."

He didn't know where the accusing growl came from, but the words rushed out as uncontrollably as his arm did, reaching and seizing her shoulder in a merciless grip. "And you have no right to say you have *tried,* madam, until the Lancer's dead body is incinerated to ashes."

She opened her eyes; wheeled an indignant glare at him. "Is that so?"

"Yes, it is."

"And I suppose you'd like me to hunt down Jack the Ripper while I'm at it? Better yet, fetch up a newspaper; there must be a few other unsolved crimes in this city you can blame me for!"

"This is different and you know it." Taylor leaned closer over her. "This maniac is not the Ripper, Miss Marsh. He's worse. The streets of Whitechapel were enough for the Ripper; the Lancer has struck in separate locations each time, all over the city." He tried to infuse some calmness into his next words, but to no avail. "The Ripper was satisfied with prostitutes, but the Lancer has fixed upon the ladies of England's finest families. Your *peers,* Miss Marsh. Your friends. Your family."

She blinked just once before she started to laugh at him.

Taye dropped his hand, needles of rage stabbing him, until he noticed the thick sheen of moisture in her eyes, the shaking breaths she sucked in. The thin veneer of laughter attempting to hide tears.

"My family," she repeated shakily. "And my friends, you say? Oh, yes, my lord, tell me about the duty I have to my *friends.* Do you mean the companions who never come calling? Do you mean the loved ones who just look the other way when I approach on the sidewalk, or cross the road completely to avoid me? Or," her tone rasped harsher as she lifted her hand and clawed away the curls at one side of her face, "do you mean all the friends who don't want to be associated with *this?"*

The scar was as thin as a razor's blade—the Lancer's tool of preference for his victims' faces—but extended at least three inches through the smooth peach skin of her temple and high cheek. Without thinking, Taylor reached out. He felt a surge of outrage; his senses burned with the ridiculous notion that his touch could make her skin all right again . . . make *her* whole again.

But Gwendolen Marsh dodged him with fearful speed. "No." She dropped her hand. Her copper curls resumed their function as camouflage.

"I'm sorry," he murmured. "I'm . . . sorry."

Her lips tightened with frustration. She had heard those words at least a hundred times. "I didn't show it to you for your pity."

Taylor compressed his lips and stepped close to her again, closer than he'd dared this entire confrontation.

"The apology was because I frightened you," he clarified quietly. "I'll save my pity for when the Lancer strikes again and you have to go to sleep every night, wondering if you might have helped stop him."

Her stare flicked back up to him. Taylor looked down at her. His nostrils caught the tender child scents of talcum powder and cake soap . . . funny, with her deep green eyes and riot of copper-gold hair, she looked more like a tigress defending her cubs.

"I cannot help you, Lord Stafford." She stepped back, then returned to her haven by the window. "I'm sorry. I am. I—I just want to get on with my life now. I want everything to be right again. I just want to be *normal* again."

"Gwen . . ." Bryan's voice came from behind Taylor, imploring. "You're not really considering this. Think of all the good you can do!"

Taye grasped his friend's shoulder. "No, Bryan," he ordered. "No more. Let's go."

They gathered up their hats and scarves in silence. Taylor waited while Bryan bid Miss Marsh a quiet good-bye, then turned toward the door when his friend did the same.

He suddenly stopped. Bryan threw him a puzzled glare, but even if Taylor wanted to explain himself, he couldn't. Instead, he yanked off his right glove, dug his hand into his corresponding coat pocket, and pulled out the solitary calling card he kept safely embedded there.

He walked over to Gwendolen Marsh, lifted her hand one last time, and curled her fingers around the worn edges of the card.

"I apologize for the condition it's in," he said awkwardly. "I've considered the thing a lucky piece over the years." He coughed, a nervous, pause-filling cough. "But it's my last, and I would indeed consider the card lucky if you've the need to use it—any day, any time."

Gwen responded with a silent nod—the only reaction she could summon.

She didn't know how, but she sensed Taylor Stafford nodded, too.

Without another word, he turned and followed Bryan out the door.

She watched from the window as the two men dashed through the downpour and into a coach of understated elegance. Though the weather and their similar cloaks and top hats should have made both figures anonymous, it took frighteningly little effort to discern which was Lord Stafford: his determined stride across the sidewalk, his strong, gloved hand gripping the top of the coach door as Bryan climbed in first, his easy power used as he pulled himself in after.

Then he closed the door, and the shiny blue-black carriage rolled away through the curtain of rain.

Gwen didn't know how long she stood there blinking, feeling as if she'd shifted back to reality from a strange and mystical dream . . . but when she did, a single phrase beat mercilessly at her brain:

What had Taylor, Earl of Stafford done to her?

The only answer she could find was that he'd made her angry. Furious, in fact. At Bryan, for bringing the man here in the first place. At herself, for allowing the meeting to continue. Worse yet, for permitting that half-savage to keep touching her the way he had . . . and not just along her hands and shoulders, which were still tingling at this moment in an unnerving manner. No, he'd reached down and stirred her spirit . . . churned up her frustration and fury, brought her to words and actions she thought she'd long since suppressed forever.

It had been terrifying.

It had been exhilarating.

Slowly, she backed away from the window, then sank to the sofa in front of the cold fireplace. She looked down to her hand, still folded around the crumpled edges of Taylor Stafford's calling card. His last, he'd said. His lucky piece.

When she unraveled her hand, she discovered the reason why. Beneath the printed letters of the elegant Belgravia address and his name—including all three of his middle names and myriads of official appointments—a hand-etched cupid's arrow directed the holder to the back of the card.

Gwen turned the paper over. There, written in a fluid, yet delicate hand, read the message:

Hello, you crazy fool . . . I love you.
Connie.

Then the letters blurred before her eyes . . . drowned by her tears of loneliness and sorrow.

Three

"By all the glorious gates in heaven! A lord! A true-to-life lord of the realm, here! Today!"

"Now, Hannah—" Gwen tried to calm the cherub-faced woman waltzing across the kitchen. Of course, the task was impossible when it came to Hannah Aberdeen, the tireless force who kept the inhabitants and grounds of Saint Jerome's Orphanage clean, safe, and comfortable. As Hannah executed a pirouette before the bread board, Gwen smiled—her first smile since she'd left the parlor this morning—and suddenly she was grateful to Hannah for her antics.

"And so handsome he was." Tess nearly sang the remark over a pile of onions on the chopping board. "Treated me like a bleedin' princess, he did."

"Treated everyone like a princess!" Hannah returned. "Did ye hear him thank me as they left? Imagine that, *he* thanked *me.* And the way he referred to Gwennie as 'Miss Marsh' and 'Madam this and such.' Now that's how a nabob's supposed to act!"

"Wait a minute." Gwen's smile dropped as quickly as it had formed. She set her ladle down on the sideboard with such a decided clang, the gas flame beneath the soup pot jumped. "The way he called me . . ." she murmured with growing realization. "Hannah, you were eavesdropping again!"

The woman, at least ten years Gwen's elder, looked like a four-year-old caught with her thumb in the Christmas pudding. "Now, Gwennie—"

"Ohhh, no. Don't 'Now, Gwennie' me. You once said you wanted to learn how a real lady behaves, Hannah, and I told you: a lady does not press her ear to the wall to eavesdrop on other people's conversations."

"But he was a *lord.*"

"I don't care if he was the King of Spain." More chastisements occurred to her, but Hannah could charm the whole of Parliament simply by rolling her large brown eyes and twisting her smudged apron just like that. The remainder of Gwen's lecture withered unspoken. She turned and leaned over the big black pot again.

"He was right, ye know," Hannah's knowing tone floated into the broth- and bread-fragranced silence.

"Who?"

"Ye know bloody well who."

"I know *very* well who," Gwen corrected.

"Don't skirt the issue, missy. Ye know *very* well who, and ye know he was *very* well right."

Gwen didn't respond for a long moment. As she watched the bubbling mixture swirling about the ladle, she sucked in a breath, then slowly released it. "I already told you, my meeting with Lord Stafford was a private matter."

"Rat's dung."

"Hannah!"

"I said rat's dung, Gwendolen Victoria Marsh, and I mean *rat's dung.* Lord have mercy, you could drive me to bring a whippin' switch into this home for the first time. When are ye going to wake up, Gwennie? When are ye going to pull that befuddled brain o' yers out of the sand and join us here in the modern world?"

Gwen snapped her head up. "I have no idea what you're talking about."

"Oh aye ye do, missy. Ye have every idea what I'm talkin' about. Ye had every idea when Lord Earl King o' Spain himself was here today, and ye sent him away."

Hannah's face displayed an expression of pursed concern.

She rounded the stove and stepped to Gwen's side. "Ye sent him away because he frightened ye, didn't he? Because he spoke right to your soul . . ."

"I don't want to talk about it."

"Ye have to talk about it." Hannah's hand at her shoulder squeezed gently. "Gwendolen, a horrid thing happened to ye two years ago. But ye survived, darlin', and now ye've got to ask the good Lord why. Maybe, just maybe, it was so ye could help Lord Stafford find the Lancer and send that monster to the hell he deserves."

"And maybe the good Lord has shown me enough *whys* for the whole nightmare already." She pivoted to accept a handful of onion bits from Tess. "Maybe I just want to get on with my life."

"Yer life?" Hannah stormed back to the bread board. "Yer *life,* is that what ye be callin' it? A betrothed who hasn't the decency to act betrothed, a social register consistin' of one piano recital and a trip to the seashore in the last six months, and God only knows how many days ye've spent under *this* roof."

"I happen to like being under this roof."

"Ye like *hidin'* under this roof." A finger shot out from Hannah's plump fist, which was embedded in the slightly plumper mound of dough. "Don't ye be raisin' those eyebrows at me, either. I'm ringin' yer bell loud and clear this time, and ye know it." Hannah snorted. "Look at ye, Gwennie. Ye're young and ye're beautiful. Ye should be plannin' yer ball gowns fer the next gala season, not hunchin' over vegetable soup."

"I happen to like vegetable soup."

"Ooohhh!"

The older woman threw up her hands. Gwen and Tess laughed as flying flour bits transformed their kitchen into an impromptu winter wonderland.

Down the hall, a firm knock sounded at the front door.

Hannah's smile receded into a snort of frustration. "Gotta be Reggie," she mumbled, nodding as the hall clock knelled three o'clock in seeming agreement. "Bless that husband of mine, he's prompt, but stupid. How many times have I told him we lock the front door now?" The woman bustled down the hallway with a voluminous, "Reggie! Reggie, ye big lug, what did I tell ye 'bout the doors, ay?"

As Hannah's form and voice faded away, Gwen exchanged a mischievous smile with Tess, swiping at a blotch of flour on the girl's slender nose.

"Well, Lady Tess," she said, "I believe your duties to the kingdom are completed for today. Could you check on Gertie for me once more on your way to your silver tower chamber? I want to be certain we've broken her fever for good."

Tess giggled and nodded, but the next moment the girl's smile faded. Her dark eyes reflected puzzlement as she looked across the kitchen, behind Gwen.

Gwen turned to observe Reggie Aberdeen doing his best to shake himself dry and haul in a cumbersome box at the same time.

"Hey, Gwennie," he boomed through his thick black mustache. "Well, here it is. London Orphan Asylum's donation fer the week. Regular bounty o' good, as usual." He cracked a sardonic sneer. "Let's see here . . . we got Seeger's Special Hair Dye . . . Chinese tea leaves . . . and my pick o' the week, Berman's mint-scented shavin' cream! Hey, Tessie, I know you and the other girls can really use this . . ."

But as Tess laughed and Reggie continued his commentary on the worthless goods, Gwen moved to the door and peeked into the hall. One disconcerting question knocked at her mind: if Reggie had just trundled in the back door, who was at the front?

She deemed the nervous speculation justified when Hannah swished into view a moment later, a dancing gleam in her eyes. "Well, well. Ye're certainly the popular bird today, missy."

"Another caller?" Gwen's eyes widened when Hannah nodded. "Inspector Helson?" Her eyebrows jumped in surprise at her friend's denial. *"Who?"*

Hannah shrugged in feigned innocence. "All I got to say is I could get used to these tall, handsome men hangin' around my parlor all day."

"I heard that," came Reggie's voice from behind.

"So what if ye did?" Hannah barked. But she swirled back to Gwen with the grin of a sixteen-year-old encouraging her best friend at their first ball. "Ye look splendid, Gwennie."

"I've been stirring vegetable soup for the last hour."

"Ye look *wonderful.* Go!"

Gwen shot Hannah an agitated parting glance before taking a deep breath and heading toward the parlor. The storm had gone into temporary hibernation a few hours ago; without a backdrop of deafening thunder, her footsteps sounded disturbingly loud on the faded but clean wood floor.

The clouds might be resting, she thought, but the premonition the dark sky gave her this morning still hovered over the entire day.

Then again, perhaps she'd just stepped into the role of heroine in a Jules Verne time travel fantasy, and it was seven-thirty this morning all over again.

He stood before the fireplace once more, still in that damp black rain cloak, still poised just beyond the lamp's glow. But, Gwen noticed almost immediately, he didn't fill the room the way he had this morning. His shoulders didn't rival the mantel for broadness. His stance now appeared more a cat's than a lion's.

A surge of pride filled her as she looked upon him a moment more. Let Hannah tell her she didn't see things for what they truly were. Gwen knew exactly what she saw before her—and exactly how to handle the insolent intruder.

As her heels clacked an angry entrance, she set her chin high and her head proud. "Lord Stafford, I am not going to dally with the formalities this time around," she began. "I'm simply going to ask you to leave this instant. I was tolerant of your impertinence this morning, but now—"

"Hello, Gwendolen."

A gasp robbed the remaining words from her throat. Gwen's hand flew to her chest.

She stared, speechless, into the fathomless lake-blue eyes of the man she loved. His perfect features were framed by perfectly clipped, perfectly coiffed dark-brown hair.

"Lloyd."

She sounded inane—and she felt even more witless. How could she confuse her Lloyd with that raw-edged Stafford twice in the same day? Worse, now that the right man was here, where had her first confident joy of the morning fled? Gwen barely believed her legs capable of supporting her, much less of walking to him to offer a welcome.

So she simply stood there and gaped, almost certain she was dreaming an incredibly realistic dream again, as she had so often.

"You look well," he said.

"You're really here."

An answering smile toyed at the edges of his lips. But as if he knew the display would bring imperfect lines to his face, he coughed his way back to composure.

"I've startled you," he said. "I apologize for my unannounced visit. You were expecting someone else . . . Lord Stafford, perhaps? Indulging one of your East End character's visions of grandeur?"

Had she not been through such a maelstrom of emotions already today, she'd have laughed at her fiancé's misconception. Yes, one of her demure feminine laughs that used to bring an approving slant to Lloyd's lips. Instead, Gwen dropped her head beneath a sudden and frightening suffusion of heat.

"He's nobody who matters," she replied hastily. "What matters is that you're here."

At that, she forced strength into her legs. She walked across the room to him. "Oh Lloyd—Lloyd, I know you had to take that trip north, then things got so hectic at the bank, but darling, I've missed you so."

But as she took the last step to rush into his arms, Lloyd grasped her elbows, holding her at a distance. Gwen stared at his manicured fingers as they pressed against her soup-splattered sleeves. Finally, she looked up into his face. He kept every feature carefully shuttered against her.

"What?" she asked. "What is it? Something at the bank? Or your parents? Has your mother taken another fall?"

"No!" He removed one of his hands to rake back his hair. "No, it's—it's nothing like that. But you're right; I've come to speak with you about something. Something specific."

At last, Lloyd met her gaze directly. The connection lasted for all of three seconds—and didn't hearten her in the least.

"This is going to be more difficult than I thought," he murmured. He stepped away from her, shoving his hands into his coat pockets.

"Just . . . just tell me," Gwen encouraged, though her mouth suddenly dried to the consistency of the soup droplets coating her sleeves. "Whatever it is, I'm certain we can battle it together."

"Battle it together." Lloyd laughed softly. "Oh, Gwendolen, your spirit astounds me. It was one of the first assets I counted in you."

She decided to heed his meaning, not the awkward stops and starts of his words. She walked to Lloyd again and stood before him, gathering his right hand into her left.

"Do you see this ring, Lloyd?" she said gently. "When I accepted this emerald from you, I promised I would become your wife. Your helpmate. Your support in ill weather as well as fair. So what is it, darling?" She paused. "Have you . . . by any chance been to Kate Hamilton's? Did one of the . . . *hostesses* there give you an infection?"

"Gwendolen!" Lloyd jerked away from her. "Good God!" He wiped his hand against his chest, as if just her words could contaminate him. "Where did you hear about filth like that?" he snapped.

Gwen took a long breath. "Hannah and Reggie believe the children should know the facts about life in the City." She offered it more as explanation than apology, though she didn't add her usual adamant addition: *and I agree with them.*

She tamped the unsuitable thought down as she pulled her sights back up. "Lloyd, this isn't getting us anywhere."

"No," he rebutted. "No, actually, it is. Gwendolen . . . don't you see? It's a perfect example of how far our paths have drifted apart."

"How far our paths have *what . . . ?"*

She heard her voice fading. His intention was clear—and the cadence of panic pounded louder in her blood. Gwen extended her hand, seeking an answering grip from him to tell her this terrifying instinct was wrong, but retracted it when she saw her fingers shaking uncontrollably.

"Well, of course we've been a little . . . detached lately." She forced out the words with a brightness she was far from feeling. "You've been working so hard, darling, and I've been involved with—well, with things here; no wonder we haven't seen much of each other."

"Gwendolen." Without another glance at her, Lloyd began to pace before the fireplace. "It's more than that, and I think we both know it."

"It's not more than that." She sucked in a breath to counter her wobbling tone. "We just need time. We just need *time.* What about a trip to the country? What about—what about Dorset? I hear everyone is selecting the Southampton resorts over Brighton again this spring—"

"Gwen, I don't think a holiday is going to mend this."

"We'll ask your parents to chaperone; they've always loved Dorset."

"Gwendolen, listen to me."

"We'll make it just the four of us—"

"Gwen, I'm getting married to Carolyn Tedworth on the fourteenth of March."

For a long moment, she saw nothing but a thick grey haze. She stared around the room, but furniture once familiar to her now looked foreign. Walls once comforting closed in on her. Paintings and lamp shades and even the floor beneath her feet seemed to mock her, heartlessly leering at her.

Taunts and jeers and stares. Now, she realized with anguished finality, her life's sentence.

One image managed to pierce the fog. Lloyd's face appeared at her side, clear and balanced and so perfectly noble. "I think you should sit down," she watched his perfect lips state. She felt firm hands at her shoulder and elbow. "You're very pale. I'm going to get Mrs. Aberdeen."

"No."

"Gwendolen—"

"No!"

Her shriek rang in her head as she wrenched from him, stumbling through the grey fog until she collided with something. She vaguely recognized it as the back of the sofa. She stopped, staring at its faded flowered pattern. Scrambled words and confused images and raw pain slashed through her mind, stabbing her heart whenever they could between the rapid breaths she inhaled.

As abruptly as the pain came a final realization. "March fourteenth," she blurted. "My birthday. You're getting married on my birthday."

"Gwendolen, you don't look right at all."

"This has absolutely nothing to do with different paths, does it?" The laughter died on her lips. "The only *path* it has to do with is a certain alley—"

"You know that's not true."

"The alley the Lancer dragged me down and turned me into your soiled goods."

"Gwendolen, stop it. I still care very much for you."

"Don't." She jumped away from him. Lloyd halted, but only

for a moment. Through her tears, Gwen watched him continue toward her, arms out . . . like the performer taming a wild horse in a Gypsy circus they'd stopped to view during that magical summer in Dorset, the summer just before he'd proposed . . .

Only this taming act had a significant difference to it, she thought then. *She* wasn't Lloyd's trained filly. Wildness beckoned to her like a best friend—the permit to finally surrender to the frustration, the fury, the loneliness, the pain. As she inched closer to the breaking point, a rush of such pure feeling poured through her that for a moment her mind ceased to exist.

The wildness attacked—and called her to the other side of emotion. Gwen heard herself gasp; some last hold out of rationality inside tried to scramble back to reality, then the pain sucked her in. Lloyd grabbed her again, but she flung him away, clawing at him with nails bared. At the last minute, she managed to rasp, "Let—me—go."

Then she ran. She ran as fast as she could, across the room, through the front hall, and out the front door. She ran into the cold and endless rain—to the outside, where she belonged forever now.

The Thames uncannily echoed her moods that day. It flowed grey and flat beneath her as she ran across the Tower Bridge, roiled with restless storm winds as she slammed enraged fists into the rails of Blackfriar's Bridge, then ended up a black abyss sloshing below as some clock close to Waterloo Bridge gonged midnight. Yes, a black and aimless void—she felt one with the river now.

Gwen stumbled on.

It wasn't the rain that started to bother her as she continued. No, the freezing water seemed a natural cloak as she passed empty tables in dark bistros and peered into dim boutique windows reflecting damp sidewalks. The deluge soaked her through just as her now-impossible dreams drenched her heart:

dreams of summer teas she'd never share with Lloyd, of laughing window-shopping flings never taken, of a life no longer meant to be hers.

No, it wasn't the rain or the wind or the cold that hurt her so. It was her heart.

And her shoes. Yes, her shoes . . . they suddenly felt heavy and unnecessary. Gwen forced herself to stop for the first time in hours, backing into the doorway of a closed milliner's shop to do so. She ripped at the laces atop the square-heeled ankle boots, coughing once, twice, as she did. Why did it hurt so much to breathe?

One shoe came free. The other. She threw one out into the street. The other. She coughed again, wincing with the pain searing down her throat.

"What's this?" a deep voice boomed just beyond the doorway.

Gwen froze. She looked on in dread as a tall constable walked to her shoes in the middle of the empty street and picked them up with studied curiosity.

Oh, God. Dear God. The blue-suited enemy plucked, prodded, and even smelled her shoes before turning around to scrutinize the doorways on either side of the street.

"Oh, God!" she gasped. The need to run filled her senses as full as any of the puddles in the street. But while Gwen's mind already placed her halfway back across Waterloo Bridge, her limbs failed her miserably. She slid back out to the drenched sidewalk with the grace of a tortoise.

If only the dizziness would stop. If only her head and throat didn't throb so. If only she could catch a full breath without coughing.

"Jesus, Mary, and Joseph," came that same voice of authority, suddenly next to her. "Ye're not only without a shoe, lass; ye're soaked clean through."

"Leave me alone," retorted a faraway voice. Gwen wondered who else had arrived; the speaker's sickly rasp frightened her.

"Now we'll have none o' that, missy. Ye just tell ol' Jerry

here which casual ward it is which puts ye up, and I'll drive ye back over the bridge to yer friends."

The mere implication of the words sliced through her desolation. Gwen lurched from the blue-uniformed arms with a sob. "Leave—me—alone!"

She whirled, but the pavement tilted before her. The rain drove at her from all sides. She couldn't find her direction, let alone flee there. "It hurts," she croaked. "Just let me hurt."

"Hey, lassie." The deep voice sounded again. "Ye're not from a casual ward, are ye?"

"I . . ." *I don't belong anywhere. I don't belong to anyone now. I never will.*

All night, she had sensed a great cloud looming above her. The storm finally descended. She felt herself crumpling onto the sidewalk, her neck falling back against an arm encased in drenched wool rain clothes.

Yet after a moment, even that comprehension faded to numbness. Only the cloud of semi-consciousness prevailed, from which Gwen listened to all the voices, the strange and interesting voices . . .

"Are you certain she's the one they're lookin' for, Nigel?"

"C'mon, Jerry, I'm positive. Reggie Aberdeen gave me the description himself. Said we wouldn't mistake that head o' hair, and the—"

"Yeah, I know. The scar. Jesus, what kind of madman would do this to such a jewel of a face?"

" 'Magine the same kind of a fool who broke his betrothal to her earlier today."

"Give over!"

"I swear it's the truth! Reggie's wife was more furious than a baited bear at the nabob who done it. Chased him from Saint Jerome's with a rollin' pin and a carvin' knife."

"Good. Bloody silk stockin'. I'd have killed him."

"This is it. Whooaa, Chelsie, whoa. This is it, Jerry. Saint Jerome's Orphanage. Here, hand her down—"

"Gently, you ass. She's had a time of it tonight."

"Gwennie! Give her to me, Nigel. Give her to me!"

"Hannah . . . Hannah, just let her go until we get inside—"

"Oh, dear God, Gwennie. Gwennie, can ye hear me? Put her there, on the sofa. She likes the sofa. Reggie, she's so cold. She's so blue. Tess, put some tea to boil, and bring more blankets."

"She needs a hot toddy more'n hot tea, I'd say."

"Nigel Brownsmith, ye'll clean yer mouth of that vulgar talk beneath this roof, this very min— Oh, my God. Listen to her cough. Reggie, did ye hear her cough?"

"Yes, lovin'. I heard her."

"She still hasn't woke up. Gwennie, please wake up! What are we goin' to do, Reg?"

"Sshh. Hannah, yer tears won't help her. We gotta think calmly about this."

"And . . . what do *ye* think?"

"That Nigel's right. Gwen needs more than hot tea now . . . more than anything we got to give her here."

"But we can't take her to the *hospital.* Reg, she'll die in that filthy place!"

"No. We can't take her to the hospital."

"Then *where?"*

"Her aunt Margaret—"

"Never gave a fig fer anythin' but her bleedin' cats, let alone Gwennie."

"Let alone at this time o' night."

"Wait a minute . . ."

"Hannah? Hannah, I don't fancy that gleam in yer eye. What are ye doin' there? What's that paper in yer hand? Hannah?"

"Nigel! Where'd that layabout get off to? Nigel Brownsmith, bring the carriage 'round again, *now.* I know where we're takin' her."

The voices faded then. Gwen sank deeper into the fathomless cloud, surrendering to its black, velvety nothingness.

* * *

Taylor slammed the leather-covered pages shut with one hand and tossed the book to the thick Persian rug under his feet. Not even Tolstoy succeeded in putting him to sleep to-night. Or more exactly, he corrected, this morning; he gave a dry grimace to the hall clock as it chimed once to mark the hour.

The rain didn't help. Taye pondered why the whole of Britain hadn't been set afloat by the torrents yet, and collided with Ireland.

Yet, typical of this restless state of his mind, he had to laugh at the notion. He rose from the wing-back chair before the waning fire and stretched.

As quickly as it had come, his smile evaporated. Only letting the rain get under his skin, he told himself. Only letting this cage of water and wind keep him pacing like a shackled lion at the circus.

It certainly wasn't the haunting image of pain-filled emerald eyes, proud shoulders draped in lace, and a razor-thin scar slicing through a proud profile.

It certainly wasn't the gentle thunder that still rumbled through his chest . . . knocked insistently at his mind, sometimes so loud he thought he could really hear it . . .

Taylor snapped his head toward the double-sided doorway. The rapping came again, more rapid and urgent. It didn't sound like his chest. It sounded like his front door.

Granna appeared in the doorway, awash in a robe of ribbons and lace. Yet even in the frothy garment and at her age, she skewered Taye with a glance of her sharp hazel eyes.

"Where's Alistair?" she growled.

"It's one o'clock in the morning, Granna. I released him hours ago."

Her face puckered, contemplating that. "Then saints, Taye," she snapped. "Have you forgotten *all* the manners I taught you?"

"No, Granna."

"Then answer your door!"

One o'clock in the morning or not, he paced across the room to do her bidding. Granna followed with her fat, bright candle.

"Good gracious," Taylor heard her gasp when the light revealed their callers.

A round-faced woman with the biggest brown eyes he'd ever seen shivered on the step. Next to her stood a man but an inch shorter than himself, face framed in wild black hair but balanced by an honest, hard-working gaze.

The man cradled a soaked, shoeless, and unconscious Gwendolen Marsh.

"Help us," the big-eyed woman pleaded. "Lord Stafford, please . . . help us."

Four

Taylor watched a finger of sunlight bashfully tap at the window of the Emerald Bedroom. The storm had finally passed, leaving in its wake a pale, unnatural stillness.

Just like the pale, unnaturally still woman lying in the bed before him.

From the moment he'd ordered Hannah and Reggie Aberdeen into the house and up to the bedroom, he hadn't taken his eyes from Gwendolen Marsh's inert form. His brain couldn't comprehend that the warrior in lace he'd sparred with yesterday morning had become this unconscious waif with blue fingers he'd cradled until Dr. Ramsey finally answered his summons—then nearly crushed when the doctor declared too quickly and too ominously, "Pneumonia, my lord. She's got herself a good bout of it, too."

Asking what the devil happened didn't cool the frustration brewing in his gut, either. No, his agitation just churned harder and hotter as Mrs. Aberdeen told him of the events following his and Bryan's departure from the orphanage. After the account, Taye had responded with one slow, entirely too deep-felt curse: "Bastard."

Bastard. The slur came again from that unrecognizable source in his gut. How easy it had been to envy Lloyd Waterston. How painfully easy, when this woman had mistaken Taylor himself for the man, illuminating the dim parlor with that survivor's gleam in her eyes and that victor's glory in her smile. Her expression had packed the force of a physical blow . . . and inflicted as much damage to his unsuspecting muscles, nerves, thoughts.

Yes, how easy it had been to wish he was Lloyd Waterston. How easy it would be to strangle the imbecile now.

Taylor snapped back to the awareness of cold water sluicing down his arm. He looked down to realize he'd allowed the washcloth in his hand to stand proxy for Waterston's neck. He forced his fist loose from the dripping towel and his attention back to the motionless face against the pillows. As he watched, glistening drops of sweat beaded on her peach-smooth forehead. Her fever was peaking.

"Damn it." He hardly heard the chair tumble behind him as he leaped to his feet. "Damn it, fight it. Send it packing the way you threw me out, you little shrew." He moistened and folded the washcloth. *"Fight!"* he demanded, gently placing the cold rectangle on her clammy skin.

She didn't take long to show him what she thought of *that* idea. Her lips began to race with rapidly whispered words; her hand flung to the pillow beside her head.

Taye understood only every third word, but one rang out clearer than the others. "No!" Then, more slurred and rapid, "Stop—I can't—breathe—*no.*"

He hesitated just an instant before lowering himself to the mattress beside her. He leaned over her, trying to listen better, driven by some stupid male instinct to destroy the dragons of her dreams. But when he came close enough to hear, her lips stilled.

Then the air stilled.

Pull away. Pull away, you fool.

He didn't.

He drank a long, lingering gaze of her. He took in her dusky auburn lashes, resting against her sculpted cheeks. He marveled at her rose-dark lips . . . fuller than he remembered, smoother than he imagined. He studied each sworl of sweat-moistened hair clinging against her neck . . . and gave in to the craving to brush the copper strands away, one by one.

When he'd settled the last tendril into order, he allowed his touch to follow the line of her hair across the pillow, until his hand brushed against the curled-up tips of her fingers. Quietly, carefully, Taylor meshed their fingers together.

"So small," he said in wonder, amazed at the contrast of the ovals of her nails next to the brutish square tips of his. "But strong."

He looked back to her face, to her profile which jutted a little too high and much too proud, even in sleep. Unable to control the force that drew him, he slid a finger to her scar and traced the three-inch line.

"No use arguing, sweetheart," he murmured. "It's true. You may get away at the hiding game with the others, but I know what you're really made of. I know what you've been through, and I know what you can survive." He moved his finger down her damp cheek. "And you can survive *this*."

She only sighed and shifted again. This time her legs pushed at the bedding, pulling the cover free from her upper body, yanking Cook's borrowed nightgown halfway down one smooth shoulder.

Taylor had barely recovered from that unexpected sight when her leg moved with sleepy abandon . . . and curled perfectly, almost naturally, around his knee.

His face bunched into an awkward frown. Her limb weighed no more than a down pillow, yet the contact, intimate yet innocent, tortured him.

This was dangerous.

The next moment, Gwendolen Marsh's knee slid softly up to nestle in the juncture between his thighs.

This was very dangerous.

Blood sang through his ears and pounded through his chest. The hot, sweet melody of his pulse took seconds to bring all his body to full, quivering alert. He swallowed with a seemingly steel-banded throat. Those efforts seemed child's tasks compared to the pain of sitting upright, fighting against the flood of arousal and need, of heat—and *guilt* running through his body.

Taylor bolted from the bed and stalked to the window.

He gripped the frame with shaking hands. He looked out unseeingly upon big white clouds as pure white heat still sizzled down his body.

"Jesus," he growled. "Jesus, Stafford, pull a rein on yourself." *First stealing gawks at her in the orphanage parlor, now letting an accidental brush harden you like lead—what the* hell *are you doing? How the* hell *do you keep letting her stray you from the purpose?*

"Noooo!"

The sharp cry from the bed scattered his thoughts once more. Taylor whirled. Gwendolen moaned the protest again as she twisted against the pillows, her arms flailing, her head thrashing, the sheets tangling. The washcloth flew to the floor. She breathed hard and fast, her breasts and ribs silhouetted perfectly beneath the cotton nightgown.

And her lips moved again. But now she formed words. Distinct, fear-filled words. "No. Let me go. Please. *No!*"

She gasped for air like a drowning woman. Taylor's already strained nerves shattered. He dropped to the mattress and hauled her to him in one movement.

"Miss Marsh." The formality sounded asinine, considering he had the fevered, half-clad woman in his arms. "Gwendolen," he finally shouted. "Gwen. Wake up. You're dreaming."

"Nooo!" The vigor of her strugglings astounded him. "Please. Please don't hurt me. Please don't kill me!"

Her grip tightened around his arm. Her nails clawed at his shirt as another cough wracked her body. "Just let me go. I won't tell anyone. Oh, God. Oh God, somebody help me!"

At that, for the second time in a minute, Taylor froze in disbelief.

There, he realized, there *somewhere* in her mind, the woman remembered every detail of her encounter with the Lancer that January night.

So this was what Francis Drake felt like when he discovered his first buried treasure.

Taylor clutched her as if he held a bolt of the rare silk her skin resembled. "It's all right," he told her. "Listen to me. I've got you, sweetheart. You're going to be all right." *You* have *to be all right.*

As the echoes of his last word filled the room, her eyelashes fluttered. Her eyes opened. For an interminable moment she gazed at him in dazed curiosity, lifting weak fingers to his jaw as if to discern he was real.

Then she moaned—just before her head drooped with the weight of unconsciousness once more.

"Oh, no, you don't," Taylor commanded. She shook with the force of another spasm. "Fight it. Damn you, I said fight it!"

He heard the rustling of skirts at the door, but didn't look to see who was there. Instead, he leaned forward, cupped water from the basin and splashed it into Gwendolen's face, battling to make her russet lashes blink at him again.

"Saint Jude have mercy," Hannah Aberdeen gasped. "What happened?"

"Nightmare. She started to cough. The fluid's bad." Taye fired the segments at her, and one phrase tumbled after another without pause. "Doctor," he ordered. "Send Reggie for Ramsey again. *Now.*" He heard Hannah rush from the room, but never once looked up from the still, small form in the bed.

Each minute of the next half hour ticked by as if a snail powered the clock. Taylor and Hannah attempted to lessen the torment by trying to pour sips of water past Gwendolen's lips, but they watched in mutual frustration as she choked most of the liquid back at them.

Finally, Reggie ushered in the thin, bespectacled Dr. Ramsey.

Behind him, sandy hair falling into eyes so wide they rivaled the sky outside for vastness, rushed a panicked Bryan Corstairs. "I went to the orphanage to apologize for upsetting her yesterday," he explained, "and Tess said—"

Bryan halted short when his stare fell upon Gwen. "Mother of God. She's dying."

"The bleedin' heavens she is." With mother-hen efficiency, Hannah backed him and Reggie toward the door. "Listen, ya cod's heads, Dr. Ramsey knew what to do for Gwennie last night, and I'm sure he'll be just as knowin' now." She braced her hands to her hips like an army commander. "That is, if he wasn't so crowded."

Taye knew the woman included him in the dictate. Complying with Hannah's order was another matter.

With each of her spasms, Gwendolen's grip on him tightened. Yet as he leaned her back against the pillows at Dr. Ramsey's direction, she gave a high-pitched sob; her hands clamped harder at him. She didn't want to let go easily.

And Taylor didn't want her to. Damn it, he needed her now as much as her nightmare-plagued spirit needed him. Any moment the key to the mystery might tumble from her lips. At last, he had found the link to the puzzle. The answer to finding the Lancer.

The answer to his prayers.

"She's frightened," he murmured. He looked to Ramsey, seeking justification to stay. He knew what the situation must look like, his limbs intertwined with the patient's in more than proper proximity. Frankly, he didn't care.

He cleared his throat with unmistakable authority. "A nightmare," he began again. "I think. Probably brought on by the fever—"

"My lord." Hannah Aberdeen arrived like the infantry called in to rescue. "It'll be all right," the woman assured, her voice as strong yet comforting as her hands at his elbow, pulling him toward the door. "Me 'n' the doc will fix her up; don't ye worry."

He looked down into Hannah's face. Her big brown eyes smiled up at him. Her bowed lips and rosy cheeks echoed the sentiment.

"I promise she'll be thankin' ye fer yer hospitality in no time," she said. "Even if I have to choke it out o' her."

Taylor responded to her pledge with the same gallant kiss he'd used on those plump knuckles in the Saint Jerome's front hall. Just as then, he collected the reward of Hannah's smitten flush and befuddled smile.

As he turned and left the room, he felt confident in counting Hannah Aberdeen the first ally won over from Gwendolen Marsh's camp.

The sound of ice clinking against crystal decided Taye's direction. He headed down the hall for the billiard room. Behind him, the case clock rang nine times for the morning hour, a decidedly accusing timbre to the gongs. He didn't care. He needed a drink. And some time to think.

Time to think about just how he was going to gain Gwendolen Marsh's trust . . . and cooperation.

In short, how he was going to accomplish the impossible.

"You look like hell." Waiting with his characteristic cross-legged stance against the billiard table, Bryan offered the disparaging words and a glass of brandy in the same movement.

Taye attacked the latter first, downing the amber liquid in a gulp. He poured his own refill before sinking into a chair before the fire at the other end of the room. "I know," he finally answered, dropping his head against the soft brown suede of his refuge.

"You look like you were up all night with her."

"I was."

A moment ticked by. But only a moment, before Bryan wheeled in front of him and emitted an angry snort. "Do you mind telling me what the hell is going on? Precisely one day ago, Gwen barely accepted your calling card. Now I arrive here and she's clinging to you like she's mistaken you for Lloyd again."

Before he could think about it, Taylor's foot shot out and

toppled an innocent footrest. "Lloyd Waterston," he snarled, "is why she's got that fever to begin with."

Bryan's mustache twitched like a hare appraising a fox's scent on the air. "That makes no sense. The man is her affianced."

"The man isn't fit to wash her smalls."

"Isn't fit to—? Taye, what the hell are you about? You're acting as if Lloyd ran off and married someone else."

Taylor only answered by downing his second fill of brandy in a frowning gulp.

"Carolyn Tedworth." Bryan's statement was quiet and even, but echoed Taye's own fury. "The dog crawled off to Carolyn Tedworth, didn't he?"

Taylor still didn't trust himself to words.

"Holy Mary," Bryan growled. "I'd heard rumors at some of the parties since Christmas, but that's all I thought they were. Rumors. Damn. *Damn* that bastard."

Taye seconded the comment by rising and slamming his empty glass onto the mantel. "She ran from the orphanage while Waterston was still standing in the parlor. Hannah said they didn't hear a cry out of her. Took them a half hour before they found that coward Bryan trying to sneak out. He wasn't even going to tell them what had happened."

It made no difference that he, not Hannah, recounted the events now. Once more, undiluted rage clamped a vise-hold on his throat.

"They scoured the city for six hours before getting her back," Taye finally continued. "She was soaked to the skin. She'd thrown off her shoes somewhere—"

"Thrown off her shoes!" Bryan's stare was as oddly jarring as his interruption; for the first time since the man had offered Taye much-needed friendship in White's library after Connie's funeral, an unmistakable sheen of moisture glistened in that light-blue gaze.

"Confound you, Gwen," Bryan muttered in a tone that wavered as badly as his hand pouring brandy into his glass. "Unthinking duck was the cause of her own pneumonia."

"No. Lloyd Waterston was."

Bryan's silence bespoke his consensus to that. He spun toward the sprawling window opposite the fireplace. Drinking deeply, he stared over the velvet greens and satin roses of the garden, the deeper hues of Hyde Park on the horizon.

"Hell and hounds, Taye," he muttered. "She had her pick of the bloody litter that season. I don't know how she did it, but despite all the lessons and tutors and discipline that 'loving' aunt of hers tried, she turned out nothing like the other twits they foisted upon poor London." The sandy blond head tilted back in a wistful pose. "And she enchanted them all because of it. It was just . . . the way Gwendolen was."

His friend's statement brought a handful of questions brimming to his mind, but only a single curiosity burned its way to Taylor's lips. "The way she *was?*"

Bryan turned. With a slow grimace, he replied, "The worst scars that woman carries aren't physical."

"Well, yes," Taylor agreed. "Losing her memory—"

"Was only the beginning."

"What are you getting at?"

Bryan shook his head with that same odd, faraway contemplation. "She was, quite honestly, one of the most captivating women anyone had ever seen. Gwennie had something beyond those gowns and jewels you saw in those ballrooms. She had . . ." His brows bunched as he searched the horizon for the right word. "She had a *light* . . ."

Taylor admitted it. He'd probably have jeered at Bryan, had the same embarrassingly romantic swill not taken his own mind by surprise yesterday morning. Instead, he found himself joining Bryan by the window, urging the man on by his silence. Surely it could only do him good, he reasoned, to know as much about the woman as possible.

You mean . . . to find the weakness behind the wall another voice agreed from inside. A resolved, trusted voice. *To find the best route of attack into the fortress. Remember the purpose, Stafford. Remember Constance.*

"She wanted all life had to offer, she'd always tell me," Bryan went on. "She didn't want two or three children, she talked about seven or eight. She said she wouldn't be just her husband's wife, but his friend. She always dreamed of her home, not her house."

To Taylor's disappointment, the account only merited a shrug. "Every chit in London talks like that. They suck that drivel along with their tea and tarts."

"Not Gwennie."

Bryan's rebuttal came out as more hoarse air than spoken words. "*Not* Gwendolen," he repeated, after clearing his throat and shaking his head. "She lived that drivel. She wanted to be that drivel. She craved everything safe and secure and acceptable about that drivel."

Now Taylor turned. It didn't take an Oxford scholar to note Bryan's impassioned overtones—undoubtedly a fierce protectiveness nursed through the months of hell the man had seen her through. But something told him the statement said more about Gwendolen Marsh than that.

Something told him she'd survived a few glimpses of hell long before the Lancer got his hands on her.

"So Waterston must have seemed the bloody Redeemer to her," he offered with dry but careful distaste.

"I do think thou hast the gist of it." Bryan edged the Renaissance words with cynicism.

"Did he really propose the night before she was . . . ?" Taylor didn't know why he implied the rest. He just knew his lips couldn't create the image. His mind barely tolerated the scenes of a laughing, vivacious Gwendolen suddenly taken prisoner, dragged into a black night, face sliced open by a maniac's plunging hand—

"Yes," Bryan answered. Then a quiet, strange laugh crossed his lips. "And I don't think I'll never forget that night, either."

"Go on," Taye encouraged.

"The girl was so excited, she snuck out of Margaret's house to show me the ring. Can you believe it?" Bryan's lips compressed so hard, only his dark-blond mustache remained to be seen. "They planned to break the news officially at Carolyn Tedworth's annual soiree," he continued. "Two weeks after Gwen's attack. Lloyd and Gwennie attended, but she could have been a potted palm for all the attention the bastard gave her."

"And they didn't make the announcement."

"Oh, they made it." A gruff snort. "Let me rephrase that: *Gwen* made it. Her 'beloved' was clearly more content chortling at Edwin Rotterdam's jokes than participating in the sham. Five minutes later, Lloyd and Edwin cut out for Brooks's. He never came back for her. *I* took her home."

Bryan turned back to the window, but his eyes clearly didn't see the view. "This time she sobbed on my sofa. For hours," he finished.

"Christ," Taye muttered. No other word would come.

"The sixes and sevens about the whole thing is, I haven't seen her cry since." Bryan's tone held more than a little wonder. "Even when the looks began on the street . . . when the invitations stopped coming . . . even when Lloyd stopped coming 'round, she'd just look at me with a glint in her eyes that sometimes scared the holy ghost out of me. Sometimes, I was sorely tempted to grab her and make her cry again. Anything but that look." He shrugged. "I know it sounds batty . . ."

But it didn't sound batty. Not at all. Taye knew just what flickering, searing, consuming glint the man stammered about. He knew just what unnameable feeling Bryan tried to express.

He remembered his own determined stride across that orphanage parlor, only to have his entire perspective ripped from him by a gaze gleaming like emeralds and snapping like a forest fire. Courage and pain, boldness and terror, the battles she'd fought so long—they were all there at once, glaring into him in a single moment—

A single moment where she unmasked the woman she'd once been.

The warrior she really was.

Taylor took a deep breath. His thoughts collided in his mind like two thunderclouds heavy with meaning—ripping a lightning bolt of comprehension down his spine.

The answer to his dilemma didn't lurk in some dungeon of Gwendolen Marsh's subconscious . . . no, the solution had glared him in the face five minutes after he'd walked into that orphanage. It had only taken Bryan's accounts to fill in the spaces and balance the ledger.

She had what he most needed: a portrait, however blurred or brief, of the bastard he'd hunted from one end of London to the other.

And, by God, he had what she most needed A title. Solid social standing. Unconditional acceptance. Unshakable respect. And now, with his year of mourning over and his official passage into bachelor status again, he also had more social obligations than he knew what to do with. Or gave a damn about.

Until now. Now Taylor considered the trays full of calling cards and the desktop piled high with invitations, and he knew just how much he gave a damn about them. Just how fully he meant to take advantage of all that vellum and Roman script.

Oh, yes. He'd take her to every last ball of the season if he had to. He'd adorn her in silk and velvet creations that would turn even the Prince of bloody Wales into a panting hound at her skirt train. He'd dance under a hundred chandelier lights if the effort ignited just one light in Gwendolen Marsh's eyes.

The light of remembrance.

Gwen didn't want to leave the darkness. *Just a while longer,* she begged. She rolled over, curling herself deeper into the soft and enveloping warmth.

But the humming beckoned to her again. Like sleighbells cutting a night fog, the gentle music parted the veil of her senses. And like a child on Christmas Eve, she yearned to follow the sound, even through a cold and snowy night.

She opened her eyes.

It appeared as if holiday magic had indeed been at work. In amazement, she surveyed a room reminding her very much of a mystical fairy's glen: ivy-patterned wallpaper, rich oak paneling, deep-green carpeting—and even her own good-luck fairy.

"Hannah," she called in a weak murmur.

The humming broke off into a shocked choke. Her friend's head popped up from her embroidery hoop. Hannah's eyes flew wider than Gwen ever recalled the brown circles capable before.

"Saint Michael be praised." Hannah threw the stitchery behind in her haste to leap to Gwen's side. "Bosh. All the bleedin' saints in heaven be praised! Ye've come back to us, Gwennie. Thank ye, God; thank ye!"

"Hannah, I—"

"How ye feelin'? Hmmm, ye're cooler, but that's never been no great sign in my book. Yer hands are still clammy. I don't like yer color, either. Open yer mouth; let me see yer tongue."

"Hannah, please—"

"Open it."

"Hannah." It took a considerable effort to batten down her friend's strong grip. "I'm fine," Gwen insisted. "Tired. But I'm fine." She patted the plump hands. "But Hannah . . . what is this place? Where am I?"

Hannah's brows knotted together. When her friend's round brown eyes beneath darted toward the ceiling, Gwen scowled, too.

"Lovey," the woman ventured, "what do ye remember about—about what happened before yer fever? Do ye recall that day, any of it?"

"Of course I do." Gwen tried to ignore the uneasy emotion behind her own reply. "I'd been up with Gertie, then I received Bryan and that Lord Stafford fellow you gave me such a difficult time about."

"He was a prince, Gwennie."

"He was an *earl,* Hannah."

"Earl by title, prince by soul. He gave his last callin' card to ye, sayin' ye could use it any time, any day, if ye needed to."

At that, Hannah looked up with tear-shimmered eyes and shaking breath. "Let me tell ye, missy, after what that blighter Waterston drove ye to do to yerself that night, ye *needed* Lord Stafford's help. I just thank Blessed Mary he upheld his word as he said he would."

Gwen sat upright. Bells of alarm clanged through her brain. She leveled a hard, stunned stare at Hannah. "Oh, my God."

"Now, Gwennie, just lay back down fer a minute. Here; let me fluff yer pillows. I won't have ye expendin' yerself—"

"No. Stop it. Stop it! Hannah . . . you and Reggie—you brought me to Lord Taylor Stafford's *home?* Is *this* his—Oh, dear God!"

She fell back to the pillows. "Of all the places!" she cried. "For heaven's sake, why not the hospital? And I have a home, Hannah! You know where I live!"

"Home!" Her friend made such an adamant scoff of the word, the bed bounced. "You call that tomb of a townhouse and the walking corpse who owns it a home?"

"I believe Aunt Maggie would have risen to the situation."

"We sent Nigel Brownsmith 'round to your Aunt Maggie," Hannah said. "She didn't 'rise' from her bleedin' coffin at all. The butler told Nigel that if ye'd gotten yerself into trouble, perhaps it'd be a good lesson to ye, show ye not to consort with East End riffraff."

Gwen couldn't react to that for a long moment. She sighed and raised her eyes to the ceiling. Panels papered in a design of tight-twisted green and gold rings spread above her—as if all her trepidation and fear had risen and splattered against the roof.

"I suppose," she finally conceded, "one day hasn't hurt. It's still morning, isn't it? If we leave quietly now, I can send a gift tomorrow to show our appreciation to his lordship—Hannah, what is so amusing about this?"

She couldn't ignore Hannah's growing smile any longer. A wise smile Gwen had seen before—and knew better than to trust.

"Oh, lovey," her friend replied indulgently, "ye've been sicker than ye think."

She rose to one elbow. "What are you saying?"

Hannah answered by way of another question. "Tell me this: what day is it?"

"Tuesday, of course." Gwen scowled impatiently. "Yesterday, Reggie brought over the Orphan Asylum's donation, and you made the week's bread. Don't you remember? You always make bread on Mon . . . day . . ."

Her head jerked and her gaze snapped toward the tall windows—as her assertion faded into a zealous chorus of London church bells.

"Lord in heaven," she rasped.

It was *Sunday.*

Another piece of her life, gone. Blank, black . . . unremembered. Almost a week this time. *Almost a week.*

"Now do ye understand how far down at the heel ye were?" Hannah scowled. "We almost thought ye weren't comin' back to us, Gwennie. As I said before, thank the Almighty fer Lord Stafford. Why, fer the last six days—"

"Lord Stafford." The name fired a fresh volley of confusion and dread across Gwen's mind. "Oh, God. Lord Stafford!"

She yanked her hand free from Hannah while using her other arm to toss back the covers and help swing her legs to the floor. "I've got to get out of here."

"Ye've got to *what?"*

"He'll be at services now, too. We've got plenty of time. There must be a servant's stairway in the back. We'll just slip out and hail a cab back to Saint Jerome's."

"A pig's arse we will! Fer glory's sake, ye're still in yer nightrail. Gwendolen Victoria, get back in bed!"

But Gwen expected the attempt Hannah made to restrain her; she dodged the older woman's lunge by feigning right, then darting left, toward the door. Only a wave of coughing and dizziness stopped her, striking after she'd taken two steps.

"Ye see? Yer ears are still so full of infection, ye can't walk! And yer lungs will drop ye dead in front o' that cab before get ye into it!"

"I can't—" She forced out a rasping cough to clear her throat. "I can't stay here!"

"Ye have no choice!"

"I—can't—stay—here." Gwen gave in to the temptation to lean against the polished mahogany bed post. She'd pause just for a moment, she decided, to rest. "Dear Lord, Hannah . . . don't you see?" she asked between more painful coughs. "I've been here at that man's expense . . . for six days. I am indebted to him . . . for very nearly—my life! Don't you know what he'll want . . . in return for that?"

"Awww, Gwennie." Hannah rose from where she'd fallen on the bed. Gwen pushed back from the post in reaction, enduring the ringing fuzz in her head to put a few safe steps between them.

But the only surprise attack she faced was the soothing, almost sad cadence of Hannah's voice. "Gwennie, the man isn't like that."

"My foot he isn't."

"Fer glory's sake, he's shown us nothin' but kindness since we got here. What will it take to prove it? This list o' notes written by the fine doctor he's had tendin' to ye every day *and* a few evenin's? These scraps o' shortbread on this plate, from the meal he carried up to me himself last night while I was watchin' ye? Or the necktie he left behind over on that chair, because he stood there so long glaumin' at ye himself, I told him to sit down and take off the nasty gag?"

"What?" Gwen gaped at the dark-blue strip of cloth Hannah pointed at. "You let him sit and *watch* me?"

"Gwennie, the man cares—"

"About what an asset I'd be to his search for the Lancer!"

She brought her hand up to her temple. A drum beat of pain behind her eyes accompanied the bell choir in her ears. "That's why I've got to go." She tried to speak, not wince, her way through the words. "That's why I've been here too long already. Don't you see? This is exactly what that lunatic hoped would happen!"

"Gwennie—"

"Every moment beneath this roof is another moment I'm indebted to him. And just what recompense do you think his honorable lordship will ask? None, of course," she answered herself in a dry tone. "He'll request nothing in return for his *kindness* except for one—oh, how will he phrase it?—one 'small favor.' Only the 'small favor' of my memory. My thoughts. The mind I've had ripped apart a few too many times already, thank you."

"Gwennie— "

Gwen ignored Hannah's tight-lipped plea. "No, thank you, indeed." While shoving her feet into a pair of worn slippers near the bedstand, she spotted Hannah's cloak on the green satin lounge. She grabbed the covering and shrugged it around her shoulders. "Taylor Stafford will have to track his demon to hell by himself," she said.

"Oh, by all the souls in perdition. Gwennie, listen to yerself! Hackin' yer livin' lungs up! Look at ye, pitchin' like a teacup in a tempest!"

"I'm fine." Gwen tugged the cloak closed and stood up. "You see?" she retorted, forcing back another cough. "I'm perfectly fine. Now we've just got to make our way out before . . . he comes back. Before . . ."

The name teetered on the tip of her memory; why couldn't she recall it all of a sudden? Why couldn't she say it? The name of that man, the one with the hazel-sharded gaze and dominating stance . . . the warrior come to take her prisoner of war, to die in his ridiculous quest for the Lancer.

She moaned as the memories of his hard, tensed jaw, his

strong fingers, flashed across her brain. She raised her hands, trying to block the images, then she willed her feet forward, fleeing from the thoughts of those iron-hard arms, that intense and determined face—

Suddenly she found herself trapped between those very arms—gasping up into Lord Taylor Stafford's unflinching face.

"Oh. Ohhh, no." Gwen's vision reeled in the sea of her senses. She felt her body following in a slow, surreal descent . . . with no lifeline in sight to pull her out of the abyss.

Five

"Easy." Unlike the rest of the chaos in her head, his voice came close and cool and temptingly calm. His presence was a strong haven—too strong.

"Easy," he directed again. "Stop struggling. I've got you. I've got you now."

You've got me, her mind screamed, *oh, yes, right where you want me!* Yet her body obeyed his gentle commands as if he spoke directly to her muscles. Her head sagged on his shoulder.

She felt her feet leave the floor as he settled her in his arms. He moved into the room with her, his step firm on the carpet. His pulse thumped a steady rhythm his corded neck beneath her hands.

When he slipped her back into the bed again, she pressed her face into the pillow. She closed her eyes, awash in shame that her arms didn't possess the strength to maneuver the bed-clothes back over herself . . . appalled that his lordship gently performed the task himself.

"Wishing to stroll through the morning air already, Miss Marsh?" he asked evenly. From the foot of the bed, Hannah loosed a hearty snort at that.

Despite her mortification—perhaps because of it—Gwen opened her eyes and scrutinized him from beneath her lashes. Slowly, like sparks of a fire catching on to kindling, Taylor Stafford responded with a wide upturn of his lips.

It was the first time she'd ever seen him smile.

He had sinfully white teeth, and the expression formed deep

creases in his cheeks. Amazing. How could a base warrior suddenly appear so much a valorous knight?

"I don't think Dr. Ramsey has ordered morning walks for you just yet." Somehow he maintained that commanding, unnerving smile through the whole statement and into his soft addition of, "I'm sorry."

Gwen realized he meant it. Intrigued, she raised her gaze to fully meet his.

His smile vanished.

But that strong mouth remained parted in an expression more beautifully powerful than a smile. The man made her forget to breathe, she realized in another horrifying revelation.

Nervously, Gwen licked her suddenly dry lips. At the same time, she heard Stafford's own breathing catch. She watched his eyes lower; his hooded gaze locked, trancelike, on the skin she'd just moistened.

Then, as if he'd never allowed what must have been a heinous breach in the mighty Stafford bearing, he swallowed and looked away. Gwen wondered if the disconcerting attraction she felt was an aftereffect of her fever. Then his lordship leaned an inch closer to her. Close enough for her to see the gold and black flecks in his eyes. Close enough for her to feel the gentle caress of his intimate murmur . . .

"Well. It's good to see your spirit returning." He pulled away, but his voice still vibrated through her. "Welcome back, Miss Marsh."

And that was that.

And that was that. Gwen watched him rise from the mattress without another word. He rolled and buttoned the sleeves of his casual riding shirt, then left the room with that powerful, determined stride.

Before she could say something. Anything.

"Now what did I tell ye?" Hannah barreled around and settled on the bed like a faithful sheepdog. "I didn't hear a request fer any 'special favors' there, missy. I didn't see the man ask fer his 'recompense' before he caught ye from embarrassin' yerself in a dead faint!"

Gwen shifted wearily against the pillows. "Give the man time. He's just waiting for the perfect moment to strike."

The older woman expelled a heavy sigh. "Gwennie . . . lovey, I know ye haven't got a reason in the world to believe me . . . but darlin', ye've got to trust someone, sometime."

"And you think the person I trust should be Taylor Stafford?" She couldn't suppress a laugh.

"I think he'd be a bloody good place to start."

With that, Hannah rose again. But her lips pursed before she mumbled something about going to negotiate with Cook about some food for Gwen.

The door closed behind her with a bang that sounded more like a rifle shot in the quiet of Taylor Stafford's home.

The analogy fit, for Gwen felt like a target. In the last few moments, she'd endured everything from confusion and fear to exhaustion and exasperation . . . to anger and guilt. Anger at this broken-down body of hers, for introducing her again, of all times, to the experience of true helplessness. Anger at Reggie and Hannah, for disregarding the possibility of alienating themselves from her if they brought her here—and saving her life by doing so. And anger at Lord Taylor Stafford, for not only taking her friends up on this lunacy, but being so beautiful, for being so blasted *nice* about his unexpected guest.

Then followed her familiar nemesis of guilt, a litany of shame for indulging in all that anger in the first place.

"Ooohh!" She vented her frustration from clenched teeth, backhanding a dent into the pillow. She squeezed her eyes shut in fury and exhaustion.

And then she prayed.

She prayed for sleep and for strength. She prayed for the swiftest recovery from pneumonia ever seen by the medical sciences. She prayed that by this time tomorrow, she'd be falling asleep amidst the blissful chaos of Saint Jerome's, not trapped in this quiet, too perfect lair . . . or anywhere near the piercing-eyed warrior who ruled it.

As fate would have it, Trafalgar Square roared with an uprising the next day. In a display of unity not witnessed since the unsolved Ripper murders three years ago, a mob of all classes challenged the police's continuing failure to corner the Lancer. Curses were hurled. Knives were flashed. Shots were fired. Bodies were counted.

The saints Gwen pleaded to had an overburden of new souls to attend. Her prayers went unanswered.

A full week after she'd first opened her eyes to the finery of the Emerald Bedroom, she felt yet another cough tug her lungs. She tried to let the rose-hued furnishings and hanging ferns of the south sitting room impart the peace she knew they were there for, but her mind was far from quiet.

The silence. Lord, always the silence. It terrified her. Gwen still glanced out each window she passed just to reconfirm Stafford House actually sat on Wilton Crescent, not some secluded meadow. A meadow where time seemed to falter, where the muted elegance of days long gone by still prevailed in the rugs, paintings, and furniture of every room. Where even the birds in the trees outside knew the difference between singing their tunes and twittering them. Every morning, the warblers' voices lifted in a serenade to charm the listener. The house invited its residents to expose their most intimate thoughts, most hidden feelings.

Their deepest fears.

No. Gwen shoved up from the chair, refusing to give way to the images breaking through the chinks in her weakened mental barrier.

The memories came, anyway. Visions of steely arms lifting her against a linen-clad torso . . . feeling little-girl small nestled against it. That same broad expanse of chest leaning over her as she lay among the soft bedcovers. And the not-so-girlish arousal, warm and liquid in the core of her, when she saw a certain dazzling white smile and felt a reassuring caress. A man's touch that bade her to trust, to open herself again.

No.

"No!" she repeated aloud, pressing a hand to the blue-green serge of her house gown where it covered her racing heartbeat. "Stop it, Gwendolen," she scolded herself a moment later. "Stop doing this to yourself. This isn't helping you get better. You have *got* to get better. You have got to get out of here."

You've got to get away from him.

There. She felt stronger already. She drew in a determined breath. She closed her eyes and forced herself to enjoy the aromas of hot tea mingling with dewy grass. A faint smile crossed her lips as she eavesdropped on a maid's quip from down the hall. Her senses expanded, listening to the soft horse huffings from the stables—

Then she was suddenly aware of measured masculine breathing from the doorway behind her.

She whirled.

His mighty lordship didn't look in the least bit ruffled at finding her here. Not even unsettled. With his hair wind-tossed into a riot of dark waves and his face still bearing the high color of a morning ride, Taylor stood dominating the portal like a warrior chief in control of all he surveyed.

Especially her.

Her surprise turned into panic. "For God's sake," she snapped. "Don't you ever announce yourself the way decent people do?"

He didn't smile—his expression was a precise replica of the odd look he'd speared her with in his guest bed days ago.

Days ago? It seemed a month.

"The scenery and conversation were too stimulating from where I stood," he finally replied. "I quite forgot the social niceties."

The man's tone blended right in with the cool, gentle air. In contrast, Gwen felt her cheeks flare like twin Guy Fawkes

Night fires. Blast him! He'd heard the latter part of her passionate, *private* admonitions, that much was evident. Pray God the man didn't truly possess some magical warrior's gift to read what she'd been thinking, as well.

"What I said was none of your business." Gwen turned on her heel. She heard him follow, heard his black wool trousers rustling. Legs shaky, she sat again in her chair. With assured fluidity, he moved into the windowseat opposite.

"As charming as that blush is," he said, "I don't know what you're ashamed of."

"That's—that's not the point. I am not ash—"

"A little self-encouragement is all right, Miss Marsh."

Again, his words transported her back to those unnerving moments after he'd settled her barely clothed form between his sheets. Why—*how* did he always do that? How did he strip her next to nothing, body *and* soul?

"Listen," he began again, with a shrug that looked as though he didn't shrug often. "I'm sorry I eavesdropped. But your ramblings weren't state secrets, sweet. You're determined to recover quickly; the whole household knows it. And, from what Dr. Ramsey says, your progress is astounding. Even Hannah's pleased."

Now his dazzling smile made its slow, teasing entrance. "But I'm afraid Granna's forecast is trailing toward the gloomy," he murmured in mock gravity. "Something about checking for hidden infections; that we'd better keep you here at least a few months longer."

Gwendolen only responded with a tight-lipped glower.

His smile grew into a grin, then a chuckle.

"I suppose you find that as funny as hiding in shadows and watching women think you their betrothed," she accused.

He stopped chuckling.

"Well. You are indeed recovering swiftly."

The words caught Gwendolen off guard. No, not the words, she amended—but his tone. The man made the assertion like a friend who knew her inside out. No, that wasn't it, either.

Not a friend . . . someone closer. Someone who had the right to whisper at her like that, penetrating her like sun through morning dew . . . promising to melt her mind and memory away just as ruthlessly.

"I . . . am feeling better, thank you," she replied.

She looked around the room, at anything but him. She noticed the bookshelf along the wall; specifically, a Stafford knot emblazoned in gold across an aged book cover. Appropriate, she thought. Her stomach felt coiled in the same design.

"Excellent," his lordship responded. He sounded like a colonel snapping approval of his battalion. "Excellent. Then you shall be looking forward to full recovery by the time of . . . the Duchess Edinborough's grand ball next month?"

At that statement, the book, the bookshelf, and the world reeled out of focus for her. Gwen squeezed her eyes shut, weathering the jolt of pain. The man was either insane or sadistic. Attending one of the year's most glamorous events with her was like showing an open gate to a chained prisoner.

"The duchess has made it quite apparent I am not included on her guest list this year. Thank you, however, for your concern." She drew out the final word as if she intended to sear his ears off.

But his mighty lordship tilted one side of his mouth up. "I think things have changed since you last checked, sweetheart." To her chagrin, his voice swirled over her like a balmy caress.

"Stop it." Gwen fought the sensation. She stood up. "Stop it, *now.* You're not a daft man, Lord Stafford. You know, as well as I do, just where I stand with Duchess Edinborough and her friends."

He tilted one brow with maddening confidence. "I just know where you'll be standing the eve of her ball."

"Where I want to be. In Saint Jerome's kitchen, helping Hannah with supper."

"In Edinborough Court's main foyer, helping *me* avoid Lady Leticia's dance card."

"Pardon me?"

"So you see—" In an eyeblink of motion, he looped an arm around hers and pulled her shocked form down next to him on the window seat. "You have an invitation, after all."

Gwen shook her head, still not comprehending what he looked so blasted self-assured about.

Then, like fireworks bursting in the sky, understanding flared. "You mean . . . by right of your invitation, you expect me to attend the ball? With you?"

She searched his face for a polite denial. His mouth was set in a resolute line. His jaw formed nearly right angles in its determination. And his eyes . . . no longer twinkled in mirth but gleamed with the solemnity of what he proposed. He was power defined—polished, confident, and unyielding.

He looked utterly sure of her answer. It wouldn't be no.

"No!" she cried. "Ohhh, no! You've spoken with Bryan, haven't you? Confound him!" She balled fists as she shot up and across the rose-patterned carpet. "He thinks I should be the center of every dance floor, the gossipmongers be damned."

"The gossipmongers *should* be damned."

She whirled from the safe territory behind the cherry-wood writing desk. "Well, I'm not going to be the one to damn them for you. I've told you before; I'm not the one!"

Gwen braced herself for the retaliation. None came.

Her heart began an audible pound. What now? Stafford did nothing but begin to uncoil himself from the window seat, slowly, so slowly . . . and rose to his broad height with the knowing ease of some mythical creature.

She swallowed as she gazed at him. Lord. He was incredible. Amber-streaked sunlight flowed in from the window behind him . . . and he was backlit and shadowed like a primeval being.

He didn't advance a step. Instead, he spread his hands before her in a show of complete candidness. "I am not one of the 'idle nobility,' Gwendolen. I hold controlling interest in one steel mill, three shipping companies, and a few dozen champion Thoroughbreds." He almost smiled, and his perfect teeth peeked between his lips again. "I just need an escort to rescue me from all those fortune-hunting debutantes."

Gwen gripped the desk harder. She felt her fingernails turn white with the pressure. His words and his gesture declared surrender—but how innocently so?

She knew what path the man had walked the last year. His life was ripped apart first by a murdering maniac, then by the gentry gossip grind. Just like her. And just like her, she doubted Taylor Stafford had survived this far on simple innocence.

She doubted Taylor Stafford *needed* her for anything.

Except the very mind and soul she'd refused him already.

Her blood throbbed harder. Yet now the pulse flowed hot, not cold. Now her body coursed with anger, burning away every drop of her previous fear.

Did he think he could snap his mighty earl's fingers, produce one of the most coveted invitations of the year and she'd trip over her feet to cooperate with him? She was not a pawn on his personal chessboard. She never would be!

Gwen stepped out from behind the desk. As calmly and evenly as she could, she squared her shoulders and met Stafford's steady stare.

"Leticia Edinborough is not a fortune-seeking debutante," she told him.

At least he had the decency to nod agreement. "So her dowry would make me the English Vanderbilt."

But then a funny wince furrowed his brow; he clucked his tongue before breaking into a teasing grimace. "But that *voice,*" he quipped. "I've heard more pleasant singing from the ducks at my country house."

The heat in her veins climbed to indignation temperature. She didn't have to stand here and banter with the man. If he didn't want to take her seriously, then she'd reciprocate in full measure.

"You'll get used to it," she snapped. She settled her skirts and wheeled toward the door.

He cut her third step short like a broad brick wall. Gwen

dared not look up. She already felt Stafford's gaze searing the top of her head, bathing her in the molten-gold intensity of his gaze that she knew all too well. But avoiding meeting his eyes meant taking in the length of him, hard and long-legged and warm . . . Oh dear, how had the room gotten so warm . . .

"Were we finished?" His murmur broke the silence.

The challenge yanked her eyes up, ready or not. As she looked at his hard and angry features, a dam welled inside and began to crack. She recognized only one solution for relief to the flood of frustration, confusion: to get as far away from this man and his heartless games as she possibly could.

"My lord," she said, "we are very well finished. And despite what Mr. Corstairs may have advised you, *I* suggest you keep your social plans to yourself in the future."

She tugged her skirts higher. "I am not for sale, Lord Stafford." She intended each word to burn an indelible brand upon his conscience. "Not at any price."

She whipped past him in a storm of skirts and fury.

Taylor stood awash in the arctic aftermath of her censure, muttering a string of incensed oaths of his own—until something out the window, on the far side of the lawn, caught his eye.

He moved back to the window seat. He arrived there in time to witness a vision in a pretty house gown. Gwen paced up and down the garden, attempting to even her breathing, calm her anger, and smooth her hair while simultaneously avoiding Granna, Hannah, or any of the house servants they'd recruited as guards.

"Well, well," he murmured, "so we're hiding a human being under that armor after all, are we, Miss Marsh?"

He watched her slow at the bend formed by the rosebushes, taking note of the guilty pleasure she took in smelling the opening blooms. A smile lit up his lips as she touched one full red blossom . . . She had a look of such supreme and unguarded joy on her face that Taylor blinked at the sight in disbelief.

It occurred to him, in that moment, that he'd never seen a

woman belong somewhere more. She looked Gaea come to life, fingers brushing the flower petals with gentle possession, breeze flitting her gown around the perfect curve of her goddess's waist and hips. Her long legs didn't step across the sunlit carpet of grass. They glided.

She was beautiful.

A stunned curse sprang off his lips as his feet shot to the floor. But neither action snapped the sensation inside him . . . the avalanche of want and need and sheer shock. Disastrous desire careened down his spine, buried his chest, smothered his abdomen, then lower—ah, dear God, lower.

He spun. In three steps that felt ten miles, Taylor made it to the doorway he'd been able to stand so casually in five minutes ago.

Not again, he vowed. This would *not* happen again. *This is the last time you stand here needing a cold shower because you let that shrew catch your backside unguarded. This is the real thing. Stafford. The last chance. The only stab left in the hunt.*

With that thought, he forced himself upright again. On a tight oath, he swung back toward the window, eyes narrowing in search of only one thing.

The hunted.

She'd disappeared, most likely around the bend toward the hedgerows. No matter. Though he couldn't see her any longer, she was out there. He knew it. Out there for the taking.

And this time, he *would* take her.

"Not for sale, sweetheart?" He burned her own words back into the air she'd chilled with them. "Oh, no. Everyone's for sale, my dear Miss Marsh. Everyone. I just haven't found your price yet."

A slow, slightly predatory smile inched up one side of his mouth. "But I will find it, sweet Gwen. If it takes me the rest of both our lives, I will find your price, down to the last precious ha'penny."

Six

She would have made a fine lady for some medieval Stafford in his mighty castle, Taye concluded, had providence dealt her hand that way. She held her walls against his siege longer than he thought possible for any female alive.

He'd not wasted any time in beginning the assault, either. He left the scene of their ill-fated confrontation and didn't pause until the Stafford carriage reached Regent Street.

Then he did a little shopping.

From Liberty's, he sent her Ottoman silks and Duchesse satins, imprinted with designs only seen on the finest ball gowns of the season. To scent the mountains of fabric he'd purchased, he ordered an assortment of perfume, sachets, and toilet water from Penhaligon.

Gwendolen sent the packages right back to him, unopened.

The next morning, an entourage from Harrods called at Stafford House, bearing gloves and shoes and fine-feathered hair ornaments. Granna purchased half their stock.

Gwendolen didn't leave her room.

He ordered social stationery from Frank Smythson's, on exclusive Chinese rice paper. She used one sheet, upon which she inscribed one message:

You've addressed your parcel incorrectly again, sir. I would suggest Windmill Street. I hear many fine whores reside there.

Perhaps, he concluded, it was time for reinforcements.

Late in the afternoon during the third day of his fiasco, Taylor retreated to the billiard room, indulging in an hour's worth of licking the embarrassment from his wounds and the brandy from his tumbler. Feeling bolder if not better, he rose and scribbled a message to Bryan, requesting the man's presence for an "urgent consultation" around ten that evening at White's. If the note's purposely vague phrasing didn't bring Bryan running with eyes agleam and mustache twitching, nothing would.

Now the gold glow of late afternoon bathed Taye's path back from the carriage house, where a trio of stable boys had leapt at the chance to race the blocks to Bryan's townhouse and back. Taylor began his walk back to the mansion at a brisk pace, but something stopped him. He lifted his head—to find his gaze captured by the garden roses, still blossomed to the day's light.

The petals seemed ethereal in their opened glory at this unusual hour. Like the lips of some magical garden nymph, he thought poetically, parting for the kiss of her satyr lover . . .

Or like Gwendolen Marsh's mouth when she'd bent that morning to revel in the blooms.

His thoughts lurched at the same time his heartbeat did. Where the hell had that image come from, so swiftly, so easily? He'd banished the scene from his mind with a vehemence the very day he'd watched her there, after taking terrifying inventory of what it did to his thoughts . . . and his body. But now—what the hell happened?

Taye didn't want to know the answer. Logic stepped in, advising him to turn back to the house. *No more,* that familiar, guttural voice ordered again. *No more!* He couldn't afford wasted foolishness on romantic visions, soaring blood temperature levels . . . or other rising physical functions.

But as if the roses called out with siren voices, his feet took a step across the grass. Another. A dozen more. He stopped in front of the first bush; reached a thumb out to the petals of a lush pink bud.

You're being stupid, the voice growled. *This is folly. Sentimental insanity.*

"Shut up." With an angry tug, he pulled the bloom off the branch. "I've tried everything else, haven't I?"

He returned to the billiard room by way of the back stairs this time. En route, he skirted through the dining room long enough to swaddle the twenty or so blooms he'd picked in a linen napkin, then hand the awkward assemblage off to Colleen, the upstairs maid. He ignored the servant's knowing grin as he gave her delivery instructions for the Emerald Bedroom, wiped his thorn-stabbed fingers—then cursed himself as the century's biggest idiot.

Once back in his domain, Taye lit a cigarette from the fire flames before sitting back to await his departure time for White's. And Gwendolen Marsh's newest rebuff.

Six o'clock came. So did seven.

Her rejection note did not. Not even an angry bombardment of napkin-wrapped roses.

"What the hell?" he muttered, scowling toward the hall door.

It was then that he saw Colleen whisk by. Carrying a cut-crystal flower vase.

His lips curled up in a slow, relishing smile.

"Well, well." He gazed back at the fire through steepled fingers. "It seems you've just begun the bidding, Miss Marsh."

She should have thrown the flowers back in his face.

It had occurred to her, on more than a few occasions in the last three days, to ask herself why the idea hadn't entered her mind the moment Colleen brought the haphazard bouquet to her. But something had clutched Gwen from throat to toes when she took the roses . . . something as sweet and heady as the scent wafting from the blooms themselves.

He'd seen her, she'd suddenly realized, on that morning when she'd fled and found solace in the garden. He'd seen and he'd remembered her affinity for the roses.

And perhaps, in a small way, he'd cared.

Nevertheless, he'd considered her with something more than his credit line. No florist's wrap or satin ribbons could have been more beautiful than the bloodstained napkin he'd sacrificed for her happiness. Had the man presented granite stones in the same condition, she'd have accepted them with the same awkward smile and mumbled thanks to Colleen.

And the same utter surety that she'd committed her first fatal mistake.

The peaceful calm of the next morning helped little to assuage her premonition. After every bump or shutting door throughout the house, Gwen expected his lordship to appear, a deadly smug look on his face, with another battalion of Regent Street couturiers. At his order, they'd advance, assault, then retreat with their spoils of measurements and gown orders before she could rise from the rubble to protest . . .

Even the poetry volume she'd pulled from the south sitting room's bookcase didn't distract her from starting at the *whack* of Stafford House's front door. When she realized it was only Colleen accepting the day's post, Gwen settled back into her big chintz chair again, expelled a relieved sigh—and called herself three kinds of a coward.

A gruff chuckle from the opposite chair cut into her self-censure. Granna's curls danced with silver light as the woman shook her head. "Well," the dowager countess offered, " 'tis better, at least, than the damn silence."

Gwen's mouth dropped. But the shocked gasp she expected wasn't there. Nor a polite change in subject after the elder woman's blatant profanity in broad daylight.

No . . . a laugh spilled from her throat. A shy giggle at first, then not so shy at all.

"So I see I am right." The hazel eyes Taylor had so clearly inherited twinkled with delight.

"Yes, well. I don't imagine you've been wrong in a very long while, Granna."

"And you're a very intelligent girl, Gwendolen."

Gwen laughed again.

Granna did not. The countess rose and walked to the window, but didn't settle into the cushioned seat there.

Instead, she quietly demanded, "You're not very happy here, are you, Gwendolen?"

Again, Gwen's jaw faltered on hinges of surprise. Her gaze dove to her lap. "Countess—"

"Granna," the woman corrected—for the hundredth time.

"Granna," she complied, but not gaining an iota of comfort. "It's not that I don't . . . enjoy Stafford House. Your home is beautiful. It's just that—"

"It's just that my bull-headed grandson is making things bloody hard on you."

It seemed Taylor Stafford had inherited more than his grandmother's eyes. Oh, if Gwen designated the current Earl Stafford the reigning knight errant of drumming a person speechless with one statement, then his Granna was the man's liege lord of the craft.

"Now, come on . . ." Granna turned and brandished that unforgettably bright gaze again. "Out with it, my girl. I won't stand for shilly-shallying; you know that." She stabbed a finger toward the floor in emphasis. "I know Taylor didn't very well send 'round all those lacy gloves and hair bobs for *me* last week. I am also of a suspicion it wasn't the first game he's tried to tag you into playing."

The woman cocked her head and waited.

Gwen screwed her hands together and panicked. Good *Lord.* What was wrong with her? This was the scene she'd written off as impossible—the chance to win a real ally to her cause—and now her lips struggled around words that wouldn't come.

Tell her. Tell her. *This whole mess will be over and you won't have to worry about silly ball gowns or foolish flowers or the possibility of facing roomfuls of stares ever again.*

Or facing any more of Taylor's questions again.

Instead, she heard herself blurting, "He didn't mean any real harm, Granna—"

"Ah, ha!" came the triumphant cry. "I am rarely wrong; you said it yourself! Dear God, what's he put you through? That boy's persistence would have a nun considering suicide."

Gwen could not help an awkward laugh. "All right," she conceded. "He certainly is persistent."

"And stubborn."

"Well . . ."

"Unthinking."

"Well, no . . ."

"And overbearing. And undergroomed. I should have taken hedge cutters to that savage's mane of his long ago."

"Stop!"

Yet as the protest exploded past her lips, she wondered *where* it had come from. Granna hadn't uttered a single syllable Gwen hadn't fired at the man herself the last three weeks.

The only possible answer terrified her. She wasn't rational anymore. Taylor Stafford had driven her to, and finally over, the ledge of coherent reasoning.

"Damn and blast!" She flew up from her chair to pace in raw confusion. "The truth?" she cried. "You want the truth, Granna?" She spread her arms as she threw a helpless stare across the room. "The truth is, your grandson is the most befuddling, infuriating, frustrating—man I've ever met. He infuriates me. He terrifies me. And he—" She emitted a loud huff to mask her dread at uttering her next confession. "And he . . . exhilarates me."

She groaned and dropped back into her chair. "Ohhh, no. The truth is, Granna, I don't know *what* I should feel about your grandson."

It must have been the wind. Or an echo of the servants speaking to each other. Yet in the soft silence that followed, Gwen could have sworn she heard, in Granna's distinct gravel of a voice:

"Good."

Then she felt him materialize at the doorway.

She longed to lob her head off at snapping in such instant response to his power over the room—over her. Though dressed utterly unconventionally, in a white open-necked shirt and grey country trousers, he stood confident and composed . . . and big. So big, he made the wingback chairs look like dollhouse furniture. And so rugged, he stole more of her breath than a North Sea wind.

He looked exactly as her imagination conjured him a moment ago.

What are you? she longed to scream. *Emerging from shadows, materializing in doorways, appearing simply from a picture in my mind . . . what in this world* are *you? What are you doing to me? I don't want this! I don't want you!*

But Taylor Stafford didn't heed her thoughts now. With that maddening half-smile playing at his lips, he sauntered to his grandmother. A hint of spiced cologne and fresh stable hay surrounded him. He responded to the countess's command for an embrace and kiss. They exchanged what looked like casual pleasantries; Gwen couldn't make out their words through the dizzy buzz in her head.

Then he turned that spectacular gold-green gaze upon her. ". . . morning to you, too, Miss Marsh."

His greeting broke into her stupor not a moment too soon. She blinked at him, feeling more ridiculous than before. "Yes, well," she finally replied, not wanting to hide her vexation. "It *has* been a good morning. We'll see from here on, won't we?"

"I imagine we will." He dipped his chin just as he dropped his voice: in a smooth, clear show of challenge.

She couldn't have been more thankful for Granna's interjecting step between them—until the countess looked up and asked, "Where did you say Colleen needed me, Taylor?"

"In your wardrobe." Though he answered his grandmother, he stared over the woman's head at Gwen. "Something about your purchases arriving from Harrods," he added, "and 'no bloody room' to put them anywhere."

"Ah, yes. That would sound like Colleen, wouldn't it? Gwendolen, I am most sorry. This is, I'm afraid, a pressing matter if I'm ever to find anything in that closet again. Our chat was most interesting. I hope we can take it up again soon."

"Of course, Granna."

But she watched another Gwen perform the response. An artificial Gwen, part of a decorous facade she'd shined to perfection over the years, when Margaret Marsh's niece, of all people, wouldn't dream of showing the agitation truly burning her soul.

Those times just like now.

She waited half an instant after Granna's farewell before donning a harder shell over her pretense. She whirled and marched back to her chair. Scooping her shawl under one arm and the poetry volume under the other, Gwendolen concentrated on keeping her movements sharp and aseptic. She would not soften or falter, no matter how close he stalked up behind her, so silent, so smooth, so big. He stepped nearer. Nearer . . .

He stopped. So did she. *No. No!*

Still behind her, Taylor tugged on the poetry book. It slipped from her grip to his with a teasing shush.

"Wh-what arc you doing?" she demanded past a suddenly dry throat.

When he didn't reply, she turned on him.

A mistake. A grave mistake. Her skirts swirled around his legs as her feet stumbled atop his . . . her legs fitted against his.

Only the poetry book, lodged between them, protected the secret of her pummeling heart from detection by his towering chest. He surrounded her, filled her world with his unyielding body and his unremitting gaze, and it was—oh, it was—

Insufferable!

Incredible.

Gwen stumbled back, barely saving her balance with a jerk of her skirts. "What are you doing?" she snapped again.

"What are you reading?" He made the quip as if she'd breezed him a compliment on the tailoring of his shirt.

"My lord, I don't appreciate—"

"Ahhh. The romantics."

His tone lifted so perfectly, Gwen almost thought his interest real. But caution stepped in with able timing; as he opened the book to her marked page, she felt as if those powerful fingers pried at her soul.

"Don't. Don't! My preferences are a private matter!"

He easily dodged her lunge. "And such exemplary preferences. The Brontës." One brow cocked her way. "Now don't tell me; I want to guess. Would Gwendolen Marsh be a devotee of Anne's diplomacy, or the lightning and thunder of Emily? A difficult wager to place. Let me think . . ."

Gwen halted just short of locking toeholds with the man again. "Neither," she retorted. "*Byron* is my favorite poet."

Following the trend of this whole unnerving encounter, the man answered her with a brighter show of his teeth. She nearly fell apart. How she longed for the imposing stranger she'd first confronted at Saint Jerome's. She could contend with *that* brooding warrior. This provocative rogue hit too close . . . dredged up too much. He reminded her too much of the way things used to be. The person she used to be.

"Well, well," Stafford finally drawled, striding to the window seat and swinging one knee up to the cushion without a glance up from the volume in his hand. "So the lady does enjoy verse of more dramatic impact. But Byron . . . you surprise me there, madam. A man of such controversy. A man who took risks. Many, many risks."

He looked up at her. Gwen instantly noticed the change in his gaze. The subtle, smoldering copper light . . . the heat of knowing challenge and quiet confidence.

"You don't strike me as the kind of person who likes to take risks, Miss Marsh."

He stunned her speechless for a moment. But only a moment, before the safe shelter of anger sprung up and heated the comeback in her throat. "I don't strike many people as the true person I am anymore, Lord Stafford. And I dislike—no, I *resent* you for trying to bait me like this."

She jerked her shawl around her shoulders and prepared to leave without a backward glance.

She never expected the words he filled that silence with. She never imagined that commanding voice affecting her the way it did now, reaching out like gentle fingers instead, wrapping around her senses as he began to read: " *'By that lip I long to taste . . .'* "

She stopped. Slowly, she turned back. "Wh-what are you—"

" ' *. . . by that zone-encircled waist . . .*' "

"Stop that."

Her order fizzled into a weak choke. To her horror, Gwen felt herself gravitate to the window seat and slump down to the cushions opposite him.

Then she listened. She listened with all her being. She listened to his voice not only caress the poem, but reach out and embrace *her.* His eyes and lips didn't just follow the text, they *became* Byron's vow of devotion to a wide-eyed Maid of Athens. His murmur projected just loud enough to reach the confines of this window seat alone . . . for her ears alone. His facial expressions were gentle, charming, and . . . for her eyes alone. The way he curved one side of his mouth upon certain words . . . the raise of his lashes every few moments, caressing her like the black velvet they resembled . . .

" *'By all the token-flowers that tell,'* " he read on. " *'What words can never speak so well . . . by love's alternate joy and woe.'* "

She didn't blink or breathe, waiting for the next stanza.

It didn't come. Instead, Taylor leveled his gaze at her, all warmth and light and hazel penetration, inundating every inch of her paralyzed being. "The words of a fighting man, wouldn't you say, Miss Marsh?"

She still didn't blink or breathe. But now, shock held both back from her.

"A *fighting* man?" she finally sputtered. *By Saint Peter, Michael, and Matthew,* as Hannah would say. The man might smile like Don Juan and stare like Romeo, but his poetic interpretation belonged somewhere in the Stone Ages.

"Of course." He smiled with slow, maddening ease. " 'Love's alternate joy and woe.' The man who wrote those words knew about the struggles in life, not just the easy times. But that didn't mean he was afraid of the rough roads. Byron was a man who knew learning occurs from the 'woes' as well as the 'joys.' "

At that, his brows crunched again. "Yes, Miss Marsh. I would say your choice of poets fascinates me."

And at *that,* Gwen suddenly understood. Oh, yes; his whole purpose flared to light like the explosion from a pistol—and ignited her with equally violent fury.

The arrogant, manipulating viper! Who declared him the accountant of her personal courage? What had possessed him, thinking he'd break her resistance by exploiting the beauty of poetry for his own twisted purpose? What had possessed *her,* assuming a handful of roses and a few lines of poetry changed a heathen into a prince?

He had no right to control her life. And she intended to show him so.

Her gaze never faltered from the dark face before her as Gwen leaned forward with her own little "request." "And just who is *your* favorite poet, my lord?"

His eyes widened—though the reaction maintained the slow, purposeful demeanor seemingly woven into the Stafford genes. "I think words can be different things to a person, at different times in his life."

"And I think that is an evasive, if not faint-hearted, answer."

"On the contrary." As a strangely triumphant smile took over his lips, he returned to flipping pages with an alacrity that prompted Gwen's nerves to hammer. "I hardly consider it faint-hearted to seek out the words which will speak best to me or for me, even if they aren't what I want to hear."

Then her heartbeat came to an eerie silence. The strong-fingered hands rested on their new selection in the poetry book.

Taylor began to read again.

" 'On Another's Sorrow,' " he pronounced. "By William Blake."

Maybe this was *not* such a brilliant idea, Gwen decided, as the pain of her losses ran through her anew. "No," she blurted. "I don't think I'll enjoy this at all, my lord."

" 'Can I see another's woe, and not be in sorrow, too?' " he began. *" 'Can I see another's grief, and not seek for kind relief?' "*

"I asked you to stop."

He still didn't listen. But he forced her to do just that, once more. And try as she would to fight, to gaze out the window, to close her heart against him completely, she heard him. She heard each stanza read by that mesmerizing voice, rising and falling and pressing at her emotions as if the ghost of Blake himself had appeared to Taylor Stafford and infused him with the same anguish that the piece was conceived in—the same human yearning to reach out to another human being, even in their terrible, grieving times. The same longing to say *I understand you . . . I understand your pain.*

Gwen's eyes flew open. Taylor's words resounded in her head with crystal-bell clarity. She watched Taylor's head rise from the book, his lips move through the last lines of the poem by heart. Then, most incredible of all, his gaze met hers with and shared his true message:

I understand.

For a long moment, she only sat and stared—and struggled to breathe. Then she asked him the question that had haunted her since the day she met him. "Wh-what are you doing to me?"

Stafford swallowed—but said nothing. At last, he shut the

poetry book and stood gracefully. He walked to the bookcase and slid the volume into its slot. Gwen watched his every move with mortified fascination.

When he turned back to her, hard angles once more defined his face. Yet his lips parted again on that quiet half-smile; his intent gaze caught and captured hers.

"I have seen your grief, Miss Marsh," he said softly. "One day soon, I hope you'll let me ease it."

He turned and strode from the room.

In the ensuing stillness, Gwen sat numbly for a minute. Perhaps two. Then she slammed her fingers to her temple, battling to contain the thoughts ricocheting a hundred directions at once—a sensation not much different than that first dazing morning Taylor Stafford had thrown her into a spin of utter confusion.

As she had on that long-ago morning, she struggled to get mad. Very mad. She had every right. The man smothered her one day with blatant bribes, astonished her the next with roses stained in his own blood. When he was near, she thought of nothing but getting away from him. When he departed, she thought of naught else but his soul-piercing eyes, his thick dark mane, and his towering stance that blocked rational thought as well as doorways.

Yes, she had every right to curse the snake a thousand times over. And she *would.*

As soon as she stopped this racing rush of her heart, this crazy churning of her stomach, this heightened awareness of every sound and scent and sight around her.

In short, as soon as she stopped feeling so alive again.

Seven

Why was she doing this?

While the thought crept a maddeningly sure path down her spine, Gwen's course down the forest-green carpeting of Stafford House's north hallway fared no better than a cat's first agitated foray through a water puddle.

Lord, Gwendolen, came a rebuke oddly resonant of Aunt Maggie's drone, *it's not as if you're breaking into the Tower of London.* Indeed, Stafford House had welcomed Hannah and her more like family members than guests. From Granna's gruff affection to Colleen's detailed care, down to the youngest house maids and garden boys, she'd been assured even the basement of Stafford House lay at her disposal.

But she cared more to explore the mating habits of African butterflies than anything further about Taylor Stafford, even if he did live in a luxurious paradise of a house. The man only wanted one thing from her and would clearly resort to any tactic to triumph in his cause. She didn't need any more "tidbits" than that.

But that was what she thought before.

That was what she thought before one portentous morning two weeks ago, when Stafford House's master entered the south sitting room to wish his granna a pleasant morn and stayed to read poetry as Gwen had never heard it read before. Before he posed questions that kept her pacing half that night, searching out the answers in her heart and soul.

Before she'd found him waiting in the sitting room again the next morning. And the next.

And every ensuing morning, without fail, after that.

Yes, Taylor Stafford curled those long legs of his into the window seat every morning. He cocked those dark eyebrows of his at her at least fifty times each day. He wielded that wide white smile over and over, even daring a few laughs, until Gwen thought he'd actually guffaw like a *Punch* caricature one day.

He'd made *her* laugh.

Sometimes they shared just an amused chuckle. Other times, the moment came full and brilliant and buoyant, often in response to some silly love play of the birds on the lawn. And often they just sat in silence, no words needed from the other to communicate, *Yes. I understand. I still feel the hurt and frustration, too.*

Drat the man!

Drat him for every second of those magical mornings. For each one of those too-swift minutes, soon becoming those fleeting hours. Gwen hadn't thought of Lloyd once—and felt disturbingly devoid of shame about the fact.

Drat him that on the first day he took a predawn leave of the house for a business meeting in Oxford, Gwen missed the mesmerizing lout.

Oh, she certainly tried *not* to. She dressed leisurely, opting for a comfortable shirtwaist and wide-bowed skirt, and descended to the south sitting room in anticipation of some peaceful solitude.

She didn't feel peaceful. She felt lonely.

Thus, an hour later, she found herself tiptoeing around the opposite side of Stafford House. The most private part of Taylor Stafford's world.

Looking for what? an inner voice blasted at her. She didn't want to know anything about the man! She didn't care!

She wheeled toward the south wing again.

"Hullo," a high, small voice said.

The sheer innocence conveyed in the greeting would have stopped Atilla the Hun in his boots. Gwen's flat soles—and her heart—presented much simpler conquests.

She turned and looked back down the hall.

Then froze in pure astonishment.

There, toy sword and shield dangling at his sides, injecting an unblinking hazel stare into her, stood a boy-size version of Taylor Stafford.

"Hullo there," the child-Taylor repeated. Black curls fell over the boy's high forehead, as he cocked an inquisitive look at her. "You're the princess from the south wing, aren't you?"

Even if she'd had time to recover from her first jolt, the question didn't rank high on her what-to-expect-next list. "Princess?" Much of her wonderment didn't have to be acted. "There's a princess in the south wing? Truly?"

The boy stepped closer. "You didn't know?"

Gwen shook her head, battling the temptation to finger those silky black curls back into place. "I've . . . been sleeping a lot lately. I'm afraid I missed the excitement. Why don't you tell me about it?"

"That's odd." The solemn mouth wrinkled, straight brows lowering in a scowl so Taylor-like, her initial instinct now rang as truth. She gazed upon the future Baron Roseby, Earl Stafford.

He had a *son.* A sturdy-shouldered, proud-jawed, absolutely flawless son.

A little boy, she suddenly realized, who would never hear his mother's lullabies. Would never feel her morning kiss. Then later, a young man who would never see Constance's gentle tears on his wedding day . . .

Taylor Stafford's desperate search for a killer began to make more sense. Stunning, wrenching sense.

Gwen *knew* she shouldn't have wandered here.

"Yes. That's very odd," the boy repeated then. "You see, father says the princess needs to sleep a lot, too. He says that's why it's important to be quiet and good."

"Well." Gwen compressed her lips to steady her smile. "You certainly snuck up on me without a peep."

"I did, didn't I?" A dimpled grin broke free. "Father will be proud."

"I'm certain he already is."

At that, she knelt. She tilted her head in an expression to match her soft inquisition. "But doesn't your father allow you to run or play outside? Doesn't he ever play with you?"

"Oh, all the time." Black curls cascaded on the bobbing head. "But now we play more quiet games. Father doesn't like to tussle as much as he used to. Not since—"

A deep scowl possessed the child's face again.

"Not since what?"

"Not since the monster came and took Mother away."

The boy lifted his gaze to her again. Despite her staunchest command to herself not to, Gwen almost broke the connection. The young eyes held as much hope as Loch Ness at midnight. "It made Father very sad," he uttered. "And very tired all the time. So you see, he doesn't like to tussle much anymore."

"Yes," she whispered. "I see."

"But maybe—maybe when the princess wakes up, she'll tell Father to tussle again!"

Like his father, the young earl spoke with total determination. Gwen chuckled. "Maybe she just will."

"I hope so." The child squirmed against the confines of his high-buttoned collar and stiff blue jacket. "I really thought princesses were supposed to be more fun than this."

"Oh, I'm certain they are—if you'd give them a chance. Perhaps your father's guest was ill. Maybe she needs her rest to get better."

The child's innocent, near-onyx eyes appeared to ponder this, deep in thought. Then, as if a lightning jolt of understanding had struck the corridor, he grinned at her again. "I was ill once. I had to stay abed for days. I remember now. My friends said I was no fun anymore. But Granna said I was plenty of fun, and that one day I'd show them."

"And you did, didn't you?"

An even wider grin served as his agreement. "I like you." The proclamation came complete with a regal sweep of the play sword. "What's your name?"

"How about if you just call me Gwen?"

"Then you call me Danny. You see, Granna calls me Daniel. And my friends call me Danny. I like that better. But Father calls me the best of all." The boy squared his shoulders beneath the jacket he'd just fought against. "Father calls me his 'mate.' But only Father can call me that."

While nodding back, Gwen assumed an expression as gravely earnest as his.

"I must get back to my dragon," Danny piped then. "I was in the middle of stalking him through St. Hubert's Wood."

"Ah." Gwen rose. "Then I shall not detain you, Sir Danny."

"Detain me?" The dark curls took a new tumble with the scowl he sliced at her. "No. You're coming *with* me."

Unfortunately, she didn't know whether to frown or laugh. "With you?"

"Well, of course." Danny lifted the painted wood shield with one elbow and offered the crook of the sword-bearing arm to her. "You see, Lucifer—that's the dragon—will only come out if a beautiful princess calls him with the magic words."

Now Gwen only wanted to cry. *Beautiful.* When was the last time someone looked at her and used the word? When was the last time anyone *looked* at her, aside from this lad's father, with his nerve-razing scrutiny?

And yet this perfect, profound little being gazed at her and said *beautiful.*

It was enough to make a girl feel like . . . a princess.

"What are the magic words?" Gwen asked while accepting the proffered elbow. Though in her opinion, they'd already been said.

"Uh—um—I don't know yet." Danny tugged her down the hall. "They're written on the enchanted stone at the top of the waterfall in the wood. But it's a very hard climb. Lots of rocks and bramble bushes and—and nasty gnomes who want to bite off your toes for dinner. That's why no princess has agreed to try it. But you will, won't you, Princess Gwen?"

"Of course. The safety of the whole village depends on the success of our quest, does it not?"

"Yes!" Danny discarded his whisper to a more enthusiastic cry. "You're right; it does! Let's go!"

Faced with the ultimatum of either welling up with happy tears or breaking into a traitorous smile, Gwen followed her knight down the green carpeting toward their enchanted wood.

The first shriek sliced the air as Taylor finished shrugging out of his cloak. When the second outcry pierced his ears, he hurled the garment to the front hall's Aubusson rug and bounded up the main stairwell, three steps at a time. At the top, he spun right—toward Danny's room.

Had the doorframe not been nailed down, he would have torn the oak strip away with his lunge into his son's bedroom. Heart pounding in his throat, he charged forward, ready to kill the villain who'd caused Danny's screams with his bare hands.

Instead, he froze dumbfounded in the portal.

Waist-deep in a mound of bedclothes, surrounded by bright-eyed stuffed animals and stoic-faced play soldiers, Danny paused with toy sword held high and beamed a wild, happy grin.

It was the biggest smile he'd seen on his son's face in a year.

"Hullo, Father!"

"Hello, mate," he managed to answer.

But when he thought his pulse nearing its normal status again, another face poked from the heap on the bed. A head—no, a mussed and magnificent halo of gold-copper curls emerged. Beneath that, a deep green stare appeared . . . a gaze he'd found himself thinking of more and more lately, whenever he beheld the blossomings of coming spring on London's trees and bushes.

"Hullo," Gwendolen called to him.

"Hello."

He smiled.

She smiled back.

The muscles in his limbs clenched with the frenzy of an army putting itself on alert.

Not a second too late, that awareness received a shove back from the brink from forty-two inches of exuberant six-year-old boy.

"Ooof!" Taye absorbed most of his son's assault with a bend of his wool trouser-clad legs. "Aren't you tilting a little roughly today, Sir Danny?"

"And so I must!" Danny made a sweeping indication to the bedclothes—and that mirth-sprinkled stare still peeking out from them. "I am guiding my lady fair through the wood of the treacherous gnomes."

Despite the urge to return Gwendolen's smile with a chuckle of his own, Taye dutifully knitted his brows. *"Not* the treacherous gnomes."

"Toe biters," she confirmed.

"Toe biters!" Understanding the dramatic cue, he frowned harder.

"Nastiest creatures in the shire!" Danny cried. Delight flushed the boy's face; he shot excited glances at the *two* grown-ups he'd successfully recruited for his adventure. "Princess Gwen and I last accosted them beyond these rocks. Over here— Come, Father."

Taylor followed his son's lead around the foot of the bed, but threw a silent-mouthed, *Princess Gwen?* at his co-conspirator beneath the covers. She replied via a barely suppressed laugh . . . and her lovely face became suffused with a peach blush.

"There! There they are! Do you see them, Father?"

Taylor positioned himself behind Danny so the child

wouldn't see the smile he could no longer check. He heard the exhilaration in his son's words, but it might as well have been his own lips bursting with the excitement—his own soul, once writhing like a wolf caught in a trap, set free by a peach blush for his eyes only.

His own blood, singing with the power of Princess Gwendolen's smile.

He felt like running. He felt like shouting. He felt like kicking the arses of some nasty toe-eating gnomes.

"Yes. Yes, I do see them." He seized his son's shoulders with just the right pressure of anticipation.

"Quick, Father; behind this tree! We have to wait for the perfect moment to attack!"

"And when is that?"

"Now, of course!"

The two of them let out a raucous whoop. Gwendolen laughed and cheered. To the rhythm of her bravos, they dove and slashed, grappled and fought their way across the bedroom full of imaginary bramble bushes hiding evil-eyed gnomes.

By the eighth routing, the maneuvers began to grow quite dramatic—but certainly *not,* Taylor reasoned, because of the praise their princess showered more abundantly on the younger knight in the room. Still, four more flattened gnomes later, enough was enough. He purposely flew out of an elaborate dive and straight into a dashing belly roll. If *this* move didn't command her applause—

So intent on watching for Gwen's reaction, Taye didn't see the wall crowding his way until it was too late.

His crash and the silence hit at once.

For a long moment, Taylor stared at his haphazard position, legs crunched against the oak wainscoting, upper body sprawled along the burgundy carpeting.

Then he threw back his head and laughed. He laughed harder than he remembered laughing in the last two years. Danny joined in with exhilarated giggles.

But the now-familiar female laugh didn't join them.

Driven by a feeling too far beyond puzzlement, Taye looked to the bed.

He found Gwendolen's gaze already upon him. He caught her in the midst of a futile effort to bite back a radiant grin.

She was, he determined without thought or hesitation, breathtaking.

"The princess!" Danny suddenly screamed. "Father, what are you doing sitting there? One of the gnomes has sneaked onto the hill with the princess!"

"So one has." He made sure their "damsel on the hill" saw his slow, devilish grin. "How did we let that happen?" he teased, stalking closer to her—and the mound of toys, blankets, and pillows she commanded. "We've got to rout out the vermin if it takes tearing down that hill ourselves."

"If it *what?*" Gwendolen's features snapped from the confusion he'd just stimulated to an comprehending gape of panic. "Ohhh, no!" Scattering two pillows and three teddy bears, she scrambled toward the headboard. "The princess needs no rescuing from the hill; thank you, gentlemen!"

Danny copied Taye's hearty laugh of dismissal. "When say you we charge, mate?" the six-year-old challenged.

"Now, of course!"

They yelled. She screamed. They leapt; she rolled. They pounced, at last forcing her to join their wild chaos.

An imbroglio of tangled limbs and sheets and laughter later, they came to the mutual conclusion that the gnome had gone screaming for higher ground. They let up three cheers of victory, and for good measure, a rousing "God save the Queen!"

And then Taylor came face-to-face with her.

He breathed hard, wiping a sheen of sweat from his forehead. So did she. His tie had gone askew, his shirt and waistcoat rumpled beyond recognition. So were the proper bow and ruffles of her shirtwaist. Half of London would have swooned nose first into their etiquette manuals from the spectacle.

Taylor wouldn't have traded away the moment for all the riding ground in Ireland.

His smile fell.

He couldn't deny the feeling as truth. Yet he couldn't accept it, either. He wouldn't.

Ah, God.

Just when the bloody hell had he begun to look at her like that?

For once, Danny's shattering squeal came as a blessing. After putting up a challenging enough "resistance," Taylor allowed his son to assault, conquer, then roll him to his back and assume proper position of "conqueror" astraddle his torso.

"Cry *mercy.*" Danny instructed from his lofty throne.

"Mercy."

The boy lowered a finger to Taylor's sternum. "Who's the bravest knight in the shire?"

"It would certainly be *you,* Sir Danny."

His son flashed the same cheek-splitting grin Taylor had entered with. Taylor desperately tried to pretend the expression didn't again detonate his heart into shards of pure joy.

But Danny's next action was even more astonishing. Without a second's hesitation, his son turned that rare smile to the woman sitting next to them. "And what say *you,* princess? Does this knave say the truth, or do I chop his head off?"

At that, her dark-green eyes flashed more like a denouncing queen's. "Now, Sir Danny, you know I won't tolerate any head chopping in my kingdom."

He should have expected the unexpected by now, but Taye found himself blinking in wonder as his stubborn dervish of a son nodded assent to the mandate. "Well," Danny proclaimed. "You'll live another day, Master Stafford."

Then the boy rolled away—and scrambled straight into Gwendolen Marsh's arms. She laughed that vibrant laugh again, and stroked the hair from his eyes.

Taylor stared at the action, motionless, speechless.

Danny never let Constance touch his hair like that.

"Father?" His son's query broke into the suddenly hot, heavy air. "Can Princess Gwen come to dinner tonight?"

Taylor found his throat strangely dry and tight. Still he forced air into a reply as his gaze poured over her face. "I don't know, mate. Does Princess Gwen *want* to come to dinner tonight?"

She raised her head. The vibrant spectrum of her stare met—and intertwined with—his gaze.

His nerve endings couldn't have exploded more had their bodies entangled with the same unthinking intimacy.

Her lips parted on a hesitant smile. "I would be honored to dine with you, gentlemen."

Again, she affected him with the potency of a physical touch. Her words, so simply murmured, entered his ears . . . caressed his soul . . . stroked his blood.

"We dine at six," Taylor heard himself grate in a strangely formal voice. Then he only longed to get out of here, to escape the tempest whipping through his mind and body.

He tore through the hall, down the back stairs, across the lawn, and into the calming emptiness of the carriage house. He ripped his jacket from his shoulders and wrenched at his tie until it hung limp from his neck. Then he slammed back against a dark damp wall, gulping in the scents of leather and hay and horses, embracing any smell to forget the innocent essence of Danny mingled with the heady scent of *her:* of lace washed in fresh rain, of soft peach skin cleaned with wonderful, ordinary soap. He embraced any thought except the memories of battling invisible gnomes, of rolling among soft sheets and against soft, curving woman, and of meeting an emerald stare over the head of his happy son.

And he struggled to feel anything, *anything,* other than this sensation which clung to him more doggedly than all those scents and sounds and images put together. This pounding, arousing, torturing, terrifying feeling . . .

This sensation he remembered only as happiness.

Eight

Gwen leaned across the planter to get a better look at the bug. It must be the well-tended soil of the Stafford grounds; she'd never encountered a beauty like this half-beetle, half-spider before. As she pressed farther in, branch-fingers of the holly bush caught at wisps of her hair, but the tugs distracted more than stung.

If only her memories of this morning would diminish to mere distractions.

The insect—and Gwen's patience—scrambled out of reach. She released a huff and shook her head, but the images assailed her anyway, every moment of those hours in the north wing, swirling in her mind like beads of fresh dew twirling on a spider's perfect web. The visions came differently each time, changing hues as with the light, but each view was just as beautiful—yet as strange—as the first.

One contained Danny's face, at first questioning and curious, then grinning with the satisfied joy of childhood. Another memory sparkled with the hour she and Danny had spent "building the fortress," piling their "stones" of pillows and bedding atop Danny's bed until the creation towered so high it fell over, and they'd laughed and started all over again.

But then the images came with a third face. The sight of Danny's wide grin as he'd looked to the doorway of his room and seen his father, the larger version of himself, standing there. And that soaring, sinking feeling returned to her stomach, remembering the way Lord Earl King of Spain Stafford turned from Danny to look at her . . . to smile at her . . .

As if she were something more than just a stepping stone on his quest.

"No," she said, crushing a hand-sized canyon in the damp earth as punctuation. *"No.* Stop it, Gwen. *Stop it.* Don't think about it."

"I'm sorry," a deep, instantly recognizable chuckle offered from behind, "but I think the groundsman has already tried the strict approach. From what I can remember of his account, it didn't stop the caterpillars from eating one leaf less."

She clenched her fingers into the dirt, annihilating the hand canyon she'd made there. Gwen gaped past the equally filthy ball of her other hand, down the length of her once-ivory skirt, then up into the reality of half-smiling features she'd just or dered from her thoughts.

The rest of his mighty lordship looked just the way she remembered him from this morning, too. That same dangerous rogue's look, with those waves of hair teasing about his face and, despite what must have been his valet's best effort with comb and pomade, curling rebelliously around his ears. His imposing shoulders and strong arms. That beautiful masculine body, crouched over the shined boots completing his crisp black dinner attire.

Dinner.

"Oh, my word," Gwen gasped. "Dinner!"

After a gape at the darkening sky, she slapped both hands to the instant flush of her cheeks. Mortification set in with the realization she'd just smeared dirt all over her face. "Oh, God . . ." She tried to rectify the situation with the backs of her hands—succeeding in only making the mess worse.

"I'd completely forgotten about din—not that your invitation wasn't important, my lord—I just—Dr. Ramsey finally said I could spend a few hours outdoors, and when I saw this planter needed a few weeds pulled—not that your groundsman doesn't keep it lovely—" *Well, Gwendolen, why don't you just stuff some dirt clods into your mouth for all the good your tact is achieving?*

But her further self-castigations were prevented by a comforting thump on the ground next to her.

Gwen turned wide eyes to the sight of Taylor, Baron Roseby, Earl Stafford, on his dinner-suited hands and knees, peering at the plot of earth she'd just vacated.

"You're absolutely correct," he said. "This planter needs to be weeded. I'll see to it after our morning reading tomorrow."

Gwen's mouth opened. Closed. Opened again. Perhaps she'd be able to form a coherent reply if he didn't stand and follow his declaration with a stare of such encompassing, engulfing hazel light, making *her* feel like a drop of water making rainbows in the sun . . .

No. Not a waterdrop. Something more. Standing here in this quiet, potent twilight, in the glow of this man's quiet, potent stare, she felt something more profound . . . something beyond this world. Something beyond the warm curl in her stomach when his gaze embraced her like this; something more than the scattered vibrations at the tips of her toes and the back of her neck. Something more than just the physical awareness he wrought . . .

She felt like a star. Yes . . . energy and light surged through her like the heavens reflecting the sun's glory. The sensation filled her so much that she looked to the real firmament overhead, certain her body couldn't possibly hold so much life and that a good portion must have exploded into the dark canopy above.

Alas, only a handful of white pinpoints ventured forth in the sky yet to announce the night. A pine-scented preamble of an evening breeze accompanied them. Gwen took in a long, reverent look. "It's beautiful."

"Yes." The reply came with such confidence, she turned a wondering glance to see if both she and Taylor looked at the same sky.

He fixed his intent hazel stare on her.

She stepped back. Her fingers flew to her lips, suddenly tingling with a fascinating, frightening heat. She whirled, searching the chaos of her mind for the most composed voice she'd perfected during her tenure at Saint Jerome's.

"It's getting dark," she stammered. "And it must be past six." She gave a nervous laugh. "Danny's probably decapitated all the dining-room candles in a fit of hunger by now."

"Don't worry about Danny." From behind her, his voice was low and caressing.

"I think it's a little late for that." She laughed again as she raised her hem for the trek up the slight incline toward the house. "I'm a woman, my lord. Worrying is siphoned into a woman's blood."

"I said not to worry. Danny isn't waiting for us."

She dropped her skirt. She turned to shoot a quizzical look down at where she'd left Taylor standing, but found herself backstepping once more. He'd gained six inches toward her.

"Wh-what do you mean?"

"I mean my dervish of a son passed out from exhaustion hours ago." He made no move to close the gap between them again, but kicked the grass nervously with his elegantly shod feet until he'd adequately blazed a path to her toes.

"I was going to rouse him for our date anyway," he explained. "From what Cook tells me, he was a devil of a nuisance at her heels, making sure 'Princess Gwen's' dinner was prepared perfectly. But when I went to his room and saw him snoring there . . ." Now a boyish grin broke through Taylor's controlled mien, completing the picture started by his wind-tossed hair. "Well, who in their right mind would dare interrupt a snoring man?"

Gwen crossed her arms with a teasing smile of her own. "In other words, you couldn't do it."

"And *you* could have?"

"I didn't profess I could. But if the situation is dire enough, a body must cast aside any personal apprehensions for the good of the kingdom as a whole."

"Really, now?"

His pointed tone wasn't necessary. As a hush abruptly permeated the garden, so a terrified silence fell over Gwen's soul. Only the ominous beat of her heart sounded, reminding her just how stupidly she'd baited, set, and caught herself in her own trap.

She clutched her arms tighter to her sides, wishing she could disappear, but knowing she must stand here and face the convenient twist he'd make of her statement. Dreading the condemnation in his eyes when she turned down his next petition for help.

If, she amended, she had the strength to turn him down again.

Dear God, she prayed, *please give me the strength. Because I certainly don't have the courage to say yes . . .*

The pine-touched breeze swirled between them. A cricket began its steady overture; the bushes and trees swished a soft obbligato.

"Well," the smooth, low voice finally murmured. "That's an interesting piece of advice to think on, Miss Marsh."

Then he lowered both hands behind his back, loosely clasped them there, and began to walk back into the shadows of the garden. Gwen watched him in perplexed awe—until he paused, jerked his head up as if he was missing something, and didn't stop searching until his gaze fell upon her again.

"What are you still doing there?" With a curious half-smile, he beckoned her with a soft but confident tug of his head. "Come."

Gwen continued to stand there. A million voices screamed the order to whirl and run as fast as she could back to the house. *You lummox; don't you see? He's saving the attack for the garden! He's going to get you all alone,* then *trick you—perhaps seduce you—into complying with his plans!*

But a single whisper in her heart echoed Hannah's long-ago words back to her: *An earl in name, Gwennie, but a prince in his heart. Ye've got to trust someone sometime, Gwennie. Ye've got to trust.*

Gwen closed her eyes in a quick prayer for guidance.

When she opened them again, she smiled. A whisper of wind touched her cheeks as if to express approval of the other whisper she must heed. Then the breeze moved on, down the slope, ruffling the black-clad figure at the bottom.

She followed the wind.

When she stopped at Taylor's side, he smiled and cocked his dirt-smudged elbow toward her. After just a moment of hesitation, she smiled back and slipped her soiled hand into the bend of his arm.

"Where are we going?" she asked after an easy silence of a few minutes. Though they'd hardly walked miles from the mansion, once more she found it difficult to believe this verdant world had an end to it: a wall lying somewhere beyond the oak and pine trees lining their way, a city full of joys, sorrows, and real life beyond that.

"Aren't you hungry?" Taylor said in way of answer.

She turned a puzzled expression to him. "I hadn't thought about it."

"Cook told me you didn't eat lunch."

"Would you stop for lunch if the doctor allowed you out for the first time in weeks?"

"All right, all right." He released her hand, and raised his own to signal defeat. "You have a point; I give up. Truce? At least through dinner?"

He appeared too good to be true, standing there with arms raised like some archangel from a chapel ceiling—in fact, he looked so good that Gwen wondered exactly what game he played with her now, and considered denying his request out of pure suspicion.

But even if she decided to follow the inclination, the next moment would have seen her hopelessly unable to form the words.

Taylor stepped back to reveal a page from a fairy tale come

to life. Where else would the glow of a hundred golden candles make it seem like day again in the glass-enclosed gazebo they stepped into? Where else would alabaster unicorns and marble pixies dance beneath hanging stained-glass doves, all prancing their praises to a "sky" of flowing white satin, the material bunched up here and there to form "clouds" tied with peach and blue bows? Where else would a table be set with such intricately hand-painted china and such flawlessly prismic crystal that Gwen stopped short, afraid she'd break some magic spell if she dared take a step closer?

"Wh-what is this?" she stammered. "Where are we?"

Taylor nodded toward the familiar lights and windows of Stafford House, just twenty feet away. "About back where we started from. Just at a different perspective."

"You can certainly say that."

His eyes crinkled; her surprise obviously pleased him. "I didn't know whether you'd like it. I didn't know whether to—" His pleasure yielded to a discomfitted grimace. "Well, after this morning—"

Gwen didn't let his rare moment of unease go by unstudied. Could it be, she pondered, he recollected those hours in Danny's bedroom with the same feeling of confusion as she?

"Well," he finally continued, "I just wanted to thank you for making Danny so happy. And I know the garden makes *you* happy."

"It does. This does." She willed a smile to her lips. "Thank you." She braved a step forward. She reached out to run a finger along the rim of a wineglass adorned with burgundy-tinted cherubs. The chalice was a work of art, so lovely she couldn't imagine drinking from it. So lovely . . . so perfect.

Too perfect.

She jerked her hand away. "It's so beautiful," she whispered, trying to express the words and not the tears. "I can't—I shouldn't even be touching it. I'm filthy. Just look at me."

"I am."

Oh, *Lord.* She shouldn't feel this way at a mere murmur

from him. But his reply came close enough to stir the curls at her temple . . . to blow suffusing heat down the length of her body. Gwen couldn't find the power to resist. She raised her head—to find her nose and lips just a breath away from Taylor's firm features and commanding mouth.

"You're not such a burden to look at," he said. His head descended further, dipping toward her, drawing her into the magic of his eyes, his voice, his strength. He filled her sights. He was beautiful . . . so beautiful. "As a matter of fact," he murmured with a gentle smile, "I think the dirt brings out your eyes."

"The dirt?" She blinked, then pulled away, compressing her lips. "That's not funny."

"Ssshh." He curled a hand around her waist before she pulled back more than a few inches. He cracked a wider smile as he tugged her toward the opposite side of the gazebo. "Come here, worry wart. I want to show you something."

"Whatever you say, milord," she quipped. "You couldn't possibly stun me more speechless than you have already."

But she was wrong. He could and had rendered her speechless again. As Taylor guided her down the gazebo's far steps, Gwendolen combed her brain for the appropriate phrases to describe the scene he revealed.

No words came close. Here lay the real secret of the gazebo: the fantasy of a garden it concealed. In awe, Gwen gazed at the laughing waterfall, the welcoming roses and fuchsias, another chorus of marble cherubs and forest sprites. The nymph statues lined their way down the lush yet slippery knoll, until they arrived at the edge of the small pool where ripples reflected the steady-burning torch lights.

"Come." Taylor tugged her down to the grass next to the pool. "Let's see what my private staff can do about cleaning us both up."

"Private staff?"

"Ssshh."

This time she couldn't argue. Taylor released a barely audible breath as he pushed up his sleeve, then glided his broad hand and forearm into the water.

She watched in fascinated awe. She couldn't think of one "proper" English gentleman she'd ever danced with or been bored by who'd be caught dead like this, dressed to the gills in their dinner finery and hunched like an Indian stalking wild trout in a reflecting pool. Not even for a woman. Not even Bryan. Certainly not Lloyd.

Lloyd. She tensed at the unexpected, uninvited thought. She waited in dread for the press of pain upon her chest.

But the agony didn't come. It didn't have time to. In true warrior-hero fashion, Taylor's waving hand commanded her attention into the liquid world where his hand still drifted.

With a start, she wondered why she hadn't noticed the resplendent orange stones in the pool before. She scooted closer to look; there seemed to be more of the odd rocks on his side than hers.

Suddenly, she not only leaned against Taylor's arm, but seized the defined muscles there. "My lord—those stones are moving."

A soft chuckle. A relaxed nod. "Yes, they are."

"My lord, those stones are . . . fish."

The chuckle didn't come again. And the nod, she noticed, had become an unblinking stare upon her. "Imagine that."

"Those fish are . . . are eating your hand." She didn't know which made her more flustered: the proof of her statement taking place at this moment, with all those piranhas lunging for his fingers, or his disregard of the incident to gaze that way at her.

"Come here," he finally ordered. Taylor took her arm now, guided her closer to the water.

"Ooooh, no." She dug her walking-boot heels into the moist earth to aid her resistance.

"Come here."

"Taylor—"

"Come here."

She knew her strength, as formidable as it was compared to a few weeks ago, was a squashable pea to his graceful might. But she didn't give in without a grimace to denote her unwilling participation in this tomfoolery.

She didn't even break when Taylor's brandy-rich laugh came close and warm next to her ear, or her captor's touch gentled to feel like a very element of the water he guided her hand into. She only thanked God he couldn't hear the protests of her senses or the wild thrumming between her breasts as his hands glided over hers with the subtlety of a waterfall's mist, yet the power of that fall's roar.

God help me. Gwen couldn't let him see that no other man had affected her like this. She couldn't, no matter how excruciating the temptation to give in to this strong-fingered hold, to lean back and fit into the perfect circle of his broad torso and long arms, to let herself feel safe again . . . finally, incredibly, *safe.*

No! She would *not* yield to such delusions. That's what such fantasies as fairy kisses and stout-shouldered knights were . . . visions as unsubstantial as the torch smoke and water mist on the air. Hopes as false as believing Lloyd had ever cared for her beyond the image she'd make on his arm. Dreams as unreal as thinking Taylor Stafford gave a fig about who her favorite poet was or whether gnomes ate her toes—or, for that matter, whether the Lancer returned to finish his work.

Conceptions as pointless as ever feeling safe with a man again.

No, she'd *never* surrender herself to him.

"Gwendolen."

But his voice came so strong and so close, entering her by way of her ear . . . exiting by way of a shiver that opened every pore to the power of the crisp night air, the spicy night scents, the intoxicating night magic.

"Gwendolen. Look. You're perfectly safe."

Gwen obeyed him.

She smiled. She erupted with a laugh of wonder. "The stones are eating my fingers, too."

"No. Just nibbling."

More moments went by, marked by the splashes of golden fish moving from his hand to her fingers beneath the water. "They're *koi*. From Japan," Taylor explained. "And they're very good at taking away garden dirt just in time for dinner."

Gwen peered closer to discover the *koi* indeed possessed industrious little dirt-suckers for mouths. She tilted a knowing eyebrow back at Taylor. "That's spoken like somebody who's used this place for such a purpose before. Perhaps a lad who was late to dinner a few times himself?"

His guilty grin confirmed her suggestion. "I wonder if Mum ever realized what a haven of boyhood deceit she'd really created." He turned and stared into the night, as if some faraway scene would reenact itself there and provide him with an answer.

"I imagine she did," Gwen offered. "Mothers are, after all, women." She paused, looking over the powerful cut of his profile, now taking on more solemn lines with his thoughts. "Your mother . . . she's gone now?"

A muscle in his jaw tensed. "Yes. When I was fourteen. At least in the physical sense."

"But her mind . . . had gone earlier?"

He exhaled. If Gwen wasn't mistaken, an expression of relief washed over his features. "Yes," he repeated. "We never really knew what happened. The doctors, the specialists . . . none of them could figure it out. But the woman I called Mother disappeared completely before my thirteenth birthday. All that remained was this—" he lifted hard, unseeing eyes to the sky, "this shell of a woman, sitting in her room, staring out the window with that damn letter in her hand."

"Letter?"

Taylor didn't answer for half a minute. He still tilted his head upward. His hair cascaded over his shoulders and his eyes looked beyond the stars, clearly immersed in the universe called memory.

Suddenly, he sat up, yanked his hand out of the water and dragged dripping, shaking fingers over his face. Gwen also extracted herself from the *koi*—and turned to the harsh, wet features that a minute ago had joined her in laughter.

His sights lowered to the fish and the water again. "If there was any Englishman more in love with Queen Victoria than the Prince Consort, it was my father," he said in a faraway voice. "I swear to it; he would have slayed dragons for his 'lovely Vicky.' "

After raising his right hand in demonstration of the statement, he let his palm fall, hitting his thigh with a dispassionate slap. "Unfortunately, all the dragons in the kingdom had been killed by 1879. So Father had to settle for rioting Zulu Indians in South Africa. It was one of their spears that skewered him from behind on the field at Isandhlwana."

"Dear God," she gasped.

"One of Victoria's own envoys delivered the letter of notification to us." His voice roughened, but an odd smile broke past his lips. "We were at Wharnclyffe . . . our country home, Wharnclyffe—you'd *love* the flower beds there—well, we were there, Mum and I, out on the moors. That's where the envoy found us."

The smile fell. Impenetrable anguish worked back over his features.

"Go on," Gwen urged. Taylor stiffened harder. She grasped his hand. "*Go on.*"

He swallowed. "I . . . I just remember that Mum didn't read the letter then. She looked into the messenger's face, and *knew* exactly what the thing said. She fell down onto her knees, weeping . . . weeping and screaming. She screamed for my father, over and over."

The waterfall's rhythm filled the ensuing pause. Gwen swallowed what felt like a boulder, wrestling with the shocking longing to hold more than his hand. "What did you do?"

At that, a glimmer of surprise marred his forehead. But only for a moment. "I had just become the Earl Stafford. I did what the Earl Stafford was supposed to do. I knelt down and held the Countess Stafford while she began to lose her mind."

"But—but he was your father," she stated. "You must have loved him very much, too."

"I loved him." He nodded once, tightly. "Very much."

"So how could you—how did you—who was there to help *you* through?"

"I told you." He turned to her again, dark-copper gaze more unflinching than she ever remembered. "I had just become the new Earl Stafford. Effective then and there, on that moor, not in some ceremony after boons were given or banns posted. In that moment, I became the guide of our honor, our unity—" he motioned toward the glow of Stafford House through the treetops, "our homes, our livelihood. From that day on, I was guardian of it all, and of everyone who relied on it, from Granna down to the youngest housemaid."

Looking away once more, he presented a profile worthy of some portrait hall in Parliament. "It was my duty—and my right—to be there for my mother."

For a long moment, Gwen sat and regarded him with an equally even posture. Then, softly, "But you didn't answer my question. My lord Stafford, *who* was there for *you?*"

She half expected the response she got. Taylor, Earl Stafford since a calamitous afternoon on a windswept moor, dug his stubborn Stafford heels deeper into some mental stronghold and lifted his firm Stafford mouth into a maddening half-grin. "The meal has arrived," he stated with a glance over her shoulder. "Shall we dine, my lady?"

The last blasted thing on her mind was dinner, no matter how delectable the aromas drifting to them from the gazebo. But when Taylor started back up the knoll and beckoned her with the curled fingers of a strong hand, Gwen accepted the offer before thinking twice. Before thinking at all. Knowing only that somewhere, in some moment tonight, this man had become more than the Lord-Earl-King-of-Spain, or the anger-filled warrior, or even the alluring charmer who had begun to make the grey mornings her favorite part of the day.

Now she looked only at this person who had revealed his life and his self to her as nobody else had. This friend who made her feel a foreign yet magnificent sensation . . .

He made her feel valuable.

And *that* was a miracle of a feeling she never wanted to let go.

The moon shone from its crest in the sky when they started back for the house. As the overhead countenances of Cassiopeia and Orion looked on, the night's orb illuminated the path in a magical silver glow and flickered the surrounding trees, bushes, and grass with teasing white-cool fingers.

Yes, Taylor conceded, it was a captivating sight—but not the most intriguing blend of moonbeams and reflection tonight. That honor went to the woman walking at his side. The copper whorls of her hair glistened with a lambent life of their own. Her gaze radiated the color of green moonstone. And most intriguing of all, that mouth: that unrighteously full mouth, uptilted in an expression of pure night mystery.

"It must be good," he finally stated.

Her head came up as if he'd aroused her from a hundred-year sleep. Her eyes swept his face with a dazed look he could only deem adorable. "Hmmm?"

"It must be good . . . the thought which absorbs you so. I believe I saw your mind up there, having a spot of tea on the moon."

To his wonder, she laughed at the quip. Her smile glowed in the dimness as they crossed to the back door of the south wing. Taylor found his eyes straining to see her other features; when they reached the door, he fumbled there for a moment.

The gas lights in the foyer sparked their warmth. The soft

glow in her eyes now burst into emerald brilliance. The cream of her skin looked like satin in the gentle light.

"If you must know, my lord, that highly favored thought was about you," she said before crossing the portal.

Taye stood there still holding the door latch. Christ. Her confession might as well have been a Zulu assault on *his* system. Every muscle in his body screamed a plea to speed back to the *koi* pool and drown the rapidly rising temperature of his blood. Somehow, he made it through the doorway instead. He crossed the hall to the back stairway, where he gripped the banister in a sham of a casual pose.

"Me?" He managed to meet her remark with an equally light mien. "I thought you've barely tolerated my presence of body, Miss Marsh, let alone sparing me extra thoughts."

"So did I." She tilted her frowning brow to the balustrade, very near his hand. She didn't see his knuckles tighten on the polished mahogany, longing to stroke away those furrows himself. Thank God. "But you must confess, Lord Stafford, you hardly took care to appear the Prince Charming when we first met."

He dared a bemused half-smile. "And I appear that way now?"

For a moment, she clearly debated how to answer him. Then she smiled. "Maybe a little, tonight. I've never had my own waterfall and *koi* family before. And I've never dined on lobster legs and chocolate truffles in a satin-lined gazebo." She emitted a nervous laugh. "I'll admit, I wondered when it would all turn into six mice and a pumpkin."

Taylor switched to a puzzled scowl. "I find that difficult to believe from the niece of the esteemed Margaret Marsh. Surely, madam, you've experienced more opulent evenings in your world travels than this."

"World travels!"

The exclamation came punctuated with a gape he'd normally term melodramatic. But as she turned away, shaking her head,

Taylor glimpsed a cloud descending over Gwendolen's happiness. A very real, very dark cloud.

"You must joke," she continued in a mutter. Her voice shook more than enough to confirm his impression. "Believe me, my lord, jaunts to Paris and New York were *not* on the itinerary for Margaret Marsh's niece. I was much too busy with Latin tutors and French tutors, dance lessons, riding instruction—"

"But you had friends," he insisted. "Veronica Spencer . . . you two used to be ladies of the court around the bench in her garden."

"Yes." She gave her assent softly, sadly. "There was Veronica . . . and a small crowd of others. There were daughters or little sisters of Aunt Maggie's more intimate acquaintances. You know the sort. They were picked as the 'proper' influences on our weekly visits and teas." A half-cry, half-sigh escaped as her gaze took on the sheen of remembrance. "Thank God. Those were special times for me, those afternoons in the garden with Nicky or Beth or Diana . . ."

"But that's not all there was." Taye stepped forward, as if by doing so he'd also discard this unsettling new impression about Margaret Marsh's famous act of charity toward her early-orphaned niece. "That's *not* all there was. I . . . I still remember your coming-out ball. Our salon rattled with talk about the affair for weeks. Constance swore your aunt sent to China for that shiny blue trim on your gown. *I* had to listen to a litter of smitten pups who thought she'd gotten the bloody stuff from the gods and you were Venus incarnate—"

Gwendolen's sharp stare severed his chuckle. Her harsh whisper plummeted him to stunned silence.

"I would have traded that gown and a thousand more like it for one smile from my aunt."

A solitary tear escaped an emerald eye before him. Taylor slipped his hand free of the balustrade. He pressed his thumb to that tear, keeping it there until his own skin absorbed the drop.

"What is it, princess?" he murmured. "Certainly your Aunt Maggie didn't banish smiles from your life *all* the time."

But her nervous jerk back told him how dart-tip accurate he'd hit. "My lord," she rasped awkwardly, "surely you of all people must know that 'oversmiling is the weakness of degenerates and wantons.' "

She wiped hastily at eyes above her forced, bittersweet smile. "Thank the saints Aunt Maggie didn't see me tonight, yes? I must be the tart of the Continent after all that smiling you forced me to."

Damn. *Damn.*

Before he deliberated his actions, before he rationalized away the furious fire invading his blood, Taye used the balustrade to swing forward, grab her by both shoulders, and yank her close. Body-pressing, breath-sharing close.

And then, suddenly, he smiled at her. Not just a smile of his lips, but a message begun deep in his chest, swelling past his throat and lips and up into the very force of his gaze.

"From now on," he ordered softly, "you'll smile whenever and wherever you want to. And I'll think you the lovely woman you are and will be from now on." He tightened his grip . . . bringing her closer. "Is that understood, madam?"

Her answering smile came swift and luminous. "Understood completely, my lord Stafford."

Her tearful words undid the last tenacious threads of his composure. For the next minute, Taylor did nothing but drink in the sight before him: this vision he likened to a butterfly stretching and pushing at the grey confines of her hopeless cocoon of a world. And he felt a lad of eight again, encouraging the miracle with awe-filled eyes . . . anticipating that final, glorious moment of her freedom, yet dreading that instant when her rainbowed wings would spread and fly from him.

Heady joy and blatant terror crashed through him—especially when that butterfly's night-cooled fingers trailed sun-hot chaos along his jaw, then up his cheek.

Especially as she said in a trembling, trusting whisper, "Thank you."

"No." Taye shook his head as he grated the protest. "Be quiet . . ." *It is I who should be thanking you butterfly. It is I who should be* showing *you.*

A breath hung suspended between them. Another.

Before he comprehended it happening, Taylor felt her hair between his fingers as he cupped the nape of her neck in his hand. He gathered her slender form into his arms, so pliant, so perfect, blending and molding against his hardening body.

Then he only saw the light. The emerald light of her eyes as an unseen power pulled his face toward hers, lured his breath to share the sweet tang of hers . . . and drew his lips to the lush, full tilt of hers.

Nine

Gwen's heart halted in the middle of a beat. Her mind spun into a whirl. Her fingers slid from Taylor's jaw to his neck, where she gave in to the temptation to immerse her fingers in his hair. The strands filled her grasp, thick and dark. His gaze thickened in proportion to the aching heat in her own blood.

Oh . . . oh, dear Lord, what was she doing? She should be bolting up the stairs. She should be terminating, with fervored speed, this unspeakable disgrace of an embrace, this approaching sin of a kiss.

But she didn't feel sinful. She didn't feel outraged or shameful. She felt helpless, breathless . . . driven by age-old feminine instinct to bring his hardness and warmth closer as his lips descended fully upon hers.

And she knew the feeling was right.

She could only liken the awareness to the formation of a cresting, crashing wave. Like the influence of wind and tide upon the sea, his kiss stirred an uncontrollable force in her mind and soul. Rolling, pressing, rising, Taylor's mouth awakened her to wondrous new movement; his touch taught her heartbeat to race the wind. The sensations grew until she found herself anticipating some unseen shore to crash upon . . .

When Taylor pulled away, she saw he battled a similar surge inside himself. His eyes resembled the concentrated glow of the lamps. His chest rose with harsh, labored breaths.

Yet she found his confusion oddly comforting. Without a doubt, Gwen knew he not only understood this runaway lightning bolt within her, but clung along on the journey for dear life himself.

With dragging hesitance, Taylor released her. He sucked in a breath, the sound loud against the quiet of the slumbering house. He stepped back, but his gaze never left her.

For one more moment, he stood there—and in that moment, a darkness swept over his features again, potent, meaningful. He closed his eyes and swallowed; a muscle spasm rippled from his shoulders down to his splayed, tense hands.

He was an awesome sight. As she stared at him, Gwen wondered if he might kiss her again.

Her pulse leapt in terrifying, exhilarating apprehension.

But then he whirled and disappeared into the shadows toward the north wing. She stood and listened to his retreating footsteps, only one thought reverberating through her clamoring senses:

Thank heavens.

Six days later, she stood in that same back foyer in streams of morning sunlight. The bright dawn was a rarity; Gwen sent up a prayer of thanks for the sparkling weather as she slipped out the door to take a long look over the dew-twinkled garden.

Her last look.

She inhaled deeply of earth and grass, of pine and ferns, noticing her lungs filled to capacity without pain. An hour ago, Dr. Ramsey had pronounced her eyes and sinuses clear, as well. He proclaimed her head in perfect condition.

But what would the physician conclude if he'd examined her thoughts, instead? Would he nod so confidently if his stethoscope discerned her heart's erratic feelings, and not its recuperated beat? Would he deem her strong enough to travel if he detected the exhaustion of her soul, the effort of trying to smother the wish that had suddenly, shockingly taken over her heart in the last week . . .

That she could stay here, just a little while longer. That she could stay and feel alive and beautiful and . . . *whole* again.

As she had at least a hundred times in the last few days, Gwen laughed at the ridiculous idea. Saying good-bye to her precious flowers and trees, she lifted the hem of her mauve serge traveling suit to return inside and pack some last things before Reggie arrived to take her home.

She stopped short with the approach of a tall, broad form dressed in a grey pinstriped suit that fit entirely too well. Taylor closed the last few feet between them with steps as awkward as the tiny smile on his face.

"I'm going to miss you smiling in my garden like that," he murmured. "I haven't regretted giving you that order last week for a moment."

At that, Gwen turned away. Her flush certainly made its way down to her toes. It was the first time either of them referred to their clandestine kiss—though Gwen had known that moment jarred Taylor equally when they'd mutually exchanged sleep-deprived looks over the next morning's scones.

Yet even with that acknowledgment between them, something had changed. Something that clung to the atmosphere whenever they glanced or talked or so much as passed each other in the hall. A heaviness snuck into the air . . . a strange, frightening warmth swirled into her blood.

This morning offered no shift in the picture. A brisk spring wind rustled the trees and a nip edged the air, but tension settled over them like a dense summer haze. Gwen twisted her fingers together until they throbbed in an effort to form her reply with composed decorum, not an echo of the emotion threatening to melt the back of her throat.

"I have found much to be happy about at Stafford House in the last weeks, my lord. For that, I thank you."

Taylor didn't twist his fingers. But he kicked at the ground until an impressive divot littered the turf between them.

"Funny," he muttered. "You stole the words *I'd* prepared for this."

Their gazes met.

The heat thickened.

As Taylor continued to look at her, his laugh lines tightened. His widened smile sobered. And became . . . what? Gwen searched his face and her heart for the answer. Both echoed back a lingering uncertainty, like the final notes of a symphony she didn't believe was over. When her senses strained for the next measure, only the clattering of a carriage on gravel reverberated in her ears.

"It's time," she said through suddenly dry lips.

Taylor squinted against the sunshine toward the front drive. "Yes."

"Reggie's early." Why did it sound like a complaint?

"I don't blame him."

She glanced away. She already knew the stare he used to accompany such bold statements. And she couldn't bear to meet that spellbinding hazel intensity. Not now. Please, not now.

But the next moment, he issued just the command she feared, steady and low. "Gwendolen. Look at me."

She closed her eyes and shook her head.

"It wasn't a request." A firm hand curled beneath her chin, urging her face up.

Unable to help herself, Gwen opened her eyes.

He filled her vision, all rugged and sunswept glory, even in his tailored attire. Gwen absorbed his features like a condemned woman watching her last sunset. "I—" she stammered, hoping appropriate words would follow.

But Taylor shook his head and slid his thumb across her lips. "Ssshh." He penetrated her with his gaze, paralyzed her with it, rendered her nerves and limbs useless to flee.

"Please," she managed in a hoarse whisper. "Please, don't . . ."

Please please *don't do this to me. Because then I'll yearn to do something for you. Something like break down and agree to your hypnotists and your questions. Something like believe in your reckless fight to catch an uncatchable killer . . . or that I could ever make a difference in your world.*

If his soul heard the silent plea of hers, he chose not to acknowledge the message. He slid a step closer, blocking out the sky and the world an inch more . . . then another.

Then his hand moved to the back of her head. And gently, slowly, his lips dipped to take hers.

His kiss seared her with more heart-stopping intensity than her memory recorded. Oh, so much more. How could she have forgotten this dizzy tingling in her blood, this enlivened humming in her ears, this sudden pooling of liquid heat between her thighs?

The explanation surely couldn't be that these feelings were brand new. Certainly every kiss shared with a man couldn't be like opening a gift of sound and sensation each time . . .

Yet as Taylor's other hand rose to cradle the side of her face, Gwen dared to believe in the impossible, just for a moment. Borne on the boldness of the conviction, she entwined her fingers with his.

She heard his throat catch, felt his lips slant harder over hers. Her nerve endings raced and her heart soared with the birds in the sunshine above.

Some servant in the house called to another, reminding them of real life just steps away. Taylor pulled away, but only far enough that their gazes met.

"Promise me," he murmured, his husky tone for her only, "promise me, if you need anything—"

"I promise."

But as the words spilled off her lips, her heart prayed forgiveness for the lie. Even now Gwen conceded that if she so much as looked back at Stafford House again, much less considered taking refuge here, she would have to bring her past with her. She would have to bring the nightmare back . . . live it over again. Not because she still envisioned Taylor stalking her for it—but because she would give it to him.

A cry of "Here they are!" rang out from the house. Gwen

broke away from Taylor; he stepped a proper distance from her. They looked anywhere but at each other.

"Taye! Gwen! For God's sake, there you are!"

Their gazes reconnected in bafflement. The cry didn't come from Hannah or Reggie. They watched Bryan dash across the lawn, magenta tie flying, trailed by a wide-eyed, jacketless Danny.

Their friend halted a few feet away, panting breathlessly. His gaze bounced from one to the other of them.

Taylor scowled and shook his head, as if trying to interpret Bryan's urgency. "What?" he finally pressed. "What the hell is it?"

"The Lancer!" Danny squealed after a second of impatient waiting for the grown-up to catch his breath. "He struck again, Father! The killer struck again!"

Gwen witnessed Taylor's face transform into something she didn't know. Harsh hate washed his features. His dimpled jaw became a gaunt mask. The lips she'd kissed moments ago now thinned to a white line of rage.

Unshed tears reflected in the depths of his unblinking glare.

And in that moment, Gwen knew something in her soul had been wrenched inside out. Forever.

"Early this morning." Bryan nodded confirmation to Danny's words. "A confounded millionairess." He produced a folded copy of the *Chronicle* from his inner coat pocket.

Taylor seized the paper. He snapped the front page open. "In Regent's Park?" he demanded. "As we'd calculated he'd go?"

Bryan's fallen expression already gave the answer to Gwen. Her friend voiced the information at the same moment Taylor read it: "The complete opposite. East End." His sand-colored mustache quirked. "Three blocks from Whitechapel, if you can believe it."

"Damn." Taylor hurled the pages to the lawn. They scrunched beneath his first forceful stride back toward the house. "Was

that your carriage we heard on the drive, Bry?" he called over his shoulder.

"Right. Gregory's driving today. I told him not to bother getting off the box. Gathered you'd want to make for the site as soon as possible."

"You gathered accurately. And after we've examined the scene, we'll go to the coroner's, even if I have to bribe every guard on site to get us in."

"I don't think that will be necessary." Gwen interjected the statement from where she walked behind them. However, once the men jerked to a simultaneous stop and spun confused glances at her, bypassing the pair presented no further dilemma.

"Gwen!" Bryan called.

"What the blazes are you talking about?" Taylor's growl came at closer range. He clamped her elbow, forcing her to a halt. "Damn it, woman. This is *not* how I want you involved in this. We aren't going on a bloody pleasure trip to Harrods!"

She felt his gaze on her, animalistic and frightening. Nevertheless, Gwen took her time about turning and directly meeting his scrutiny.

"I know what I said, my lord. Bribing the guards won't be necessary. As a matter of fact, Hannah tells me this is my best color and one of my most attractively cut dresses." At that, she even felt herself quirking a bemused smile at him. "All you have to do is use *me* as a bit of . . . distraction."

"The hell I do." His pointed tone threatened to slash her resolve like razors to silk.

"Well," Gwen responded slowly, carefully. "The hell with your hell."

Despite the shocked flare of Taylor's nostrils, she couldn't believe *her* lips had delivered the words. Yet the calm she'd forced for her delivery began to translate into real confidence. Gwen straightened, liking this new reserve of fortitude she'd found inside.

She liked *herself,* period.

"My Lord Stafford, don't you remember Bryan warning you about my stubborn streak when I'd gotten a thorn beneath my saddle?" She squared her shoulders higher. "Well, I've got a thorn now. And you'd better get on for the ride or step out of my way."

For another long moment, Taylor looked torn between thrashing her or flogging himself. Either option clearly flustered him.

Yet while he muddled through the moment, Gwen found herself taking secret, strange satisfaction from his confusion. She couldn't help beaming him a satisfied grin when he stepped back from her, then bowed in mocking etiquette and gritted, "After you, little fool. By all means, after you."

Ten

Taylor was right. The cold and dirt of Princelet Street surpassed even the neighborhood around Saint Jerome's. Gwen didn't deny her relief when he stopped her at the side of the carriage, ordering her to wait where she was with Gregory, Bryan's huge driver, as temporary chaperon.

Then the concern in his gaze darkened to something black and unrecognizable. She found herself touching his elbow as if she could reach into his soul that way, but he turned without another pause, stepping toward Bryan—and the scene sprawled before her now.

Across the street, the gap between two grime-covered lodging houses formed the alley where the millionairess had met her end at the Lancer's hands. The strangest collection of people she'd ever seen overflowed from the aperture. Barefoot waifs and scarf-clad immigrant women strained for a morbid glimpse as earnestly as the wool-wrapped gentry who'd emerged from shiny carriages and cabriolets.

Aristocrats she identified by name.

That realization prompted the coldest shiver of all. Gwen inhaled sharply and burrowed deeper into the coat Taylor had shrugged out of and thrown around her before leaving.

"Miss Marsh?" Gregory frowned at her, concern in his baritone voice. "Are you certain you wouldn't be more comfortable inside the carriage?"

"It could have been me," she suddenly said. She whirled to the driver, but Gregory's kind face became background haze to the image dominating her mind. A scene of her own blood splattered in that alley, sniffed at by stray dogs, curious beggar children, and the people who'd danced at her own engagement party . . .

"It could have been me, couldn't it? They would have stared like that around the alley where I was nearly murdered."

"Miss Marsh, don't dwell on such morbidities," Gregory urged. "You needn't trouble yourself with thoughts like—"

"No. No, that's precisely it. Perhaps I should have *troubled* myself like this a long time ago."

She looked back toward the thickening crowd. Voices argued and elbows jostled for better viewing positions—echoing the din inside her. A slew of startling new perceptions pounded away at defenses she'd painstakingly erected and entrenched over the last two years. Walls she'd built to close out the pain forever.

But the pain had always found a way in anyway, hadn't it? Pain knew no boundaries.

And maybe the only thing she'd sealed off was herself.

A hundred coats couldn't fend off the chill gripping her then. Every sight and sound attacked her naked senses. Gwen felt the cold Thames wind blow down the damp, rotting street. Her ears rang with the mindless gaiety of these people, in affront to the tragedy before them.

She longed to look away, to shut her ears forever. She didn't. She couldn't; not anymore. She stared with stinging, all-seeing eyes, even when Taylor materialized from the hell, tie discarded and shirtsleeves hiked, his hands and forearms smeared with soot—and blood.

"Bastard photographers," he muttered tightly. "Any clue we could have discovered has been coated in flash powder."

"Anything to sell a paper, Taye, you know that." Bryan's voice came from somewhere to the right of her; Gwen didn't look to see exactly where. She couldn't stop staring at those crimson-covered hands.

"Right," Taylor snapped. "Even if more innocent women are killed in the process."

"But they're *genteel,* innocent women, my friend. Beautiful story-makers, even in death." Her friend's sardonic snort clung to the air, then dissipated like slow cigar smoke. "Hell, especially in death. Look at the lot of those dandies, circling like vultures after one of their own. Now I wish *I* had a Kodak."

At that, Gwen's knees gave in to the horror. She whirled and scrambled into the coach.

She vaguely remembered Bryan climbing onto the plush seat beside her, then another form and those *hands* filling the space opposite. As the carriage pitched forward, her stomach rolled. She squeezed her eyes shut and barely suppressed a surge of bile.

She reopened her gaze to the sight of the hands wiping into a clean handkerchief. Dark red stains corrupting sinless white linen. Soot and grime dominating scent and soap. Evil screaming out its victory over innocent life one more time.

The thought reverberated through her mind—not for the first time, but with the same gut-gripping impact. Because for the first time, she finally realized every horrible implication that fact carried . . . the life lost, the outrage gone unpunished.

The hands left behind to wipe away the blood.

A huge door of understanding flung open inside her. The resulting vacuum sucked her emotions from her, then slammed them back into her heart with shattering force. Gwen heard herself gasp, but didn't know if she could breathe. Her eyes stung, but no relieving tears came.

"Gwen?" Bryan's voice registered somewhere at the edge of her consciousness, vibrating with worry. "Hey, Gwennie, are you all right?" She felt his hand clutch her elbow, cool and insistent, but couldn't bring herself to grasp him back.

But then another hand moved over her. Warmth and strength encompassed her fingers, before the other voice pierced her stunned haze, low and even.

"Gwendolen," Taylor beckoned. "Look at me."

Without thinking, she complied.

In the dimness of the carriage, he still appeared a hollow imitation of the kind and laughing man she'd come to know. But there, in the recesses of his eyes, a deep amber glow formed . . . like his touch, the look reached to her with his quiet understanding, his steel courage.

And despite the horror and the pain, Gwen found the ability to utter her next words.

"It's hers." She lowered fingertips to the cloth in his other hand. "It's her blood . . . isn't it?"

The answer came mercifully devoid of inflection. "Yes." But as soon as he said it, he hurled the cloth to a dark corner. "And now that you know, don't look at it anymore."

Again, her gaze followed an instinctual impulse up to his face. Taylor now shoved his opposite arm against the window ledge, his coiled hand supporting his harsh, detached profile.

And as his glare seemed to depart the carriage for another time and place, so did his voice. His murmur changed to the bewildered tone of one recalling dreams too long neglected.

"I held Connie's scarf so long, it took me three days to get the stains from my hands. It was her favorite. The gold silk I'd given her for her birthday. It was ruined when they gave it to me. But I couldn't stop looking at it."

His gaze and his hand dropped. He uncurled his fingers, staring down as if a swag of crimson-splotched gold still hung in his quaking grip. "I just—couldn't—stop."

"Taye," Bryan interceded. He leaned and shook his friend's shoulder. "That was then. You've got to stop *now*."

"No." Gwen blurted the protest before thinking about it. Yet when she looked back to Taylor and his strained grimace, she knew exactly why she'd spoken.

"Don't stop," she told him. "Tell me what you felt. Tell me what you did."

For a long space, he only breathed hard through tight teeth. He clutched her hand again, his grip locking with the desperation of a man pulling himself out of quicksand. "No," he grated. "Bryan's right. Got to stop. Get my feet on the ground."

"And get your hands off my new carriage interior," Bryan added. The two friends gave humorless chuckles at the sally.

"It's a nice color," Taylor returned, fingering a window curtain. "Sort of a plum, eh? Are you quite certain you don't want it broken in a bit? I could just rip a little texture into the cushions and—"

"I had enough of your *texturing* last time, Stafford."

With speed stemming from incredulity, Gwen stared back and forth between the two of them, probing for some indication of a private jest beneath their words—finding none.

She finally fixed her gape to Taylor. Half anger and half disbelief bred her choked allegation. "You are *not* telling me you ruined the inside of a carriage with your bare hands."

"Not *a* carriage," Bryan sniffed. *"My* carriage. And he didn't just ruin it. He—" His mustache jerked. "Let's say I've seen monsoons hit with more discretion."

She still stared at Taylor. He didn't look back. He dropped her hand. He turned his head toward the window once more, his profile a harder, bleaker sight than before. The gaze she'd once compared to nothing less than fire or a warrior's ferocity now stretched flat and unblinking as he looked to a dark place beyond the passing buildings and sidewalks.

Somehow, without a doubt, Gwen knew what he saw there. He'd taken himself back to that day . . . back to the minutes he'd traveled these same streets on, perhaps, just such a spring day as this. Waiting through the miles in silent rage and wordless grief; dreading when the impersonal black letters would swing into view: *City of London Coroner's Office.*

Waiting for the first moment of the end of his life.

Stop, Gwen castigated herself. Surely her runaway emotions had gotten the better of her with such melodrama.

Yet she'd come to grasp the truth already. Somewhere during her weeks at Stafford House, she'd learned this man with a deep and immutable certainty. Taylor Stafford didn't give half of himself to anything or anybody—from the business meetings he often didn't return from until well after the household's retiring hour, to the afternoons he defied both fashion and decorum to lavish upon a wildly adoring Danny . . .

To the vows he'd pledged to Constance Stanhope on the day he'd made her Constance Stafford. He'd promised to protect and honor her, to be her defending knight forever.

And thus, on the day they'd buried the Countess Stafford with soil and lilies, the Earl Stafford had buried *himself* with anger and agony.

The conclusion rang like a bell in her mind once, twice—then flared through every inch of her like a black sky set asizzle by lightning. *You don't understand,* she'd once snapped at him, but now she knew, with the culmination of every voice which had whispered it to her for the last three weeks: Taylor Stafford understood exactly how she felt, down to every last tormenting, pain-filled moment.

From the midst of that galvanizing realization, she realized what she must do—despite the fear, despite the sorrow.

Or perhaps because of it.

"My lord—" Gwen blurted, fearing the tide of courage would recede from her heart as swiftly as it had snuck in. She didn't trust her lips to his Christian name, acutely aware of the emotional jumble that might very well tumble free with the familiarity . . .

I'll help you, Taylor. I'll remember what I can for you. I'll try to remember. God help me, I'll try . . . for you.

"My lord—"

"What?" He flashed a sharp glance to her, but once confronting her pensive frown, his features shifted with concern.

Taylor leaned forward. This time, his words came more gently. "What is it, princess?"

"Princess?" Bryan echoed in obvious surprise.

But Gwen forced herself to ignore the commentary. She concentrated on the strength of the hazel gaze before her, on the mixture of color that gleamed like every precious stone alloyed together at once. A light she'd find safety in.

A light she could trust.

"Whoa." Gregory's baritone sounded from the box atop the coach, cutting the moment to an end.

They rocked to a stop. Gwen's shoulders sunk. She watched that rigid shell form over Taylor's features again, as if he could use his stare to break down the cold, ominous stones comprising the large, bleak building before them.

He didn't look at her again.

So she'd have to wait to voice her pledge to him. But nothing could stop her from making good on her promises beginning now—and she would.

With that silent vow, Gwen set her chin, straightened her shoulders and followed the men out of the carriage.

An hour later, Taylor did *not* make her task easy.

"No," he growled at her for the fortieth time. He leaned dark and imposing over her, his features ravaged by exhaustion. He'd transformed his hair into a riotous mane with repeated rakings of tense hands. His jaw was a beard-stubbled rock of tension.

"Damn it, Gwen," he muttered. "I agreed to your chancy notion of flirting with those guards—"

"So you and Bryan could spend all the time you needed to study the coroner's notes." As she leveled the retort, she matched his hands-on-hips stance.

"Yes. And for the hundredth time, thank you. But—"

"But what? But I'll fall apart now, is that it? Don't you think I've proven I can survive a little pressure, my lord?" She raised both eyebrows and ran a hand across her scar.

"Standing in the hall with some smitten pup is not comparable to keeping on your feet in the investigation room with a—a—"

"With a dead body in front of me?"

This time Taylor's brows jumped, registering the effect of the bold statement she'd gambled. Knowing she didn't dare show a moment's vacillation now, Gwen countered with a higher tilt of her chin, a tighter press of her lips.

A nerve pulsed in his jaw—undoubtedly reining back a curse. "You can't do it."

"I have to do it."

"You don't know what it's like!"

"No," she agreed softly, "I don't. But I know I have to face this. I know I should have faced this a long time ago."

"Gwennie." Bryan stepped in, scratching his temple uncomfortably. "I don't think *this* is the experience you need to—"

"It's *exactly* the experience I need." She pivoted back to Taylor, looking up into the deep grimace still clenching his features. Acting on another reckless instinct, she reached and pulled his fisted hand into hers.

Before either he or Bryan could hurl stunned stares, she spoke again. "You were right, you know," she softly told him. "I've been as dead as the other victims. My lord—Taylor—it's time I wake up. Weren't *you* the one who taught me I can only escape my past by confronting it?"

"Good God," he muttered. He shook his head in what looked like regret. "If I'd have known I had such a cunning student—"

"You'd have taught her what else, Lord Stafford?"

The clipped but familiar voice echoed from down the corridor. An involuntary tension seized Gwen's belly. Anxiety pummeled her heart as the erect-postured forms of Inspector Helson and his assistants paced closer.

She stiffened and stepped back, though an odd comfort overcame her when Taylor moved forward with an equal tension binding his tall form. He shifted half a step closer to her, perhaps just by instinct, nevertheless making it known to all that she belonged here with *him*. Gwen found herself making her own subtle move toward him . . . admitting the veracity of his claim.

"Helson," Taylor acknowledged. His tight tone belied a past with the law official abounding with stand-downs like this, most likely set in this same hall. Knowing both combatants the way she did, she assumed the walls gave in before either of the men.

"My lord," Helson stated back, tone equally guarded. "I'd like to say I'm surprised by the presence of you and Mr. Corstairs in a hallway off limits to anyone but the police, but alas, my fascination lies with the new friend you've coerced into your little quest."

With that, Helson's gaze circled and pinned her. Gwen yearned to step yet closer to Taylor, to escape into the arms which had come, unbelievably, to signify comfort and protection for her.

How would it feel, she wondered, never to face Helson's emotionless scrutiny again? Or the questions . . . dear God, the questions. Still haunting, still harrowing after two years . . .

Where did he touch you, Miss Marsh? What did he say to you? Do you think the Lancer would have raped you if you hadn't gotten away? What articles of clothing in particular did he cut away? What do you mean, you can't *remember?*

She balled her fists and shoved away the memories. She focused instead on what that clipped voice said now, on how Helson condescended to Taylor the same way he'd so capably dehumanized her. The same leering manner in which he curled his thick-mustached lip. The same disdainful glare he slanted down his platypus-long nose at the man who had saved her life in more ways than one.

As her observation continued, her dread began to dissipate. In its place, fury invaded. Just as that morning at Saint Jerome's with Lloyd weeks ago, a thick haze crowded her vision and filled her head.

But unlike that tumultuous moment, Gwen didn't turn and run. She didn't want to. One moment she stood entrenched in Taylor's shadow, the next she took a wide step out, chin raising, shoulders squaring.

"I beg your pardon, Inspector." Her voice rang through the air like a bullet into Helson's throat. At least it was how he appeared, eyes popping at her and mustache crunching up his nostrils.

She couldn't resist flashing a hint of a smile before continuing. "For the sake of your records, sir, Lord Taylor did not *coerce* me into anything." She gave a quick flick of the smile at Taylor. "It was I who did all the coercing."

Helson stopped blinking. Instead, he harrumphed a nervous cough. "I'm afraid I don't—"

"You don't have to do anything," Gwen interjected. "Mr. Corstairs was witness to the exchange; I'm certain he'll corroborate my statement."

Bryan nodded with swift and admirable solemnity. "Aye. Saw the whole thing. I'll corroborate. Sure."

After waiting a moment for that to sink in, Gwen stepped forward. She paced close enough to assure Helson saw the anger in her gaze. "I suggest the next time you accuse someone of 'coercing,' Inspector, you confer with the 'coerced' first."

A soft snicker echoed through the hallway. Whether the sound emanated from the men behind Helson or the pair bordering her, the stark walls made it impossible to tell. The inspector shifted and grimaced. Gwen didn't alter her stance or stare.

"I see," Helson finally stated. "And so, if I may be so bold to ask, what is this woman doing in an area clearly marked off to police only?"

"Just trying to catch a killer, Inspector. The same thing I believe you're trying to do."

She purposely lilted the statement to sound more a question. The tension in the hall thickened. Gwen watched Helson's cheeks darken to red then purple, splotch by ruddy splotch.

But she didn't surrender her stance.

"Do you realize I could have you arrested on this spot,

young lady?" The threat vibrated with a low, almost evil cadence.

"I don't think so." Gwen coiled every muscle to ward off the fear from her voice. But she repeated, softly and steadily, "No, I don't think you'd do that at all. You'd think first, Inspector. Very hard. You'd think about those riots last month in Trafalgar Square. Then you'd realize those scenes were child's play compared to a mob that learned Scotland Yard still couldn't find the Lancer, but arrested his only surviving victim."

The platypus nose flared. "You wouldn't dare."

"I wouldn't have to dare. The *Times* and *Chronicle* have ears everywhere." She threw a pointed glance around them. "Perhaps even here."

Helson's face seethed to a deep shade of fury. His lips twitched; his eyes bulged.

"Get out," he finally growled. "Leave this building now, all of you. Pretend you weren't here. And by Judas, I mean that! You were *not* here!"

"Indeed," Gwen replied, snapping her gloves from her reticule—less from propriety than to busy her shaking hands. "And a good day to you too, Inspector."

Helson led his group on with no further words. But the stomps echoed for half a minute after their disappearance.

Gwen released a breath in a multitude of shaky spurts.

Only then did she hear the boot steps approaching behind her with slow but familiar surety.

She turned to meet Taylor's gaze. And held her breath again. Gwen tried to excuse the possessive light in his hazel depths to a reflection of the afternoon sun through the narrow windows . . . but then she noticed they both stood in shadow.

He stepped closer.

Then she didn't *want* to breathe. She didn't want to feel, didn't know what to do with the pinpoints of awareness seizing her muscles and waiting at the brink of her bloodstream.

Dear God, what was happening?

She tried to rationalize the moment away. Saints, it was only a stare. Taylor had stared at her plenty of times. Even his kisses sparked inner alarms despite all their warm and delicious awakenings. But this . . . this quiet, potent moment between them, only made her long to close the remaining inches to his broad chest, let the flood of tension flow and beg him to take away the horror Helson's presence had dredged up.

It struck like a hailstorm of confusion, this tug-of-war inside. Somehow, her mind had crossed the line beyond mutual respect or even newly forged friendship—and delved into the realm of utterly unknown, utterly terrifying feelings.

Taylor broke the silence—but not the tension—with a low, brief cough. "You'd better watch it, princess," he said in that intimate murmur of his. "People may actually think you're on my side."

Gwen swallowed and glanced away. "And if they do?"

"*You* tell *me*. What if they do?"

A scriptwright couldn't have presented the opportunity more ideally again. And Taylor stood there, her leading man, waiting for her *coup de grâce* . . . the lines she'd been bursting to recite before they'd left the carriage. Before they'd triumphed over Helson together.

Yet before she'd turned and he'd looked at her with a gaze burning like some ancient heathen ceremonial fire. Before he'd claimed her in that same basic, primal way . . . consuming her. Awakening her. Terrifying her. Changing her.

Changing everything.

Gwen turned and paced back down the hallway without answering his question.

Everything had changed. Irrevocably. Undeniably. Taylor didn't understand how he knew that, but now, studying Gwen's sleeping face against the cushions of Bryan's otherwise empty carriage, he knew.

He attempted to focus his deliberations elsewhere . . . anywhere. But as Bryan's matched greys clopped steadily down the midnight streets, the cadence played a perfect match to the pounding of his thoughts, the thrumming between his ribs.

The inner chaos had begun at dinner. Bryan insisted Taye and Gwen join him at his St. James's townhouse, assuring his cook's ability to expand pheasant for one into pheasant for three. The meal passed as a pleasing enough affair—until Gwen's eyelids drooped while they still awaited dessert.

A now-familiar impulse conquered Taye then, pressing and possessive, driving him to scoop her up, hurriedly decline Bryan's offer to prepare the guest bedroom for her, and instead ask for the use of his friend's coach to return them to Stafford House.

As the memory swept him, so did that same pressure on his muscles and bones, like a hangover without the precluding oblivion. Hell. He still hadn't recovered from the first time the sensation plagued him. That moment when he'd watched a belaced-and-bustled woman step out of the shadows in the coroner's hallway, eyes blazing queenly green fury, and give Inspector Helson of the mighty Scotland Yard a dressing down no sensible *man* would have attempted.

And had done it for him.

Not only that, but done it as if somewhere between all his blundered attempts at charm and persuasion, she'd really come to believe in his fight . . . as if she'd come to believe in *him*.

From that moment on, all Taylor wanted to do was grab her, sweep her into the carriage and get her back beneath the roof of Stafford House. Back where he alone could watch over her, keep her safe, keep her warm.

Keep her his.

"Christ."

He rasped the oath with shock and fury, at the same time grateful Gwen had fallen asleep the moment her head hit the squabs and slumbered through his indiscretion. He rammed the window open to inhale the cold night air, hoping the damp carried some secret remedy for temporary insanity.

Protectiveness was one thing, he told himself, the "right" and "noble" thing. But this sudden jolt of overprotectiveness—

Insanity. Idiocy. You fool. You fool!

He dropped back against the cushion again, taking a longer breath. Maybe, he hoped, the day was just collecting its toll from him. Yes . . . yes, that must be the story. The alley and the onlookers. The blood and the body. The memories and the frustration. Each ordeal had gathered force, pushing harder at his senses, until all he wanted was—

Until all you want is what?

As if his mind lay in wait for just that prompting, he again turned his head toward the sleeping woman next to him.

His gaze drank in Gwendolen's moonlit face . . . the arch of her neck . . . the swells of her breasts, rising and falling with each sleep-steady breath. So close. So warm. And so lovely. Ah, God, so lovely . . .

No. Damn it, no!

Taylor ordered his stare away.

But he couldn't stop looking at her.

He'd never been more thankful to hear the crunch of the carriage wheels on the gravel drive of Stafford House.

Yet with the sudden swivel of the coach, Gwendolen shifted. She curled up against his shoulder instead of the cushion. She sighed, then moaned and flitted drowsy, trusting blinks up at him. Taylor's lungs clamored for another quaff of night air.

"Are we home?" she murmured, intimate tone more befitting the fireside.

Or the bedroom.

Not an Arctic freeze could help him now. "Yes, princess," he managed in a hoarse murmur. *You're home. You're safe* came a more forceful promise from deep inside.

Gregory snapped the coach door open. Gwendolen jerked upright in surprise and blinked again. Taylor disembarked first, then offered his hand up to help her. She swerved, but frowned stubbornly, and waved away his aid. Jerking up her skirts, she started out the carriage herself.

She missed the step by a foot and careened toward him with a shriek.

Taylor caught her around the waist with one arm and her legs with the other. He bent his head a moment, checking his smile. The feel of her against him once more, soft and scented and *safe,* proved the only quenching to the tormenting heat in his blood.

And yet, unbelievably, the spark which spread the blaze farther . . .

Gregory came sprinting to help, but Taylor waved Bryan's big driver away. "Is everything . . . all right then, milord?" the man asked anyway.

"Fine, Greg. Thank Mr. Corstairs again for me."

He wondered why his tongue felt thick with the well wishes toward his friend—or why he didn't pause for the usual parting hand shake he exchanged with Bryan's driver. Yet Gregory nodded as if he understood. The big man gave a respectful tilt of his top hat, climbed aboard the box and eased the carriage back down the drive.

Surprise swiftly overtook confusion as Taylor entered a front hall still flooded in lamplight. Gwen squirmed against him, squinting at the onslaught of incandescence.

As Taye looked down at her, another gust of blistering sensation blew at the doors of his composure. A collection of curls now fell into her sleepy face, making her look that much more innocent, more beguiling . . .

More arousing.

Taylor coughed. "You've . . . had quite a day, madam," he stated. He battled to think of balancing ledgers or getting a tooth pulled or scooping horse droppings; anything to yank his tone—and his thoughts—to safer ground.

But then she responded to him with a smile. Soft. Warm. Inviting. "Yes, my lord." And she used that same unwittingly intimate tone she'd begun in the carriage . . .

Ah, God.

What the hell was he letting her do to him?

"Thank you for rescuing me from my death fall," she at last said.

Taye attempted a cursory shrug. "Thank you for rescuing me from Helson."

"You didn't need to be rescued."

"Oh yes, I did."

She laughed and smiled a sheepish smile. Taylor laughed and flashed a stupid grin.

He wanted to kiss her.

The thought attacked with fierce, feverish speed. Oh yes, he wanted to kiss her. Now. Here. Holding her in this unconventional position, in a scandalous, shameless way. And by the way her emerald gaze darkened to a near onyx, he knew Gwendolen envisioned the same hot, desperate scene.

They couldn't have scrambled apart faster had the Metropolitan Line just laid new rail through the foyer.

"Oh," she blurted, raising quivering fingers to her lips. "Oh, dear." Taylor's gut twisted harder with the sight of her unease, with the self-condemnation of knowing he'd incited it.

"I—" Gwen tried to begin again. "I—well, as you said, it's been a long day."

"I'm certain Colleen has anticipated your extra night's stay," he took over. Taye concentrated on recovering the breaths he'd forgotten to take in the last moments.

His effort went rewarded when the white tension of her lips yielded to a trusting smile again. "Sleep well, Taylor," she told him, moving toward the stairs.

"Good night, princess."

She'd climbed just two stairs when Alistair's distinctive cough echoed through the foyer. Stafford House's head butler approached with an unusual haste to his usually confined pace.

Taylor turned with an instant and concerned frown. "Alistair, what is it? Danny? Granna? Where are they?"

Alistair shook his thin-haired head. "Master Daniel and the dowager countess are fine, my lord. But you—er, rather Miss Marsh, has a guest."

"A guest?" Gwen hurried down off the stairs. "For me? Here? At this hour?"

"Yes, miss. He very clearly insisted on waiting."

"He did, did he?" With that, she emitted a surprising laugh. Her eyes twinkled as she looked up to Taye in explanation. "I should have known Reggie would insist on making camp in the drawing room. I'm sorry, Taylor. I should have warned you."

"Miss Marsh." Alistair punctuated the interjection with another discreet cough. "Mister and Mistress Aberdeen went back to the orphanage hours ago. They said they would return tomorrow after tea. I'm afraid *this* gentleman was not so considerate."

Her smile drained away. She whipped the ensuing frown to Taylor. He read her silent, fearful question: *Helson? Could he have had second thoughts about arresting me?*

Only one action surfaced as the right reply. Taylor stepped forward and slipped his hand over hers. *Come on,* his soul murmured back to hers. *If he's here, he'll have to arrest us together.*

As he guided her across the foyer, Gwen told herself to focus on Taylor's warmth and not the cold reverberations of their footsteps on the marble floor. She pressed her lips together and fought the urge to cling to him with *both* hands.

Before the polished oak doors of the main drawing room, Taylor stopped. He turned to her. Their eyes met. His gaze flickered like firelight through brandy, warm and soothing. One side of his mouth tugged up, enveloping her with his undaunted confidence.

She was glad he was here. So very, very glad.

She nodded to him. Just once. But without hesitation. He stepped from her and pushed the two doors back.

Gwen retained the vague awareness of Taylor's frame tensing like a piqued lion as she gasped like a dazed idiot. No matter. She *felt* like a dazed idiot.

"Lloyd," she finally stammered. "Lloyd. what are you doing here?"

Eleven

He stood in the middle of the room, the picture of refinement in his formal dinner attire, stock still perfectly tied. At Gwen's gasp, he broke composure only with the arch of one smooth eyebrow.

"Well." Lloyd tugged on the crisp cuffs at both sleeves. "Here you are, at last."

The pronouncement flowed across the room with the same mixture of cadence and control that reminded Gwen of many a summer afternoon at his feet. She'd been so swept away in those redolent days, so captivated . . .

But now she gritted her teeth against the shocked clutch of her stomach, the uncontrolled spin of her head. Now she heard the serpent behind the smooth slither of a voice.

And she watched. She looked on as the face, once enrapturing and perfect, became as cold as the Michelangelo statue Lloyd had always reminded her of.

"You'll never imagine who I met up with tonight," he finally said. He strolled the room as if he'd called at noon, not midnight.

Until Taylor stepped forward and blocked the way. He took little pain to disguise the contempt coiling every muscle in his body. "Guess what, Waterston?" he snarled. "We don't care."

Lloyd just arched the other brow. "Inspector Helson, of our own Scotland Yard," he went on. He stepped around Taylor as if bypassing a bothersome part of the room's architecture. "He told me some things, Gwendolen. Disturbing things." He stopped when he stood nearly toe-to-toe with her. "I, of course, set him straight—in front of quite a crowd at the Haltermingers' dinner party, I might add."

"Lloyd," she said through locked teeth, "I don't think this is the time or place—"

"I told him he'd finally let the investigation get the better of him. I told him he'd started to hallucinate things if he saw you two not only fawn over each other in the middle of the coroner's office but proceed to laugh at him as you frolicked off in the same carriage together."

"For heaven's sake," Gwen retorted. "That's not true!"

"It isn't?" Between slow blinks, Lloyd scrutinized her, then Taylor, then her again.

"Of course not." The whole situation suddenly struck her as absurd. Gwen couldn't stifle the awkward smile tugging at her composure. "We did *not* laugh at him."

Her gaze met with Taylor's as she pressed restraining fingers to her lips. The crinkles around his eyes affirmed her perception of the ludicrous scene.

She had no idea Lloyd saw things differently.

Gwen's heartbeat clutched as his enraged face filled her vision and his long fingers coiled into her shoulders. She felt hairpins pop loose as he jerked her back and forth. Her vision blurred. Pain attacked her temples.

"Blast you, Gwendolen. This is not a game!" The smell of after-dinner cigars and brandy permeated his breath. Red veins bulged in his eyes as he clamped her tighter, shook her harder.

It took her several stunned seconds to realize he'd been hauled clear from her, then thrown against the marble mantel across the room.

Gwen peeled her hair back with quivering hands. Taylor dominated the carpet before her, breathing with hard, fast fury. He stood on wide-braced legs with arms curled slightly behind him, as if some invisible restraint posed the sole barrier to him tearing Lloyd apart with his bare hands.

"She's not yours to command anymore, Waterston," he finally seethed. His lips barely moved—though his jaw grinded at the turbulent pace set by his racing heart and lungs.

Lloyd's right cheek twitched like a dying mosquito. But his reply matched Taylor's tight fury word for word. "Maybe she's not, *my lord.* But her *business* very well is." He flashed a glare to her again. "Dear God, Gwendolen! Would you think about what you're doing for once?"

With that, he pushed from the marble. Gwen instinctively retreated. Taylor pounded a threatening step.

Lloyd raised his hands, as if presenting a truce flag. "Gwen—just this time, listen to me," he charged. "And just *think* about things. You've already compounded the Lancer affair with that orphanage foolishness, and now—" He flung a look around the room as if they stood naked in the Sistine Chapel. "For Peter's sake, you've taken up residence at Stafford House. Stafford House—as in *the* Staffords of Buckingham—from the *sixteenth* century."

Gwen sighed heavily. "I know which Staffords, Lloyd."

"Then how did you expect this little arrangement to go by unnoticed? Did you really expect to live here with him, in the middle of Wilton Crescent, with no chaperon to speak of?"

"With no chaperon?" Gwen repeated. "Is that what you think?" She barely quelled another laugh. "Have you ever met the Dowager Countess Stafford?"

Taylor's nearing presence instilled her with more conviction. He moved closer, large and solid, while continuing to glare Lloyd down as if truly intending to produce a battle lance the next moment. "Her honor, as if you really give a damn, is being protected with all seemly precautions."

"Well," Lloyd huffed. "Of course I give a— Of course I care. Surely you, Stafford, can understand that."

She could have sworn Taylor mouthed an expletive crude enough to make a sailor cringe. "This ought to be good," he muttered aloud.

At that, Lloyd inclined his head closer to Taylor's, as if sharing one of those concepts female ears couldn't possibly understand. "I'm certain you've been forced to facilitate a few of these . . . delicate separations yourself, my lord. The damage can be irreparable if not handled just so. And while I admit my reputation in Town is good, it is not sterling enough to withstand much more of all the rumors and scandalmongering. Everyone knows Gwendolen and I aren't *associated* anymore, but they haven't stopped *affiliating* us with each other."

Before continuing, he cleared his throat and shot a pointed look at Gwen. "Which means, madam, I'm still spending a good amount of my time explaining your actions. And if I can be frank about the matter, Gwendolen, it has not been enjoyable."

Silence draped over the room like a funeral shroud.

Gwen took a step back. She yearned to run from this monster again, from the fury and frustration he reintroduced to her heart. But her legs barely supported her now. The craving struck to swing her palm full force into Lloyd's face. Yet her arm hung useless and numb at her side.

Worst of all, something deep inside acknowledged his words as the truth, however final . . . however painful.

She thanked God for Taylor's voice, cutting through her fogged senses with low but commanding calm. "Well," he began, matching Lloyd's throat-clearing with perfect precision. Too perfect. "I'm certain Miss Marsh appreciates your call for candidness as much as I."

"She does? You do?" A full half minute passed before Lloyd remembered to collect himself. "Well, indeed," he drawled then, running a self-sure hand down his stock. "Of course you do. I knew that when I came here. I realized I could depend on your experience and aplomb to grasp the intricacies of this situation, my lord."

"Quite." The same even control modulated Taylor's voice—though as accompaniment, he wielded a look Gwen had never seen before. A potent, predatory look. Something told her to step away as one side of his mouth curled up and he loomed closer over Lloyd.

"Now get out," he at last snarled.

Lloyd's hand stopped stroking. "I beg your pardon?"

"Complete candidness, Lloyd." Taylor turned into more a stranger with every inch of the slow, savage smile he bared. "That's what you said, wasn't it? Man to man. Surely you understand, with your *aplomb* and *experience*."

For a moment, Lloyd stood there and blinked—like an animal comprehending, too late, a forest fire was upon him.

He took a tentative backstep. Taylor compensated, stomping forward. "I—" Lloyd stammered. "My lord, I don't think I—"

"Then let me be frank, mate." Without warning, Taylor shot both arms out. He coiled quaking fists into Lloyd's lapels and jerked. Hard. "Isn't that what you wanted . . . *Lloyd?*" He drew the name out in nasal mockery as he hauled the man six inches closer, bringing them chest to chest. "Utter honesty, right, *Lloyd?* Then listen closely, *Lloyd*."

"Now see here!"

"I don't think I'm the one with the vision problem."

"Unhand me!"

"Shut up."

Gwen gasped from behind the Renaissance chair she'd latched on to. She watched Taylor's shoulders tense and flex, jostling Lloyd up and down. Lloyd's eyes bulged and his nostrils puffed, transforming perfection to disfiguration. She wondered—wished?—that she dreamed this unreal scene, that she imagined Taylor's vehement show of fury tearing at some secret core of her—riveting her attention, though she begged release from the savage sight.

"You bastard!" Taylor seethed. "How dare you come here prattling of honor and character—how dare you, when your pathetic lack of either drove this woman here in the first place!"

"Now see here!" Lloyd managed to squirm an accusing finger loose. "I'll be happy to discuss this like gentlemen when you cease this unlawful mistreatment!"

"Mistreatment?" The return vibrated with caustic humor.

"Only you'd have the gall to utter that, Waterston. What do you think you did when you marched in to Saint Jerome's that afternoon and spit this woman's hopes in her face?" Another violent tremor rippled the muscles of his back. "Say it, god-damn you. I want to hear you say it."

Lloyd struggled like a flounder on a fish hook. "I did what was best for everyone involved. There was no other way out of the catastrophe!"

"Jesus."

Gwen knew he'd lost control when she barely heard the disgusted oath. But before she could act, Taylor's fist flew; Lloyd shot out the doorway and across the front hall. He came to a stop only by colliding with the Aubusson carpet six feet away.

Taylor inhaled deeply, in and out, as if trying to summon control he didn't think he had. He stalked into the foyer and leaned over Lloyd's prone position. He glared down with glittering, unbridled fury. His upper lip curled with revulsion. He took in another breath; the far reaches of the foyer echoed with the potent wrath of it.

Finally, he uttered, "Listen to me and listen well, Waterston. I'm only going to waste the effort once on you." He leaned down an inch further. "If you ever defile my doorway again, I'll have you arrested for trespassing and anything else I can drum up. And believe me, there *will* be a trial. And it *will* be more publicized and scandalous than your worst nightmares. And if you ever come near Gwendolen again—" his fists began to coil and uncoil, "if you ever look at her, or speak her name, if you ever *think* about her, I'll know it. And I'll come and kill you." He straightened. "That's a promise."

He looked to Alistair then, who'd materialized from nowhere. Taylor dragged his hand through his hair while forcing down more harsh breaths. "Get him out of here, Alistair. Get him out of my home. Now."

Gwen vaguely acknowledged that the butler carried out the deed; after several minutes, she looked around and realized Lloyd had disappeared. But her most keen sights and senses tunneled on the man still standing in the middle of the foyer. Taylor's dark hair tumbled over his tight mask of rage. He still held hands curled and ready at his sides, as if expecting more pompous demons to come flying through the door at her any moment.

He was furious and wild and dark.

He was painfully, absolutely beautiful.

She stepped toward him. For the first time, she comprehended the teary mist marring her vision. Her heartbeat clamored in her throat again. Yet this time, the pulse resounded through her ears, through her head, demanding to possess her, louder and louder with each moment.

Taylor snapped his head when her skirts swished on the tile. She halted as if a lion pounced before her, slashing out a warning claw—and not too sure one hadn't. Fire roared through his eyes, hot and gold; wildness emanated from him like summer sun behind one of Trafalgar's bronze lioncels.

She swallowed on a suddenly dry throat. She swayed on suddenly liquid legs. "Taylor." The syllables came as a question and an offering in one. "Taylor . . ."

He slammed his eyes shut, as if her voice pained him. "Go to bed, Gwendolen."

"But I—"

"It's over, damn it; just go to bed!"

He spun and didn't look back as he bolted from the foyer. After an eternal pause, a distant door slammed like a cannon blast.

Gwen stood in the following silence for a very, very long time. *Oh, God,* her soul wept. "Oh, God," she whispered.

She wrapped both arms around her middle, battling the hot-cold spasms beginning to attack her with each remembrance of the scene just played out on the tiles below her.

The hot swept like a wave of fever, strange yet uncontrollable, and achingly, solely feminine. With each wave, she remembered Taylor standing here so large, so furious, so primitive—so unlike any creature she imagined possible on this earth.

But the cold preyed as suddenly and relentlessly, a pervading chill when her mind replayed his snarled warnings at Lloyd.

His threats at Lloyd for *her.*

Then the waves came mixed of both, heat and chill, as she remembered afterward, and his stare. *That stare.* That gold light piercing her like a lion's eyes seared the night, hunting her down with intensity and—

Wanting.

Gwen gasped. Her hands dropped from her mouth to her skirt. The action released sensation up from her woman's core to her breasts . . . heat and chill, confusion and terror. Her heart pounded against her corset, hard nipples throbbing against stiff lace, warm ache spurred by a heated hazel gaze . . .

"Oh, God!" she cried in fear . . . and in need.

She jerked up her skirts and tore up the stairs, two at a time. She dashed down the hall, as fast as she could. She bolted into the Emerald Bedroom, slamming the door shut with her back.

She opened her eyes in the moonlight-slivered darkness.

She saw only a leonine head of hair, a tormented black-and-gold gaze. Taylor's gaze . . . devouring her.

"Oh, God," she murmured past fast, hot tears. "Oh, Taylor."

An hour's flight along the walkways of Hyde Park only served to whip Taylor's blood into a more turbulent frenzy. As his stalks made echoing crunches on his return trek up Stafford House's drive, he resigned himself to a sleepless night in the library, gulping back more brandy than he could handle, battling to forget every moment which had turned him into this enraged, unthinking beast.

Yes, he'd try to forget the flood of fury when he'd watched Waterston reduce Gwen to a tramp with one sweep of that arrogant gaze. He'd slam back a huge swig to forget how good it would've felt to strangle the hypocritical life from the sonofabitch.

Then he'd drink himself under the table to quell the guilt. That twisting, hot attack in his gut, when he'd let the bastard go with nothing but a good blow to the jaw.

But he knew he couldn't kill Waterston when he'd looked up and seen Gwen standing there. Proud. Brave. Not crumpled in a shocked swoon or shooting him a glare to indicate he'd turned into a barbarian, but gazing at him with so much respect and reverence, all he'd wanted to do was fly across that foyer and drown in that life-giving green gaze . . . surrender his senses to that full, trembling mouth.

He'd bloody near scorched himself alive with the vision. But his stalk through drizzle-drenched Hyde hadn't helped. His brain still raged afire; his body screamed a parched plea for the nectar of Gwendolen's life and hope and—

What? *What, goddamnit, do you want from her, Stafford? Just her little part in your purpose, wasn't that it?* Isn't *that it? Just the facts she can give you, then get away clean, right?*

Right?

His abrupt stop sent echoes of squeaking boots through the recesses of the front foyer. He looked up. Up toward the south wing. Toward the Emerald Bedroom.

He cursed.

A bead of sweat slithered down his jaw. Gritting back another oath, he backhanded the wet distraction away. Another step, slow and sliding; he thought of the haven of books and brandy waiting on the other side of the foyer.

He looked up again.

The main stairwell stared back in smooth-carpeted silence.

He lifted a foot to the bottom step. He pressed his weight to it. Quiet pervaded every inch of the house. He heard himself breathing. And he heard the whispering, soothing rationalization of his mind: *Just for a moment. Just to make certain she's sleeping well.*

Taye didn't look back as he ascended to the second floor.

He wiped more sweat from his brow as he proceeded down the hall—grimacing in self-rebuke at his suddenly damp hands and slowing stride. But despite his effort otherwise, he eventually stood at the door of the Emerald Bedroom.

"For Christ's sake," he growled to whatever body part would stop thudding long enough to listen. "You've seen a sleeping woman before."

Not a woman who sleeps in the bed you once held her in, begging her to stay alive because she did something to you even then, Stafford. Because she probably looks beautiful against those sheets now, healthy peach skin against those pillows, copper hair glinting in the moonlight . . .

Because when you see her like that, you might not want to leave.

A chunk of something between anger and rebellion gripped him. He mouthed an angry, salty oath, and reached a determined hand to push the door open.

His fingers gripped the knob tighter when Taye beheld the empty bedclothes. Moonbeams highlighted the green counterpane, the rumpled white sheets and blankets . . . and a lady's lace-trimmed robe, laid neatly over the lounge at the foot of the bed.

The rest of his body tensed at the last observation. She surely could not have gone far in her nightrail, he reasoned.

Or was it possible she'd left behind *all* her bedwear—in preference for traveling clothes? Taylor clenched back another unexpected and unwanted stab of anxiety.

Then the awareness of her overtook him.

He turned toward the open-draped window.

The moonlight poured in between the flitting curtains, bathing her in silver-white light . . . soaking through her nightgown as if the material were no more than gossamer in the path of a tidal wave. Her breasts and hips and buttocks had been transformed into shadow and curves and mystery.

The silhouette affected him with the subtlety of a lightning blast.

But her face stole the mobility from his limbs. Like a mythical sea goddess in her ocean of moonglow, she looked up to the stars with eyes ashimmer as if to call each a precious friend. She'd raised her left hand to the slightly opened windowpane; her fingers were pale from a term of clearly intense pressure.

Especially pale, Taylor noticed then, the stark white band on her ring finger where an emerald engagement ring once had been.

His throat tightened on a heavy swallow. He didn't know where she'd put the jewel—and frankly, he didn't care. He only recognized, with shattering, terrifying speed, what the act signified. She'd torn down the last of her walls. She'd laid her castle bare once more. It meant his siege was over . . . and now it was time to seal the possession.

He bolted forward on legs made of fire.

He stopped short when her fragrance hit him. Evening wind and fresh soap. Pure femininity. A torture of arousal.

Gwen turned as he halted. Her fingers flew from the window to her lips.

Tears, Taylor realized. That bottomless shimmer in her eyes wasn't starfire. Those ocean green depths glittered with sad, searching tears.

Pain sliced his chest in two. Anger and self-doubt wielded the merciless blades. "I . . ." he began. *I'm sorry. Not because I lost control down there, but because you saw it. You saw the monster I really am and now there's nothing I can do to change it and there's everything I want to do to change it and—*

"I didn't mean to frighten you," he blurted.

"You didn't frighten me," she murmured back.

Taye shook his head. "No. I'm not doing this well." His voice sounded pathetic. Hoarse. Grating. Full of the need wracking him from head to toe. "I meant—earlier—"

"I know what you meant."

Her hand slid up the side of his face. Their gazes locked. Their breaths rose and fell, in ever-increasing speed, together.

Taylor drank her in, pressed her fingers tighter to his skin . . . and knew only greater desire and hotter need, replacing the terror. Her words, so purely spoken, so lovingly given, had toppled the last of the doubts and the fears . . . had solidified all the laughter and tears and happiness and tension of the last weeks into this inevitable moment of awakening.

And he realized it then. Realized it; accepted it. *Inevitable,* his soul repeated. *Inevitable . . . meant to be.*

There was no other direction to take but forward, through the destined portal.

He plunged.

She whimpered as he slanted his lips over hers, a feminine mewl of gratitude, of surrender. Taye pulled her body close next. His hands tangled in her unpinned fall of hair. His fingers raked down her back and her thighs. Soon, he trailed back up to knead fistfuls of her nightgown and slide palmfuls of her skin.

She didn't respond in kind. No, she came back with more. She returned every movement of his with eager, desperate unselfishness, nearly causing him to stumble away in shock. But he stayed and felt her explore his nape and mess his hair, grasp his shoulders and grip his tensing upper arms, then clutch his neck again as she molded herself closer, tighter against him. Against his arousal.

He battled for some last reserve of control, but the dam had been broken . . . the flood at last unleashed. And it was "so good," he murmured aloud. Jesus, the flood felt so good.

He drove his mouth harder, implored her lips to open for his deepening intimacy. He shuddered when she responded with as much trust and passion. He nearly exploded when her tongue, at first shy and untried, warmed to his mouth's mating dance. Her body joined in the surging, sensuous rhythm.

Taylor groaned, sliding his hands around her bottom, urging her onto the swelling in his trousers. It had been so long. And she felt so bloody good.

"God," he rasped as he tore his mouth from hers. A touch

of consolation dawned to feel her breath as staccato as his, her eyes as glazed as his probably were, and her lips—

He refused to look at that tempting red fullness. *Her eyes,* he commanded himself. *Just keep focused on her eyes and think of how you caused that confused, chaotic . . .*

Beautiful emerald light.

He forced himself to breathe and straighten her gown at the same time. The former was impossible. The latter yielded disastrous results in the vicinity between his thighs.

Her eyes, her eyes, look at her eyes.

"Gwen," he grated. "Sweet Gwen. If I don't leave now, I won't be able to stop."

He stepped away, trying to let her go. She held him tighter, pressing her lips determinedly. Her eyes pooled and glowed. Another shimmering drop escaped down her cheek.

"Then don't leave," she pleaded in a trembling whisper.

Twelve

Like the silver night beams around them, her words floated on the air, suspended, waiting . . .

Real?

Gwen's soul pressed the query to her. But oh, what was the answer?

Taylor gave it to her. He stopped his retreat . . . instead concentrating a gaze into her of such deep copper heat and need, she knew the words were real. And she knew she'd never meant anything more in her life. She'd never yearned for anything harder than the thick flames in his eyes, now upon her, licking through her, enflaming her blood and marrow. She never needed anything more than the fire that stare promised: a conflagration high and hot enough not only to cremate every ugly moment of this day, but transform every shadow of her life into brilliant day again.

And now, her heart confessed, she was ready for that light. After two long years of this hopeless night, she longed to greet the dawn.

And she wanted no other to show it to her than the man waiting a heartbeat away.

She stepped closer to Taylor. Their hands intertwined. Their gazes swirled and locked. Their bodies moved together without thought, an innate oneness . . .

He squeezed her hands harder. His head lowered. He stopped inches away, his dark and rugged glory filling her vision, his eyes raking her, exploring . . . assessing . . . possessing. Gwen heard the stark catch of his breath; she rejoiced in his body constricting once more against hers, fingers squeezing, thighs pulsing, chest trembling.

He expelled the breath in a ragged rush. Then again, he captured her mouth beneath his.

Sweet surrender, some dim corner of her mind thought. Sweet, aching, burning release; a pressure she hadn't known the full force of until now as he unbound it within her, within him. Every glance and smile they'd ever exchanged, every silence at the end of a poetry line or warm glow over some shared anecdote about Danny, all the precious moments had added to the bittersweet tension. Every hour of all these treasured days, leading to this. *Meant* for this.

He parted her lips once more, with increased urgency. She yielded with a moan. His tongue dominated with magical sensations: hard desire and soft sensuality, giving in long, passionate sweeps, then taking with slow, agonizing abandon.

They broke apart with rasping reluctancy, breathing hard, trying to understand the needing, searching facets in each other's eyes. Finally, a look of decision intensified Taylor's features. He stepped backward. He caught her limp fingers and pulled her with him. Gwen swallowed, her gaze unable to leave his broad, taut form . . . and the shadows of the bed behind him.

His lips parted on one word of gentle bidding. "Come."

Come, his golden eyes promised her.

Gwendolen let him guide her closer.

Without words, he sat on the rumpled covers she'd left behind. His eyes lowered, as if contemplating the moisture on his boots, perhaps some stray lint on the floor. Gwen stood awkwardly, longing to touch him, yearning to delve her fingers into his thick hair, frightened to do anything beyond breathe.

In an abrupt move, without looking up, he pulled her to him. He drew her between his legs as he burrowed his head beneath her breasts, against her heartbeat. His hands moved around and up her thighs, his fingers caressing, molding, learning her shape.

Gwen's throat caught in mute joy. Her eyes closed; her arms raised. Finally . . . She raked her fingers up through his hair. She pressed her cheek to the top of his head as she pulled herself closer, even closer. She couldn't get close enough.

"I want to be one with you." She winced even as she whispered the words. Surely Aunt Maggie's tutelage had been correct. She was on her way down the road toward a wanton downfall. She had to end this shame now; this sweet, atrocious scandal . . . just after another moment. *Oh, please, just another moment . . .*

But the next moment came, and Taylor answered her with a kiss that stole her breath and her reason. Gwen looked down as he raised his head, his eyes now closed, his mouth . . .

Oh, his *mouth.* His lips and tongue kissed and suckled her breast, savoring the taste of her through her nightgown. She stared, fascinated. She watched, spellbound, as his tongue's path inched higher, higher.

Her sweet cry of pleasure caused Taylor to groan as he moistened the fabric around her tightening, tingling nipple. He rocked her, toppled her into sensations she'd never dreamed existed.

And there was more. Dear God, there was more . . . she knew it as his hands began to move on her, finding her other nipple, coaxing the sensitive point into the same hard crimson as the bud beneath his mouth. His other hand slid up, over her shoulder, down her arm . . . taking the sleeve of her nightgown with him.

She lost her remaining balance. She fell forward. His safe, sure arms caught her and settled her into clouds of pillows and sheets that cradled her bare shoulders and back.

Night air wafted its way across her body, and she opened her eyes. She blinked, not sure whether the beauty before her was just some trick of the night shifting through the curtains. Yet the incredible sight remained: soft moonlight upon the pale lawn of Taylor's shirt, and his dark hands, sliding buttons from their slots, exposing his naked skin to her, inch by inch. She watched, but she could not control her trembling reaction to it.

His sculptured collarbones . . . the planes of his chest, his sinfully symmetrical abdominal ridges, then . . .

Then lower. *Lower. No. Yes* . . . Her widening gaze descended. *Oh, my,* she thought.

Her eyes flew back to Taylor's face.

He'd been watching her as she watched him. His own stare had transformed from leaping flames into smoldering heat.

Instinct told her what that difference meant.

It meant he was going to take off the rest of his clothes.

It meant a rush of tension into her every nerve ending. It meant watching him peel back his shirt, then drop the white mass to the floor—while looking at her. He tugged off one, two boots—never wavering in his purpose, not lowering his stare a fraction.

Then . . . oh, then his fingers moved at the front of his trousers, pushing fine fabric over his hips and down his legs.

Gwen blinked at the hard, bold beauty of him, appalled with herself for looking, but unable to tear her gaze away.

"Touch me," he told her then. He grasped her hand and drew it to his chest, after placing soft kisses on each of her fingers. "I've been cold for so long. You're so warm. *Touch me . . .*"

Gwendolen did.

He dipped his head to kiss her wrist, his profile tight with anticipation. Gwen would have been thankful to die here, now, with this sight of him, the scent of him . . . the feel of him.

Unable to resist, she raised her hand to explore him. He sucked air between his teeth.

She emitted a soft gasp of her own. Gwen considered this new phenomenon she'd caused, stroking and circling his puckered skin. She watched him swallow, but he allowed her to continue, wordlessly telling her of the sweet torture she dealt him.

At last, Taylor grasped her fingers, lacing his own through them. His grip trembled against hers. Their entwined limbs sank into the pillows. His muscled body descended and molded to hers.

His kiss was like the feel of his body: strong and sensual, consuming, completing. He covered her with heat and life and power. His sinewed skin pressed against her softness.

"Yes." He breathed the word against her neck. His lips and tongue suckled there, teaching her again, she realized. Showing her time-old rhythms, pulsing a primal beat through her blood, filling her senses with instinct's sweetest song. "Oh, yes," he encouraged. "Don't stop."

They moved like that, faster and hotter and wilder, until Gwen swore she'd scream with the fever in her blood. At that moment Taylor pushed her wet curls away from her eyes, fully exposing her face to the molten gold desire of his stare.

He drowned her scream with a hard plunge of his mouth. When they broke apart, his breath mingled with hers in scalding rushes of desire.

"Burn for me, sweetheart," he gasped. "Burn *with* me."

"Yes." She arched into him, meeting his kiss with abandoned thrusts of her tongue and lips. His groan reverberated through her, exploding heat in the core of her womanhood.

And she opened to him.

Taylor's hands worked feverishly at her gown, pushing the material over her legs and hips, pulling it from her thighs. Gwen reached up to pull him close, closer, so he could lower his lips to hers again. She moaned hungrily into his mouth. "Please," she begged. *"Please."*

"It's all right," he answered. "Soon."

As if to prove just that, his hand slipped along her inner thigh. He stroked higher, touching delicate curls and slippery flesh.

Gwen inhaled. Dear *saints,* this couldn't be real. This couldn't be *her,* feeling pleasure so intense, so shocking and hot, she'd surely ignite from the flames any moment.

Aunt Maggie *was* right. This feeling was debauched, decadent. It made her writhe like a heathen. It made her cry out like a harlot. It wasn't proper or seemly or pure.

It was heaven.

"Please. Taylor, *please.*"

Her conscious thought ceased. His lips ravished hers, wet and wild, her tongue delved deep and intense. The fire inside her flared higher. His hard thighs slid between hers. He was moving, probing . . .

Penetrating.

She gasped again. Taylor moaned. It was exquisite, this joining. The bed and the scrollwork ceilings and all of Stafford House seemed unreal, far away in the realm of mortals. Their joining was fated, glorious, a fusion of souls.

"It's wonderful," she whispered. "I never thought . . ."

"I know," came his reply. "I know, sweeting."

She felt his arms quiver. Hesitantly, she brushed the back of his head. "It's . . . not over, is it?"

Taylor groaned. "No. Oh, no. We're just beginning. We're just—" A second tremor seized him. He moved farther into her. His control shattered. "Hang on. Hold me. Hold me—tight—I can't stop—*now.*"

He filled her. He gasped with the pure pleasure of it.

Gwen cried out with the sudden and jarring pain. In that second, she'd been hurled back to the Emerald Bedroom four-poster, back to tense reality, to sharp pain stabbing the most vulnerable part of her. Despite her staunchest effort, tears squeezed out the corners of her eyes.

"Damn." Taylor's murmur blended with his lips on her cheek. "You're crying. I made you cry. Don't cry."

"I'm not crying! I . . . I'm being childish. I was—" She swallowed, struggling for the world-wise tone that wouldn't come. "I was betrothed for a good while, my lord. I knew what this would be like."

"You knew nothing."

The normal voice he used then sounded like a cannon blast

after their whispers against the house's silence. Taylor rose up on his elbows and the intensity in his eyes filled her soul.

"Look at me," he told her. "Look only at me. Trust me." She winced as he moved inside her again. *"Trust me."*

He withdrew for another long, deliberate stroke. "Gwen," he rasped. "You don't know how good it can be. You don't know how incredible."

No, Gwen admitted, she didn't think she did. But she wanted to. She needed to . . . now, here, with this man's gaze holding her safe, with his body showing her the way. She shed fresh tears as he set the rhythm anew, opened her to the bright and beautiful sensations warming her. Igniting her. Arousing her.

Gwen moved her hands on his back. She hesitantly slid her foot along his leg. Taylor's hold tightened around her body; she felt his hardness stretch inside her.

She suddenly wanted to be full of him.

He shuddered as she arched her hips against him, pulling him deeper, tighter. His lips and tongue worked at her neck, hotter, wetter. Her hands traced a path down his back until she cupped his straining buttocks, urging him on deeper inside her.

"Jesus." His harsh, amazed rasp blasted warmth into her ear. "Jesus Christ, sweetheart."

His mouth found hers again. He invaded and conquered, in time to the quickening pace of his body. Then he buried his face in the curve of her neck. He burned the skin there with his last fierce oath as her feminine core burned with the hot flood of his climax.

Slowly his movements eased to satiated glides. "So warm," he finally murmured, stroking her shoulder, her breast, "You're still so warm . . ."

He kissed her then, absorbing her quiet tears with gentle lips. A breeze reached their slick bodies; he pulled the dark-green counterpane over them, enclosing them.

For a long while, he lay with her and rocked her, seeming to know this haven of softness and silence was the only world she wanted. Perhaps the only world she'd ever want again.

Gwen recognized that strange idea at the borders of her consciousness, but she couldn't think about it right now. Now she existed for this bond joining her to a proud, noble man. This man, this moment had given her so much—her happiness. Her dignity.

Her life.

Thank you, her heart whispered as she entwined her limbs with his. *Thank you,* her soul cried. *Thank you.* She wrapped her arms around the broad warmth of him.

And as exhaustion worked its spell upon her, dragging her eyelashes down, her face nestled against his musk-scented skin, her lips formed one more silent phrase:

I love you.

Taylor blinked groggily. Meeting only grey light, formless shadows. He blinked again and squinted. Dim patterns focused above his eyes. Circles, tangled together like the thoughts that wouldn't straighten in his mind.

Dreaming, came the comforting notion. Yes, that was it. The sight was just a funny dream, these circles reminding him of the Emerald Bedroom's ceiling. Surely he'd awaken soon and forget this strange disorientation, as if the true Taylor stood back and watched a stranger lying here squinting and dreaming.

Truth be known, he didn't really care. He'd rather be the impostor Taylor if it meant basking in this warmth, surrounding him in sensual scent and physical satisfaction. He'd rather die in his sleep if it meant an eternity of holding the silken nudity he rolled over and pressed into.

Connie, his mind murmured absently. His imagination repeated her name as a question. It had been so long since she'd visited his sleep—had she always smelled this clean, like summer rain? He remembered her fragrance differently. Sweeter. Heavier. *No matter,* he told the dream with a smile. *I like this better.*

She moved against him. It *had* been too long. She felt so real. She pressed her back to his front. So real . . .

His sex grew to fit between the spheres of her perfect bottom. He cupped his hand around the lush curve of her shoulder, then her breasts . . . *Connie. God. Connie, I don't remember your breasts feeling like* this.

He lingered over the swells, delighting in the feel of her skin coming alive under his touch, contracting, hardening. She sighed, pure feminine response, a sound that stirred him and moved his hand back up to her shoulder, through her hair. Connie's midnight thick hair . . .

His fingers froze. His half-parted eyes flashed open.

He didn't hold a waterfall of darkness. Dawn-kissed curls coiled around his fist. Copper curls.

Consciousness. Racing, remembering consciousness. The overhead circles were real because the room was real. The patterned ceiling, the dark oak furniture, the thick, snowy sheets—

And Gwendolen wrapped in the soft mess, sleeping next to him. Bare-breasted, beautiful . . . a goddess of sensuality.

Gwendolen.

It wasn't a dream.

He thought it was a dream.

Because, came the harrowing, heinous realization, he'd dreamed of her like this so many times before.

Dear Christ.

When had things *changed?* When had he broken the line from needing her in his plan to needing her in his bed?

The answer, he admitted dismally, didn't matter. The damn bridge had been crossed, *that's* what mattered. Now he had to get back to the other side as swiftly as possible, back to the right before he'd made it wrong . . . back to Connie and the quest. Yes, the quest was all that mattered. All that *could* matter.

He clenched down the immediate yearning to thrash aside the sheets. A few simple kicks would disentangle his body, but if he awakened Gwendolen and she smiled at him, kissed him, *thanked* him—

His soul might burn the bridge before his head had anything to say.

He had to leave. He had to leave now.

He rolled silently from the bed, ordering himself to disregard the blood-splotched nightgown he pulled from around his leg.

A shiver jerked her eyes fully open. Gwen moaned in discomfort and pulled the blankets tighter around her, wondering why she'd grown so cold after passing the night in such blissful warmth.

The answer struck her at the same instant she realized her nudity beneath the covers.

Taylor. *Oh, Taylor.*

The memories throbbed like the ache lingering between her thighs. Part of her pounded in shock and mortification, remembering her hands on Taylor's body, her sighs, her hips sliding beneath his in a hedonistic dance that surely no other proper ladies of London knew about, much less abandoned themselves to.

But the other part of her closed tighter around that ache . . . embraced the precious vulnerability now branding her as whole, as woman, as—

Loved?

Uncertain silence replied. Gwen pressed her lips together as the hollowness pervaded her soul. She rolled over in the blankets, drawn to the other pillow by a rich masculine scent. Taylor's cologne, lingering along the linen . . . joined by remnants of the sinuous dark-brown hair she'd clutched last night.

Against the white fabric, the strands now looked black. Gwen stroked one of the inky slashes. How different things appeared in the light. How drastically the dawn changed the whole world.

How easily it could change people.

Would it change Taylor? How would everything change between *them?* How would he look at her in this day's new light, tempered by the silver shadows of the previous night? Would he still favor her with that dimpled half-smile of his? Would the gold flecks of his eyes still come alive when she entered the room? Would he hold his powerful hands out to help her, to hold her? Was he waiting even now in the sitting room, a special poem in hand to share with her?

The wish to be with him transformed into need. She had to see him. She had to look into his eyes and see everything was all right. Things would be different—but gloriously different. Their pasts had been thrown away and locked out as firmly as they'd tossed Lloyd into the street last night. And the moonlit magic of a few hours ago had been just the beginning . . .

Gwen relaxed her lips into a hopeful smile. She even managed a quiet laugh at her bashful shielding of her body to an absolutely empty room.

She rose and hurried to the closet, scanning the contents for the easiest garments to slip into. A pleat-front shirtwaist and a narrow dark-blue skirt trimmed in Hussar braid met the requirement. She buttoned her shoes, then attacked her hair. The wild reflection of the red-gold mass made her think *warrior's woman,* and sent another permeating flush down to her knees. With trembling fingers she finally worked the strands into a thick braid, which she coiled atop her head and hastily secured with pins and pearl combs.

She left the most awkward task for last. With another secret smile, she pulled the bed sheets free, rolled them together—and hoped Colleen had too full a day to notice an odd crimson splattering upon her day's laundering.

She didn't know what led her to the north wing, instead of going directly down to the south sitting room. Her mind's eye already completed the perfect scene in the latter: Taylor dominating the window seat, one waistcoat button undone, shirtsleeves rolled halfway up his forearms . . . a kiss smoldering in his eyes.

But at the bottom of the main stairs, a tangible presence stepped into the foyer, calling Gwen as discernibly as a real beckoning from Taylor. She even smelled him on the air, wool and leather and rich cologne. Like a child at the scent of a tart vender, she migrated toward the call.

Still, she stopped in surprise when Taylor's voice reached her from a half-closed door at the end of the hall. Surely her imagination created the sound, yet he seemed so real, so close . . .

"Come to me," he summoned. "Talk to me."

The low cadence *was* real. Warmth swirled through Gwen's stomach as confirmation. She placed a hand to the giddy sensation and smiled. She only removed her fingers after she snuck up on the portal and moved to press the door back.

The wood obeyed her on silent hinges—just before she swallowed back a stunned choke.

After that, she didn't know which occurred first. The torment, she decided. Most certainly the torment. The slow agony of taking in the portrait dominating one wall of the room with thick-eyed, queenly gowned confidence. Then the horror of recognizing the figure as Constance, Baroness Roseby, Countess Stafford . . .

At last, the dread came. Piercing. Suffocating. Choking her harder each moment she looked at Taylor, his legs braced before the cold fireplace below the painting, head dropped between his arms. He gripped the mantel as if believing it the Ark of the Covenant, about to impart divine secrets to him.

"Connie . . ." His voice shook with such violent desperation, Gwen doubted he'd look up if she'd come singing into the room. "Connie, don't go away now. Last night . . . I . . . it was never meant to happen."

Gwen flung a hand out for the doorframe. Even then, she fought to stay on her feet. *Never meant to happen!*

Taylor still didn't hear her. He shook his head, pounded his fist atop the mantel. "What the hell happened? Everything was supposed to be simple. Innocent. So bloody innocent. You know that, don't you? A little charm; a smile once in a while. Do you remember when I'd flirt with your mother and her friends at Sunday tea? I can be a rogue when I want to be; we both know it."

He dropped his head again. Gwen's heart turned over at the sight of him, beard-stubbled and disheveled and beautiful. No, not beautiful! Why did he have to be so beautiful?

"That's all it was supposed to be," he continued. "Some poetry in the morning. A few quiet dinners in the evening. Just enough to let her see my good side. Just enough to convince her to help me."

His hands coiled again, his tension as palpable as the aura emanating from the poised, perfect painting. "This road's been so long, Connie. So frustrating. So many dead ends, so much chaos . . . feeling so goddamn lost." A harsh sigh escaped him. "But last night—I was worse than lost. Last night, I *wanted* to be lost. And I . . . I was wrong, Connie. It was wrong. It was a mistake."

The words clung to the heavy-scented air, curling like the nausea in Gwen's stomach. She gulped back hot bile once, twice. Stinging heat flooded her eyes as he continued to mete out his lethal confession, oblivious to her silent agony.

"I betrayed the purpose," Taylor went on. "And I'm sorry. Speak to me, Connie. Say you forgive me, so I can continue our fight."

Gwen's grief at last transcended physical restraint. Her outcry began in her soul, echoed through her being and pierced the silence, raw and hurting. She watched Taylor spin at her, but the moment passed like a nightmare, shuddering and slow.

Her sob died away. Silence descended once more. He stared at her, hard, unblinking. She looked away, anywhere . . . everywhere. Her gaze collided with more pictures of "Connie" Stafford, inundating the room, on tables and adorning wall shelves, a few finer portraits lovingly hung on other walls.

Lies, every chamber of her heart echoed. Every rapturous day here, every moment—lies. He'd read her poetry and looked into her eyes, slayed deadly gnomes and let his fish suck her fingers. He'd made her feel a part of his life, his home—when she was no more a part of Stafford House than a housebreaker in the night.

"Bastard." She rasped the word through traitorous tears. "You lying, treacherous bastard."

"Gwen." The word came weighted and gruff, just as he'd uttered it last night against her breast, warming her skin . . . lying to her in his bed. He pushed from the mantel, arms raising. "Gwendolen."

"Don't!" She jerked back. "Don't touch me! Don't speak to me. That shouldn't be too hard for you, my lord. 'Innocent amusements' are simple to forget. Even panting, doe-eyed virgins like me!"

"Stop it. Gwendolen, last night—"

"Must have been incredible torture for you. How *did* you do it?" She laughed to save herself, triggering a tone of mock fascination. "How did you remember to call my name instead of hers? It was amazing, your lordship, truly amazing. Even at the height of your passion, not a single faux pas. Even when I thought you couldn't think at all. Even when you—" She choked, drawing air in sharp spurts, pressing a hand over her eyes to hide her pain from him. "Oh, God, even—when—you—"

The memories flooded her. The visions of his face above hers, damp with exertion. His lips against her throat, wet with their mingled sweat. His climax inside her body, full and hot.

None of it meant for her. None of it at all.

"Let's go to the drawing room." His hand closed around her elbow, the firm yet gentle hold she'd come to ache for, she'd come to love.

Fool! her soul screamed. *Simpering, stupid fool!*

She struggled in his hold, flailing at him, punching as hard as she could. When she broke free, she swept her arm across the eerie horizon of the room.

"Which one, Taylor?" she whispered. "Which picture did you see last night when you came to me? When you slid yourself inside me?"

"Gwendolen."

"I want to know. Which one replaced the scar and the hideous curls and the face you couldn't bear to look at?"

"Stop it. Stop it right now, damn it."

"Which one! Tell me, hell take you! I want to know how you saw Constance last night when you used *me!"*

With sharp, sobbing breaths, she awaited his answer.

Thirteen

Her sobs sliced the silence—sharp, wrenching bursts, as if the Lancer had returned to finish his deed and impaled her heart with his dagger, again and again.

But a faceless criminal didn't wield the blade this time, Taylor thought on a wave of rage. Another destroying bastard did. The bastard reflected back at him from Gwen's glare. He looked at the somber, sloppy image of himself in those green pools, and in that moment wished the Lancer would come after *him.*

If he could just hold her again. If he could just grab her, make her listen. He'd make *himself* listen, good and hard, as he confessed the gamble he'd taken with both their feelings in the last weeks, and lost—miserably. Lost to the irresponsible recklessness of last night, the desperate unreality of it. The heaven of it. The wrong of it.

He had to hold her one last time.

Yet when he moved forward, she flinched back. When he reached for her elbow, she winced as if a beast's paw slashed at her. He ignored the similar pain clawing his gut.

He switched to the force of instinct. With speed acquired from years of taming terrified colts, Taylor feigned left, then lunged right. He prepared to follow the motion through to the floor, but Gwen struggled with more coordination than a three-month-old foal.

He ended up backing her against the doorframe. Their stares locked; they both breathed hard. His legs encased hers as he seized her shoulders.

"Just—listen—to me," he said tightly.

Her muscles tensed beneath his grasp. She drew back her lips to snarl a retort.

A shriek pealed from the floor above, instead.

Taye saw his alarm mirrored in Gwendolen's eyes. Without thinking, he grabbed for her hand—then noticed she'd already slid her fingers between his. Together, they raced down the hall to the front foyer.

In the year and a half Colleen had been in his employ, Taylor had never seen the lass's face drained of so much color. The maid stumbled down the main stairs, shaking like an equally sapped fall leaf. A dusty rag dangled from her right hand, a wrinkled sheet of paper from the left. She stopped when her teary gaze befell Taylor and Gwen, as well as Granna and a handful of other curious servants.

"Milord," Colleen blurted. "Oh, milord, he's gone."

Gwen's fingers went stiff and chill in his. She knew, Taylor concluded vaguely. Like him, she already knew the disaster Colleen cried about.

The case clock knelled seven o'clock—the hour Danny normally trotted down these steps to greet him good morning. The chimes died away into the funereal silence. Sickening fear clutched his gut.

Somehow, his legs carried him up to the first landing. At the edge of the pounding in his ears, he heard Colleen's weepy account: "Went to wake 'im as I always do . . . bed empty . . . toy sword and shield gone . . . this note on his little pillow . . . Oh, Master Daniel!"

Danny. Oh, God, Danny.

He yanked the paper from her. The sickness surged and swamped his brain. Everything faded from his view but the scratchings he peered down at, the familiar, awkward letters . . . each pencil stroke bearing testament to countless hours of labor, just him, his son, and the A-B-C's in the study together.

Deer Mate . . .

He swallowed leaden despair, noting the reference to himself as the only perfectly spelled word on the page.

I hav goon too halp yoo deestry— a six-year-old's rendition of the Lancer filled the ensuing space: red eyes, sinister frown, bloodied knife.

Yoo wil bee prod ov mee I wil gett himm.

I luv yoo. Yoor sun, Danny.

His sun. His son.

He stood there, frozen in terror, knowing he'd faint, amazed he didn't. Taylor turned, searching for—what? He didn't know. Words wouldn't come. Thought and reason existed somewhere beyond fury and frustration. Distant. Impossible. Danny. What did he do now? Where did he go? Danny. *Danny.* God.

Then she entered his vision. He reached out to where she materialized, just below him but rising steadily up each stair, an angel coming to catch him with her shining hair, earnest eyes, and gentle, calm movement. Surely a miracle, Taye concluded dimly. She couldn't be real.

Her fingers alighted on his whitened knuckles. She *felt* real; her cool skin, her welcome touch. Fresh morning scents emanated from her hair, her skin, mingled with the musky traces of last night . . . the traces of him. Christ. He yearned to run *to* her and run *from* her at the same time. *Don't leave. Don't leave me now, princess.*

"Let me see the paper," she requested softly.

With quaking muscles, Taylor handed her the note. He didn't look up. He couldn't meet her eyes.

The paper rustled between them, the only sound in the crypt-quiet vestibule. He yearned to shatter the silence with a throat-ripping roar. He yearned to shatter *anything.* Danny. So help him God, if any bastard out in those gutters so much as splattered Danny's shoes with their filth—

Her handclasp saved him from himself again. Through the violent haze of his senses, Taylor gripped back. He listened to her voice, steady and assured across the foyer.

"Alistair, tell the stable to bring his lordship's carriage and fastest horses around. Colleen—there now, wipe your eyes—I need you to fetch me some articles from Master Daniel's room. Cloth toys or worn clothing, things with a scent that dogs will pick up."

"Dogs! Saint Mary, ye don't think ye'll need *dogs*. Miss Marsh?"

"I'm not sure. I—I don't think so. I hope not. But if we do, we'll have to be ready."

With a sweep of unexpected speed, she turned. She caught Taylor—and the stare he finally lowered to her—completely off guard.

In that instant, he felt many things, but none of them equaled the ache to wrap himself around this woman, her dignity, her strength, and never let go. The admission staggered him. Humbled him.

Terrified him.

Still, he let her lead him down the stairs and to the door, never taking his eyes from her straight and strong shoulders. Without a doubt, this inferno of dread would consume him whole without this angel to pull him through it.

The familiar onyx blue of the town carriage came into view. As he slammed the front door and stumbled across the drive, Taylor only let himself care about one thing: not losing sight of her.

She didn't protest the intimate position he took on the dark sapphire cushions next to her, instead of the seat the footman had warmed for him opposite. She didn't flinch when he pulled her hand to his lap and retwined their fingers, despite how he most likely crushed her hand with the force of his terror.

Yet she didn't look at him, either. She only spoke when the coach spurted down the drive. Leaning forward then, she clearly commanded:

"Saint Jerome's Orphanage, Brick Lane. And hurry!"

* * *

Everything happened in a blur after the silent torture of the drive. In contrast to the damp morning quiet of Brick Lane, they stepped into a whirlwind of sound and energy. Children's shouts sallied up and down Saint Jerome's clean wood staircase, punctuating squeaks and creaks that echoed of memories and laughter. The chilly air warmed as Taylor followed Gwen toward the redolence of spicy porridge and fresh bread and heated marmalade.

"Johnny!" He recognized Hannah Aberdeen's robust bellow from the midst of the homey smells. "Johnny Goodfellow, stop teasin' the tots 'n' get yerself down here. The ashes haven't been emptied 'n' last night's stew pot looks like ye narry touched—"

The woman's voice choked to a stop at the same moment the youthful chatter died away. A half dozen pairs of eyes swung their direction. A half dozen marmalade-stained mouths popped open in curiosity. Only the contented bubbling of porridge on the big black stove gurgled through the silence.

Then the day's blur thickened.

"Gwennie! Yer lordship! Gracious, milord, ye didn't have to trouble yerself with bringin' her back. Reg 'n' me, we were just waitin' on a decent hour to come round—"

Hannah accomplished the impossible, interrupting herself twice in the same minute. "What's wrong?" she suddenly demanded. "Gwennie, ye're as pale as a sheet. Yer lordship? What the heavens?"

Gwen took the woman's hand with her fingers so pale, Taye noticed, they bordered on translucent. "Hannah, we need your help. You and Reggie, Nigel and Jerry, and anyone else we can gather."

"Wh-why? Gwennie, what's happened?"

"Dan—Master Daniel—left us this note this morning."

"Now what's this? Oh, sweet blessed Mary!"

"We've prayed to her already."

"He could be anywhere in the city!"

"We don't think so. He was with us yesterday when Bryan

brought news of the Lancer's latest attack. We discussed the location of the body in front of him. The East End was mentioned several times."

"Then what in perdition're we waitin' upon? Reggie! *Reggie!* Come quick! Give a shout across the alley to Nigel; tell him to put a fire on it, too! Gwennie needs us. She needs us now!"

If Saint Jerome's teemed with activity before, the dwelling exploded from the spark of Hannah's call. More precisely, Taye determined, at the proclamation of Gwendolen's name.

Another room's worth of children pounded down the stairs and joined the huddle already at her skirts. As Gwen finished embracing them all—even the blushing boys who didn't solicit her greeting—more humanity joined the throng. Men and women of all shapes and sizes, ages and dialects swooped over her like the Queen's guard closing ranks over the crown jewels.

It didn't take long for Taylor to discover why. Though she still never looked at him, she began to explain this nightmare in a tone that clearly made all of them feel as if the challenge they faced was complex, but certainly beatable. Taylor absorbed her confidence, too. For a moment, he closed his eyes, willing her strength to seep into his skin.

Subsequently, the crisp male voice at his side came as a surprise. "Yer lordship . . . er, beggin' yer pardon a moment . . ."

Taylor opened his sights to a weathered face with a drooping grey mustache but a sharp silver gaze that met him eye-to-eye.

"Nigel Brownsmith," the man supplied over a firm handsclasp. "I'm the bobby in these parts, so they say. Found Gwennie the night that guttersnake Lloyd Waterston drove her out into the rain. I vow we'll bring yer little one back just as snug, and in time fer supper, too."

It didn't startle Taylor to realize he believed the man. He struggled to utter his thanks, to Nigel Brownsmith and all the life-toughened faces around them, but a heavy breath ravaged his words. He returned Brownsmith's nod and hoped his crushing hand grip communicated his sentiment, instead.

The man lowered silvered brows and emitted a gruff cough. "We'll be needin' a description of yer lad," Brownsmith told him. "The more detailed, the better. And o' course, anythin' that would make him stand out—any special qualities or features."

"Of course." *Special features? My boy has* special *glowing from every last pore, damn you. Damn you. Thank you. Just find him. Please help me find him.*

Nigel repeated the description Taye gave to him around the crowd, whose numbers now spilled down a narrow hall and into a room Taye recognized as the parlor where his life had first been touched by Gwendolen. His life now so damn dependent on her.

With that comprehension, the white vertigo came again. Taylor dug fingers into the splintery tabletop for balance, feeling stupid and alone—and too bloody vulnerable in the drenching fear-fog.

Only gritted effort brought his head up again. He raked a gaze over the crush of braided and bowlered heads, seeking a barely tamed halo of light copper framing an angel's countenance. Gwen's face, etched with the calm and courage he could find nowhere in his own ravaged hollow of a body.

He spotted her as the group started breaking into search parties. Reggie Aberdeen and two other men clustered with her at the far end of the hall, at the doorframe of the parlor. Taylor shoved from the table and wound through the crowd to her.

"Yer lordship." Reggie echoed the other men's salutations at his arrival, yet added a nod of friendly familiarity. The man swung his burly head toward the parlor, noting the groups assembling there, too. "Everyone's makin' to move out now. Don't ye sweat about it; we got everythin' from Old Street to the Tower Bridge covered. And what with Gwennie with us down by the river and you joinin' the groups through the streets up here, we'll find that boy—"

"No." Taye heard the vehemence in his voice. He didn't

care. He barely acknowledged the startled glances he collected, either.

"No," he repeated past the clenched jaw he usually reserved for the toughest bastards in business meetings. "Miss Marsh and I will stay together. It will be—" *It'll be the only way I can keep on my feet, damn it.* "It will be more remunerative."

The word hit the nerve he intended on the two immigrant men and the simply-educated Reggie. Their eyes widened in befuddlement before they acceded to male pride and nodded vigorous agreement to his "important" point.

Gwendolen didn't concede so easily. Taye watched her lips disappear against each other in an effort to control the glare she scorched up at him. She turned her gaze toward the parlor, out that same lace-curtained window she'd hidden at weeks ago.

"Your 'logic' is lunacy," she retorted lowly. "You and I are the only ones here who can instantly recognize Danny. We'll find him faster if we separate."

"We don't separate." He pressed his hand to the wall above her shoulder in subtle command . . . in dire entreaty. Swallowing a granite lump down his throat, he dipped his head over her ear and added one more word in a clenched murmur. *"Please."*

She still didn't look at him. But she nodded—a single, stiff motion before stepping away from him with the haste of a woman who'd just struck a deal with the devil.

Taylor didn't care. They'd find his son now, he was certain—that was, if the stubborn little knight-errant didn't find them first. Even in the labyrinth of Stafford House, Danny could find Gwen before his father had covered three rooms. The bugger was drawn to her like—well, Lancelot to Guinevere.

Then again, Gwendolen Marsh seemed to have that effect on anything good and beautiful in this world.

Even countless hours later, in the waning light of the day, Taylor looked across the carriage and drew eager hope from her gentle features. Just as quickly, he condemned himself the selfishness. Dark rings of fatigue and despair tramped across her face. Her eyes drooped, heavy and unfocused in the diluted sunlight of the late London afternoon. Her lips showed chapped patches from pressing together into too many silent prayers. She'd bitten her right thumbnail to the skin between the fervent pleas. In her other hand, she clutched Danny's favorite stuffed animal: a grey felt whale named Ahab that smelled nothing like the sea hero it was named after, but everything like dust, stolen sweets, and bubble soap—the bouquet of a happy six-year-old boy.

The scent she'd give to the police dogs when they returned to the orphanage in four blocks.

The thought had briefly taunted Taylor's mind back at the Spitalfields. But now, watching Gwen's fingers corkscrew into Ahab's faded bottom fin, simple taunt became stark reality. He swallowed back bile from his empty stomach. He closed his eyes, but the white dizziness returned, a gloating ice storm of fear.

Dear God, his soul called out, *don't you dare take my boy away, too. Damn you, don't you dare.*

As he opened his eyes again upon the weary, beautiful woman slumped on the seat opposite, he added one more silent invocation: *And please make her look at me just one more time. Just once.*

At that moment, Gwen's lashes raised.

But she barely flicked a glance at him. Her attention turned and centered on some sight out on the sidewalk. A tart vendor's lively jingle grew louder. Taye leaned back and shut his eyes again, stifling the angry realization that a few stale pastries elicited the response he sweated prayers for.

Her voice sliced into his broodings like the pierce of a candle into the black of midnight.

"Stop the carriage."

He looked in time to see her thrust her head out the window—in time to see her gaze ignite with brilliant emerald hope. Her hair swirled in the wind; the smile at her lips erupted into a disbelieving laugh.

"Stop the carriage!" she exclaimed louder. "Now!"

But she pushed open the door and jumped to the ground before the wheels could comply with a full stop. Biting back his confused curse, Taylor bounded out of the coach after her.

He'd just hit the road when a broken laugh escaped his own lips. He passed Gwen in a handful of strides as he took in the ridiculous, miraculous sight before them.

"Hullo, mate!" Danny called from a perch atop the tart peddler's pushcart. His son's sticky smile matched the wagon's cranberry-colored paint; Danny's dirtied legs swung happily in time to the jostling tin bells. The toy sword still bobbed in the air from one grubby hand, but the shield had been entrusted to a rusty nail along the side of the vehicle—no doubt to allow freedom for sampling treats.

"Danny." For the hundredth time today, Gwen put volume to the words lodged behind the boulder in Taye's throat. He felt her rush past him, but didn't—couldn't—rip his gaze from his boy. *His boy,* whole and healthy and alive.

"Danny, you've given us a fright," she chastised in a maternal lilt. With gentle but thorough proficiency, she inspected small arms and legs, checking for damage through the layer of dust Danny looked right at home in. "We've been searching all day for you," she added in more stern rebuke.

Danny's frown combined surprise and indignation. "I left a note. I even drew a picture. I wanted Papa to be proud of me."

"And I am." Taylor congratulated himself on managing at least that. He moved closer, each step a brutal battle against the craving to seize the little hellraiser to him. "But," he qualified, "I was proud of you before, Daniel Taylor Randolph."

As he invoked the familiar words of correction, he assumed the adjoining stance of warning. Yes, at last, *here* was firm and familiar ground. Taylor braced both feet to the sidewalk while locking hands at the back hem of his coat.

Danny's mouth stopped in midchew of a cheese pastry, also in recognition of the posture. "Yes, sir," he mumbled.

"You've frightened a great deal of people today." More control pumped back into his blood. "You will, of course, spend your free time tomorrow penning them thank-you notes. That should put those writing skills to good use."

The little shoulders slumped. "Yes, sir."

"Now thank your friend for his kindness."

He hid the smile of pleasure at his son's amazingly polished compliance. Danny hopped down from the cart as smoothly as he dismounted from his pony at Wharnclyffe. Then he turned to the tart vendor with the same aplomb he afforded his good-nights to visiting dignitaries and duchesses. His black curls dipped in a deferential nod and he extended a firm grip toward the man's paw of a hand.

"I thank you for a most happy day, George," his son said as if reading from his etiquette tutor's textbook. "I'll never forget any of it. I—"

Danny's voice wavered and broke. He jerked free of the handclasp and launched himself into George's sugar-caked apron front. "Oh, George, I shall never forget *you!*"

The man humphed an awkward chuckle, jostling his generous belly. "Aw, c'mon now," he scolded. "Ye know the rules o' the route, Danny Boy. No hackin' the lassies, and no frownin'. Now get along to yer da and come visitin' again soon."

"I will. I promise. I mean it, Georgie. I'll never forget you!"

"I don't think any of us will." Taylor smiled, but his tone shouted dead solemnity.

He brushed his son off toward the carriage. Yet when he had the privacy he wanted with the tart vendor, he grimaced with indecision. He couldn't decide whether to offer George every farthing of his assets or just follow the man home as his servant for life. So he stood there, numb and exhausted and euphoric and exhilarated, wondering if he'd be capable of coherent speech again.

"George." Again Gwendolen appeared to his rescue, an angel seemingly called by the simple force of his need. Stepping forward, she prompted, "Mister . . . ?"

"O'Toole, m'lady," the vendor supplied. "George O'Toole, at your service. And o' course, yer lordship, as well." He bobbed a deep nod at Taylor, several sweeping bows at her.

By his third dip, Gwen pulled him to a stop. Tension outlined her posture again, clearly drawn there by the man's assumption of her as Lady Stafford.

"Please," she bit out. "You're too kind. His lordship is grateful for all that you've done, but I really cannot—"

"Of course ye can." O'Toole turned her hand over, bestowed a reverent kiss on her knuckles. "Your modesty makes ye even more lovely, m'lady, but accept my praise for your motherin'. He's a splendid lad. A splendid lad. Yer lucky, the two o' ye; don't forget it."

"Yes, well." She hastily withdrew her fingers. "I'm certain Lord Stafford wishes to repay you for your kindness—"

"Oh, no. No. I told ye, I thank *ye* fer borrowin' him today." The man's generous bottom lip quivered; he dropped his gaze to the sidewalk. "The . . . er, the missus and I haven't been blessed with wee ones. We've tried, but the doctors said the soot in the city air has weakened Jennie too much. Her lungs and her heart barely sustain *her,* let alone a new life inside her."

As suddenly as the tide of emotion broke over him, O'Toole's spine stiffened and he covered the space to Taylor in two lumbering strides.

"Treasure them, m'lord," the vendor murmured. He lifted a sad, pleading stare. "Ye've a fine lad, and a fine lady. Ye've been truly blessed."

Tell him, a voice ordered inside. *Tell him the truth, damn you, and show Gwen you've got at least a crumb of decency in you.*

But he didn't. Couldn't. He looked away from George O'Toole, staring down the emptying East End street, only to liken his soul to the sunlight being crushed at the bottom of the smoky grey sky.

They arrived back at Saint Jerome's to a choir of cheers. The chant grew to a chorus as the good news jumped alleys and window ledges down the street. The pounds of sugar Danny had consumed since dawn were hours from full depletion; he raced ahead to the kitchen, disappearing amidst children anxious to hear of his adventures.

Reggie, Nigel, and the waterfront search groups arrived shortly after. In a flurry of concern, Reggie rushed to his wife, who distributed more ladlefuls of her happy tears than the cider bubbling on the stove. The rest of the day's searchers either crowded into the parlor or bid farewells, returning to their own hearths and families.

A tenuous quiet befell the front hall.

Gwen's cloak rustled distinctly as she let her stance sag for the first time today. Standing behind her, Taylor yearned to fulfill the vision of lifting his hand to her nape, fingering away the damp curls lodged there, and rub away her tension. His traitorous arm actually raised twice. Both times, he checked himself with a noisy betrayal from his own wool garments.

After his second awkward commotion, her frame stiffened again. "Was there something else, my lord?" She questioned the stairwell more than him.

Taylor drew in a heavy breath. "As a matter of fact . . . yes."

"Well, I don't want to hear it."

She whirled and shoved through a side door, into the orphanage's office. With as much unthinking reflex, he went after her.

He slowed his steps when he saw the room allowed her no escape route but the door he blocked. For a moment, he simply looked at her. Back still turned on him, she stopped before a scuffed oak desk, arms outstretched to her sides, fingers pressing the tops of two child-size chairs from which he easily imagined some misbehaved urchin apologizing to her.

Only this time, the wretch should have *his* ugly face.

No, Taye contradicted himself, not even that. A rap of the ruler and an apology note wouldn't right the wrong this time. What the hell would? He didn't know—but his gut jerked with the need to find that answer.

And *that* terrified him.

"I wish to thank you," he tried to begin. His murmur floundered like a one-winged duck across the few feet—the million miles?—between them. "Gwen. Princess—"

"Don't." Her hands coiled around the chair tops. Raw pain drew her tone to a rasp. "Don't you dare call me that again."

He took another long breath. "Fine. But you won't hold me back from what I came here to say." He took another step forward, clicked the door shut. "I couldn't have survived without you today, Gwendolen. I . . . just wanted you to know that. I wanted you to know—I owe you my life."

She responded with a laugh.

He recognized the sound immediately. She erupted with that harsh half-sob he remembered so well from the first day they'd met. The sound of utter hopelessness which had twisted his consciousness then—and ripped him asunder now.

Yet the agony died away as a mere skirmish preceding the tearful glare she spun on him now. *"You* owe me nothing," she spat. "I didn't do this for you. If *you* were missing on the streets of Whitechapel, I'd say it was where your blackened, self-centered soul belonged in the first place."

Taylor said nothing. Just weathering the furious fire of her eyes became an effort tantamount to crossing the Cheviots on foot.

"What?" she finally taunted. "Nothing to say, my lord? No charming wink or chit-melting smile this time? Well, good." She looked away. "As a matter of fact, now that Danny is safe I would just as soon never see your wretched face again."

Again, silence descended. Gwen's slow but angry steps

clacked on the floor as interruption. Taylor's muscles clenched with the observation that she headed straight for him.

Two feet away—close enough for him to touch—she halted. Her hands rose to her hips. With slow reluctance, her eyes raised to his. "But there, you heartless bastard, is the dilemma you've trapped me in."

Taylor scowled through the following pause of confusion. His mind scrambled through every word of their exchange. Certainly he'd missed some important detail between her first stinging outburst and the steamed sigh she released now.

"Dilemma?" he finally asked.

Her response took him aback. No exasperated glare or stinging retort. Instead, her chin raised and she tightened her bottom lip—a look not only surprising, but captivating. Right down to thc unexpected swelling of his groin.

"Despite how far a ride you told *Connie* you could take me on," she explained with withering clarity, "I am neither witless nor blind. I realize more children are certain to follow Danny now. They'll read of his exploits and try the same stunt."

Taylor deployed every battalion of self-control to temper his voice to a noncommittal, "Yes. They probably will."

"But not all of them will be so lucky."

"Probably not."

"Then the Lancer has to be stopped."

Taye held his breath for fivc seconds. Five more. She said nothing else, merely paced a few steps beyond him, then stopped.

He turned to the corner where that telling silence dwelled. "Then you're going to help me."

She whirled. The emeralds in her eyes glared at full fire again. "No—*wrong.* I'm not helping *you.* I'm doing this for all the Dannys I want to keep alive. I'm doing this for every dead woman who's been gawked at and gossiped about for the last two years." She pulled her spine straight again, squaring her arms at her sides before adding lowly but evenly: "And I'm doing this for me."

The following stillness strapped both of them in place.

Only the faded shrieks of the children filtered around them, like ghostly echoes of the laughter which had once spilled so easily from those pale lips in her face now . . . the laughter *he'd* shared only yesterday. The laughter they'd muffled from Helson until they'd escaped to the haven of the carriage, before he'd held her warm and close all the way home. Before they'd come home to Lloyd Waterston, and Taylor had almost called the man out. And yes, before his blood had gone singing through his muscle and his being, casting out better sense—erasing everything but the obsession for her body beneath his.

Drowning the laughter forever with the stupidity of unthinking lust.

Taye wanted to slam his eyes shut against the remorse, the self-damnation. Some merciless force kept his gaze glued to her face.

He suddenly recognized that force as pure wonder. The realization that now, even after the hell he'd put her through, Gwendolen Marsh rose from the flames a brilliant angel, flashing-eyed and copper-haloed; so magnificent, Taye yearned to pull her close once more just to look for the gilded wings sprouting out her shoulders.

But he didn't. He ventured as far as brushing a wayward tendril of hair from her cheek. "For what my view is worth," he told her then, "I'm proud of you."

For a moment, an amazing moment, the anger in her gaze diluted. In its absence, a green tenderness expanded that conjured memories of moonglow, silken skin, and soft moans.

But only for a moment. All too swiftly, he watched her defenses spring back into place as instinct wore off, pain and hurt taking over. "Well, your view isn't worth anything." She whisked her stare away. "If it's the truth at all."

"Then I'll just thank you."

"I don't want your thanks, either. I told you, I'm not doing this for you."

Slowly, he stepped to her again, ignoring her visible tensing at his approach. "Then what in the kingdom can I grant you, princess?"

Another marked stiffening. Then in clear, unfaltering command, "A promise."

"All right. A promise it is."

She dropped a succinct nod. Then hands on hips again, she turned to face him. The stance pulled her coat back from her wrinkled shirtwaist. The top button of the blouse had slipped free hours ago; Taye watched her pulse beating in the smooth column of her neck. His gaze dropped to the pebbles of her nipples, still hard from the cold.

And in that instant the comprehension blasted him, like the torrid furnace of a runaway train. He still wanted her. Dear sweet God, now more than ever, he wanted her.

"The promise is simple," her cold tone spattered into that blaze. "In exchange for my cooperation, you will also give me yours."

Her deliberate step echoed strangely, almost musically through the room. She leveled a stare as glassy and green as any bewitched mythical lake. Yes. She was magic. A temptress. An angel. And so close. So beautifully, torturously close.

"You will never touch me again, Taylor Stafford," came her low, threatening order. "As God as your witness, you will swear not to touch me ever again."

Fourteen

Gwen couldn't wait for an answer. She stepped forward, determined to get to the door, committed to plowing through him if she had to.

She didn't have to. Wordlessly, Taylor moved aside. She burst out into the entry hall and stumbled her way to the stairwell. Clutching the worn banister with both hands, she fought for air, but a simple breath would mean giving in to wracking sobs. Dizzy pain assaulted her, but to sit would mean complete collapse.

And she'd never let him see her pain.

She turned that commitment into a vow. She didn't care what price the feat extorted. Especially from him. She didn't care, no matter how real the tension in his shoulders looked when he followed her into the office. No matter how tight the cords in his neck strained when she banished his touch from her forever. No matter how bright the sheen in his eyes gleamed as their gazes locked one more time . . .

Oh, that molten gold light, penetrating to her core despite every inner wall she threw up against the hot assault. Making her think he knew precisely how difficult the words were for her. Making her think he understood.

"Lies," she attacked that thought in a harsh breath. "The snake never understood to begin with, you nattering fool. It was all *lies*."

She kneaded her hand up the rail, wishing she could snap the wood as mercilessly as the rip dealt to her heart. Concerns for Danny had kept the wave of anguish at bay all afternoon, but now the boy's laugh rang out from the kitchen, leaving no dam for the pain drowning her deeper with each recall of this morning's horrifying scene. Taylor praying at the altar with Constance as reigning goddess, confessing his sin of bedding the merchant's daughter. Apologizing for giving Gwen the most wonderful sensations her body had ever known . . . the farthest heights her spirit had ever soared to.

Apologizing.

Nothing . . . nothing. She had been nothing to him.

She pressed trembling hands to the sting at her eyes. She clenched her teeth in a prayer for composure. Impossible. She sunk to the stairs, body convulsing, tears breaking past the battered defenses of her soul.

March wind hit her as Saint Jerome's front door opened.

"Gwennie?" a frantic male voice also slashed in. "Holy blazes, what happened?"

A grateful laugh replaced the sobs. "Bryan." She flew up as if borne by wings. "Thank God. Bryan."

He caught her outstretched hands, encasing them in his alarmed grip. His gaze raced over her as if searching for some hidden bleeding gash. "Are you all right? Are you hurt? Gad, you're shaking all over."

"I—I'm just cold." The excuse spilled easily from her lips. Too easily, for the first lie she'd ever told her friend. But she'd force herself to tell Bryan she was dying of pneumonia before divulging the real sickness eroding at her. The unspeakable scandal. The unforgivable shame.

"I was in bloody Chiswick all day on business." He sounded more a recalcitrant husband imploring to his wife. A spontaneous smile flashed to Gwen's lips at the adorable portrait he presented.

"I returned a half hour ago," Bryan continued. "The maid said your message came this morning. When I read it was urgent—when I saw how fast you'd scribbled it—"

"I'm sorry; it was a mess." Then in a sad, quick murmur, "Everything around here has been a mess."

"No, you silly duck. *I'm* sorry. I wasn't here with you." With an unexpected sweep of motion, Bryan hauled her against his chest. "By Saint Chris, Gwennie. I worry so much about you."

Gwendolen didn't move for a moment. The affection came as a strange surprise from Bryan—and sent an unusual squirm of discomfort through her joints.

Then a reprimand echoed from her brain: *You're all right, you simpleton. This is* Bryan *holding you now . . .* Certainly she just reacted to the unknown, smoky smell of him and the abrasion of his overcoat on her chapped cheek, not to the image playing itself out in her mind of Taylor leaving the office this moment and assuming what he would from the scene. Knowing Earl Stafford's morals with the clarity she did now, Gwen didn't doubt the lowest conclusion would spring to the man's mind.

With strength she didn't know she still had, she stepped back from the embrace. "I'm fine," she insisted, folding her arms at her chest. "Just tired. Very tired."

"I can see that." Bryan scowled as he took in the fatigue rings beneath her eyes. "Gwendolen, what the devil happened today?"

Just thinking about how to answer that sunk her to the steps again. Hints of smoke and street mist refiltered into her senses as Bryan crouched to her level. Yet now the scents seemed a welcome presence, just the solace she needed.

She attempted an account of the day's events. She survived the report, but only by averting her eyes and painstakingly refining the true ordeal at the heart of her exhaustion. She left out the hours spent mere feet from Taylor . . . the moments she'd look across the kitchen at his pain-wracked profile, disheveled hair falling over his grimacing forehead, or those hours in the carriage, staring at his hands clasping his knees, nearly kneading holes into his trousers.

No, she didn't say anything about the ordeal of hurting with him . . . of hurting because of him.

And she completely omitted the torture of the last hour. Truth be known, she yearned to blot it from memory forever. The agony it had been to look across the orphanage's office, into those unblinking gold eyes—and burn with more rage than she thought possible because that molten stare still inspired her body to a torrent of need. Because she still envisioned clutching that dark head to her breasts, still longed for those hard hands on her body, not caring that the giddy sensations were lies or Taylor's fingers used her like no more than a rook in a chess game. Reducing her to nothing but the hunger *he'd* taught her. A shameless tart. Lord Stafford's whore.

Just as Aunt Maggie, Inspector Helson, and everyone in every tea parlor in London had predicted.

"Great God." Bryan's mutter mercifully caught her before the tears threatened to break again. "After all that, you found the little chap a block away?" At Gwen's nod of assent, he shook his own head, and wrapped an arm around her shoulders. "You poor waif. By now you must feel like last week's bread."

The observation hit dead accurately—and *should* have been comforting. But within Bryan's embrace, uneasiness again crept its strange hold back over Gwen.

She fidgeted beneath the hold that *should* have been soothing, wondering how long it would take to become accustomed to a human touch again. The Lancer's violation had left her flinching for months. But the Lancer hadn't lied about his intent. The Lancer hadn't disguised his attack beneath linen sheets and whispered desires.

The Lancer had been fair about destroying her.

"You're right," she replied in a swift rush. "I *am* very tired. And I'd like to go home."

Bryan threw a puzzled glance up the stairs. "You won't be staying here tonight?"

At that moment, Danny's giggle pealed down the hall. Gwen knew Taylor would indulge his son as much time with his new friends as possible. The Staffords would be here for hours longer.

And she was definitely not a Stafford.

"No," she answered. "No, I don't want to stay here."

"Oh, of course. Your things are still at Stafford House."

"No!" She grabbed the banister and catapulted herself up. "Not Stafford House. Bryan, I—I want to go *home.* To Devonshire Street. Now. Will you take me?" *Before that office door opens and I have to face that gold sword of a stare and that warrior's body again. Before I have to remember the beautiful, despicable way that bastard used me.*

Her friend also stood. For a long moment, Bryan just looked at her with that same intense, worried stare he'd pointed upon her at his entrance.

This new side of him wasn't unpleasant, Gwen admitted. She might even find herself charmed, if half her attention wasn't so focused on that office door, sure to open any second . . .

Finally, Bryan's mustache lifted. His understanding rogue's grin appeared beneath. At that, Gwen knew everything would be all right again—someday.

"Have Gregory help you into the carriage," he instructed while opening the door for her. "I'll give your good-byes."

Bryan didn't say anything more until they stopped for a passing dairy wagon at Gray's Inn. Sir Francis Bacon's catalpa tree blocked the streetlight from half his face as he turned a gently probing stare upon her.

"Suppose you tell me *everything* that happened today, duck."

Gwen tried not to openly gape back, but after a long pause, she still couldn't translate the unfaltering blue-grey of his gaze. "I don't know what you mean." Silently, she defended the words as only half a lie.

"I think you do." He sighed, glanced out the window. "It

was very odd back there, Gwennie. When I said your farewells and made your excuses, everyone was rather agreeable. Hannah even promised she'd light a candle at mass tomorrow for my scoundrel's soul, to thank God I'd convinced you to return home and rest."

Despite her apprehension, Gwen couldn't hold back a smile. "She lights a candle for you every time."

Bryan didn't return the humor. He turned back to her, staring that intent way at her yet again, as if she were a ghost, about to waft away at an eye's blink. "Everyone was splendid," he continued lowly, "until I got to Taylor. The man wouldn't look at me—especially when I said your name. I don't even think he spoke. He just drummed his fingers on the balustrade. And that man—"

"—never drums his fingers," she stated in unison with him, before caution or common sense could stop her.

Now Bryan blinked. Slowly. Carefully. Gwen dug self-conscious teeth into her lip, fidgeting beneath his regard like she hadn't fidgeted since Aunt Maggie had once plopped her ten-year-old bottom on a cushionless chair and demanded she reveal when, where, and why her little friend Nicky Spencer had run away from home.

After twelve hours in that chair, she hadn't given in to her furious guardian. How harrowing could another quarter hour with her best friend in this velvet-padded carriage be?

Bryan's knowing tone came as a deeply disturbing answer to that. "I see," he said softly. "So . . . I wasn't imagining things the other day in the coroner's hall. You and Taye have gotten to know each other quite well in the last weeks, haven't you?"

She made a noisy show of smoothing her skirt. "Not that well."

But once she made the assertion, her hands relaxed against the ink-blue fabric. Not a syllable of the statement had been a lie. Taylor Stafford was more a stranger to her this morning in that eerie shrine of a sitting room than the man she'd first sparred with in Saint Jerome's parlor.

"Gwennie." For the second time tonight, Bryan's touch came without preamble. His fingers curled around her wrist, cool and direct. "Gwennie, what did he do to you?"

"Nothing." Again too late, she realized how blatantly her swift blurt implied the opposite. She bit her lip with the intent to draw repentant blood this time.

"So help me God if he's hurt you, friend or no, I'll call him out *tonight.*"

An awkward laugh released her throbbing lip. "For heaven's sake, Bryan. What makes you think such a thing?"

"Nothing in particular." Only a fool could have missed his triple underlines of irony. "Only that neither of my closest friends has looked me directly in the eye tonight. Only that both of them look as if they're mourning me, although I sure as hell was fleeced out of the unique experience of dying. Only that every time I say Taye's name that nerve beneath your scar does the fanciest jig I've ever seen."

"All right, all right! Enough; I'll confess to the sordid details." Gwen gave in with another weak laugh, waving her pocket kerchief.

But again, her friend didn't jest back. Bryan leaned forward again, to that same point where the shadows cloaked his face. The catalpa hid everything except the nearly opaque blue of his eyes. Finally, lowly, "You agreed to help him find that bastard, didn't you?"

Gwen hesitated. Then nodded. "I had to."

"Said who? You, or him?"

"Oh, *Bryan.* What the heavens do you think?"

"If he forced you in any way so help me God I'll—"

"—call him out; I know." She shook her head in bewilderment. "Lord. If I didn't know better, I'd think you were looking for any reason to kill somebody tonight."

She chuckled again.

Bryan didn't.

The carriage rolled back into motion. They rumbled up Southampton Row, then turned left, past the university, in silence.

"It's all my fault, you know," he finally muttered. Gwen thought she heard him hiss an oath, as well. "I pushed Taylor on you in the first place. Now it all seems a dangerous, crazy-headed, *bad* idea. I should have listened to you, duck; you were probably right. You're not ready for this."

Gwen spun at him so fast, her hasty braid of this morning finally slipped and fell down her back. "Stop it," she ordered. "Stop it right now. First of all, you don't have to speak for me anymore. You won't assume I'm not 'ready' for anything. I've let too many people do that for too long. I've let everyone hide me for the last two years, Bryan—and more women have died as a result."

The carriage slowed for more cross traffic, as if fate knew the pause of quiet that should have followed.

Gwen pressed back to the cushions. She redirected her gaze out the window. Clouds blew in off the Thames, scudding across the London buildingscape—the same way bursts of feeling bumped then meshed inside her. It was strange, how different shame and heartache could be when turned into storm fronts of anger and bitterness. And determination. Cold, unhesitant determination.

"Bryan, it's not whether I *am* ready now. I *must* be ready. We have to catch this monster. And we will."

"Then I believe you." He tilted a quiet but encouraging smile. "But not, I repeat, *not* at the expense of your sanity or your life."

Gwen smiled in return. "That's what you're here for."

This time, Bryan didn't rise to the quip. But his eyes answered her, very distinctly, turning a blue she'd never seen in his gaze before. A color she could only liken to the core of an intense flame.

Gregory's "whoa" broke the odd moment. Reluctantly, Gwen turned her sights to the row of townhomes looking down upon the carriage in stylish judgment. The most imperious residence on the block lay across the walkway from them, identified by an ornate address shingle of "Marsh" illuminated by a privately installed lamp. The front curtains had been drawn for the evening, but the rainbow glow from a crystal Tiffany lamp radiated onto the walk, as if promising passing leprechauns a haven for their pots o' gold.

Oh, how looks could be deceiving.

But the Marsh Mausoleum, as Hannah would snort it, was home—the only place Gwen could call such tonight.

Then why couldn't she envision anything but satin-covered gazebos and moonlight-filled bedrooms when *home* whispered through her mind?

"You're shaking again."

She jerked her head as if caught in the middle of a daydream. She'd heard Bryan's chastising tone, but murmured a guilty, "What?" in response.

He smiled indulgently. "You're shivering like we've parked in Antarctica."

"I am?"

The smirk compressed into a concerned scowl. "Gwennie." His fingers curled around her arm, pressing with concern. "Are you certain about doing this?"

"This is my home." She forced the last word out. "Of course I'm certain."

"Not just this." A trace of exasperation sprinkled his reply. "About everything. Are you positive about Taylor's plan . . . about Taylor?"

He knew. Gwen struggled to dispel the fear as swiftly as it seized through her mind. Her fingers worked the side seams of her cloak in time to the echo of Bryan's words in her memory: *Taylor wouldn't look at me . . . he wouldn't even talk.* She believed her best friend without thinking; Bryan had probably exchanged no more than a hello and good-bye with Taylor—but somehow, with some infuriating, secret male intuition, he'd walked out of Saint Jerome's with her humiliating secret in firm hand and mind.

"Yes," she finally answered, raising a cool, determined gaze to her friend. "Lord Stafford and his plan are as important to me as finding the Lancer. As important as taking back my life from that monster. And until that happens, nothing else matters." At that, she betrayed herself with a visible tremor and a leaden swallow. *"Nothing."*

"Well." Bryan's comeback flew with an unusually airy tone. "That's good news, then."

"It is?"

"Of course. Now I won't have to decide who my seconds would be if Taye fancied making *you* part of his conquest."

Grateful his breeziness called for an answering laugh, Gwen nevertheless concentrated on hiding her relief behind the mirth. So a divine lightning shaft hadn't pierced Bryan with the knowledge of her and Taylor's intimacies. But that lingering blue fire she witnessed in his eyes dictated just how serious his lethal threat was if he ever found out.

As if she needed *that* factor added to the wobbling scales of composure inside her. This new protective streak of Bryan's had only helped tip the balance dangerously toward collapse.

It all began to take a weighted toll on her. She was suddenly anxious to see her bed and stay there for a week.

Gwen drew in as measured a breath as she could before smiling and saying to Bryan, "Good night. Thank you for coming for me."

He flashed his ready jester's grin. " 'If all the while I think of thee, dear friend, all losses are restored and sorrows end.' "

Now her laugh came effortlessly. "Do you ever read anything printed beyond 1650?"

His mustache wiggled. "Would you prefer I spout Brontë and Byron?"

Her convulsing throat cut the laugh short. "No."

She used the pretense of gathering her skirt to cloak her shaking hands. Disembarking from the carriage shielded her pained grimace. But nothing concealed the memories from her mind. The echoes of a sure male tone sliding over rhyming pentameter . . . the remembrance of dark, defined features awash in the south sitting room's morning light. The memories of Taylor stealing her breath, her thoughts—her trust.

"No," she repeated when Bryan followed her out onto the walk. On a strange but urgent impulse, she reached her gloved hand up to affectionately tap his cheek. "You stay just the way you are, Bryan Corstairs. I need one thing in the world I can depend on."

For a moment only his forehead moved, bringing dark-blond brows over confused eyes. Yet when he opened his mouth to question her, she slid meaningful fingers over his mustache.

Then she turned and rushed up the three marble steps.

Her heart raced harder as she grasped the polished gold door latch. She paused for a last moment of respite, pressing her forehead on the carved mahogany portal as she directed two requests heavenward: one for the upcoming trial of facing Aunt Maggie's judgment . . . another for the looming ordeal of facing Taylor in her moonlit dreams.

Even after the bitterness of their last departure, his magnificence filled her eyes with tears. Even in the realm of dreams, he flooded her body with heat.

Without asking, Gwen knew what to do. She stood motionless, waiting for him, watching him stride through the night mists to her. A breeze spiced of his cologne billowed his black mane around his face, eased his lawn shirt off one muscled shoulder. His thigh-high riding boots made no sound. She wondered if he merely floated on the clouds, closer, closer . . .

Her senses came alive, sparkling and wanting, as the dark-gold fire in his eyes grew visible. His gaze conveyed his love, screamed his need, promised his protection, forever.

She stepped into his arms. He pulled her tighter, blanketing

We have 4 FREE BOOKS for you as your introduction to KENSINGTON CHOICE!

To get your FREE BOOKS, worth up to $23.96, mail the card below.

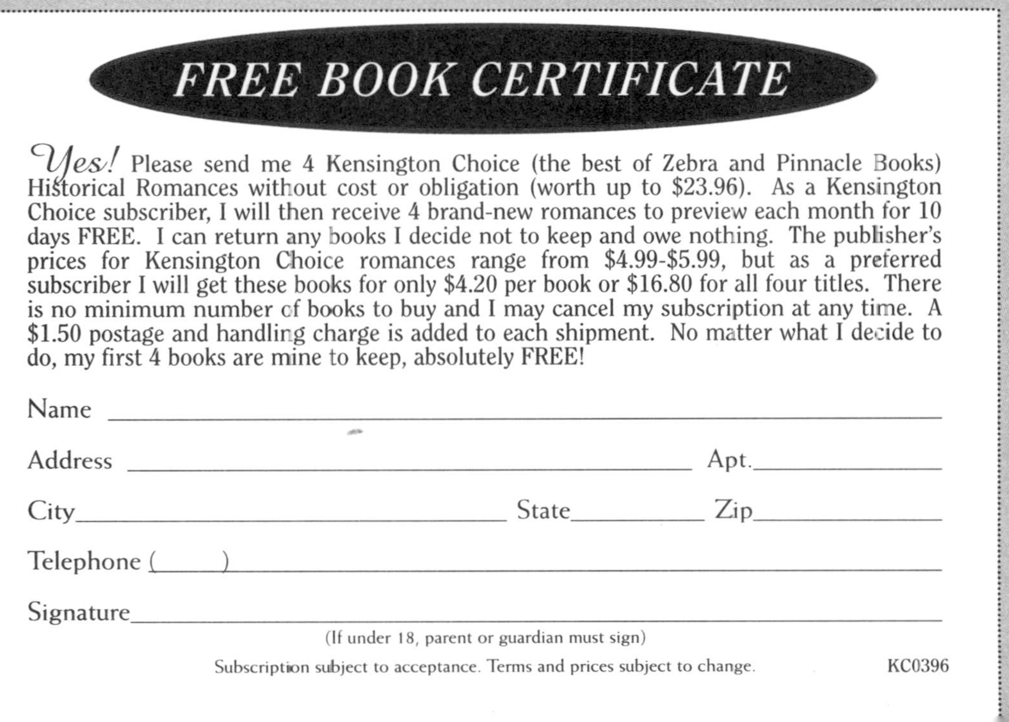

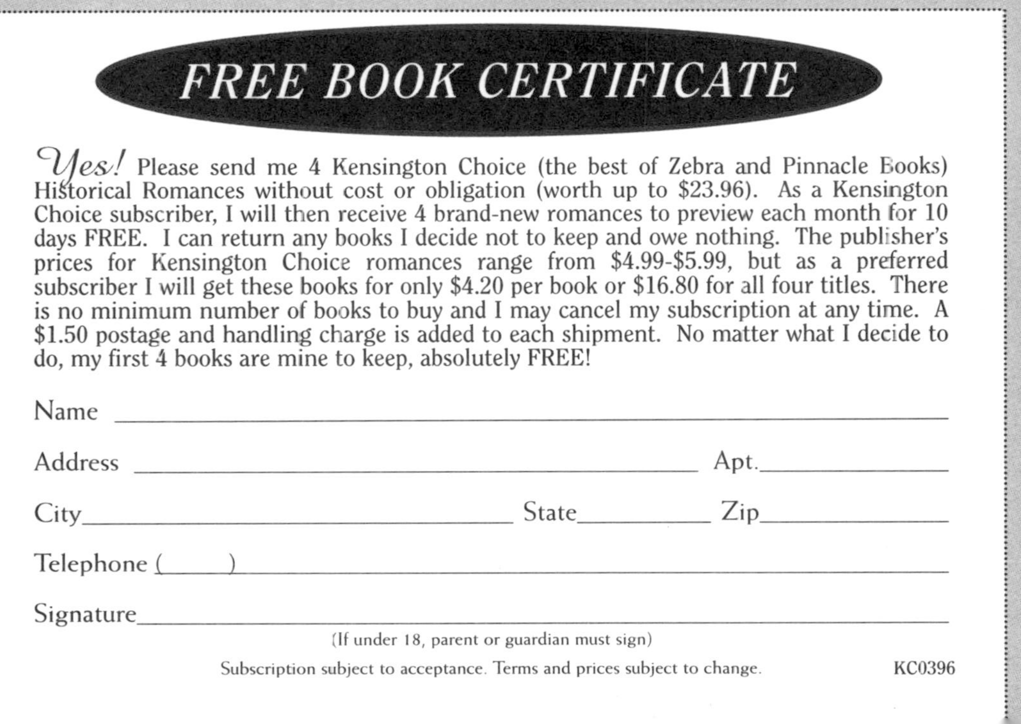

FREE BOOK CERTIFICATE

Yes! Please send me 4 Kensington Choice (the best of Zebra and Pinnacle Books) Historical Romances without cost or obligation (worth up to $23.96). As a Kensington Choice subscriber, I will then receive 4 brand-new romances to preview each month for 10 days FREE. I can return any books I decide not to keep and owe nothing. The publisher's prices for Kensington Choice romances range from $4.99-$5.99, but as a preferred subscriber I will get these books for only $4.20 per book or $16.80 for all four titles. There is no minimum number of books to buy and I may cancel my subscription at any time. A $1.50 postage and handling charge is added to each shipment. No matter what I decide to do, my first 4 books are mine to keep, absolutely FREE!

Name ____________________

Address ____________________ Apt. ______

City ____________ State ______ Zip ______

Telephone (   ) ____________________

Signature ____________________

(If under 18, parent or guardian must sign)

Subscription subject to acceptance. Terms and prices subject to change.

KC0396

We have 4 FREE BOOKS for you as your introduction to KENSINGTON CHOICE!

To get your FREE BOOKS, worth up to $23.96, mail the card below.

her with his strength. *Nothing will ever hurt you again,* he whispered. *You're home. You're mine.*

Taylor, she sobbed back. *I love you.*

Give me your life, he pleaded against her lips.

Give me your life, she sighed in return.

Oh, Connie came his harsh rasp. Connie, my love, my heart.

Cold. Suddenly, she stood cold and alone. An arctic gust slammed her unclothed body at the same time horror stormed her heart. She whirled, shivering, clutching at the grey nothingness surrounding her, wanting him, hating him. *No! No, don't go; she's not there. She's dead. She's* dead! *But I'm here. I'm alive. I love you. I love you . . .*

Only a moan answered. His moan, thickened to the pitch she knew as his passion song, followed by the hot breaths she could feel on her skin again from the sheer desperation of her imagination.

She spun about once more.

Through the grey mist, they materialized. The siren was faceless, nearly formless, drifting in and out of sight when the fog desired it—as if the woman *were* the fog. But Taylor—

With a tortured sob, she gazed at every hard, beautiful inch of him. The sculpted mounds of his arms as he braced his body for entry. The sweat beading down the valley of his back as he arched, ready for release. The urgent strain of his buttocks as he made love to his ghost, moaning again. The harsh ecstasy on his features when he found his completion inside her.

Gwen wrapped her arms around her nakedness and looked away, her hot tears the only warmth she felt now.

She retreated into comforting darkness. Remembrance came with no pain now; the void had been good to her before. She could forget in this enveloping dark. Cease to think. Cease to hurt. A few more steps and she'd be safe.

Blinding white light suddenly attacked her conscious mind. Grey fog and masculine cologne became morning glare and lemon tea. The calls of street hawkers drowned Taylor's passion cry. A moment later, the bustle of carriage traffic joined in—only faded by the more distinct rustle in the room with her.

Aunt Maggie's petticoats.

"Well, young lady." The huff marched at the same cadence as the military footsteps around the bed. "Are you going to play Taylor Stafford's princess and loll the day away, or actually attempt to do something productive before noon?"

Gwen pried her eyes open into the merciful dimness of her pillow. Her swollen cheeks and stiff lashes still bore the salty evidence of her nightmare—for the third morning in a row. She'd said good night to Bryan exactly as many evenings ago.

Blast you, Taylor Stafford. I won't let you do this to me.

She meant it. With the strength gleaned from that anger, she rolled over and forced herself to sit up, directing a steady gaze across the room. "Good morning, Aunt," she said clearly. "Thank you for waking me personally."

"Yes, well." The fleshy jowls jiggled as the lace-capped head pivoted. "You look appalling," the woman decreed.

Strange. The disparagement didn't yank the bottom out from Gwen's confidence as it normally would. Instead, only one tranquil reply glided to mind. "You're probably right."

Her aunt's grey-green eyes narrowed as if scrutinizing a trick mirror. Still, the woman's tone softened with her next ruling. "You're much too pale."

"Yes. I know."

"You need to get out. You're not in mourning, for heaven's sake."

"I know." This time, the response took more effort. More than a few times in the last days, she'd longed to go find some dead body just to have an excuse to don black, shut herself off from the world and weep without control.

"Well," Aunt Maggie said again. Her lips pursed; she turned a disgruntled glare out the window. An unorthodox flush of humor tempted Gwen's own mouth. She'd clearly befuddled her poor aunt by not bounding out of bed and beginning her usual single-minded quest to escape the house.

"I think a ride in the park would be out of the question," the large woman continued, albeit cautiously. "Though most in Town agree that philanderer Waterston was responsible for your betrothal fiasco, you did nothing to help yourself by taking up residence at Stafford House." A begrieved snort followed the heavenward roll of her eyes. "Thank the fates his lordship has droves of grateful business partners, and the Dowager Countess came out to speak for you herself. Otherwise I don't know what kind of damage—"

"The dowager countess?" Gwen bolted upright in bed then. "Granna? Granna went into society to speak for me?"

Her aunt provided no answer but a startled jump of thin grey eyebrows. "Good Lord. You're on a familiar basis with Racine Stafford. Does that demand a ride in the park or not . . ."

The droning faded beneath the trumpetings of emotion in Gwen's mind and soul. She remembered Granna's steady but slow steps about Stafford House; she knew it was difficult for the elderly woman to fight age and stiffness just to rise in the morning. Yet the dowager countess had ventured to stuffy tea parlors and interminable dinner parties to defend the honor nobody believed Gwen had anymore.

The gratitude and love stemming from that comprehension summoned the next natural images from memory: her mental portraits of Danny. Danny, giggling with her as they chased butterflies in the Stafford House garden. Danny hugging his face against her scarred skin, seeing the beauty nobody saw anymore.

For these two, Gwen flung aside the covers and stepped out onto the chilly wood floor. For these two, she paced into her closet and searched out an appropriate walking gown for the day. For these two, she would be strong—because they believed she could be.

"Gwendolen?" Aunt Maggie's demand came muffled by the tunnel of clothes she'd immersed herself in. "Gwendolen?"

The sound came sharper. The fleshy face scowled at the open end of the closet. "Are you ignoring me again?"

"Hmmm? No, Aunt. I'm not, truly. I just have a number of things to do today. I'm anxious to get started."

"A number of things?" Jowls shook with the outraged sniff. "What kind of things?"

The bedroom door opened. A lamb-eyed maid bobbed an apologetic curtsy. "Pardon me, Miss Marsh. I don't mean to interrupt your dressing—um, but—this message just arrived from Lord Stafford's footman. He—um—said it was important . . ."

"Yes." Gwen rushed past Aunt Maggie to accept the opulent white square. "Yes, I think it is, Esther. Thank you. Thank you very much."

She turned the envelope over and broke the distinctive seal, a sole Stafford knot in the middle of scented dark-blue wax. But she didn't hear the seal break. Aunt Maggie's renewed tirade drowned the sound.

"Gwendolen Victoria! You didn't answer my question. And now this—what is *this?*"

Then, not even Aunt's ravings could rival the pounding of her heart. The cacophony began at Gwen's first sight of the familiar, bold pen strokes. Taylor's writing.

She reread the cordial but succinct missive four times. She pored over each powerfully symmetrical word, surrendering to the fortitude she hated he could still give her, but accepting the warm courage with the shameless gratitude of a street beggar.

Two days later, adhering to the message she'd memorized backward by now, she handed her card out to a footman in the crisp Stafford blue-and-gold livery. Half a minute later, the footman returned from the front steps to help her down from the formal coach his lord had dispatched for her.

Gwen climbed the old stone steps even as she longed to dive back into the coach and speed home. She paused at the looming front door, listening to the muffled dongs of the hall clock. The chimes repeated eleven times to declare the morning hour.

The door swung in before she lifted her hand to ring. She prepared a smile of greeting for Alistair, suddenly realizing how much she'd missed the droop-eyed servant.

Alistair was nowhere to be seen.

Taylor dominated the portal before her.

"Good day, Miss Marsh," he said softly, politely. He'd dressed in a similarly polished manner, from buttoned collar and brushed satin waistcoat to pinstriped trousers atop black patent ankle boots. Tall. Elegant. Breathtaking. Perfect.

As he regarded her, she saw him struggle to reflect his smooth tone with his features. But the intensity of his eyes was his betraying Judas kiss. The look sluiced liquid warmth down the traitorous recesses of her own composure.

"Good day, my lord," she managed to stammer back.

Seriously, respectfully, he offered his hand. Slowly, hesitantly, she gave him her fingers.

Their eyes met again. *Look away, look away,* her aching heart ordered.

She couldn't have ripped her gaze down if a steam train barreled through the house.

"What do you say?" Taylor asked her then, concern evident in the casual tone he tried to affect. His lips battled down a tender, awkward smile. "Are you ready to be hypnotized today?"

Fifteen

Taylor wondered what insanity drove him to ask the question. Certainly she knew she was the one, standing there staring at him with her parted lips and wide emerald eyes, hiding the hypnotic powers.

He'd spent all week telling himself he didn't miss her. By this morning's scones and ham, he'd finally thought he believed the litany.

He had, of course, made a mistake. A big mistake. An error almost as glaring as his stupidity of last week—that fateful morning, and the sight he'd never forget . . . Gwen poised at the door to the gallery, face still twisted from her aching outcry, lips as white as her knuckles around the doorframe. He also recalled, all too well, the strange clutching in his own muscles, as if the lie he'd just gutted her with continued its sweep to *his* soul.

Yes, a mistake. He'd show her he understood that, no matter how high the wall she'd thrown up against him doing so. And he'd show her without violating a fraction of her mandate against his touch, with the honor she regarded as no more than gutter swill at this point.

He'd show her that her life mattered.

Then he'd get out of it forever.

No matter how much the act killed him.

Kill him it just might, Taye ruefully concluded, ordering his gaze not to indulge a third drink of her in the last minute. Everything about her hit him as familiar and strange at once:

the scent of peach toilet water wafting from skin he knew as equally soft and smooth as the fruit, the Louis XIII jacket flaring over hips still branded in his memory and his dreams, the newly determined rise of her chin despite the unsure tremors of the lips above. She'd pulled back her curls beneath a simple peacock feather hat, save for the ringlets styled over too-red eyes and too-pale cheeks.

She was beautiful.

He wanted to grab her and hold her and tell her everything would be all right. He had to settle for taking her hand and looming over her like an awkward moose.

"Dr. Post is waiting in the library," he told her. "I thought you'd be comfortable there. The chairs are softer and the fire grate larger." *It's also the room farthest away from the south sitting room and its poetry books.*

He knew she reached the same conclusion by her own glance toward the south wing. As they crossed the foyer, Taye wondered what she'd do with the knowledge. He dared to hope it tugged at some last tiny thread of tenderness in her memory, for whatever slack that string could deliver to this tension between them.

Another mistake.

She stopped. Her head rose. Their gazes met for the first time since she'd caught him damn near praying to Constance's portrait.

In that instant, he knew she'd rather face reporters from every penny tabloid in Town instead of him. Her gaze roiled more dark and turbulent than any rain-swept sea he'd encountered.

"The library will be fine," she finally said. With the same tight, polite snap of her tone, she tugged her hand free of his. She pivoted toward the library, either not aware or not concerned about the faceful of peacock plume she gave him. Taylor guessed the latter.

"Damn it," he growled. He batted the feathers away while

stalking to block her path. He grabbed her hand again, prompting an incensed glare, which he ignored.

"Not like this," he told her. "For Christ's sake, Gwen, don't go in there like this."

Her stare narrowed. An incensed breath pushed from her nostrils. "Oh?" she replied with mocking honey. "And how, pray tell, would you like me to do it, my lord? Better yet, why don't you tell me how Constance would do it? The woman is perfection embodied, isn't she?"

His arms cramped from the battle not to grab her and shake her—hard. *"This* is what I'm talking about. Don't go in there like *this*. Don't do this to prove something to me."

If he wasn't mistaken, she looked ready to laugh at that. The bitter twist of her mouth salvaged her glare at the last moment.

"I am perfectly clear about my reasons for this," she said with chilling calm. "But if I wasn't, you'd be the last person I'd consult about misguided vengeance. And you'd certainly be the last man I'd seek it for."

Then she brushed past him again—making sure another assault of peacock plumage took care of the little she hadn't made clear.

They paced the rest of the way to the library in silence.

Dr. Post looked the way Taye imagined his Grandfather Julian would have aged to be, had a wild boar on a hunting expedition in North Scotland not gotten to the earl when Taye was five. The physician had a head and beard of distinguished silver waves, contradicted by dagger-straight cheekbones, a nose which couldn't be missed, and a topaz gaze which *wouldn't* be missed.

Despite the physician's imposing mien, he rose to meet Gwen with a gentle assuredness that relaxed her spine and even coaxed a hesitant smile. Post settled her into one of the burgundy wingback chairs near the fire, then took his own place in a more functional desk chair in front of her. Feeling even more the useless moose, Taylor stepped back and slumped a reluctant shoulder against a row of volumes ranging from Greek Drama to Egyptian History.

"Well," the doctor began in his crisp-cool voice. "Everything seems to be in order. How are we feeling today, Miss Marsh?"

For a renowned physician, the man asked an ass's questions. *Why don't you look at her?* Taylor silently snarled. *She's barely slept. Her hands are shaking.*

But surely Post would observe the incapable state of "the patient" in a moment. Then they'd call this whole thing off. Then, Taylor ensured, he wouldn't have to confront the terror ramming at his heart. The dread of remembering as Gwen remembered, of screaming as she screamed—of reliving the agony of those days after Helson had calmly told him his wife lay lifeless in a West End alley . . . and his life lay in tatters around him.

In short, he wouldn't have to feel anymore.

God only knew the catastrophic results if he tried *that* again.

"I feel fine," came her soft answer to Post. "Maybe a little tired."

A little? Taylor vented a rumbling cough in lieu of a disbelieving laugh. Both doctor and patient's gazes flashed to him—Post's questioning, Gwendolen's challenging. Taye squared his jaw and leveled a challenge right back. As he expected, that swiftly swung her attention back to Post.

He did *not* anticipate the account she gave next.

"I visited the site of where the Lancer—of where my incident occurred—a few days ago," she stated. Post's eyebrows jerked; Taye gained a little assurance knowing somebody shared his surprise.

Gwen went on in explanation. "I hoped the trip might stir my memory of things. I wanted to go this morning, too, but I didn't. I followed Tay—Lord Stafford's instructions; I rested and had a big breakfast."

"Yes. Excellent," Post murmured back. He felt her wrist for her pulse and scrutinized her eyes. "That's what you should have done. We never know how long a session will be; you'll need your strength. Now, did his lordship explain the remainder of the procedure to you?"

"Not really. We've both been quite . . . busy this week." Her response conveyed nothing but a measured calm to rival Post's. But then the telling instant came: as Post scratched some notes on a nearby pad, her lashes flickered . . . her gaze dropped. Taylor fought the craving to hold her again. Post went on scribbling.

"Well, then," the doctor finally said. Post smiled that grandfather's smile. "Allow me to offer a brief explanation of what I'm about to do." He leaned forward, resting elbows on knees. Gwen smiled back, and Taylor knew, in that moment, she gave her trust over to the man.

Gwen's trust. Did the bastard know how lucky he was?

"There are many stages of hypnosis," Post began. "But what they all are, in one form or another, are voyages into your subconscious. The voyage we're embarking on today is not an impossible one, but a deep one. To complete this journey successfully, you must want to go, with all your being."

After a quiet instant, Gwen nodded. "Yes . . . yes, I want to go."

"Good," Post replied. "I want to go, too." He took one of her hands between his. "Do you believe that?"

Gwen nodded and smiled again. Her growing trust shined brighter from her eyes—throwing up the walls around her and Post yet higher, closing Taylor farther out in the cold.

Damn it, he growled at such petty, stupid thoughts. *He* was the one who'd wanted this session, who'd pushed for this breakthrough. Now the miracle would at last take place. In a few hours, they might have some clues, some real pieces for the puzzle. As a matter of fact, he wished they'd hurry up about the whole wretched mess.

Didn't he?

"All right, then." Post stood, his august stature commanding primary interest in the room again. "I will summon my assistant in now. His name is Dawson; he'll be transcribing the session and aiding me with my materials. You needn't worry; like me, he is well studied in the work of Dr. James Braid, who brought hypnosis into the realm of science to begin with."

Gwen tilted him a bemused smile. "I'm not worried." She was the picture of composure, Taye thought. Perhaps too perfect.

"Excellent, excellent," Post crooned. He turned and opened a side door. A man entered, as squat as Post was tall. Dawson came complete with a parade of leather volumes and rolled charts, which Post and he locked heads over with the intensity of Napoleon restructuring the world map.

After several minutes, Taylor gave up trying to hear what they consulted about. He pushed away from the wall of books and paced across the room, still feeling as conspicuous as an odd-numbered dinner guest.

"Taylor?"

The urgent press of her voice halted him. When he turned and looked, Gwen's Mona Lisa composure had been stroked over by an intensity more fitting an intimate Degas scene.

He *knew* the refined portrait she presented had been a forgery. But the verity didn't set off the vindicated triumph he'd normally revel in—only a vise that clamped harder between his ribs with each step he took back to her.

"Where are you going?" That same exigency underlined her tone.

He knelt beside her chair. "To get a glass of juice. Would you like some?"

"Oh. No. It's just that—I thought you were leaving."

"I wasn't."

"You won't, will you?" At last she, too, noticed the fervency of her words. As if searching inside for the Mona Lisa face again, she dropped her head. "I mean, after they begin. You're not going to leave . . . right?"

The juice could ferment into wine. Taylor rose only to take over Post's chair, sliding forward until his knees came threads from her skirt. Three seconds barely passed before Gwen reached for his hands with a compulsion he hadn't experienced since Danny used him for balance when taking his first steps.

"You made me promise not to touch you." He wondered if he made the light tease to ease her tension or his. Either way, she didn't counter the remark.

Nor did she lighten her hold.

"Gwendolen."

He said the word as a bidding. The lift of her head said she knew it, as well. Her gaze didn't follow suit, but he'd live with that. Scraping up every degree of gentleness his barbaric male soul would surrender, he infused the feeling into two simple sentences.

"Gwen, I won't leave you. I'll always be here for you."

As easily as fate awarded the moment, time cut it to a cruelly premature end. Post and Dawson rustled their way back across the room. Gwen yanked her hands free. Taylor gave up his position to Post. He looked back to her as he returned to his stance by the bookshelves, but now her eyes followed Post with an expression mixed of hope and nervousness.

"All right, now," the doctor instructed. "Rest back, slowly . . . slowly." Gwendolen obeyed, but only after checking the depths of the chair as if to assure no spiders or skeletons would seize her.

"Now, Miss Marsh, I want you to take one deep breath . . . good. Another. Excellent." Post checked her pulse again. "Now close your eyes, and take two more."

As she complied, the man beckoned to Dawson without turning from her. The assistant moved forward with surprising speed, placing a waist-high candlestand between doctor and subject, touching a match to the fresh wick of the plain white candle.

"I am going to ask you to open your eyes now," Post intoned. His voice came so steadily, the candle flame barely swayed, his rhythm seemingly set by the weavings of the blue-white smoke. "You will open them slowly, steadily, and when you do, the only subject you will concentrate on is the candle in front of you. Just the candle. Do you understand?"

Gwen's nod reflected the same manner as her opening gaze: slow, a lingering half-movement. Post didn't waver his eyes from her, but Dawson nodded confidently in answer to Taylor's questioning look. The hypnotic suggestions were already taking effect.

The candle flame undulated through ten minutes of Post's soothing litany . . . ten more. Following Dawson's hand-signaled advice, Taye didn't gaze into the candle himself, but now even he sagged sleepily between a volume of Aeschylus and a critical overview of Sophocles. He began speculating they'd gone too far and Gwen would end up reliving some January night from her tenth year instead of her twentieth.

A laugh from the big chair set him jerking to both feet again. A laugh he'd never heard before: light, carefree, adoring. If he didn't step over and view the sight with his own eyes, he'd have sworn Gwendolen Marsh had slipped out of that chair and paid another to take her place.

"She sounds like a lovestruck maid," he whispered into Post's ear.

"Because she *is,"* the physician countered at regular volume. He motioned for Dawson to remove the candle, then placed his hand over Gwen's.

"Gwendolen?" Post called. "Can you hear me?"

She rolled her eyes and laughed again. "Of course I can hear you."

"And can you feel my hand on yours?"

"Yes."

"Excellent. Now if you feel this touch on your hand any time during the session, you will immediately see the candle's flame once more. The image will help us sustain or deepen your memory if we need to. Does that sound all right?"

She dipped her head demurely, a gesture straight from *The Habits of Good Society.* "Whatever you think is best."

Post swiveled to glance up at Taylor—but he couldn't take

his eyes from this woman before him. She had given him only peeks at this Gwendolen before, in those unguarded moments when their eyes met or their laughs coincided. But she'd always slam the shutters of herself closed again, as fast as she could, frantically repainting the picture.

But now this . . . damn, this was a bloody mural unveiled at once. She'd never shown him this. Not even when he'd made—not even when he'd become the same being with her.

Numbly, Taye nodded for the procedure to continue. Post turned to the eighteen-year-old Gwen still smiling at them, eyes young and twinkling.

"Gwendolen, can you tell me what day it is?" he asked.

"Saturday. January fifth. Eighteen eighty-nine."

"You sound very excited about an ordinary Saturday."

"That's because it isn't an 'ordinary' Saturday." Her shoulders lifted as if a spasm of pleasure tingled down her spine. "My fiancé is taking me to the theatre tonight. Perhaps you know him? Lloyd Waterston?"

"I'm sorry," Post replied. "I don't."

"He's wonderful." She didn't miss a beat. "He's with Gresham's Exchange, you know. Lord Chelham says he's going to go far. We're sharing a box tonight with the Chelhams—his lordship and her lady. I'm wearing my gold satin gown with the Roman neck and the long train."

Taylor gripped the back of Post's chair with the vision she inspired in his mind. With the gown matching those starbursts in her eyes, she'd undoubtedly had every man in the building longing to be Waterston that night.

"And what play do you see?" Post prompted next, bringing her forward to the evening's events.

"Oh, I don't know." She hid her bashful smile behind a fan she thought she held. "I just know I love it. We're at the Lyceum, so Ellen Terry's in it. I could watch her do anything. She's beautiful. Just beautiful. Don't you think?"

"Indeed. And after the play . . . what do you and Lloyd do now?"

"Lloyd and Lord Chelham are taking turns predicting Gresham's overseas dividends for the quarter." She clamped the imaginary fan shut with an agitated snap. "They're being quite indecisive about the matter, too. Lady Chelham and I are waiting by the rail of the box. She's very well informed about everyone leaving the other boxes." Her voice took on a pinched tone for what Taye recognized as a remarkably accurate imitation of Yvette Chelham: "There's the Duke and Duchess of Shropsbury. *Gad,* what a hideous gown. That's last year's green, isn't it, Gwendolen? And who is *that* in Anthony Bernwhile's box with him? Not his wife, I'll tell you that."

At that, her face screwed up in a grimace. "I think Lloyd and Lord Chelham's conversation is more interesting."

"Me, too," Post told her. "Now . . . you're finally ready to leave the theatre. Is it late?"

For the first time during the session, she paused before responding. "Yes," she said slowly. Her gaze searched the air over Post's head, as if she peered through—

"Fog," she defined, nodding her head. "It's foggy, too. Cold. Damp." She coiled her arms and hugged them close, shivering against the murky night she felt once more. "Lloyd helped me into my cloak back in the theatre, but it doesn't seem to be doing any good." Her features rekindled into a momentary giggle. "Lloyd— Oh, stop! I can't believe he stole a kiss right here on the walk!"

Post's eyebrows raised. "In front of Lord and Lady Chelham?"

"Oh, no." She waved the closed "fan" at him. "Their carriage was waiting at the curb, of course. They've long gone. There's . . . there's some sort of trouble with Lloyd's brougham. They're taking an eon to figure it out." She retracted her hand, curling in against her throat. "Lloyd's gone to check on the problem himself."

Now her voice began to shrink, edged with an unsteady rasp. "He wants me to wait here, next to the potted trees, where the wind won't chill me."

Post's tone also softened. "Are you warmer now?"

No answer.

"Gwendolen?"

She winced. With a vehement jerk, she struggled to free her other hand from his. Taylor remembered a sight of such terrified despair only once before in his life . . . by the time he'd happened on that she-wolf in the Cheviot forest clearing, the creature had gnawed halfway through its leg trying to break free from the steel trap.

"Gwendolen?" Post prodded again. When Taye impulsively surged forward, the doctor hauled him back.

"I'm warmer," she finally stammered. "But then, I'm not. I'm . . . I'm frightened."

"Why?"

"I don't know!" She still squirmed in Post's grip. "I feel something—" Her breath caught on a sharp gasp. "No. *Someone.* Someone's watching me."

"Who? Do you see this person?"

"No. Nobody. The street's empty. They're closing the doors to the theatre. No—don't—I'm afraid."

Her words spilled fast and urgent, emulating the pulse slamming in her neck. Taye's heart pumped to match the wild beat, some damnfool part of him thinking he'd ease her terror by sharing the sensation.

At that moment, he knew why Post had come so highly recommended, and accordingly priced. Every thrash Gwen attempted only consolidated the man's unwavering hold and firm tone.

"Gwendolen," Post stressed, "don't be afraid. We're right here. Take a deep breath and think about what happens now. What do you do now?"

Her scream vibrated with the neck-arching, limb-straining sound of pure terror.

Taylor lunged for her. Dawson appeared from nowhere to hold him back. Post battled her flailing arms and taut torso into the chair again. "Gwendolen!" he shouted. "Think of the candle!"

She panted and trembled, eyes flung open so wide the emerald centers were lost to the horrified whites. "No-no-no," she rambled. "No-no—please no-oh God, no!"

"Bring her out of it!" Taye ordered. "For God's sake, Post, it's too much!"

For that, he found himself the subject of Post's indignant topaz glare. "Lord Stafford, as you informed me yourself when we signed the contract, *this* is the goal we've been waiting for. I assure you Miss Marsh is in no danger. She will remember none of this—*if* you'll step back and allow me to conduct my session properly!"

With a forced set of his teeth, Taye shuffled back.

In the chair, Gwen began to cry.

Post lowered himself to his own seat. "Where are you now, Gwendolen?" he asked evenly.

"I don't know." Her voice cracked with her fear, a high and plaintive mewl. "Dark—it's so dark . . . a back street . . . an alley. It smells like old fish and—and mud. I hurt. He's got my arm twisted. He's dragging me farther from the lights—it's so dark! Oh, God . . . please don't kill me!"

Post leaned forward. He stressed his next question with strict clarity. "Can you see him?"

She thrashed her head from side to side. "No. No; he's behind me. I can't breathe. He's tied my arm around my back—squeezing my middle now—so hard! His other hand is—is over my face." She stopped, her forehead scrunching with realization. "Glove. His glove smells like Lloyd's—soft leather. Good leather."

Taylor exchanged a wondering look with Post. "What else?" the doctor pressed. "Is he wearing cologne?"

But she seized again, her mouth dropping on a silent scream. "The glove is gone. He's spinning me around—" she emitted a guttural grunt of pain. "Wall. He's thrown me against the wall. Oh, it hurts—my head. My arm. It all hurts. Please. Oh, please, stop. I won't tell anyone. *Please,* stop!"

Post pulled her hands tighter in his. "Who, Gwendolen? Who are you talking to?"

"Can't see!" Tears waterfalled down her cheeks. "I can't see anything! Just that cravat around his neck—so white, snowy white—and a tiepin, a red tiepin. Blood red—coming closer—there's—there's a picture in the stone. I don't want to look, I don't want to. A lion. It's a picture of a lion, on its hind legs, and roaring—why can't I do the same? Why? Why are you doing this to me? No! He's pinning me back! It hurts! Oh, God, it hurts! Don't kill me—don't kill me—don't kill me!"

"The candle," Post interjected, stroking her hands. "Breathe deep and think of the candle, Gwendolen."

"Shut up."

The growl came so low and so hating, even Post froze, then backed several inches away from her. Taylor looked from him to Dawson. Stunned scowls answered him on both accounts.

"What the hell?" he muttered. He looked back to Gwen's stiff, blank face.

"Dear God." Post's voice resonated with amazement—a fact that did *not* shine comforting light on the scene. "Could it be?"

"Could it be what?" Taye snapped. "Damn it, what have you done to her?"

Post coughed uneasily. "My lord, she's not only remembering the bastard, she's emulating him . . . perhaps *become* him."

"For Christ's sake, I said shut up!" Gwen—or whatever had overcome her—snarled again.

"Bring her out of it." Taylor curled his fist into Post's sleeve, intending to proceed to the man's flesh next if need be.

The doctor's sharp amber stare swung around at him again. "And if I do, the possible psychosis she suffers will be on your hands."

Taylor began to realize what a truly idiotic idea this was.

"You're a pretty thing," Gwen continued, one side of her mouth curling in a sardonic sneer. "Oh, yes. So very beautiful." Her deep-throated laugh reminded Taye of many a snide masculine snicker around the fire at White's. " *'A beauty truly blent,'* " she went on in a slow murmur, " *'whose red and white Nature's own sweet and cunning hand laid on. Lady, you are the cruelest she alive, if you will lead these graces to the grave.'* "

"What is *that?*" Post murmured.

"Shakespeare," Taylor supplied. *"Twelfth Night.* Twisted to a purpose the old bard probably never imagined in his nightmares. The bastard is even sicker than *I* imagined."

Gwen's shriek snapped his head up. "A knife!" she cried in her own voice. "Oh, God, he's pulled out a knife!"

Post snatched her hands again. "Gwendolen, it's all right. Nothing is going to happen to you. Just describe what's happening, as calmly as—"

"Please, oh please, no! No!"

Her upper body reared from the chair, every muscle straining, hands clawing tangled masses of hair from her flailing head. In the next instant, she slammed back against the cushion, whimpering, quivering. Her fingers arched in stiff desperation, the talons of a ladyhawk arrowed down in flight.

"He's leaning over me. He's pressed up against me. Oh, God. His breath . . . stinks. My clothes—my coat—it's ripping—he's slashing it. So cold. My head hurts." She began to sob, hard, tight gulps of sorrow. "Not my dress! Not my wonderful dress, please! Don't tear my dress!"

Post didn't spur her to further talk. His taut facial lines said each of her despairing, humiliated chokes prompted the same images in his mind as Taylor's: the scene of this vibrant creature being stripped to the barest requisites, physically and mentally.

Suddenly, on a decisive sniff, Gwen ceased. "No," she seethed between locked teeth.

"Gwendolen?" Post prodded carefully.

"No, damn you! I won't let you do this to me!" Her legs shot out, toppling Post backward into Dawson, continuing to kick into midair like a colt that wouldn't be broken. "Get away from me! *Get away!*"

"Post!" Taylor yelled, whirling between her and the two-doctor heap. Frustration and helplessness wracked him. And fear.

"Good God," the doctor rasped, trying to pull his leg out from under Dawson's chunky rump.

"Post, for God's sake!"

He stared at Gwen writhing in the chair, battling off a murdering lunatic with every last holdout of strength in her slender limbs. Only then she stopped on a shaking scream, eyes wide as she pleaded, "No, *no,* not my face!" She snapped a clenched hand to her scar, breathing with the violent speed of terror.

"Oh, God," she sobbed. "Dear sweet God, help me, please!"

Taye bolted from the chair and sped across the room.

"Gwen!" he bellowed. "Sweetheart, it's all right! Stop!"

She raced and collided into the bookshelves he'd been leaning against. Sophocles and Aeschylus came out into her frantic hands, discarded after she peered into the empty space they left, uttering an oath of fearful desperation.

She dashed to the arched window next. The velvet curtains yielded to her angry jerks. An unintelligible victory cry erupted from her; she pressed excited hands to the thick glass, finally deciding on an area of the large pane that appeared to meet her approval. She raised her arm in preparation to smash the glass with her bare hand.

Taylor tackled her to the floor two seconds before she could do that.

Her scream filled his ears. Her fists and knees battered every vital organ the length of him. The pain was nothing in tandem to the fear and fury pulsing through his heart and soul.

"Post!" he managed to command in a bellow. "Bring her out of it *now!*"

"My lord—oh, dear heavens, my lord!" came the doctor's answering shout, "I don't know if I can!"

Sixteen

Six hours later, Taylor clenched back what felt like the six hundredth tremor through his muscles—then unfurled his hand to run a caress across Gwen's hair. She shifted in his lap, warming his neck with her sleep-heavy sigh.

They'd finally freed her from the trance—a feat he felt certain in terming the most terrifying experience of his life.

After ten more minutes of grappling with her on the floor, Post had resorted to slapping her, at which point she ceased to breathe for a full half minute. At last, thank God, she'd collapsed into Taylor's lap, sobbing; after fifteen minutes of that, her agony ebbed into this leaden slumber.

The library's leather couch crunched as she again wriggled for comfort. This time she curled her head down, to spread heat into his chest. Yet after her breathing evened, the center of him still smoldered with an inundating warmth. It took only a moment of introspection to recognize the sensation as utter relief sparked into fierce possessiveness, as rage toward Helson now transformed into fury at himself.

Just as the resolve never to touch her again was annihilated by this fear of ever letting her go.

"Ah, Gwen," he whispered, raising his gaze to the angels painted in the wall frieze as if he'd see her face adorning one of them. As if she'd smile down and soothe his turmoil with an easy answer to his rasping query:

"Gwendolen Marsh, what the hell have you done to me?"

"Mmmm." Her drowsy mumble tickled his left nipple—*not*

the consoling solution he'd requested from on high. With a resolved swallow, he dipped his eyes to her again.

She already blinked up at him. "Hello," she murmured.

"Hello," he answered huskily.

"Where are we?" She managed a weak look around.

"Still in the library. Do you recall anything about the session?"

Her brows drew together. "No. But the trance must have been long. I'm very tired." She licked her lips, then pressed them together. "And very sad. Did I . . . remember it all?"

Taye hesitated only a second before tightening his arms around her. "That doesn't matter right now. There'll be time later. Another day, when you feel better."

"Yes." She reclined her head against his shoulder. "When I feel . . ."

He heard her long, difficult gulp. Taylor moved his hand to her hair again. He didn't know which strands wound tighter, the copper coils around his fingers or the savage-sweet ties around his gut.

"It's all right to cry," he told her in another rough grate.

Slowly, gratefully, she nodded. Openly, quietly, she drenched his neck and his collar with her tears. She didn't say anything, but Taye knew no words existed for the feelings. He knew it because the same speechless frustration clamored at the restraints of his own soul, and he hated the sensation with unutterable violence. He hated the anger that the hypnosis session hadn't purged a drop of, as he'd hoped—as he'd expected.

And he hated the questions. Always, *always* the questions. Why did God allow monsters like the Lancer to be born? Where the hell was that bastard now? How did he eat or sleep, knowing what he'd done to an angel like the woman who wept into Taye's shoulder now?

And why, *why* hadn't he been stopped?

Yes, Taylor hated the questions. Plaguing his eating, his sleeping, his breathing, now joined by a hundred more mysteries which had attacked his brain while reviewing the details of the session in the last silent hours.

But most of all, he hated himself, because during those moments of reflection, he'd realized his most agonizing quandary of all.

He cared for Gwendolen Marsh more than he thought himself capable of feeling for anyone again.

And he'd hurt her. Perhaps unforgivably.

Most likely, unforgivably.

That conclusion brought on the terror. The panic of not only acknowledging his mire, but mulling over just how deep he'd sunk into this emotional morass. Of wondering what irrefutable force pulled him closer to her every day.

Of deliberating what the hell he was going to do about it.

At this moment, no verbal answer to that challenge made sense. The only rightness in the world lay cradled in his arms, sniffing out the end of her tears, emitting a soft hiccup before she whispered words that filled his senses like starfire.

"I'm very glad you're here, Taylor."

"Me, too, princess," he finally managed to rasp back. "Me, too."

He had that look again.

Gwen only intended to look up from the notes in her lap long enough to stretch her neck and relieve her eyes. But she'd just tilted her head back against the dark-cocoa velvet of the study's Morris sofa when she started at Taylor's unblinking hazel gaze trained on her over a steeple of strong brown fingers.

The surprise didn't stem from the pose itself. She had no doubt Taylor had entered the world gaping steadily at the world. No, the man's outer command hadn't changed at all.

The difference emanated inside his eyes. The meaning came from behind his cryptic look, as if questioning her for an unknown something. It lay in the way he looked so suddenly yet painfully vulnerable.

It also caused the vexating dent in the defenses she'd sworn to hold against him.

The admission brought on an increasingly familiar wave of confusion—and fury. Blast him, they'd come to an agreement about working calmly and *platonically* to find the Lancer. Nothing more. Nothing less. And stares full of hidden questions and composure-crashing meaning were definitely not part of the bargain.

Yet obviously, his lordship had deemed it correct to change the rules. Well, Gwen determined, she'd show him what she thought of *those* tactics. Now.

She snapped her head off the back of the couch. Her shoulders followed, squaring straight at him.

Then she demanded, in two clipped bites, "What's wrong?"

His answering placidity worked the opposite effect on her nerves. "What makes you think there's something wrong?"

"You know what." She slammed down the notes and coiled her hands together into a fist atop the stack. "That—that *look* of yours. For three weeks, ever since the hypnosis, you've been staring at me like I'm about to glow in the dark. Like I'm about to answer some vast metaphysical quandary for you."

Taylor demolished the finger steeple to lean back in the Renaissance revival chair he filled. "Maybe it's not you I ask the solution of."

Gwen paused. A retort eluded her puzzled thoughts. What in the world was the man about? She was certain only of his obsession to see the Lancer's head on a stake.

Gwen turned quizzical brows toward the Renaissance chair.

He didn't wait for her there. Instead, she found the man crossing the space between them, then settling on the couch beside her. The furniture looked diminutive when forced to accommodate his broad torso and long legs, but he slid onto the cushions with a grace befitting his demeanor.

With that same knightly command, Taylor pulled the papers

from under her hands. The notes consisted of the composites they'd worked together for each of the Lancer's victims, Gwen herself included. Each report detailed everything in the woman's life, from her favorite breakfast meat to most-frequented dressmakers.

Taylor directed his gaze to the list on the top sheet, but gave his soft question to her. "Come up with any striking similarities yet?"

"No." But the answer came diluted of her previous ire, a faint breath of a syllable. Gwen's energy now went to combatting the effect his proximity played on her heartbeat. Blast him! Blast *her,* for this unacceptable, uncontrollable reaction.

"No," she repeated with more conviction. "The only other victims *I* knew personally were Nicky Spencer and Frances Pinkingham, Baroness Kilvert's ward."

"How many of the remaining have you simply met?"

"Just Lady Carrington; briefly during interval at the Haymarket one night."

"And how many of you have been courted by the same men?"

At that, she stiffened. "Only one man ever courted me properly, my lord. The man who put an engagement ring on my finger. Unlike what every newspaper reporter in Town wants everyone to believe, not all of the victims were flighty maids pursued by half of London." She lifted a knowing eyebrow at him. "Did you forget two of the victims happened to be married and devoted to their husbands? I think one of them was named Constance."

"I didn't forget."

As she expected, the rebuttal came swift and hard. As she *didn't* anticipate, Taylor raised a glare so cold at her, she knew why the poets labeled some shades of gold "frozen sunlight."

To her further surprise, he didn't torture her longer than a half second with the look. No, the true shock struck via his next statement.

"But you're right," he conceded. "From time to time, an

overzealous admirer or two from Connie's debutante days came sniffing around in hopes she'd become the bored Countess Stafford looking out for some sport. But Lloyd Waterston wasn't one of them. I don't think I'd forget *that* bastard's distinctive stench." A bitter smile curled his lips. "So I think we can safely conclude none of you shared the same thwarted inamorato."

He looked away during the last conclusion. He leaned forward with his elbows braced to both knees, raising his hands to rub the weariness from his eyes. Gwen sat in silence, watching him for a long moment . . . then ignored every strident scream of her logic by scooting forward herself, closer to him.

God help her, but she couldn't stop the action more than she could hold back the tides. The tension in his fingers, the nearly visible knots along his broad shoulders, the heavy meaning of his long sigh all beckoned her with one overriding message: despite all his single-minded contriving, this was still the sole human being who not only understood, but shared her pain.

When Taylor dropped his hands and tilted a small smile of thanks at her, she knew he felt that unity, too.

They sat like that for a long moment, looking at the notes as a thin excuse for extending their temporary peace. Finally, Gwen pointed to a pair of columns on the top sheet and remarked, "The only similarity I really see is everyone's taste in gowns and jewelry. But compile any group of London women together then make a list of such things, and you're bound to see—"

Taylor swung a hand around her wrist faster than a dressmaker's needle. "Jewelry?"

"Well . . . yes. Inasmuch as I actually selected jewelry." Gwen glanced away, feeling her cheeks pinken at the admission. "Only about three times . . . once for the pearls Aunt Maggie insisted I have for my debut, again when Lloyd took me looking at wedding sets, then when I had my engagement ring. I . . . lost some weight and half a ring size after my incident."

"Where?"

That snapped her head back up. "I don't think that's any of your business. I lost weight, that's all."

Taylor closed his eyes. As he opened them, that *look* dominated his features again, only now with a bemused cast. "The jewelry," he clarified. "Where did you select the jewelry, princess?"

"Oh." Then, with a surge of understanding, *"Ohhh.* The jewelry . . ."

Their smiles rose at the same rate of slow but steady hope.

He was euphoric.

Oh, he'd never come right out and tell her such a thing; as a matter of fact, Taylor's features maintained their same fixed intensity now, as he guided his matched bays through Park Lane traffic, as they ever had when poring over police reports or Dawson's accounting of the hypnosis session.

But the electricity in the man's body told Gwen everything. The distinct snaps he gave to the reins. The loose energy of his torso as he leaned forward from the phaeton's seat. Even the lively rhythm of his boot on the dash, keeping time to the ditty of a chimney sweep they passed. Every inch of his body proclaimed his triumph more loudly than a whooping victory cry.

Concurrently, Gwen found herself joining in his pleasant tune. The trip to Kingsley Jewelers had been more a success than they dreamed. While Arthur Kingsley didn't recall selling a ruby tiepin bearing the detailed lion's head Gwen remembered in her trance, he confirmed that four of the Lancer's other victims had regularly browsed the wares he sold by the motto of "beauty through craftsmanship." Gwen's name made the fifth entry on the list. Taylor's obvious friendship with

Kingsley affirmed Stafford House, and thus Constance, as the sixth.

As they took their leave of the kind-mannered jeweler, Kingsley reiterated his promise to comb his records for any rare purchases made by the remaining three victims and abridge Taylor of his findings as soon as possible.

Finally. Gwen's heart declared with trumpets of joy. Finally, they might be blessed with a clue.

The thought alone seemed an enchantress's wand from a fairy tale, waving an extra brilliant sparkle to the late-afternoon sun illuminating every tree, flower, and even street sign they passed. Gwen tried to toss off the impression to her own elation, but everything glimmered brighter as Taylor turned the phaeton onto the length of Wilton Place, then halfway around Wilton Crescent, slowing before the lights of Stafford House.

He mastered the bays to a stop, but made no move to disembark or aid her down from the vehicle.

Instead, he turned to her, hair gleaming a mythical black-bronze, gaze shining a celestial gold. "Stay for dinner," he quietly commanded.

Instinctively, Gwen tensed. As if expecting the action, Taylor reached a firm hand around hers. "Just a friendly glass of wine and some cold pheasant." That deep-valleyed grin broke free, despite what looked like his efforts at containment. "I . . . don't want to celebrate alone," he added. The unguarded boyishness of the statement proved Gwen's undoing.

They entered the house by way of the garden—an intentional detour, Gwen felt certain in concluding. The roses looked like drops of color from heaven in the amber radiance of the setting sun. She sighed in happiness at the resplendent view, and smiled to Taylor in thanks.

The pleased glow in his eyes returned a strangely heart-stopping acknowledgment.

Despite their connected moment, something rang amiss as they entered the back foyer and traveled the south hall. More accurately, nothing rang at all. The house echoed too quietly around them.

Gwen stopped as she pinpointed the discrepancy. "Danny," she said. "Where's Danny?"

Taylor stopped then, too. He rounded off the action with an uncharacteristically nonchalant shrug. "Gave him the night off," he quipped. "Little bounder requested leave to spend the night with his granna and family friends in Sussex."

Gwen feigned a shocked gasp. "How dare he."

They broke down into chuckles—until Taylor's mirth gave way to a stunned stare. "Now that I think about it," he murmured, "since I knew I'd be alone, I gave Cook and Alistair the night off, as well."

Twenty minutes later, Gwen sat on the chopping block in the middle of the weirdly empty kitchen, gaping at a feast to put any Renaissance regale to shame. When she took in the food around her—breads and puddings, sausages and roast beef slices, fruits and jams and three kinds of cheese—she wondered what, if anything, remained in the huge ice box Taylor still had half his body emerged in.

But while the sight teased her funny bone, all her other joints and limbs lay in serious danger of melting one into another. He ruthlessly exposed her to the sight of his muscular legs, his black trousers perfectly fitted around his hard buttocks, his spread-legged stance emphasizing his muscular power.

Though she didn't want the joy of this day to end, the urge to flee raced rampant up and down her body. Dear God, she shouldn't be here . . . in this house she'd vowed not to take a step in again. And alone with just this man and two maids retired to the servants' rooms for the night. And thinking it was wonderful . . . even after she'd promised herself not to think it wonderful ever again.

She turned and glanced across the dim floor of the kitchen. The back door lay unlocked just a jump down and five steps away.

On her other side, she heard Taylor close the ice box with a satisfied whump. She felt his tall form move to the chopping board. He leaned against the counter and uncorked the wine he'd promised. Her senses filled with his rich, masculine cologne, entwined with the savory aromas of the food.

She closed her eyes and delivered a short prayer for strength. Then she turned back to him.

He didn't say anything as he handed her a blown crystal flute full of the candlelight-colored liquid. Through the next moment he said nothing, either. He offered himself openly, honestly, his hair a dark and wind-blown disarray, his white shirt open at the neck. He'd peeled cuffs up during his food hunt, revealing lean-muscled elbows. And then came his face, inundated with the most powerful version of that *look* she'd seen so far.

Finally, his lips opened on the soft, husky murmur she knew he used for her ears only.

"To you." Taylor slowly lifted his glass.

Gwendolen sipped, but only briefly. She didn't know how the tumult of her stomach would react to even that small swallow. Maybe luck would be with her and the deafening outcries of her heart would dilute the falling liquid:

Oh, Taylor Stafford, what the heavens are you doing to me?

Only a supreme command to his self will held Taye back from sending an invitation to her through the next fortnight.

That didn't mean he didn't try to conjure up an excuse to do so; *any* excuse . . . but no logical or proper reason existed. No messages arrived from Kingsley's jewelry shop, nor did Taye expect any for days hence. And after that wide, wondering, magnificent stare Gwen had unveiled on him after his wine toast over Cook's chopping block, it had taken every iota of control not to damn propriety then and there . . . all he'd been able to do not to crush his lips and body against hers between the Tansy pudding and the currant jelly.

Even now, a full eight days later, he wondered how he'd get through the next few hours of their weekly review meeting without revealing himself.

No, he corrected himself, he didn't even wonder about composure anymore. He *prayed* for it.

He heard Stafford House's front door swing open. The chime of Gwen's laugh drifted up and through his dressing-room door. She launched a round of teasing at Alistair again. Maybe she managed to get the smile she always begged the stoic butler for; it had, after all, been eight days for Alistair, too.

Taye hurried through the finishing tuck on his cravat. As he shrugged into his dark-grey morning coat, she laughed again, a ringing giggle this time.

God, he loved to hear her laugh.

God, he longed to make her happy.

Rein it back, Stafford. Each syllable of his silent order coincided with his determined steps down the main stairs, halfway down the main hall, up to the study's thick oak door. While he gathered a composing breath and jerked his grey-and-black checked waistcoat into place, he added a mental mandate: *She's not ready to be happy—at least not by your hand. There's no way you'll force it on her this time, either, you stubborn bastard. You* must *wait until she's ready.*

You must also consider she may never be ready.

As if fate entertained the notion of rubbing salt in that wound, Gwen's laugh burst out beyond the door again. Taylor raised his arms and braced himself against the doorframe, pressing his forehead to the hard oak, enduring yet another round of that magical, musical sound.

Until a separate giggle joined in with hers. Wilder. Younger. And utterly ear-splitting.

He knew only one person who squealed like that.

Taylor flung open the door to the sight of his tousled son and an equally disheveled Gwendolen poised at opposite ends of the couch. They held a leopardskin pillow each, elbows cocked back, ready to assail their respective foe at the first opportunity.

At his entrance, their laughs faded and their pillows plopped to the floor in unison.

Taye took a slow step forward. He looked first to Danny, then to Gwen. He chose the sequence of his inquest carefully, recognizing the very real possibility of losing his composure to the mussed, girlish vision of her. Her beauty threatened to take his breath away. The light green of her eyes and the rosy flush at her cheeks perfectly matched the printed leaves and flowers of her frothy spring dress.

Luck leapt to his side. He looked away in time to save his forbidding facade. "That wasn't a very wise thing to do," he said then, spreading his stance between the discarded pillows.

"I'm sorry," Danny mumbled.

"I started it," Gwen defended.

"Still wasn't too smart." He shook his head while sweeping a "nonchalant" glance downward. Then, with two panther-swift lunges, he scooped up both pillows and sent them hurling at diagonal angles across the couch, "After all, everyone knows you're not supposed to surrender your ammunition to the enemy!"

His aim struck dead on. Danny shrieked in joy with the blow he took; Gwen's curls toppled even closer to the faceful of leopardskin dealt her.

But when she peeled the cushion back, her gasp of shock became a laugh of delight that flooded the room in bright music . . . and Taylor's soul in brilliant symphony. If only for this moment, she knew happiness—because of him.

The thought rendered him so motionless, he barely felt the two pillows Danny hurled back at his own skull. He even stood there grinning like a clod as Danny leapt off the couch and into him. They both slammed to the floor, where his son flattened him to the carpet with an ear-shattering victory whoop.

But Taye considered having all the air shoved from his lungs a worthy price for the horrified "Good Lord!" he heard from the couch, followed by the nearing scent of soap and woman. He secretly smiled at the feeling of Gwen's skirts across his leg, her palm pressing soft but urgent worry across his forehead.

"Danny, get off your father." She issued the command with as much mercy as Marie Antoinette showed the peasants, despite Taye's good-natured wink at his son. "Dear God. Are you all right?"

He took a long and purposeful pause before answering. "Would you care if I wasn't?"

Her hands withdrew. But her gaze did not, and she made no move to bolt from him. *Now* Taylor's head keeled. His pulse throbbed like a steam engine. And he didn't give his son's assault an ounce of credit for either condition.

Slowly, with the torturous calm he used on Danny's pet rabbit after its weekly escape from the hutch, he rose up on one elbow. "Gwen?" With the same tentative care, he slid his other hand into hers.

She tensed beneath his touch. But she didn't move away.

"I—I believe my purpose here is our weekly review meeting, my lord." Her voice and her gaze wavered at the same nervous cadence. "What have we to go over at this point in the search?"

At that point, Taylor couldn't hold back a knowing smile. "Kingsley hasn't sent back a single word." He shrugged with deliberate casualness, while inside, praising fate for the notorious Kingsley slowness. "That's all I have to report." He grinned wider. "Now it's your turn."

She turned a perplexed scowl on him. "You're bluffing."

At *that,* he stripped away all pretense at humor. Halfway on purpose, Taylor clamped his grip tighter—forcing her to really look at him. Willing her to see the soul he now wore in full view across his face . . . the purpose that scalded a dry, stinging heat behind his eyes.

"I learned my lesson about bluffing all too well, princess," he told her then. He ignored the embarrassing grate scraping the edges of his tone. "I learned it the hard way."

She didn't strain or squirm this time. As a matter of fact, to Taye's surprise, her fingers relaxed and her gaze gentled.

"I've . . . looked over our lists again this week," she said softly. "So many times, my eyes have crossed. Besides the possibility that all the victims patronized Mr. Kingsley at one point or another, there are no unifying characteristics I can find." As she contemplated that, her lips pursed. "And to think I assumed people were all the same."

A moment went by, marked only by his son's innocent play noises at the other corner of the room. Turning his hold into a gentle massage at her elbow, Taylor at last answered, "That becomes a logical assumption to make when all those people label you a freak at once."

Again to his wonder, her reaction came immediately—powerfully. Gwendolen's scar went white, then paled to nothing; she blinked back swift and shining tears. She flung her gaze down and jabbed embarrassed fingers at her face, laboring to hide her emotion from him.

Then Taylor squeezed her hand.

She froze for a long, long moment before squeezing back. Very, very hard.

The moment was right. So blessedly right.

It was the way he'd wanted things from the start, when they'd first locked gazes across that dim orphanage parlor. When her composure had wilted like the rain-drenched flowers outside as she struggled to understand that despite the nobleman's title and the brooding face, Taylor Stafford's veneer hid a man who realized her worst scars weren't inflicted by some faceless monster down a foggy alley.

No, Taylor admitted, he hadn't even realized it back then, standing in that cold London parlor, battling the chaos of his senses and the outcries of his soul . . . but he realized it now. *This* was what he'd yearned to do. Hold her like this. Be with her through the pain like this. Heal her like this. It should have been this way all along . . .

But maybe, just maybe now, they could make it a new beginning all over again.

Seventeen

His vow was only hours old when Gwendolen literally stretched his resolve to the limit.

Beneath one of Hyde Park's oldest poplars, Taylor made his fourth reach across the picnic blanket to cover the plates still piled with cold cornish hens, cheese sandwiches, fresh fruit, and a collection of Danny's favorite candy twists. But the gesture didn't distract his imagination—or the result such thoughts dealt to the juncture of his thighs—from wandering where it did with the dream-perfect scene before him.

Only he wasn't dreaming. Dear God, he really wasn't. As Danny tumbled down the lush green incline which secluded their picnic spot from the rest of Hyde's throngs, his son called to him in very real squeals and screams. He smelled the sweet grass the boy churned up; he inhaled the damp redolence of the willows bent over the inlet the Serpentine formed here.

Taye amended that last thought as he swept a gaze over the shimmering water. More likely, he mused, the little lagoon wasn't a natural formation at all, but a manmade creation, carved at the command of some long-ago monarch to woo his ladylove between the sunshine and the dandelions.

A ladylove. There lay the most real, most will-wracking part of this scene . . . yes, there, standing at the bottom of Danny's hill, regal as only a namesake of Guinevere could be. She even came with hair pulled free from pins and spiraling long and free, medieval-maiden style . . .

Taylor leaned to adjust the cloth over the hens—and his

sitting position—again. He began to rethink his original self-acclaim for suggesting this picnic. But after their wild leopardskin pillow fight this morning, one look at the weary shadows under Gwen's eyes and the disarray they'd made of the study convinced him their meeting was doomed to failure, anyway.

Quite simply, they needed a break. And the crisp spring day called . . . though Taye truly did expect a refusal to his invitation. When he helped Gwen up from his study floor, she did *not* beam a smile of gratitude, but his picnic proposal a few minutes later, wildly seconded by Danny, came instantly rewarded by a grin he'd seen only once before.

A grin on the Gwendolen of two years ago, brought back by a hypnotic trance.

Taye smiled himself now, remembering that look. He pressed a hand to the pleasant heaviness in his chest, trying to remember the last time *he'd* felt this way.

Suddenly realizing he'd *never* felt this way.

"Father!" Danny's shriek frightened off the brown duck who'd paddled over to say hello. "Father, watch. Watch!"

"I'm watching," he assured. "I'm watching."

At a nod from Gwen, the boy dove for the ground, hands first. His legs flailed up. She caught them, straightened them and followed the excited pace his hands churned across the grass. "See?" Danny proclaimed. "See, Father? Just like the clowns in the circus!"

Unfortunately, his son hadn't mastered the art of talking and hand-walking at the same time. As Gwen encouraged the pace, Danny paused to let a triumphant grin fly loose. His body flipped over; they tumbled to the ground together. Their giggles danced on the air like the butterflies flitting around them. The sound swelled louder as Gwen found Danny's ribs and dug in. When she ceased, she succeeded in a quick escape, jumping up and running down the grass incline.

Danny caught her, but they quickly turned the game into a race. With a growing grin of his own, Taylor watched the subtle performance the woman charmed his son with: she surged ahead but feigned exhaustion to fall back, culminating the competition in a close but clear victory for Danny at the bottom of the hill. There they sprawled to the ground again, laughing and wrestling, until Gwen at last raised arms in surrender and trudged back to the blanket.

"Lord," she joked on a weary but happy breath, collapsing on the opposite side of the blanket. "You'd think that boy has never rolled around in the grass with a female before."

Taylor's smile dimmed. He contemplated her remark for a very long moment. Then, softly, "He hasn't."

Gwen said nothing. She didn't have to. He knew what her abruptly furrowed brow and pursed lips meant.

"No, Constance didn't play with him like that," he said to the question glimmering rather transparently from her eyes. He searched for more words as he scanned the edge of the blanket for an appropriate blade of grass to pluck. "It just wasn't how Connie did things. It . . . wasn't what she did."

"There's nothing wrong with that," came her equally temperate answer.

She rolled over to face him in the same one-elbowed position he'd chosen before quirking a tender smile. "What things *did* Danny like to do with his mother?"

Taylor returned her smile—for a moment.

"I don't know," he replied on a sudden scowl, in a foreign, scratchy voice. But he searched his memory deeper for the answer . . . and found only gaping, frightening emptiness. "I don't know." *Did I ever know? Ah God, Danny, was I too busy taking care of you to care* for *you?*

"Father!"

He stared at his son through a strange haze of heat, centered behind his eyes, as Danny landed an enthusiastic pounce atop him. At that, the heat cascaded to Taylor's arms, aiding the fierce hug he welcomed the boy with.

"Father, guess who's waiting on the other side of the hill?" If Danny thought anything abnormal about his father's sudden affection, the tumble of his words didn't betray him. As a matter of fact, the boy returned the embrace, planting surprisingly strong grips to Taye's shoulders.

"Wellll," Danny prodded impatiently. "Father, *guess!"*

Taylor made a convincing show of deep, hard thought. "The queen?"

"Nooo!" Danny giggled.

"Toe-eating gnomes?"

"Fa-ther!"

"Bumbo the circus clown?"

"No!" Danny rose and locked hands to his grass-speckled hips. "Harry and Corvina Greystone. And they've got their chaise out today, with the grey goat pulling it!"

"And?" Taye couldn't help baiting the hopping boy with a slow arch of his brow.

"And they want me to go 'round with them! Father, can I go? Can I go?"

"May I *please* go," came the interjection from the opposite side of the picnic blanket.

Taylor turned in time to watch Gwen's remorseful gasp combine with her embarrassed flush. When he chuckled and winked his approval of her interference, she blushed deeper and glanced away to Danny.

Taye, on the other hand, didn't take his sights off her. He took in her tender adoration of his son, the way she looked at Danny from beneath her sunlight-trimmed lashes, the way her mouth inched up with quiet feminine wisdom . . .

And knew he'd never wanted to kiss her more.

Somewhere in the tumult of his senses, he heard Danny dutifully respond to her prompt for manners. "Have a good time," he managed to answer. "Be back by four."

With a triumphant cry, Danny disappeared over the hill.

The next minute descended, silent . . . and awkward.

A breeze finally rippled across the water. Taylor couldn't think of a syllable to say. Apparently, neither could Gwendolen. Two meadowlarks sang harmony to a dove's aria. Taye dared a glance across the blanket, to see she sat straightening a bow on her dress hem with wordless intensity.

He told himself to discard every tangent of hope a pause like this might give a man . . . ordered himself that her silence and her fidgetings didn't cloak anything except some fleeting thoughts and a little absentminded movement. Three times in a row, he ordered himself to retrieve the poetry volume he'd brought; yes, Thackeray was just the sweet, safe diversion they needed right now.

At least the diversion *he* needed.

Yet when Taye made up his mind and reached for the basket, she looked up, stopping him with the power of her clear stare. "You're . . . very good with your son, Lord Stafford."

He snorted without humor. "I've made a thousand mistakes. I'm amazed he's as magnificent as he is."

"Well, I'm not!" She yanked out the bow she'd just perfected with the emphasizing finger she thrust at him. She didn't seem to care. "He's magnificent because you love him. He's giving and caring because you've given and cared. Because those are the most important things, not goat chaises or mountains of toys or closets of clothes."

Even the breeze stilled at her words.

Taylor just looked at her. He looked long and intently. And she looked back, without a blink. He thought he'd seen every facet of emerald her eyes could shine, but this undaunted conviction glittered a new and amazing light. It was as if every hell and hurt she'd been through had honed her soul to a stronger shine, until this vision of boldness and beauty materialized before him, overwhelming him . . .

Humbling him.

It was there, in that frightening realm called humility, that Taylor found the surprise of strength. The courage to utter the response clamoring at his lips and his heart.

"A magnificent example, princess? You call me that, even after what happened that night in the Emerald Bedroom? Even after what I . . . even after the next morning?"

At *that,* she averted her gaze.

Still, her features comprised a determined profile as she gazed across the water, as if the sunlit shimmers there would scroll out a response for her. Yet in another way, she appeared to already know that answer—and now searched out a less terrifying alternative.

"Yes," she finally murmured. "I do say that of you now." Her fidgetings began anew at the dress's bow. "You see, I . . . I think I understand why you came to me that night."

A flush darkened her face more with each word. The sight of it undammed a raging river of hope through Taylor—strewn with pebbles of gentlemanly warning. If he heeded propriety, he'd overlook her suggestive confession . . . change the subject, *fast* . . . pull out that damn Thackeray volume . . .

The way she darted her tongue over her upper lip rendered all of that impossible.

He waited through an agonizing pause before pressing, "And what reason is that?"

"I only mean that . . . I—I know men have needs. I mean, I've *heard* men have needs—" The blush deepened. She tugged harder at her dress. "I—I just think I understand those needs now."

The river broke the dam and became a flood. Taylor forced a steady, heavy breath into his lungs in order to suppress the jubilant roar clamoring there. He summoned the will of every muscle in his arm not to topple the picnic basket as he lifted it from between them. But the effort was worth it; he moved closer to her, blood racing, heartbeat filling his chest with thunder.

"I see," he softly replied. "And what exactly leads you to think that?"

Her head dipped lower. She inhaled a breath of her own, short and shaky . . . and arousing.

"Because," she stammered. "Because . . ."

"Because of what?"

"Well, because of . . . well, I've had yearnings myself, in the last few months. Ever since we—"

Her cheeks flamed. Sunlight streamed through her auburn waves as she shook her head, as if trying to wake herself from a dream. "Forget I brought this up. I shouldn't be—"

"What kind of yearnings?" Taylor stopped her nervous hand with the firm grip of his own.

She closed her eyes. Her throat constricted around a deep swallow. Heart pounding harder, Taylor thought of pressing his lips there. He fantasized how that warm, slender column would feel beneath his wet, sliding tongue . . .

"They come sharp, and yet aching," she whispered. "They . . . stop my heart. Then they send it racing. I get warm, then cold. I feel numb, but I've never felt so alive. Oh, this makes no sense. I must sound fevered."

Taylor tightened his grasp. "Funny," he whispered back. "You don't feel fevered."

That garnered her hesitant smile, and he deemed the expression enough. Enough to slide his hold up past her elbow, fingering circles at the curve of her shoulder, continuing the slow, questioning pattern at the bottom of her neck.

"How else do the yearnings make you feel?" he asked.

She raised an uncertain gaze. "I don't know what you're asking."

"You called them needs, princess. Needs make you want to have something. To do something." He continued caressing, up to the softness behind her ear. "What do your needs make you want to do?"

The breeze came anew, flitting through the tree over their heads, releasing a kaleidoscope of leaves around them—and a riot of color in her eyes. Or did he really see desire swirling in those green-gold depths?

"I . . . they . . ." she rasped. "They make me want to . . ."

"What?"

"I can't—"

"Do they make you want to hold me?"

Slowly, she nodded.

Taylor smiled. "And touch me?" Another nod. "And . . . kiss me?" After a still, breath-held moment, a third nod.

Like a wisp of air on an ember, her wordless confession sparked his bloodstream into a forest fire. Despite the breath Taylor took in hopes of cooling the inferno, everything incinerated to oblivion. The park, the lake, this day, the time, nothing existed but the face before him, frightened tears aglow in her eyes, mouth trembling, waiting for him . . .

"And do you have those needs now?" he heard himself murmur.

She ran her tongue over her upper lip. And nodded again.

"Do you want to touch me now? Tell me, Gwen . . . say it."

"Yes," she whispered, her fingers sliding to his face. "Yes . . ."

Clattering leftover plates as he went, Taylor lowered her to the blanket, forming his hand around the curve of her waist, then up the rise of her torso.

"And do you want to kiss me now?" He formed the words against her forehead, down the graceful bridge of her nose.

She didn't waste time with an answer. Her lips lifted to his, seeking him, hand slipping around his neck to pull him upon her, his lips and tongue into her. Their mouths fused, moist heat transferring into trembling passion down their bodies, curling into their mingling, writhing legs and feet. Following that scorching path, beyond his control, Taylor's hand left her ribs to slide down her hip, around the curve of her bottom, clutching the enticing swell as he molded himself to her. Gwen sighed into his ear, and arched to allow him better access.

Burned alive, Taylor concluded somewhere in the tempest of his mind. He was being burned alive, and Christ, what a sweet death it was.

"Taylor." Gwen's breathless cry indicated she might second him into the fatal flames. "Taylor . . . this is the need I was talking about."

He kissed her softly on the lips, then suckled his way to her earlobe. "I know, sweetheart. I know."

Then he pulled slightly away, settling onto one elbow again. His other hand slipped from her bottom to her thigh, fingers gathering her dress's flowery material up, inch by silky, heart-pounding inch.

"Taylor," she breathed, "what are you—"

"Ssshhh." He nipped gentle teeth at her bottom lip, around her chin, down her throat, and to the glimpse of one quivering, firm-peaked breast. "Help me, princess," he said. "Let me see your beauty."

As she pulled her bodice down, he glided his hand up, further up her leg, his senses reveling in the feel of petticoats and soap-soft skin, of silky drawers . . . and the slick, satiny prize beyond their yielding door.

He covered her hard nipple with his mouth as he cupped her springy curls with his palm. She gasped; whether in pleasure or protest, he couldn't fathom for a moment. She clutched harder at his back and arched her soft mound up to him; Taylor's heart crashed against his chest as he unfurled his fingers into her wetness.

Her strained outcry filled the moment he found her sensitive nub of flesh. Taylor looked to her face as he used his thumb to burn her there, his forefinger to inflame his way up her tightness.

Tears streamed down her cheeks, ecstasy shining in each sunlit trail. Taylor kissed away the shimmering crystals, savoring each salty drop more than the smoothest brandy or the finest wine.

"It's all right," he murmured. "Surrender, sweetheart . . . surrender to me."

"Taylor," she sobbed, writhing uncontrollably beneath him. Her breaths came fast and shallow.

"I'm here." He matched his strokes to the pattern her hips set. He slipped a second finger inside, her juices drenching him immediately. "I'm right here, love. Jesus, you're so wet. You're so ready. Doesn't it feel good? Doesn't it feel right?"

Her whole body answered him now. With a silent scream, she bucked against him, the walls of her grotto convulsing around him, the scent of her climax warming and intoxicating him. His own lungs pumped double rhythm to accommodate the heady force slamming through him, the wordless wonder of watching her face dissolve in rapture. In surrender.

Completely his.

He recognized that thought as the most powerful aphrodisiac he'd known. Coupled with the sight of Gwen against the blanket, breasts still moist from his suckles, face awash in sunshine and rapture, Taye didn't marvel why his shaft still pulsed torturously against the barrier of his trousers.

No. He clenched his thighs and began to slide away from her. He had to rejoice in the knowledge of the heaven he'd catapulted her to; he'd wait until she invited him to join her there.

But he'd barely rolled one leg from her than she grabbed his hip. "Don't," she pleaded. "Taylor—I never knew. Oh, I never knew this is what you felt when you—"

"Sweetheart." His voice strained with an urgency pressing harder by the second. "I can't—if I don't—"

"No."

Taye's breath clutched as her hand moved up and squeezed his buttock. "Now you," she whispered, bringing up her other hand, kneading his hip in a steady, sensuous rhythm. "I want you to feel this way, too."

He groaned. Again, he tried to push her eager fingers away. "Gwendolen—love—you don't know what you're—"

"Pull the side of the blanket up."

If he likened his heartbeat to thunder before, it erupted into a crashing tempest now. Dear God. She considered the possibility of onlookers the only obstacle to their union. As her hands began to twist his trouser buttons free, he didn't care if the entire bloody peerage watched him claim her.

"I've unleashed a minx," he growled. Then he crushed his lips to hers, hard. His knees thrust her legs apart feverishly.

They gasped together as her fingers closed over his bare flesh. Taye shuddered and gulped, his next words coming in a fast, hot breath. "Hold me—just like this, love—just for a moment."

In that very instant, Danny's distinct shriek sounded from over the hill.

Taylor groaned, reaching down and helping her refasten his buttons with the frenzy of two young lovers caught in the Hampton maze. "Well done, Daniel Taylor," he muttered wryly. "You've inherited the impeccable timing of your father."

As the carriage rolled up the drive of Stafford House in the hazy glow of that day's twilight, Gwen couldn't decide to term Danny's interruption a blessing or a curse.

She'd never wanted anything so badly as Taylor's velvet-hard passion inside her. She'd never burned for anything hotter than the pleasure she wanted to give him . . . the same incredible heaven he'd shown her.

Even now, as she stared past the parted velvet curtains at her image in the coach window, the remembrance of that hour came like watching a play unfold: it had happened, but it had been another person, a Gwen as separate from her as the swollen-lipped creature looking back at her from the darkening glass.

A stranger. Surely it had been a stranger writhing like that in a corner of Hyde Park, a stranger gasping into the Earl of Stafford's ear with insatiable desire, a stranger tearing open that same earl's trousers . . .

A stranger realizing she had never felt so complete in her life.

Gwen pressed her lips together until they trembled, staying the confused tears until she could make her hasty good-bye, race home, lock herself in her room and sort out each sob. Until she could figure why she'd opened herself to a man who'd only filled her life with more pain and frustration.

Until she could talk herself out of this tormenting desire to do it again.

"Princess?"

Despite the inner lecture, her head willingly snapped up at Taylor's address. He stood outside the coach's open door, hands braced to the roof, the pink-and-grey sunset a perfect backdrop to the white shirt fitted so well to his broad torso.

"Hullo." He imitated Danny with a gentle grin.

Gwen hated the responding smile she couldn't control. "Hello."

"Thinking?"

"A little," she hedged.

"About what happened in the park?"

She dropped her gaze.

He swayed the carriage as he lifted one foot to the carriage's step. He leaned both elbows to his knee, the movement rustling his clothes in a strangely sensual manner. Or perhaps, she thought with unnerving revelation, that was just the way she'd perceive everything about him from now on.

"Would you like to come in and talk about it?" he asked.

Gwen kept her eyes forced to her feet. She yearned to go home, didn't she? She wanted to untangle this mess *alone* . . . didn't she?

Her soul never got the opportunity to answer that. With nary his usual shout of warning, Danny came bounding back out of the house.

"Father!" Excitement even drained the volume from his breathless voice. "Father, Bryan's here to visit!"

"Bryan?" Gwen jerked her eyes up then. "At this hour?"

A glance to Taylor confirmed he shared her sentiment. They certainly deemed their friend iconoclast enough, but after the streetlamps were lit, she assumed Bryan steered his eccentric house calls towards London's more warm and willing female occupants.

"I asked him the same thing," Danny said with a proud nod. "But the other man said they were here about police things! Father, *police* things! Isn't it exciting?"

Gwen exchanged another look with Taylor. This time, a more knowing look.

"Danny." Taylor knelt and anchored his son's shoulders. "What other man? Who came here with Bryan?"

Danny shrugged. "The *police*man, I *told* you. He's tall and he has a funny nose and he doesn't smile. He must do very dangerous police things."

Taylor flashed her one more look. Again, that connection spoke their mutual conclusion without the need for words.

Helson.

Before either of them blinked again, Taylor reached into the carriage for her. With swift and sure strength, he hauled her down. Without letting her go, he made for the house at racing speed. Gwen matched him step for step.

Alistair waited next to the main stairs, lips already parting with the answer to Taylor's unvoiced question. "They're in the drawing room, my lord." He signaled to a maid standing by; she swept the doors back for them.

As Gwen followed his charge into the room, she circled to the welcome sight of Bryan on the long brocade sofa. Taylor bypassed the forest-green ottoman and marched straight to Helson, seated in an appropriately stiff-backed chair by the fireplace.

"What is it?" Taylor ordered. "Did you catch the bastard?"

Even beneath his grey-flecked beard, Helson's jaw stiffened. "No," the officer finally replied. "But we've come upon what we think is a major breakthrough in the chase." He arched an annoyed eyebrow. "If you'll sit down, my lord."

Taylor's shoulders bunched and released, then again. Sitting clearly didn't appear on *his* agenda for this meeting. His pleasure looked more like dismantling the fireplace and crashing it over Helson's head.

Gwen threw an imploring look to Bryan. Surprise set in when she saw his questioning gaze already fixed on her, that distinct spring sky blue now intensifying to a troubled winter grey.

Only then did she doubt why he didn't appear *more* stunned. Her unbound hair still weighed on her shoulders and upper back. An image exploded to mind of her reflection in the carriage window: hot and flushed cheeks, well-kissed lips, shimmering but secretive eyes. She didn't dare glance down at the condition of her dress. She prayed no telltale grass poked from her bodice or clung to the bottom Taylor had fondled so thoroughly.

It took every ounce of her courage to ignore the accusing cast of her friend's stare and convey a silent plea of her own: *For heaven's sake, Bryan, do something. Protect him from his own stupid temper!*

She beamed Bryan a grateful smile while he rose.

"Now, mates," her friend clucked, stepping into the line of glare fire between the other two men. "Let's not fuss like a parlor full of magpies over this. Anyone for a drink? I think you'll agree Helson's news calls for a celebration, Taye."

Taylor lingered next to the chair matching Helson's. At last, to Gwen's joy, he flipped the piece around and straddled the chair backward.

"I think I'll decide that when I hear the news," he rumbled back to Bryan. He folded stiff arms over the chair's back, looking to the inspector with the vigilance of a lion appraising a foe.

Helson merely sniffed, almost looking bored. Just when Gwen anticipated a yawn about to part the ugly goose's whiskers, he reached into his coat pocket and withdrew a dirt-smudged square of striking red material. He held the swatch out, sniffing again when Taylor received it with slow curiosity.

"Recognize it?" the policeman drawled. "We unearthed it in the alley off of Princelet Street."

Strangely, through the next tense moment, Gwen found her gaze dominated by Taylor, and her heart filled with increasing pride. If Taylor heard the man's condescending lilt—and she was fair certain Helson didn't breathe without his attention—Taylor didn't lift even a brow in reaction.

"Silk," he responded instead, still concentrating on the red square. "Imported. Expensive. I don't imagine this came from an entire gown or shirt."

"A scarf," Helson supplied. "Or so we're speculating."

"Good speculation," Taylor replied softly. "And the rich color . . . you could probably narrow this down to two or three shops on—"

"Regent Street. Yes. Mr. Corstairs has been most helpful in informing us of the establishments the more particular gentlemen of London frequent, most of your peerage included, I am told, my lord."

"You are told correctly."

If Gwen hadn't heard the respect underlining Taylor's confirmation for herself, she'd never have believed it possible. Instead, she watched on in more shock as Taylor stood and shook hands first with Helson, then Bryan. "You're right, my friend," he told the latter. "This *is* cause for celebration."

"Yes," Helson concurred. "Along with the details Miss Marsh recounted during her hypnosis—the elaborate tiepin, the gentleman's leather gloves, the speech patterns—Scotland Yard has deemed it wise to continue on the official hypothesis that the Lancer isn't only assaulting members of the gentry, but *is* a member himself."

At that, Gwen reached to the sofa's back for support. She and Taylor had discussed the theory—but she'd always changed the subject with unnerved haste, finding some "logical" excuse to refute Taylor's conclusions. No, she couldn't accept the wild notion . . . that the man who'd tried to kill her—rape her—had perhaps smiled at her beneath a ballroom chandelier a week prior. Maybe even wished her good morn as they passed on their way to church . . .

But here, now, she couldn't push aside the voice of Scotland Yard. Or more importantly, the evidence they'd finally turned up, still resting now in Taylor's hand.

Fury and terror ran a stream of ice water down her spine.

She turned to Taylor. Dear God, she needed his gaze, steady and calm, his fortifying warrior's mettle. "I could have been clinking wineglasses with him at interval that night," she stammered. "I probably let him kiss my hand."

He didn't let her down. The look he leveled back could have been a physical caress with its warming potency. "The important thing is that we now know for sure," he replied. "We've narrowed the field. We can look in a tighter circle."

"Beginning with next weekend," Helson announced.

"Next weekend?" The quotation marks to Taylor's echo came in the form of perplexed creases at the corners of his eyes. But the next instant, he leapt up with a bright-eyed vigor Gwen usually associated with his son. "Good thinking again, Helson. The Guardian Society's Harvest Ball; I should have remembered it myself."

But his excited words only sent Gwen sinking to the sofa. Just as her heart plummeted in her chest.

"That's one of the most exclusive events of the year," she claimed feebly. *One of the first guest lists my name was "accidentally" dropped from.*

"Exactly," Helson confirmed.

"Everyone who's anyone will be returning to London to attend." Taylor actually joined the police officer at the fireplace, tilting his head to one side in deference to Helson. "Bryan, Gwendolen, and myself, along with a contingent of your best undercover men, should have that mausoleum Moorford calls an estate covered to the eyeteeth."

"Wh-what?" Gwen squeaked. Good saints, didn't he realize? Didn't he envision the impossible sight of her flouncing into that ballroom after all these years? She couldn't do it. She wouldn't. He might as well give her a razor and let her gash her wrists; the effect on her spirit would be the same.

But neither man heard her protest. They'd already begun mapping their strategy with gesticulating gusto. "You'll need at least two agents for the gardens," Taylor asserted. "The rumors are true; sometimes they haven't found drunken guests in the Moorford forest for days."

Helson jotted the suggestion on a pad with an approving grunt. "You, Mr. Corstairs, and Miss Marsh will stay to the main ballroom and lounges, of course."

"Wait," Gwen implored again. "Taylor, I don't think—"

"Of course." Taylor nodded. "No telling whose voice may set off a spark of recognition in Gwen. Bryan's got a good eye for gems. And I just want to kill that filthy son of Satan."

"Taylor."

"We may really get him this time. Good God, we may really get him."

"Stop it!"

They turned as Gwen jerked up from the sofa, pulling up a brocade pillow as she went. "Listen to me, damn you! *We* aren't going anywhere next weekend. *We* aren't 'getting' anyone. *We* is not a possibility, so stop making your silly plans as if it is!"

She stood there twisting the pillow until Taylor's face became too painful to look at . . . his gaze, too dark and confused to bear.

Then she threw the cushion down, jerked up handfuls of her skirt and bolted from the room.

Taylor watched her from the doorway of the south sitting room. She'd tucked her knees under her on the window seat. Her forehead pressed against the window glass while her tear-glimmered gaze reflected the shadowed lawn.

After confirming the carriage wouldn't be ready to take her home for another ten minutes, he somehow knew she'd flee here. He knew the canopy of ferns and the now-shelved poetry books would beckon with memories of the peace and laughter they'd once shared here.

He knew it because the room had called to him in the very same way a dozen times since she'd left.

"Don't!" came Gwen's sudden command through the dimness. She didn't turn her head; her breath formed a momentary O of fog on the window.

"Don't what?" Taye whispered back. If she wanted a war, she'd have to work to hear his maneuvers.

"Don't look at me like that."

"You have no idea how I'm looking at you."

She laughed then—her half-sobbing laugh. "I see you in the reflection of the glass," she explained. "The way you're standing . . ." Warmth snuck at the edges of her second chuckle. "I once fancied you some kind of guardian warrior sent to me because of that stance. Because of the way you gazed at me when you stood like that. Like you understood everything."

On the last word, her voice hardened again. "Well, you don't understand. You can't. I remember that now. I don't know why I allowed myself to forget. You're an earl, for saint's sake. You could probably murder someone yourself and not know what it feels like to be thrown out like coal dust."

"Christ," Taye finally growled. He stormed across the room, making no formality about grabbing and hauling her up to his level by both slender shoulders. "What are you talking about? What are you not even giving me a chance to comprehend?"

"I can't go to the bloody ball!" she cried back. "Is that clear enough for you, Baron Roseby, Earl Stafford?"

Taking advantage of his temporary puzzlement, she shoved away. She thudded back to the window seat with a dreary finality.

"In case you've forgotten," she muttered into the ensuing tension, "I've been off the London 'A' List for quite some time. The 'B' and 'C' sets don't want much to do with me, either. Nobody wants to expose themselves to the dreaded Lancer germs, which I *surely* carry. Don't you remember?"

Taylor gazed down at her for a strange, ethereal moment. His chest twisted. How had one of heaven's own angels been degraded to this, all tearful cheeks and moonlight-streaked sadness? How had she been reduced to making courageous jokes about a monster she dreaded instead of tittering with her girlfriends about gown necklines and wedding-night preparations?

His soul wrenched harder as his survey moved lower, following the rumples in her dress, each wrinkle a reminder of the caresses he'd given to put them there—and her breathtaking ministrations in return.

Then he thought of one more image: the sight of her alone in this dark, calling out to him, calling him *her* guardian angel.

Believing he would make everything all right.

And yet . . . he *could* make everything all right. The solution swelled in his mind; so overwhelming, he wondered why he hadn't seen the picture before. The one way to keep her safe forever . . . to ensure she'd never hurt again.

With a casualness so opposite the tempest now raging inside, he lowered to the seat. He faced opposite Gwendolen, toward the dark sitting room.

"So the problem is, you don't have an invitation to the ball," he stated.

"Don't," she countered—the word now a plea. "Taylor, don't make me think you understand this time."

"Nor do you expect Lady Moorford to recognize the mistake she is certainly making, and rush off a late invite to you anyways?"

"Blast you."

He returned her glare with an intent smile. "Then there's only one thing left to do." He cocked a knowing shrug. "We'll have to make you inviteable again."

The glare narrowed. "It's confirmed," Gwen muttered. "You're insane."

But Taylor caught her chin as she turned to dismiss him.

He directed a stare into her, conveying a sole command: *no retreat. Not this time, Miss Gwendolen Marsh.*

Slowly, gently, he pressed closer to her. He moved close enough to smell her peach soap, to inhale the scent of earth and sunshine in her hair. He leaned close enough to hear her heartbeat, and to recognize the need to protect that precious pulse . . . forever.

Yes, the need.

Dear God, Taylor realized then. *He* needed *her* as much as the situation in reverse.

"No," he softly countered her. "Not so insane at all. It's possible, Princess; all of it." He reached for her hand, indeed feeling as if he'd picked up a fragile star fallen from the twinkling sky above them. "All you have to do is become the next Countess Stafford."

She blinked. Then she swallowed.

Then she gasped, "What?"

"Marry me, Gwen." He bore his gaze deeper into her, yearning to convince her . . . needing to have her. "Marry me, and come to the ball with me . . . and share days like this with me for the rest of our lives."

Eighteen

As Gwen lowered the ivory gauze veil over her face, she swallowed back the gnawing dread that she also shrouded her heart from the truth . . . that she was about to walk down these stairs, into the drawing room and commit herself to a marriage created solely out of an earl's lingering guilt and code of duty.

But remorse was the last thing she'd seen on Taylor's face in that incredible moment in the sitting room—had it been only four days ago?—and yes, even in that stunned instant, she'd studied him long and hard, examining every hard plane and carved nook of the intent, rock-still stare he fixed upon her.

All she'd seen was need.

And all she'd felt was the same soaring, reeling joy he'd given her in the park that day. The same peace and security she'd experienced in his arms during the hours after her hypnosis. And, she'd realized on a wave of elation, the trust he'd labored so long and patiently to win back from her.

That's when she'd kissed him and nodded yes.

That's when Taylor kissed her back, a kiss so deep and consuming and thorough, she'd thought the four days necessary to procure a special license, send for the Stafford family minister from Yorkshire, and make arrangements for a small ceremony would fill an eternity.

Now the time felt like an eye's blink.

As if hearing her bones tremble in reaction to that thought, a small but sturdy hand squeezed at the bobbin lace draping her elbows. "It'll be all right, you know," Granna said. As was her way, the dowager countess issued the words as command more than assurance.

Gwen tilted a grateful smile through the filmy gauze. "I . . . I just wish I had more time."

"Oh, for heaven's sake. To do what?"

"To think. To sort things out. To make cer—"

"Gwendolen Victoria." Granna's hand now dropped to cock an imperious stance at her diminutive hips. "Do you love my grandson?"

Gwen took a long breath. She glanced to the floor, then back up, knowing very well she didn't study the inside of her veil . . . but the images in her mind's eye. All the beautiful pictures she kept treasured there. All the thoughts of Taylor.

And then a smile brimmed to her lips. The look came ushered by a precious warmth, a new confidence . . . a sweet ache she never thought possible to feel again, let alone this deeply, this profoundly.

From that soul full of joy, she issued her soft but sure answer.

"Yes," she stated, raising her gaze proudly. "Yes, Granna, I love him very much."

"Well," the woman humphed, finally and apparently satisfied. "Just making sure you knew it."

Gwen's smile took on a bemused slant. "And you did already?"

"Ever since I saw the two of you look at each other that day in the sitting room. Bloody damnation, the only thing that amazes me is how long you took to ponder things out. Still can't believe Taylor was ready to let you slip by with nary a fight. Thought I taught that lad a higher trot. I almost thanked Lloyd Waterston for coming by that night and shaking you both up."

"Lloyd," Gwen stammered. "That night?"

Good Lord, she suddenly realized. Lloyd. That night. *That*

night. "Granna," she gasped, cheeks blazing, "Granna, you *know* about what we did . . . when we . . ."

"Mercy, yes." The woman waved a nonchalant hand. "Why do you think the maids didn't bother you at the crack of dawn? I only wished I'd orchestrated the whole thing myself. Didn't happen nearly as dramatically with Julian and me. My poor love had to crawl in through my bedroom window. He nearly fell from the lattice three times!" She added a chuckle to the smile, a light but wistful sound. "It was terribly romantic, though. So terribly, unforgettably romantic. Everything a girl dreams of for her first time."

As her tone drifted into memory, Granna closed her eyes for a quiet moment. When she looked up again, she patted the lace glove sheathing Gwen's hand. "The result of that night was Taylor's father, God rest his soul."

"B-but the child was conceived out of wedlock." Sheer shock pushed the words out.

At that, Granna's own eyes snapped up, her gaze no longer a contented kitten's stare but a nettled wildcat's glower. "That child was conceived in love," she leveled. "And we never, not for a moment, regretted it happened that way."

Strangely, Granna's words lightened Gwen's heart of a burden she'd kept a deep and well-guarded secret. Though the passionate hours she'd spent with Taylor hadn't created more than the following months of confusion, she'd lain awake through many a midnight hour wondering what she would have done if their recklessness had carried more permanent results. In the process, she'd encountered an astonishing mix of guilt, anger, and yes, joy and hope.

"You . . . you didn't?" she at last responded to Granna's declaration. She hated the betraying wobble of her tone, but hoped it encouraged more explanation.

The woman gently shook her head, confirming she wouldn't disappoint Gwen. "The week after Julian proposed, the nuptial parties began," Granna explained. "But the week after that, Julian received his orders for immediate dispatchment to the

Maori uprisings in New Zealand. We . . . we had three hours together after our wedding, and then he was gone for a year. The only reminders I had of him were my ring, my gown, and the new life inside me."

At that last simple statement, a silence of understanding fell warmly between them. Gwen looked down at the little woman as she felt her shame and shock disappear through the roof. In her heart, only love and pride remained—and excitement that she would soon call this family her own.

She placed her other hand over Granna's and squeezed. "It is a lovely gown, too," she whispered. "Thank you for letting me wear it today."

In standard Granna fashion, the woman just snorted before stepping back to appraise Gwen with no less scrutiny than Pitt reviewing his troops. "Yes, well, the bridal gown is only as striking as the bride," she declared. "Now tug the shoulders a little lower, dear."

"Granna!" A hot blush claimed Gwen from collarbone to forehead.

"You have lovely skin, Gwendolen. Flaunt it. And the hoop—does the hoop feel secure?"

Gwen nodded as she brushed her hands over the rows of ivory satin flounces supported by the round wooden frame and three layers of petticoats. Fine lace trimmed the elaborate drapes and lined the off-the-shoulder bodice. Above those luxurious flounces, the material shimmered with garlands and garlands of exquisite cream pearls.

"This dress . . . is sheer wonder," she breathed, afraid any louder utterance would break the spell and leave her out in the drive with a pumpkin and five mice.

"Taylor's mother wore it on her wedding day, too, you know."

Gwen looked up in surprise. "She did? You didn't tell me."

"I didn't want to sway your decision. Yet now, with you in it, I suppose we'll *have* to start calling it a family tradition."

That turned Gwen's look to a smile. The melodramatic emphasis didn't fool her an instant. Granna's twinkling gaze and quirking smile proved testimony to how long the matriarch had waited to say that.

But the comprehension brought another question to mind. "What about Constance?" Gwen didn't ask it without fearing the possible answer. "Didn't you offer the gown to her?"

Granna's reply came in two stages. The first, an instant change of her features, reminded Gwen of watching a shade being pulled over a sunlit window.

Then the words came. "Of course," the countess replied—with unconvincing flippancy. "Constance merely desired something more—oh, how did she put it?—something more 'current,' if I remember correctly."

The information rendered Gwen speechless. It never entered her mind to turn down Granna's offer of the dress. Concurrently, she never remembered feeling more beautiful than she did in the timeless creation, or more graceful as she descended the stairs, skirts and veil floating like an ivory bubble bath behind her. Nor did she ever recall being more happy as Tess and the other orphanage children met her at the bottom, breaking into reverent *ooos* and *ahhhs* at the sight of her.

Then the music started, growing louder as Alistair pulled back the double doors of the drawing room and gave a fatherly nod. She turned and saw faces, picking out only a handful of familiar images in the crowded room: Hannah, big eyes already aglow with tears, Aunt Maggie, fleshy face transformed with a surprisingly gentle expression, Danny, proudly holding the ring pillow aloft, and Bryan, an unusual portrait of reserve in a grey morning coat and banker-striped trousers. Gwen clutched her bouquet of cream-and-pink roses tighter, trembling, not knowing if she had another step inside her . . .

Until everybody faded away at the sight of Taylor, tall and broad and dark before the mantel at the end of the aisle. Her proud warrior. Her gentle-maned lion. Her protecting guardian.

And after a few steps, her beloved husband.

She suddenly yearned to hitch up her skirts and sprint down the aisle.

She settled for a more sedate pace, concentrating on the proper cadence to match the music. Halfway now . . . yes, she could do this—

An urgent grip around her elbow shattered her hard-won poise. The musicians continued on, but the crowd caught its breath on a collective gasp.

Gwen jerked an astonished stare up into Bryan's face.

"Bryan." She rasped the word frantically as she searched his tight features. If she thought his stare peculiar outside Aunt Maggie's townhome a month ago, his expression shot pure dumbfoundment—and discomfort—through her now. "Bryan, what are you—"

His breaking smile stopped her short. Gwen blinked. The nerve-rending stare had disappeared. Had it been just a play of her imagination? *No* . . . despite her current threadhold on composure, she knew what she'd seen. Yet still, now, he squeezed her arm with such affection and flashed a wink of such camaraderie, Gwen felt herself actually grinning back.

"You're beautiful," he said then. "Go on, my Lady Stafford."

With a grateful smile, she did.

As she joined Taylor before the spaniel-eyed minister, she swore she heard his heartbeat sprinting along with hers. She longed to take Bryan's cue at defying convention and turn her sights to her betrothed's face, to know for certain. But one scandal a wedding was enough. She tamped down the urge by pressing her lips together, dropping her gaze lower.

The crowd gasped for the second time in as many minutes.

Their promulgation preceded Taylor's touch at her chin by two seconds. She obeyed his silent hest in eager surprise, finding his features alight with a joy and wonder she'd never seen there before.

He gave a small laugh before murmuring, "You're wearing the gown."

She managed a nervous smile back. "Well, Granna—"

"Bryan's right. You're beautiful."

She returned his laugh. "When Granna offered, I was honored. I—"

"No." His voice jerked as hard as the way he shook his head. "No, I'm the one who's honored, my Lady Stafford."

Before the preacher uttered a word, before the guests collected themselves over the outrageous but incredibly romantic twists and turns of this wedding, Taylor raised her face higher, then dipped his head and kissed her, right through the veil.

My Lady Stafford.

She'd heard Taylor's words repeated at least twice by every well-wishing guest this afternoon. How many times did that add up to? Gwen's weary brain refused to do the simple arithmetic. No matter; it didn't change the fact that she sat here in the quiet of the master bedroom, expecting the next pop from the fireplace to really be Aunt Maggie's sharp hand clap, waking her from this incredible dream.

Lady Stafford.

She watched herself twist her wedding ring in the bureau mirror. The diamonds, set in a sunburst design which popped her eyes out but the simplicity of which Taylor *apologized* for due to such short notice, didn't feel like a dream.

Countess Stafford.

Gwen picked up her headpiece, a froth of roses and baby's breath supporting the train of exhausted gauze. She brought it up over her brushed-out curls. In her other dreams, veils never wisped her face and shoulders like this.

Lady Stafford.

"Lady Stafford?"

She whirled around. Her nightgown tangled around her legs, but even the cool press of the material didn't convince her this time. Definitely a dream, she concluded. She'd wake up any moment, heart soaring, blood pounding simply from the sight of the masculine majesty dominating the bedroom's doorway.

Taylor stood with shirtsleeves rolled, waistcoat unbuttoned, and one shoulder cocked to the doorframe. He was roguishly disheveled, dark and powerful and sensual . . .

And he was hers.

No. A dream. Too good to be anything but a dream . . .

Then he smiled. A flashing, warming smile, permeating very real happiness through her. His gaze, heating like cinnamon sticks in hot cider, sluiced real enough honey down her helpless veins.

"Good evening, my lady wife," he said again, softly . . . intimately.

Gwen rounded back toward the mirror. She pretended interest in her hairbrush, frantically searching for any spare curls she hadn't untangled yet—

From the corner of her eye she watched his image in the glass grow bigger. With every nerve of her body she felt him move closer; his height, his hardness, his power . . .

Her breath caught as his hand burrowed beneath her hair to her shoulder. She looked up to where his eyes met hers in the mirror. His gaze held her so strongly, caressed her so tenderly she barely felt his stubbled cheek grate hers or his other hand circle possessively around her waist.

She only became aware of the distinctive white envelope he held because he trailed it directly between her breasts. He cracked a white, devilish grin and murmured, "I was saying good-bye to the Roundtrees when this came for you. It's got the Guardian Society seal. What do you think it could be?"

She halted her hand where she'd begun to revel in the feel of his exposed forearm around her middle. "You're not serious," she chastised his reflection.

He replied by flipping over the envelope. Her eyes widened. Indeed, the Guardian Society seal secured the flap.

"Lord in Heaven." She reached for the invitation.

Taylor swooped the square up and out of her reach with a

devilish chuckle—especially because he utilized the maneuver to pull her flat against him, her body molded to the muscles covered only in that irresistible white shirt and those sinfully fitted black trousers.

"Oh, no," he teased. "You can reread this a hundred times tomorrow." His tone fell to a suggestive growl. "Tonight, my Lady Stafford, we have unfinished business to attend."

As his lips dropped to hers, claiming her with slow, sensuous strokes and bold, hot pressure, her senses swam again—and the envelope could have been a summons from Buckingham Palace for all she cared.

Gwen glided a hand up the arm holding the invitation. She pulled the missive from Taylor's grip and threw it over her head as she wrapped herself tighter to him.

He groaned and parted her lips wider. She answered his tongue with eager passion from her soul, tasting the lingerings of brandy and wedding cake on his lips, learning the untamed, undaunted motions of his mouth on hers. Her fingers raked at his head and shoulders as his hands stroked her waist, her hips, her thighs.

Short of breath, they parted. Gwen smiled. Her gaze still interlocked with his, she moved her hands to his chest. She slipped her fingers down, down, releasing shirt buttons one by one. Taylor's stare hooded lower, his tongue remoistening his lips as his chest rose and fell beneath her touch.

On a hard swallow, he finally stopped her feather-light caressing. "Now you," he commanded. "Turn around."

Gwen's smile fell. "Turn . . . around?"

He only molded his chin to the crook of her neck as he pressed her against him, her back to his chest. His teeth gently caught her earlobe. As Gwen arched with pleasure, she realized what he was about.

She watched herself in the bureau mirror again. Yet now Taylor joined her there in that shiny dream world. His hands roved the silhouette of her body beneath the nightgown, traveling to the center seam every few moments to wisp another button of the clothing free . . . to reveal more of her body to his gaze, staring hot and hooded from over her shoulder.

At last, he peeled the voluminous garment away. The Gwen in the mirror stood golden and warm, nude except for the headpiece and the veil framing her from behind.

She reached for the crown of roses, but Taylor stopped her hand with a kiss. "No. Leave it."

His other hand trailed the gauze train around her, swirling the material over her breasts and belly, casting the thatch of curls between her thighs into filmy ivory mystery.

"Dear God, I've waited for this," he rasped against her nape. "I've imagined you like this . . . so many times."

"You . . . you have?"

"Mmmmm . . . yes . . . oh God, yes . . ."

His words felt so good. *He* felt so good. He made her senses soar. He made her soul fly. He unfurled her world to sweet, sensual splendor . . .

Closing her eyes to the blissful feel of her womanhood moistening for him, Gwen arched and coiled and moved against him. All the while, his hands slid and kneaded, drawing the veil across her skin in a way that reduced her to a mass of shivering, erotic need.

His fingers slipped between her thighs, pressing harder, stroking longer . . . and in a few exquisite minutes, she released all her passion with a joyous cry, in a shower of tear-swept sensation. Gwen heard his harsh breathing in her ear as she writhed against him, reaching behind to grip at his neck, his thick hair.

"My Lady Stafford," he grated to her in that shining moment, "open yourself for your husband."

He spun her to face him. She opened her eyes to the sight of Taylor entering her in a long, quaking lunge. He yanked her legs around his waist on the second stroke. Gwen watched him in transfixed ecstasy. She ran eager hands across his straining torso, causing his head to fall back on a pleasureful moan. At that, his shirt fell from his shoulders, exposing the beauty of his sweating muscles, his shuddering need.

"Christ," he suddenly groaned, shaking the bureau with his increasing thrusts, "oh, God, sweet wife, *yes*."

And at that, Gwendolen smiled, for no words could have sounded more beautiful to her heart . . . no love poem could have trilled his feelings more eloquently . . . no minister's marriage vows could have assured her more fully . . .

She was now, really and truly, married to the man she loved.

Hours later, reflections of that resplendent moment still warmed a smile over Gwen's face . . . despite the ice chips of renewed fear nicking at her spirit.

She finished tying the bow at the neck of her dressing mantle as she lowered into the window seat a few feet from the bed. Dawn still slumbered hours away, but crystalline moon glow filtered past the curtains, allowing her to distinguish Taylor's tousled hair and beard-darkened jaw against his pillow.

As she watched, her husband grunted and wrapped himself tighter around his pillow. He slept deeply, the slumber of an exhausted, satiated man.

She decided not to care if the perception proved right or not. Either way, her heart now flew higher than it had spiraled a few hours ago. Her soul followed, recognizing a gloriously intimate sense of possession.

Then the memories joined her in that heaven: joyous visions of the moment Taylor had pulled her to those sheets and taken her all over again, their second union more slow, more delicious . . . more passionate.

Yet with every kiss and caress she reexperienced, Gwen's spirit parried with blades of anxiety and doubt. And confusion.

He had *not* married her out of obligation, she tried to command herself. He had certainly not done it just to procure her the momentous white envelope from the Guardian Society. She could have flung Lady Moorford's invitation into the fire last night and he wouldn't have noticed—nor, she hazarded a strong assumption, have cared.

The rational conclusions terminated there.

In the same instant, her mind answered a yawning void to the simple, dreadful query: then why?

Why did Taylor Stafford, Baron Roseby, Earl Stafford stand before his friends and colleagues and peers at that altar and pledge himself to the freak of London . . . forever?

And the fear assaulted all over again.

She combatted the sensation by looking once more to her husband, to the shadowed sheets and blankets behind him. Cushioned in those bed linens and tangled in Taylor's arms, the fear didn't seize her once. Together, they'd formed one body, one starpoint, one fire; her husband belonged to her as surely as she surrendered herself to him.

But then came the now, the *after.* And as unexperienced and unworldly as she was, she knew a marriage's foundation depended on the after. The kisses and the passion would dim and flare at will, but the sharing and the communion burned tireless flames, steady and bright through the storms of life, supported by the endless fuel of—

Gwen's throat squeezed as her mind refused to admit the word. But her heart's answering rebuke came too loud and too true to avoid any more:

A marriage needed love.

She gulped again, squeezing her eyes shut against the refrain, now knelling a daunting score down the corridors of her conscious: *A marriage needs love . . . a marriage needs love . . .*

The onslaught continued, louder and louder. Gwen braced herself for the impact of the words on the paper-thin defenses of her soul. She wrapped her arms around her sides, fingers digging into her ribs . . .

Only the blow didn't come. No, a different force jolted the deep core of her, instead. A detonation of shock, joy, and hope—all at once.

Her eyes flew open from the intensity of the eruption. Her lips formed rasping, rapturous words with the power of it:

"But this marriage does have love!"

Now she let the tears course free. She turned her sights once more to the bed. "Yes, Taylor Stafford," she confessed on an air-soft murmur, "I love you more than I ever thought I could love a man."

The salty drops spilled from her eyes and trailed slow paths down her cheeks. As Gwen lifted a hand to wipe the tears away, the moonlight ignited her wedding ring into facets of prismic beauty . . . and her lips flew upward at the sight, half laughing in hope.

Maybe now, maybe with these rings binding us, that will be enough, her heart beseeched. *Maybe, God in Heaven help me, maybe I can teach you to love again.*

Then her eyes jerked open wider.

"Could I really do it?" she whispered in hope . . . and hesitation. Oh, did this paralyzing, inundating ache in her soul really reach deep enough for two?

Yet she already knew how to discover the answer to that. She only had to remember who opened her heart to the magical force in the first place. She only had to recall the smiles, stares, kisses, and caresses which taught her how to feel again—that filled in the holes of her life again.

In short, she only had to look at the dark warrior angel asleep on the bed. After that, Gwendolen knew, without a doubt: she could do anything.

She would help Taylor conquer his past; she would help him confront, then bury the rage, the helplessness and the guilt of his Lancer-inflicted nightmare.

But first and foremost, she'd help him get revenge. Until they found and slammed the Lancer behind bars—knowing Taylor's unwavering will, perhaps they'd just hang him themselves—she couldn't loosen the chains around his heart an iota.

And right now, their greatest chance of accomplishing that lay beneath the seal on a lone white envelope on the dark-grey carpet toward the foot of the bed—precisely where Gwen had tossed it last night before losing herself in Taylor's kiss.

Quietly, she padded from the window seat to pick up the Guardian Society missive. She turned the envelope over and held it up in the moonlight.

Her Ladyship Gwendolen, the Countess Stafford,
Wilton Crescent, Belgravia

As she stared at the elegant letters, a strange, yet not-so-strange sensation fluttered between her breasts. Gwen frowned in confusion, but as she moved back to the window seat, her glower blossomed into a full and joyous smile. She recognized this butterflying sensation with sudden and undeniable accuracy . . .

Anticipation.

Hardly believable, but true; for the first time in over two long years, she looked forward to her next ball. As a matter of fact, she could barely wait. She could hardly contain her impatience to at last corner the past, lock the monster behind bars, then begin the rest of her life.

No, she corrected herself, to begin the rest of *their* life: Taylor and Gwendolen Stafford, bound by trust, loyalty, laughter . . . and, please God help her, *love.*

Nineteen

If not for the gentle strains of the quadrille filling the Moorfords's Vienna-style ballroom, Gwen vowed she and Taylor would have been greeted by an audible pin drop. With more precision than a row of Russian ballerinas, every gaze snapped and followed the Lord and Lady Stafford as they stepped from the claret-red carpet onto the Italian marble floor.

Then the storm of gossip broke.

Oh, the tempest didn't swirl in a routine lightning flash of chatter or a wind gust of murmurs. London didn't prefer anything *that* easy. But from the corner of her eye, Gwen recognized the telltale allusions. The fans flipped open because of the "heat," only to disguise curious female titters. The oiled male heads bowed together as if discussing Gladstone's latest maneuver on Parliament, with stares fastened to her scarred features the entire time. Only after that came the normal flurries of coughs, whispers, furtive glances, and outright stares.

And like an island in the middle of a flood-brimmed lake, Gwendolen stood there solitary, embarrassed, feeling the flood rise higher and higher around her.

Until a strong hand locked around hers.

At first, suffering the effect of her dread working its numbing power so quickly, she jumped. With dawning realization, Gwen raised her eyes up Taylor's arm and torso.

He appeared even more broad and magnificent in crisp black-and-white evening attire. A breath-robbing smile still gleamed from his rugged face, eclipsed only by the stare filled with as much amber heat as the moment she'd met him in the front hall in her new emerald brocade gown.

Just remembering that moment infused a blush over her face again. She relived Taylor caressing her shoulders straight through the gown's train of gold chiffon. She smiled when picturing him ignoring the skirt's brilliant golden feathers to wrap a possessive arm around her, coaxing her close, then kissing his approval of her luxurious attire—and her adult pulled-up hairstyle.

And right here, right now, he looked as if ready to do it again. Indeed, before Gwen could voice an abashed protest, Taylor took advantage of their proper pose to pull her closer to him . . .

But when he lowered his head, his lips didn't seek her mouth. To her astonishment, he leaned over and pressed a long, loving kiss to her exposed scar. Still enveloping her in his strength and warmth, he murmured into her ear, "It seems as if everyone realizes the most beautiful woman of the evening just entered the room."

"Taylor . . ." Yet she forced herself to stop at that loving rasp. The sweet ache in her throat threatened to turn anything else into a teary delivery worthy of the Drury stage.

Indeed as if taking a cue, the orchestra broke into the moment with perfect timing. The accomplished ensemble filled the room with the beginning measures of a lush waltz.

Gwen smiled at the empty marble floor, then took Taylor's hand with bold confidence. "Dance with me, my lord husband. I want everyone to see me and my scar in your arms."

Taylor's smile spread wider, filling the room with light—and her heart with joy. He eagerly obliged her request.

They whirled through that selection and three more, oblivious and uncaring of anyone but each other. Halfway through the second tune, Gwen laughed with incredulous joy. She felt as if each step and glide peeled away another day of the last two and a half miserable years.

With equal amazement, she discovered the Gwen unveiled

by those falling layers as a Gwen she hadn't expected at all. Beyond the toppling bricks of her sorrow and guilt, she did not find the content, carefree eighteen-year-old she thought preserved there for two years.

She found someone better.

She encountered a woman now, not a girl. A woman who looked with eyes of love, not infatuated gazes to disappear at morning's light. She saw a Gwen who smiled again, but who now cherished each smile as the priceless treasure it was, not a careless trinket of flirtation.

Best of all, she saw someone she liked.

Basking in her husband's soft but intent stare, she concluded he saw someone he liked, too.

The world rushed back at them via a discreet tap at Taylor's shoulder. Her husband's face reflected the same disappointment dousing Gwen's spirits. Nevertheless, Taylor acceded to the mirthful grin dancing beneath the full grey whiskers of Lord Moorford himself.

"Understand congratulations are due for you two," the older man chuckled. "Don't mind if I take a whirl with the prettiest bride of the year, eh, Stafford?"

"Not at all, sir." But Taylor's undertone of impatience went clearly lost on Moorford, who latched on to Gwen with the tenacity of a man bent on staying for a few sets.

Gwen would have bestowed a grateful smile on the Viscount Heatherton for intervening on Moorford after the next waltz—but the young nobleman's hands roved more greedily than his gaze. She found herself wondering how to refrain from slapping him before they finished the following polka.

Bryan, bless him, rescued her from having to make that decision. She'd never been more thankful for her etiquette-defying friend, stifling a chuckle as Bryan pried Heatherton free with a glacial glare and a tap dangerously bordering on a wallop.

Bryan swept her back into the flow of the dance with practiced ease—but did not meet her grateful gaze. He directed his eyes, still a hard and frozen blue, over her head and toward the perimeter of the dance floor.

"You're the talk of the party, duck," he stated with little inflection. "Seems Taye's given your social standing the Midas Touch, despite the suddenness of the wedding."

Gwen attempted to throw off the comment with a light laugh. "If I didn't know you better, I'd say their talk bothered you, Mr. Corstairs. I thought you didn't give a whit about what people gossiped about."

"I don't." Again, his words were clipped with an uncharacteristic terseness. "The whole lot can moan about the flu epidemic for all I care. It's their bloody hypocritical backwash that galls me. They shunned you last week and the week before that; now they're tripping over each other to dance with you."

"Ohhh." She nodded at him with a knowing lilt. "*Now* I think I understand the problem. That drooping mustache of yours is because of *my* feelings. Careful, duck, those feathers on your protective wing are starting to ruffle." She gave herself a mental pat on the back for the self-conscious chuckle she coaxed from him.

"Gwendolen Victoria," he admonished, "that was not fair. Especially to the poor friend who graciously agreed to come fetch you on behalf of your husband and Inspector Helson."

Again as if the evening's events had been choreographed in a play, the dance ended that moment. In an instant, Gwen remembered why she was really here.

"Helson," she repeated. "Yes, of course. Where is he?"

Bryan answered with a smooth tilt of his head. She followed him that direction, skirting the dance floor, past the refreshment buffet, until they slipped past a carved gold door and into a sumptuously appointed sitting room.

They entered not only on the inspector, but on half a dozen other men in equally ill-fitting evening ensembles. Gwen's heart went out to the obviously uncomfortable men, but their disarray did provide a breathtaking foil for the clean-hewn lines and dark-fitted composure of her husband. Heat swept every inch of her, and it had nothing do to with her exertions on the dance floor. Concurrently, when Taylor saw her, his gaze thickened, and he left the chair all too eagerly to claim Bryan's place by her side.

"My lady," Helson addressed her with a respectful nod. "You're here. Very good. You and Lord Stafford broke the ice nicely by taking the dance floor an hour ago. Now the gala is in full force. That means we have no time to lose."

During his last statement, the inspector turned to the entire room. Fish out of water they may have appeared in their formal clothes, Helson's men fell into the swim of things as he switched to concise police language.

The inspector recounted the characteristics they assumed about the Lancer so far: wealthy, perhaps wearing the unique ruby tiepin Gwen described during her hypnosis; educated, judging by the speech snippets she'd quoted and the highborn background of all the victims; and most importantly, strong.

At least powerful enough to drag a woman away and carve her to death.

At the last assertion, Gwen reached to support herself on the rococo settee. As quickly, she berated her weakness. She had nothing to dread anymore, she *must* learn that. Taylor's arms supported her with the steel force of his own concern, and she looked around at the serious faces of each agent present.

This clearly did not make the first time their leader had briefed them on the facts. Some looked as if they'd been dreaming the details of the case for the last week. And no matter where she went tonight, one of these dauntless faces would be within sight.

With growing reassurance, she listened to Helson call off the assigned lookout stations: Adams, to the front hall, Fitzhugh, between the dance floor and the ladies' lounge, Carlyle, on patrol in the gardens . . . they even delegated Bryan an outpost, playing the charming iconoclast at the buffet line all evening.

Then Helson closed the briefing and dismissed the men to their assignments. Gwen's brow wrinkled in confusion. "Inspector," she called, "I believe you've forgotten some assignments."

One bushy brow arched at her. "I beg to differ, Countess."

"I beg to differ back." She didn't falter a step as she joined him at the mantel. "Taylor and I worked hard to get this far. We intend to be a part of it."

To her astonishment, the policeman cracked a bemused smile in reaction. He lowered those quirked lips to her fingers. "But Lady Stafford, you *are* a part of it. The most important part."

"The most im—"

"As they say in the colonies, my lady, you're the belle of the ball," he explained. "Now get out there and use that to your advantage. Meet everyone and anyone you can. Watch. Listen."

Then, banishing the smile as swiftly as he allowed it, the inspector snapped, "And bring me back some bloody great suspects."

Two hours later, head pounding and feet aching, Gwen happily allowed her husband to cut in on Anthony Pringle's incessant chatter and lead her off the dance floor.

"Was he really telling you the mating habits of Indian elephants?" Taylor teased into her ear.

She groaned and closed her tobacco-stung eyes. "In vivid detail. I thought my face was going to break from feigning an interested smile for so long."

"Do you think he's our killer?" He murmured the question as he lowered her into a velvet loveseat at the side of the room, his features betraying nothing but a new husband's adoration for his bride.

Gwen longed to raise a probing finger to that expression. Barely holding herself back from the action, she replied, "Pringle? A murderer? Only if he bores the poor women to death first."

Taylor's pout now worked to restrain a chuckle. The expression made Gwen ache to touch him. She decided she would do just that, etiquette be damned, but as she raised her hand, Taylor caught it between his own. Without warning, he tilted his lips and began to suckle her wrist with his warm, wet lips.

Gwen's breath audibly caught. Those lips curved into a knowing masculine smile.

"We're both exhausted." His breath cooled the moisture on her wrist, sending tingles into the most sensitive parts of her. "Why don't you go find us a quiet place to relax in the gardens and I'll bring out a little picnic to nourish us back to health?"

Every time, no matter what, came the awe-filled thought, no matter that even now she reminded herself they were on the trail of a killer—a killer who could be watching her this instant—this man made her forget the room, the city, the whole earth with the thrust of one brilliant hazel stare. He made her feel nothing could harm her save the absence of his magical touch.

"I love picnics," she uttered back from a dry throat.

He beamed his room-lighting grin. "I know."

"I'll meet you near the fountain in fifteen minutes."

"Ten," he countered. "And Gwen—" He squeezed the blood from her fingers before he released them. "Check in with Helson's man Carlyle so he knows you're out there."

She nodded indulgently as she rushed toward the terrace. This picnic spot had to be as perfect as their lakeside idyll in Hyde. She didn't want some other couple getting there first.

As she stepped onto the wide marble veranda, she smiled and thanked the heavens for being on her side tonight. Just like the Moorfords, God spared no expense on showing off his grandeur this evening. Diamond-bright stars glittered on a canopy of velvetine blue, which sewed itself into the horizon of gently swaying cyprus and willow trees. Moonlight blended with torch glow over the alabaster fountain and the Moorfords's prized rosebushes, then faded to silvered mystery beyond the diamond-shaped maze, toward the far side of the gardens.

Those seductive shadows caught and held Gwen's attention. Her smile widened when her exploration came upon a majestic willow tree, just to the side of the maze. The tree's branches sloped toward the carpet of lush grass, promising a private lover's haven.

The scene was perfect.

She lifted her skirts to start down the steps into the garden, but stopped at the balcony edge when Taylor's fervent request bounded to the forefront of her consciousness. *Check in with Carlyle, so he knows you're out there.*

She bobbed a hasty glance down the terrace. Carlyle's distinct red head indeed came into view—at the end of all thirty yards of the marble passageway. To take a "leisurely" stroll the entire distance, taking pains not to attract attention to Carlyle, she would miss Taylor's rendezvous time at the fountain. Perhaps she'd even forfeit their ideal picnic site.

Oh, dear. Gwen scrambled to think quickly.

At that moment, Carlyle pivoted toward her. He gave a friendly jerk of his head and a gruff wave.

Gwen smiled and waved back. Well, now. Surely that constituted checking in. She'd call it a fairly efficient check-in, as a matter of fact.

She took one more moment to peer back in at the ball through the full-length windows, wanting to inspect Taylor's progress. Judging by the determined stride Gwen had watched him direct toward the buffet when they parted, he'd make it to the fountain in *five* minutes. She prayed, for once, his quest would be delayed. She wanted to be perfectly ready for him . . .

She nearly laughed aloud when she finally located him. It seemed God was indeed set on heeding her petitions tonight—even if He had to employ Aunt Maggie to the cause.

Her poor husband hadn't neared the buffet yet. He just now maneuvered a polite escape from Maggie's grasp as she praised her new titled nephew to two of the three hundred matrons she called her "closest, dearest" friends.

Stifling another giggle, Gwen turned and hurried down the marble stairs to the gardens. She sighed in happiness, her heart tripping as merrily as the water spouted by the fountain's four carved dolphins.

She smiled as she approached the Moorfords's rose collection, taking delight in the flowers' heady fragrance. Her steps made quick, pleasant crunches on the gravel path between the rainbows of bushes. She found herself unable to resist when a bloom of richest amber invited closer enjoyment. The color reminded her of the heated silk in Taylor's eyes when he shuddered and exploded inside her.

She stopped and inhaled the rose's luxurious fragrance. Then, with a guilty blush, she plucked the flower, stripped the thorns, and slipped the bloom behind her ear.

"Very becoming," said a low voice behind her.

Her heart lodged in her throat. She ordered her knees to support her dizzying whirl. "Lloyd." She stumbled back a step. Another. "Dear God, what are you doing here?"

To Gwen's wonder, his forehead crinkled. Her apprehension actually seemed to upset him.

"Has it come to this?" he quietly asked. "Are you truly afraid of me, Gwen?"

Her amazement deepened as she searched herself for the answer—and found only hurt and anger where she once stored her thoughts of Lloyd. The next moment, she found her legs not only lacking supports to stand on, but collections of tensing muscles, clenching and unclenching as she battled the urge to hike her skirts and kick this miscreant where it would pain him the most.

"The only thing I'm afraid of, Mr. Waterston, is my husband's persistence in keeping his word." She slung the statement with reckless surety. But the confident tone felt good in her throat and sounded even better on the taut air.

"Taylor and I agreed to rendezvous out here in approximately three minutes," she continued, "and I assure you he has not forgotten the promise he made if he ever found you within ten feet of me again."

At that, she couldn't resist the temptation to draw her train around her, letting her wedding ring sparkle in the torch glow—and in Lloyd's sights. "So in the interests of avoiding bloodshed all over these lovely flowers, I'll bid you a good evening," she at last leveled. She turned from him in a flounce of brocade and chiffon.

"Gwen!" came his swift protest. She didn't break her determined stride. "Gwendolen—*wait.*"

She halted. But not from the shock at hearing the man raise his voice above a refined cough for the first time. Her heart couldn't ignore the pleading desperation of Lloyd's tone . . . the pain cracking the last word he winced at her.

Nevertheless, Gwen didn't give him the convenience of watching *her* turn to *him.* She waited. Then waited some more.

Finally, his slow steps sounded on the gravel path. He moved around her side, circling to stand in front of her.

She waited again. Lloyd emitted a long, heavy huff. He raked fingers through hair that looked well past due his bimonthly appointment with the barber.

"I wanted to say . . ." But he faltered. "I'm—I'm just sorry for the way events have gone between us, Gwendolen. I didn't mean to cause you all the difficulties you suffered."

"Yes," Gwen replied with a wary lilt. "I suffered a few, didn't I?"

Despite what looked like an effort at control, furrows marred the man's patrician brow again. "But you've come through like an ace now, haven't you?" His lips jerked into a clumsy smile. "Look at you. Darling, you're absolutely beaut—"

"Lloyd." Gwen took a sharp step to the side. "I'm not your darling anymore."

"Well, yes. You're right. I—I understand congratulations are in order, Lady Stafford."

At that, Gwen wanted to both hug and beat the bastard. Yet

she'd do neither—and judging by the furtive deception in his eyes, Lloyd knew that, too. For every time she heard somebody address her by Taylor's name, actually reaffirm she was his wife, a piece more of her melted in joy.

Anger dissipated from her like ice melting off a spring sidewalk. Subsequently, despite hating herself for doing so, she curved a bashful smile at the man across the walk.

"Thank you," she told Lloyd. "And congratulations to you, too. If I remember correctly, you and Carolyn will be celebrating your four-month anniversary next week."

Then the truly unbelievable occurred. For the first time since she'd known Lloyd, he looked about to decompose. His jaw clenched. A tremor chased its way down his body and back up again. As Gwen looked on, the possibility struck her that he might succumb to some deep emotion there in front of her.

"Ah . . . Carolyn and I aren't married."

"Not—" Gwen stammered. "What happened?"

"Two weeks before the wedding, a French duke offered for her. She . . . uh . . . well, she met him years ago, accompanying her mother on a visit to his cousin, or some such nonsense. The family decided it was in her better interests to be a duchess rather than a broker's wife."

He slammed his hands into his pockets so forcefully, Gwen expected to hear fabric rending. "She lives in Versailles now," he finished in a defeated mutter. "The Duchess of la Salle, or la Soie, or some such gibberish."

Gwen ranted at herself for the sting she blinked back behind her eyes. She forced herself to recall that Shakespearean proverb Bryan always quoted her: " '*Friend or brother, he forfeits his own blood that spills another.*' " And yes, here Lloyd stood, bleeding from the very blade of betrayal he'd dealt her. He had, in all truth, set his own trap.

The only thing was, Gwen knew how agonizing that imprisonment could be.

"I'm sorry," she said, and meant the words. "I know it's not easy to give up your dreams and expectations."

Lloyd laughed harshly. "Yes," he grated, "I imagine you do know." Slowly, almost reverently, he reached and tugged on her fingertips. "But you found new dreams, Gwendolen. You're happy now, aren't you?"

As much as she knew her words would rub salt into his wound, she replied with sincerity. "Happier than I've ever been."

"And you certainly *are* lovely tonight."

"Thank you." She shifted her hand in his, wishing he'd at last take her impatient cue, give her a polite kiss on the knuckles and leave—before Taylor saw them like this.

"Why didn't I ever notice how exquisite you are?"

Because you haven't looked *at me in two years.* "I—I don't think that matters now." She flashed a nervous glance toward the terrace. "Lloyd, forgive my rudeness, but if my husband comes out and—"

"There's nothing to forgive."

Unexpectedly, his hold tightened. His grip slithered up her arm and suctioned to her elbow. "Darling Gwen, don't you remember? It is I who came here begging your absolution."

"You have it. I told you that already." Employing the aid of a rigid step back now, she jerked her arm.

Lloyd's hold didn't yield.

Gwen shot a glare up to him.

In an instant, her flaring anger drowned beneath cold trepidation. The twilight blue of Lloyd's eyes now waned beneath the black of midnight—but loomed ten times more unfathomable than a moonless sky, ten times more terrifying.

He took a step back now himself, ruthlessly hauling her with him. As Gwen collided into his wiry frame, she smelled alcohol, sweat, and a pungent stench she'd only experienced when the wind blew the wrong way past Saint Jerome's windows.

"What on earth?" she blurted. "Lloyd, stop this. You're drunk—"

"With the thought of you." His growl reverberated through

the grip hooking around her other arm. A clump of his unkempt hair fell over that flat black gaze, turning him into a stranger, a faraway being who laughed as he pulled her harder against him, forcing her farther away from the lighted path.

Fear plundered her now. Gwen rooted her feet into the grass as deep as she could, cursing herself for indulging in Taylor's generosity and splurging on these new low-heeled dancing shoes.

"This is enough!" she charged. "Lloyd, you've gone too far!"

"Oh, no, darling." She wondered how he maintained such cool calm as he fought her increasing struggles. She gasped in shock as he wrenched her around. His arm curled a vise hold around her middle. With his other hand, he stuffed dirty cloth between her teeth and around her face.

Then he yanked her hard and fast around the first hedge of the Moorfords's maze.

"No, no," he crooned on, his stale breath at her ear. "Don't you see? I could never go too far with you, darling Gwen. You like it like this, don't you? You like it in the dark, all tied up—just like you did with the Lancer."

She screamed. She cried out with all the wrenching, terrified volume her lungs forced up her throat. But Lloyd dragged her around another curve of the maze. He headed to the middle of the giant puzzle, where even if someone heard her, came the horrifying realization, they'd have no idea where or how to find her.

"Is that why you married Stafford, darling?" the stinking snarl came again at her ear. "Is that why? Because he gives it to you just like that maniac did? Is that why you married him right after Carolyn left, and made me the laughingstock of the entire social register?"

If she had another protest in her, Lloyd silenced it when he hurled her to the ground. Gwen whimpered in pain, but he followed the jolt with his ruthless weight atop her, the spindly fingers of his hand pinning her wrists over her head. His other hand raked down her body, groping, pressing, forcing her skirts higher up her legs.

Lloyd's eyes trailed up that path for an instant, then snapped to her face again. He saw her but he didn't see her, his glare glossed over with a wild, unthinking sheen.

His sweat dripped onto her from above. The dew of the grass seeped to her skin from below. But the chill from neither set off the frantic shudders through her body.

Lloyd chuckled—a low, maniacal savoring of the moment. "I'll tell you something, darling." He finally jerked her skirt high enough to clutch at her thigh. "I'm as good as your beloved husband. And I'll show you, dear. I'll show you right now."

Gwen screamed again, but the sound seemed a water drip against the waterfall of Lloyd's grunting, taunting laughter. She squeezed her eyes shut, blocking the sight of him. Hot and disbelieving tears finally loosed across and down her cheeks. *Oh God, this isn't happening—not again, not* this.

As she felt that hateful hand claw higher on her leg, she forced herself to envision the sole hope that would get her through this agony. *Taylor. Taylor, please tell me you're there. Please tell me you love me.*

The tears flowed faster as his face filled her mind, bold and commanding, hazel gaze flickering with the force of his intent. She willed the image into more detail. *Get me through this. Dear God, Taylor, don't leave me now.*

In her vision, a strong and dimpled smile gently parted his lips. *Gwen,* he called to her, *sweet, warm Gwen . . .*

Twenty

"Gwen!"

As loud as Taylor bellowed her name on his burst into the gardens, discharging birds out of the trees as if a hunting rifle had blasted instead, his call sounded pathetic and useless in his ears. His legs felt like three-ton millstones, forcing him to skirt the fountain instead of leaping over it.

Thank God for Bryan. Thank God for Bryan. His brain thrummed with the frantic refrain; he would have spun right there and embraced the friend a pace and a half behind him if they both weren't speeding to the disaster Bryan had sighted from the ballroom: Lloyd Waterston pawing, then assaulting Gwendolen in the rose garden.

"Gwen!" he boomed again, skidding to a stop in the gravel walk between the rosebushes. He scanned the darkness for the glinting aigrettes in her hair, the glitter of her gown's train.

Instead, he spied only a lone rose in the path before him, dethorned stem snapped halfway, a handful of dark-gold petals surrounding the wilting bloom.

He snatched up the crushed flower, rage roiling in his gut. His mind's eye easily created the scene of her admiring the rose . . . leaning to pluck it . . . dropping it as Waterston grabbed her.

Damn. *Damn!* What sin had he committed, Taylor silently demanded of heaven, that he suffered this sentence of helpless fury and sickening agony *again?* Hadn't the experience, on that dismal morning when Scotland Yard paid its first grim visit on Stafford House, more than paid his debt? Hadn't the hell of losing *one* Countess Stafford been enough?

"Taye!" Bryan called with a jerk of his head, "Look there."

A few feet ahead, the path gave way to a strip of lush lawn, then the entrance to Moorford's maze. Together, they dashed there—to sight a zigzagging trail of footprints cutting a clear path through the dewy froth on the grass.

Whoever entered the maze had *not* been taking a leisurely evening stroll.

"Gwen!" This time, Taylor shouted it from the churning pit of his soul.

Bryan raced in first, cutting right at the first fork in the green puzzle. Taye launched in after him, but opted for neither direction.

He barreled straight through the hedge "wall" in front of him.

He demolished the bushes in half a dozen more places before he broke through to the center of the maze. In the middle of the court there, a gold fountain trickled water dyed the same gilt color. Rare flowers and scroll-backed benches encircled the fountain, inviting paramours to dare things as unbelievable as the view: declarations of undying love, bold proposals of marriage—

Attempting to rape another man's wife.

Taylor's gaze tunneled as he stalked around the fountain, seeing nothing but Waterston's body crouched between Gwendolen's bared legs. The bastard gripped her thighs with brutal greed; her frightened whimpers punctuated his gritted profanities.

Taylor's vision narrowed tighter. Reality submitted to a crimson fog of rage. The red murk invaded his head, taking over rational thought—exploding in his violent bellow.

At that, he saw Waterston's head snap up. Good. His vindicating glare would be the last thing the scum remembered before he died.

Taylor hurled aside one last bench and flattened a bootful

of tulips before curling fists into Waterston's wrinkled brown coat and yanking up as hard as he could. The motion sent the bastard flying, red-shot eyes now surrendered to raw surprise, into the fountain. Taylor made sure Waterston's carcass found solid landing on one of the carved Cupid's arrows pointing from the base.

But it wasn't enough. Not by half. Without thought, Taylor plunged in for the kill. His boots plunked black and menacing into the amber water. He shook droplets off his face in order to aim his grip into Waterston's collar and haul the dripping worm's face to his eye level once more.

"Yes," he agreed with himself on a vicious growl, "let me see your slimy smile one more time, you bastard—before I mash it into the hog's swill it's really good for."

"Taye!" Bryan's yell penetrated the rage just as Taye cocked his elbow to full face-ramming extension. He pushed a harsh breath past his teeth, telling himself he didn't hear the call. He didn't care about anything but the scene he'd burst in on just ten feet away; wasn't concerned with any image but the sight of his wife, still lying exposed and helpless in the grass—

He spat an oath and raised his arm a notch higher.

"Taye, for Saint Chris's sake, wait!"

Bryan's call came louder. Taye heard his friend's foot scuff the rim of the fountain. "Stay out of this, Bryan." He didn't look up from Waterston as he issued the command with a deadly, deceiving calm. "Stay the hell out."

"Confound it, you don't want to kill him!"

He cracked an evil smile. "The devil I don't."

"Taylor?"

Gwen's voice first induced amazement—instantly seeping every muscle and nerve in him. Then sheer shock, wondering how two syllables from her lips blew away his fury faster than a winter wind on a damp fire.

Then pure bewilderment, as he unlocked his elbow and sent Waterston splashing into a shivering heap at his feet.

"Taylor?" came her trembling call again. Only then did he

notice the extra light upon the courtyard. Helson and his rumple-suited agents brandished a dozen extra torches as they swept across the area like bloodhounds gone too long without the scent of a juicy fox.

Taye gladly kicked Waterston toward Helson, then stumbled out of the fountain and to his wife's side.

"Princess." He dropped to his knees before the bench she'd made her way to. "Are—are you all right?"

He touched her cheek and stroked her hair, helped her cover her legs while fighting the concern to check thoroughly for bruises. He longed to hold her, yet he didn't know *how* to hold her—

He'd never experienced this . . . *uncontrol* before. Not even with Connie. Even during the frightening times, Connie just looked up, begged him to hold her, and he'd taken care of everything. He'd been Taylor the Competent. Taylor the Commanding. So effortless, so simple.

Nothing about Gwendolen was simple.

Gwendolen had walls, layers of them, painstakingly erected with each assault on the fragile castle of her heart over the last two years. Taylor had vowed to bring down those barricades, brick by brick, touch by touch, kiss by kiss . . . and lately, he'd reaped the first brief but beautiful boons of his labor. He'd watched her ramparts start to slip, the castle shining through the gloom again.

But now he watched her scramble for the bricks to build the walls again. He looked on as she pressed her lips together into a bloodless line. Her chin jutted as she strained to gulp back tears.

"I—I think I'm fine," she answered him in a whisper. "But my hair . . ." she ran her hand over her mussed curls, "and the dress. I selected this dress for you. I knew you'd like it. Now—now it's ruined."

Her voice cracked on the last word. She curled her hand into a shaking fist, as if wanting to help Taye rip apart another flower bed—and he knew her embattlements had been torn down too far for repair this time. The remaining bricks would soon crumble . . .

And he knew it would be all right to hold her.

And he did just that.

"We'll get you another gown," he murmured as he drew her close. "We'll get you a hundred more . . . Is that all right?"

She nodded and burrowed against him. Taylor looked to the night sky and wondered if even that vast, starry canopy could encompass the breadth of his fulfillment. Sweet God, she felt so good in his arms, safe again. He wanted to hold her like this for days. He'd never let her out of his sight again.

Damn it, he shouldn't have separated from her in the first place. Not tonight of all nights. Not when she needed him most, when he knew the Lancer could wait around any corner to rectify his singular bungle. And where the hell was—

"Carlyle," he continued the thought aloud. He pulled away from Gwen to repeat the agent's name, louder. And angrier. "Where was Carlyle all this time? What the hell did he do after you checked in with him?"

Gwendolen's eyes met his with a suddenly contrite cast. Her grip tightened at his shoulders. "It wasn't his fault, Taylor." She blurted the words in a defensive rush. "He was positioned at the other end of the terrace, and I didn't want to walk all the way down there. It would have taken forever, and . . . well, I wanted to find us a perfect picnic spot . . ."

He felt himself sinking back against the bench again. The explanation added yet another snag to the tangle of comprehension balling in his gut. She'd bypassed her check-in because she was thinking of him. She'd raced through the garden, unwary of danger, because her mind focused on pleasing him. She'd even picked out her bloody dress with the hope that he'd like it.

Confusion tightened that tangle—confusion, then terror. Taylor shook his head. The concepts didn't make sense. He wasn't used to this. He didn't know how to respond to this, no matter that his wedding ring lay on her finger. The Earl of

Stafford always saw to everyone else's needs, not the other way around.

A mocking snort erupted into his thoughts. "Looking for picnic places, my arse," Lloyd Waterston's dripping lips sneered at them. "She was dawdling in the garden, waiting for any well-hung stallion to walk up and slip it to her."

The bastard had a death wish. Taye came to that fleeting conclusion as he lurched up from the bench and across the clearing. Three, then four of Helson's men sprang forward to hold him, but he bucked against them like a chained beast. His senses inflamed with an equally primal fury, an instinct only to be satisfied with the sight of Waterston's blood, which he planned to pound out of the man, fistful by fistful.

"You filthy, philandering son of a bitch!" he roared. "You've been ramming so many sluts, you can't see the sun through the smoke!"

"At least I didn't marry the smoke," came the derisive reply. "How do you sleep at night, Stafford, wondering which corner your wife will be standing on next, inviting any mucker in London to take her?"

An army couldn't hold him back then. Taylor covered the space between them in two unthinking stomps. On the third step, he smashed his fist into Waterston's jaw. The bastard hit the grass with a loud thud.

Taylor barely heard the sound. Nor did he care. "Get up," he snarled. "Get up, damn you, so I can finish you off properly in the eyes of the law!"

But before he'd finished, Helson himself broke in, broad nose huffing furiously. "Blast it, Stafford! No one is finishing off anything tonight. Your business with Mr. Waterston is completed."

"The hell it is."

"The *law* says it is!"

Taylor held his retort, but stood his ground. Goddammit, Helson *wouldn't* let Waterston walk away from this. Not with Gwendolen still behind them, bruised and trembling from the maggot's attack. This time, he'd be certain the "law" did its bloody job.

He made sure his expression said just that.

Helson, though many things, was not blind. As they squared off, the policeman's gaze bespoke clear comprehension—and perhaps a little understanding—of Taye's message, but then narrowed in preparation of his own riposte.

"My lord, I'm warning you. Step back, or I'll cuff you and take you in right beside Waterston."

Raw shock compelled him to comply. Taylor blinked against a stunned scowl. "You're—you're really taking him in?"

"Taking me in?" Waterston railed at the same time. "What the hell for? I'm an honorable man, Inspector. If Lady Stafford wishes to press charges, I assure you I will avail my cooperation to the court."

"I believe I've allowed Lord Stafford to settle up on Lady Stafford's behalf." Again, Helson's reply lilted with preternatural calm. "Though he did such a fine job, I may let him take *my* turn at your opposite jaw.

"However," Helson continued among the muted snickers of his men, "there is another, more pressing matter the Metropolitan Police have to take up with you, Mr. Waterston."

The gentle splashes from the fountain comprised an ironic backdrop for the next tense pause. If Taye didn't know better, he'd accuse Helson of milking the moment like a seasoned actor. The inspector took deliberate, maddening time to produce a battered sheaf of papers from his inside coat pocket.

Finally, Helson turned back to Waterston. "Lloyd Roger Waterson, of 512 Dover Place, it is my responsibility, as Chief Inspector of the Metropolitan Police of London, to take you into custody for questioning as to your whereabouts and doings the nights of One November 1888; of One December 1888; of Two January 1889, of Sixth of January, 1889—"

"Wait a blasted minute!" Waterston started forward, only to walk into the waiting handcuffs Officer Carlyle had produced.

"Sixth of January?" Gwen's voice interjected. Taylor turned

to see her walking shakily toward the group. "That's the night I was—the night the Lancer assaulted—"

She blinked at Helson from a suddenly pale face. "You think he's *the Lancer?"*

"You've gone off the damn rails!" Lloyd lunged against his restraints, flashing a wide and disbelieving glare. "I had nothing to do with those beastly crimes!"

Helson only raised a cynical brow and flipped to a second sheet of figures. "You were affianced to Lady Stafford," he contended. "And you were acquainted with, if not close friends to, the remaining eight victims."

The assertion jerked Taylor's brows together again. He looked over Helson's shoulder and beheld the evidence, scribbled right there on the policeman's papers—but, as much as he hated himself for doing so, a puzzled protest sprang to his lips. "No. Think about it again, Helson. I barely recognized Waterston before I met Gwen. I'm certain Constance never knew him."

Helson didn't answer. Not at first. But he raised his hand to cover a cough—a disturbingly recognizable cough. Taylor used the same perfunctory sound as a stalling measure in business meetings, when deliberating how to break unpleasant news.

Finally, the inspector muttered, "Mr. Waterston took Wednesday tea at the same parlor your late wife did, my lord. Just yesterday, the Duchess Highgrove swore under oath that Waterston presented to her Belgrave Square parlor each Wednesday promptly at four. The late Countess Stafford usually arrived five minutes later."

The policeman coughed that damn artificial cough again. "The duchess also stated that Mr. Waterston seemed quite taken with your wife. He often steered the conversation toward questionable subjects, quoting classic poets *and* Shakespeare's romantic works. Very many times, he accompanied the more . . . suggestive passages with demonstrative glances and touches."

"Wait a minute." Taylor pressed forward by a single but threatening step. "What the hell are you implying?"

Helson lifted one imperturbable brow. "I don't *imply,* my lord. I am stating fact. The fact is, that as with the other victims, Waterston seemed enamored with Constance Stafford's beauty, jewelry, and social position—"

"Enough!" Taylor snapped, the word tight and low as he gritted his jaw against the bile rising in his gut. "Enough. As if Connie would have anything to do with filth like him. Just . . . get him out of here. Get him out of my sight."

Helson, his agents, and a fiercely swearing Lloyd filed out of the maze. A minute later, as they apparently exited, a roaring cheer went up. Lord and Lady Moorford hadn't missed the opportunity to make their soirée the talk of the season by moving the entire party into the gardens for the evening's unique drama.

But thankfully, the crowd dissipated after the climax. They took their torches and noise with them. Taylor, Gwen, and Bryan sat a few minutes in silence, indulging in the courtyard's renewed peace.

Taylor finally looked to his wife. In the dim light, her eyes were dark and unreadable, the color of a troubled Irish loch. She blinked slowly, taking in the soaked bricks around the fountain, the chunks of flower bed he and Lloyd had demolished in their battle, the gouge in the hedge where he'd exploded onto the clearing.

Her gaze lifted to Bryan, standing with hands shoved awkwardly in his pockets. His mustache quirked as he cocked his jester's grin at her. She laughed back, but her chin wobbled as she rasped, "Thank you. Thank you for being here, Bryan. You're a good friend."

She maintained her composure a moment more. Then she whirled and buried herself against Taylor's chest. Her sobs shook both of them and the bench.

A violent emotion churned in Taye's own gut. He shuddered from it, longing to wrap himself around her. He managed to limit the action to his arms. He rocked her, whispering soft, nonsensical soothings against her forehead and into her ear.

"I almost married him," she choked several minutes later. "Taylor . . . Taylor, I thought I loved him. I told him I loved him. And he—the whole time he might have been—"

"Shut it out," he ordered, stroking her hair. "It's over."

"I almost married him."

"But you didn't."

"I almost married the Lancer."

"But you *didn't.*" He backed far enough away so that he gripped her shoulders, a pressure that didn't come close to the intensity pressing his heart. "You didn't, damn it. You're *my* wife now, Gwen. You're safe. And you'll be safe from now on—for always."

Slowly, wordlessly, she nodded the understanding his tone commanded. She sniffed again and brought her fingers to his face.

Her touch forced his eyes closed for a moment. Just the feel of her soft skin awakened a whirlpool of sensations in his soul, threatening his own flimsy composure at this moment. He wondered if she realized what a tumult she unleashed as she curled her head to his chest again, fitting her warmth against him, through him.

"Is it really all over?" she murmured. "Can I go to bed tonight and not fear any more of this nightmare?"

Taylor raised her fingers to his lips—if only to stay his hands from wandering elsewhere. Just her mention of going to bed, in that breathy, arousing voice, conjured incredible pictures in his mind—and an aching torture in his body.

"Yes," he managed, kissing her knuckles soundly. "Yes, everything's really going to be all right, sweetheart."

At that, she clung tighter to him. "I'm so glad. And I'm so . . . tired." The last words faded into a soft yawn.

Taylor nuzzled the top of her head. "Would you like to go home, Lady Stafford?"

"Yes. Yes, home . . . away . . . alone. Just you and me and

Danny. No more visitors. No more wedding gifts. Away, all right?"

"No more *gifts?"* he teased. Over the last week, he'd witnessed her wide-eyed shock at the inundation of tokens from his well-wishing acquaintances across the country. Once, he caught her standing in the middle of the library gaping at the finery, like a stunned Alice in her own strange Wonderland of china, crystal, and linens.

"No," she forced herself to blurt before exhaustion completely blanketed her, "no more gifts. Just—*us.* Please."

Softly chuckling, Taylor scooped her up in his arms as he stood. Bryan turned from where he plunked coins into the fountain, took one glance at them and quirked a wry grin. "Say your good-byes for you, right?"

Taye smiled back. "Thanks, friend. And give my apologies to Moorford about the damage to the hedges and the flower beds."

"After you made his ball the affair of the year? I wouldn't be surprised if *he* sent a dozen roses 'round to *you,* mate."

"Well, tell him I won't be home to receive them. I'll send him a check for the repairs from my office at Wharnclyffe."

"Wharnclyffe?" Bryan's mustache twitched. "In Yorkshire?"

"No. In the Bahamas." Taye jerked a sarcastic brow of his own. "It is, after all, my real home. The Staffords have defended that land since the 1300's, long before Stafford House was built here in the City."

"But you hate that huge place."

"No," Taye countered. "Connie hated it. I respected her wishes."

"And Gwen's wishes?" his friend prompted.

Taylor edged up another slow smile. "My new bride wishes for a honeymoon. And that's what I intend to give her, in every sense of the word."

* * *

He began the next morning.

Directly after breakfast, he whisked her to Regent Street, where he ordered a gown to replace her ruined frock—and eleven more. Then Taylor hustled her back into the carriage, flabbergasted stare and all, but only smiled mysteriously when she pointed out they'd turned the wrong way on Piccadilly.

A block later, they pulled into the Charing Cross Railway Station.

"Taylor." Gwen leaned an intent, curious gaze out at the bustling crowds and the snorting trains. "Taylor, what in the world are we doing here?"

Relishing the precious beauty of her innocent look, he only wiggled his eyebrows and inched his smile wider. Wordlessly, he swung out of the carriage. As she moved to disembark, he hauled her out into his arms, instead. Ignoring her embarrassed shrieks, to the accompaniment of approving cheers, he carried her across the crowded terminal and into the private train compartment already loaded with their luggage.

"You're insane!" she gasped as the train lurched out of the station. "Where are we going?"

"Away." He spread his hands magnanimously. "You told me you wanted to go away."

"I did not!"

"You did so. Last night, before we left the Moorfords."

"For heaven's sake, I was in shock!"

"But you said it." He lolled his head back in a teasing imitation of her befuddled state, slurring his voice. " 'Away, Taylor . . . away, alone.' "

Her jaw dropped. He chuckled harder. "Well, I'm taking you away, wife," he said. He let her see the smoldering fire behind his gaze as he added in a meaningful growl, *"Alone."*

"Danny—"

"Will be fine with Granna." Using the excuse of comforting her on that account, he moved across the compartment to her seat and wrapped his arms around her. "He's joining us in a week," he consoled, congratulating himself on making her wear a new violet walking gown out of the shop. The dress's silken material drifted erotically between his fingers and the curve of her waist.

"Joining us *where?*" She only half attempted to squirm away from his mouth, now nibbling the edge of her ear.

"Mmmmm. You'll see."

At that, he drew in a stabilizing breath. Christ, he already reeled with the hot, hard effects of her nearness, her fresh scent, the damnable temptation of this dress.

"God," he groaned into her neck. "I can't wait for you to see. Then *I* can see all of you . . ."

The shimmering stare she gave him in response choked him tighter than all her other temptations combined. With another groan, Taylor hastened across to the opposite seat again.

"Get some rest, woman," he ordered, pulling out a pillow and a footrest for her. "Because I promise you won't get any tonight."

By late afternoon, Taylor guided an open-topped phaeton down a cyprus-lined drive . . . while he anxiously watched his new countess's reaction to her first view of Wharnclyffe.

The adoring tears in her eyes rained joy down his being.

Her awe only intensified as they stopped before the main house, briefly strolled the lush front grounds, then entered the Elizabethan-style, single-parapeted mansion. And slowly, Taye felt a seed of wonder burgeon in him, too. Gwen's reverence for his home reawakened a forgotten part of his mind . . . making him feel as if he saw the estate for the first time himself. He hadn't realized how Constance's preference for the "modern edge" of things, as she liked to phrase it, had tainted his own image of Wharnclyffe's beauty, preserved from the days when knights and their ladies roamed these very stone walkways.

But today, Constance's "dangerous" spiral stairways became majestic again. The heraldic banners and vaulted ceilings of the main hall were inspiring, not "drafty." And when Gwen stopped at a stained-glass window and proclaimed the estate's "mucky" lake the most romantic thing she'd ever seen, Wharn-clyffe's master declared himself a doomed man.

Taylor simply surrendered to the aphrodisiac of her. He joined her at the window, drew her into his arms, and sank his lips against hers in a long and thorough ravishing.

Then he yanked her up the stone steps to the master bed-room without another word spoken—or needed.

"Thank you," she whispered when they got there, soaking fervent kisses to his face and neck. "Thank you, thank you; it's all so incredible. Thank you for bringing me here!"

Taylor chuckled at her enthusiasm—a desperate maneuver to disguise the knot really choking his throat. "It's a home, sweetheart," he said lightly. "Just a building and some land, a little pond and a few trees—"

"A few trees? That forest we drove through was not a few trees, my blind lord husband!" She pushed away and spread her arms, twirling around in the space before him. "And look at this—this soccer field! It's your *bedchamber!* Look at this bed—" She jumped between the dark oak bedposts, squealing as she sunk half a foot into the wide down mattress. "Good Lord, Taylor, *feel* this bed!"

He laughed again—but didn't move. Christ . . . she was so clean and bright and beautiful, a child and a woman at the same time . . . a curse and a blessing . . . a surrender and a victory.

"Come here!" she urged again. "Feel it!"

"I've felt it before, Princess."

"It's magnificent," she told him, shaking her head in awe, loosing a number of curls from her prim married-woman twist. She lowered her copper head to the pillows, in the process settling her body into an equally enticing angle across the snow-white coverlet before him. "*You're* magnificent," she de-clared in a whisper.

Taylor gulped. Ah, God. His composure could have borne any other words, any other endearment but that. Because at that moment, surrounded by the age-old magic of this mansion, he believed her words. With every drop of his blood, he believed them. With every clench of his muscles and breath of his lungs, he believed he was her Magnificent and her Incredible, her world and her all . . .

Because, God help him, in that moment, she was his.

He propelled himself to the bed in two fevered paces, molding to every inch of her in one urgent slide. He crushed his lips to hers, primitive fire taking over him as her mouth yielded to him, offering the heat of her tongue and teeth to him.

Shock consumed him as they broke apart, both gasping for air. He realized he already ground his pelvis against her, his shaft pounding, his blood burning.

"Feel what you do to me," he rasped, tearing at his trouser buttons to free himself. "Feel it. Feel *me*."

He jerked her fingers down around his length, cupping her there, her palm spreading the moist drops already on his head. She gasped. He groaned. He slided swift hands up her hips and yanked her drawers free in one furious move.

"I'm sorry," he grated, nearly losing himself then with the feel of her naked skin beneath his touch. "I'd planned to give you such pleasure. I'd planned to make it last—"

"No!" She flung her head from side to side, her eyes barely seeing him, her stare glazed over with awe-stricken desire. "No," she gasped. "I want it *now.* I need you inside me. I need you . . ." Her words succumbed to a helpless whimper as she opened to him, guiding him to the tight, wet glove of her body, raising her hips to meet his first shattering thrust.

He grasped her and groaned, pumping in and out of her sweet, silken folds. Gwen met him stroke for stroke. Her neck arched with her incoherent cries. Her long fingers grasped his thighs, then jerked his clothing away to anchor around his buttocks. She pulled him deeper into herself, as if she couldn't get enough, deeper and harder and hotter.

Jesus, it had never been so good. It soared beyond sex, beyond even making love. With each lunge Taylor felt as if he touched a piece of her soul, just for one precious, primal moment in space and time.

Until time ceased to exist . . . in that excruciating, exhilarating instant, when the world stood still, then raced forward, around him and through him. His seed exploded out of him in a lightning-hot flood. He chanted her name over and over with the exquisite tremors, only then realizing Gwen said his own name back in between shivering sobs.

Taylor kissed at her tears, stroking her hair from her cheeks. She blinked up at him, salty drops on her lashes reflecting the beauty of her eyes, the green there as vast and deep as a rain-washed meadow.

From somewhere in that rapturous haze, words suddenly brimmed to his lips. The words could have come from everywhere or nowhere; all he knew was that he couldn't stop them. They spilled out, the timeless bonds of poetry which had entwined his soul to hers in the first place. He kissed her with them, loved her with them . . .

" 'Star of my joy, art still the same . . . now thou hast gotten a new name.' " He trailed the words across her forehead, down her wet cheeks. " 'Pulse of my heart, my blood . . . my flame.' "

Slowly, softly, Gwen raised her hand to his chest, to the cleft below his throat and between his nipples. She swallowed and shivered again, then whispered just one meaning-filled phrase to him: "My heart . . . my flame."

They explored every room, nook, and secret passage of the mansion, christening every new discovery they made with a bout of lovemaking in, on, under, or against the lucky conquest. One afternoon, Taylor took her into the tall tower. Once up on the ramparts, she scurried from parapet to parapet with the delight of a real princess returning to her beloved home.

From that day on, Taye ordered their tea served atop the round turret every day, treating her to a different view and a different pastry with each sunset—both of which she devoured with uninhibited pleasure.

Alistair delivered Danny the next week. After a reunion dinner filled with his son's loquacious accounts of *everything* that had happened at Stafford House the past six days, they took the boy to the stables, where one of the prize geldings lay with her newborn foal.

As Taye expected, Danny gasped at the sleek black foal, then began to fire questions at Seth, the young livery master attending Wharnclyffe's new arrival—and hopefully, future racetrack champion.

Seth handled the queries with good-natured ease—until Danny asked where a mummy horse found a space big enough to push out such a big baby horse. As Seth scratched his head and stammered for an answer, Taye recognized his chance to slip a silent arm around Gwen's middle and guide his wife several stalls away, to the dark sanctuary of an unoccupied bay.

She opened her mouth to protest, but he slipped his tongue inside instead. He pushed her between the wood wall and his hardening body, filling his nostrils with the intriguing blend of sweet hay and her peach soap scent. The effect became intoxicating as her mouth surrendered beneath him and her hands curled around his neck.

"Taylor . . ." She sighed back a giggle as he teased the sensitive spot he'd learned beneath her ear. "Taylor, what on earth do you think you're doing?"

"Reminding you." He worked his lips under the high collar of her prim shirtwaist.

"Reminding me? Of what?"

"That you're mine."

At that, she stifled another laugh—but Taylor drew back and leveled a stare *not* meant to tickle. "I see the way that young buck Seth is eyeing the countess's beautiful body," he growled, nipping at her lower lip. "And I'm just reminding the countess that—"

"The countess doesn't need to be reminded." She took a passionate nip of her own. "The countess wants her husband, and it's only her husband she'll have."

Taylor gasped back a chuckle of his own as she gathered her skirt high, then hooked her leg about his thigh and yanked his pelvis against hers. They stole a last feverish kiss as Danny called them to come watch the foal roll over, hurriedly straightening themselves though they knew their bruised lips and glossy gazes betrayed all to any discerning eye.

Then again, Taye mused as he followed her back to Danny's side, let those eyes look. Let them look all they want, and let them see the Lancer had finally, miserably lost. The Earl Stafford had reclaimed his life, and it was sweeter, finer, more perfect than he'd ever dreamed.

I did it for you, Constance, he sent up a brief and silent prayer, *but I did it for me, too. Yet . . . you knew that all along, didn't you?*

You can rest sweetly now, Connie. The battle has been won. Your vengeance has been wrought. Everything's in place once more.

And I'll be damned if I let any murdering bastard ruin it again.

Twenty-one

Gwen guided her spirited chestnut mare back into the stables with a mixture of regret and anticipation.

She wished she hadn't commanded Taylor to finally attend his mounting business letters. If he'd joined her on the afternoon ride, as his eyes so clearly begged when they'd parted, he'd have been with her to see the twilight begin its wondrous descent over the moors.

On the other hand, now she could join him before the fire in his study and relive every detail of the scene for him—with some embellishments, of course.

She'd tell him how the wind on the amber-green grass reminded her of his touch on her skin . . . so soft, yet a softness capable of moving clouds—and her heart. She'd recount the faded copper glow of the afternoon sun through the summer haze . . . a picture so like the warm aftermath of their passion.

Maybe, if she grew brave enough, she'd tell him of the deer family which had ventured from the forest to study her. She'd describe the father and his antlers in front, mother keeping an eye from behind, the half-grown brother next to her, and the baby sister wobbling along in the middle.

And maybe, just maybe, she'd tell him how she secretly called the majestic buck Taylor and the big brother Daniel. Then, how she'd seen herself in the doe's contented eyes . . . and finally looked to the tiny baby, and thought . . .

Her relaxed walk back to the house became a race against the throb of her heart. Passing the soft orange glow emanating from her husband's study window sweetened the anticipation. Smiling to herself, Gwen yanked up her skirts and dared a rather uncountesslike sprint to the kitchen entrance of the house.

Once there, her smile spread wider. She tugged open the door and began to rave to Wharnclyffe's cook before she passed fully into the room. "Oh, Wendy. Dinner smells wonderful. What are you fattening my husband up with tonight? Quail? Or is that pheas—"

The word fizzled on her tongue as her gaze swept the empty kitchen. Cedar tables usually populated by bowls of sauces and piles of fresh seasonings lay strangely barren and clean. Gwen's footsteps clicked distinctly on the spotless tile floor . . . another abnormality; the kitchen maids' chatter usually drowned out her footsteps.

This was not right.

She pushed back the door into the dining room. The gas chandelier had not been turned up; the mahogany table lay bare but for the burgundy damask runner down its middle. The crystal and china on the sideboard lay still and empty.

Now Gwendolen frowned.

"Wendy?" she called, her voice a stranger's with its lilt of uncertainty. "Camille? Edith?" she directed to the other kitchen maids.

The entire mansion seemed to answer her . . . with weighted, ominous silence.

Fear clutched at her throat. Gwen angrily ordered the sensation away. Flinging her riding crop and short top hat to the table, she set off through the formal sitting room and toward the front hall.

Despite her inner command for logic and calm, she cried out in astonishment when a wall of ten wide stares confronted her in Wharnclyffe's dim vestibule.

"Good heavens!" She pressed a hand to her thudding heart and reached for the security of an oak side table. "Wendy—Edith—Alistair." She named a few familiar faces in the crowd of servants, glaring in particular shock at the lofty butler. "What are you all doing here in the dark? For goodness' sake, it's almost dinnertime, and his lordship has been working all—"

"His lordship doesn't want any dinner, m'lady." The petite Camille bobbed forward with the interruption, then bit her lip self-consciously. "Begging your pardon I mean, m'lady," she mumbled. "But . . . he told me . . ."

Gwen blinked at the maid, fighting the odd force twisting her chest as she listened to Camille's words. But she couldn't dismiss the hesitant edge of tension to the girl's voice—the very same way everyone had spoken to her in the days after her "incident." As if everyone knew some huge, horrible secret but her.

"Told you what?" she finally stammered.

"My lady." The matronly Wendy stepped forward, contradicting Camille with a tone of flowery—and clearly false—comfort. " 'Tis nothing to overset yourself about. 'Tis just that it would seem best to leave his lordship alone for the night—"

"Told you *what?*" Gwen shouted the demand at Camille now, spinning and spearing a resolved glare into the maid.

Camille gulped. Then, in a sudden and frightened rush, the story spilled from her lips. "I just went in to offer him tea . . . his lordship said no. His voice sounded odd. Like a bear's growl. I asked if he was all right. Well, I can't repeat what he said to that. He told me to leave. I was worried by then. I asked if I should send a stable boy for you, my lady. That's when he—"

The maid teethed her lip again. Her eyes darted over Gwen's shoulder; obviously Wendy had wielded a warning glare.

Gwen seized Camille's shoulders. "What? Devil take it, Camille, I'm not going to throw you out! What did he do?"

The maid sighed in resignation. "He threw the crystal vase at me, m'lady."

Gwendolen released the maid's diminutive shoulders, suddenly depleted of the strength to hold on any longer. *A mistake* came the simple, almost effortless thought. This was just a mistake—or a sadistic joke. Taylor, *her* Taylor, who kissed her scar as if it were a beauty mark and held her close even after hearing the morbid details of her attack, didn't throw vases at kitchen maids. Murdering frauds like Lloyd Waterston did.

"That's ridiculous." She heard herself laugh at them all. "Alistair?" She turned, searching for the kind face in the midst of the gaping servants. "Alistair, surely you don't believe this. Why didn't you go to him?"

The butler's grey eyes sagged—*not* a successful remedy for the strange knot forming in her stomach. "My lady, I went to the study as soon as the maid related her story. I do say I found his lordship in the same strange state. Beg pardon, but I am hesitant to repeat our precise exchange in mixed company. I'm afraid . . ." The butler coughed discreetly. "Well, my lady, I'm afraid he's been imbibing."

Her reply echoed in her head as if spoken far away, through a dark mist. "Wh-what?"

"I was hesitant to presume it myself," Alistair replied into the quiet, almost surreal tension. "In my ten years of employ, I've never seen his lordship in this sort of state. Not even after the first countess—" an embarrassed frown snagged his features, "well, I assumed he was ill. His lordship promptly corrected me."

Silence pressed in on them again. Gwen stood with the small group a moment; as erect as a stone statue . . . with all of its limbs snapped off. What in the world had happened? What demon had taken over her husband in the short hours she'd been gone, transforming a trusted core of servants into a frightened huddle in the hall? What disaster had Taylor come across in his business papers that he sent even Alistair away without a word?

It didn't make sense. She almost laughed once more as she remembered Taylor's long-ago dissertation on those "qualities" of his which would bring her back into society. The Earl Stafford didn't live off his title; if one of Taylor's ventures failed, he had a dozen more to juggle. Saints, even if all the projects crumbled at once, he'd explode from the rubble, level his warrior's glare at the world and rebuild the mess with his own stubborn hands.

He wouldn't drink himself into a vase-hurling oblivion.

What the blazes was going on?

Gwen whirled from the group and steeled her sights on the study door. "I'm going to him."

Wendy and Camille's gasps of protest buffeted her like a gale wind. She closed her eyes in thanksgiving as she heard Alistair step forward to hold them back.

Forcing down a long, even breath, she raised her hand to knock at the looming door. The next moment, just as decisively, she dropped her arm. She reached, turned the knob, then stepped into the dim room unannounced.

Damp permeated the air. Heavy, unfamiliar smells pinched her nose into a grimace. Potent sulphur tendrils curled out from the dying fire; entwining with the odor of more decay: old paper, aged leather, dusty books and bookshelves. The only light came from the lamp on Taylor's desk, flame turned low, casting most of the room into shadows and dark corners.

She took another step into the room.

One of the shadows near the window moved. Tall. Broad. Leaning a forehead of unruly hair to the darkened pane.

"Taylor?" She took another tentative step. She didn't know this world, still had difficulty connecting this grey obscurity to the man who'd shown her light and life again. She refused to believe it. "Taylor?" she called softly again. "It's me."

"Get out."

She wouldn't have heard the order but for the dank stillness in the room—and the eerie gruffness in his voice. For a long moment, Gwen stood frozen, unsure how to respond, forgetting every assurance she'd dictated to herself in the hall.

In that silence, she saw his other arm raise, fingers clenched around a tumbler. He tossed back his head, hurling what must have been half the contents down his throat, giving forth a harsh gasp after.

Alistair was correct. He *had* been drinking. With a vengeance. The fact should have put her on alert, perhaps frightened her. But that option didn't enter her mind. Gwen set her chin and started toward him again.

Only instinct stopped her when he drew back his fist and drove it into the wall.

"I said *get out.*"

He issued the command twice as lowly—four times more viciously. She looked at the strained breadth of his back. She followed the line of his arm to his fist, still shaking against the chip he'd put in the paneling.

A horrible but irrefutable force pulled her closer to him. She moved one wobbling step. Another. But she issued her response clearly, steadily. "No."

He turned on her. For an instant, sharp and torturous, their gazes met. Gwen battled not to clutch her stomach at the physical blow she felt. In his red-rimmed eyes, she confronted pain and fury—and hate.

"For God's sake, Taylor." Her voice sounded small and feeble, shaking with every drop of dread flooding her—and yet that force drew her closer by another step. "What is it?"

She knew the wild urge to slap him for the laugh he sneered at her. "You're beautiful when you cry," he slurred, reaching a rough hand over her cheek before wheeling around to the desk. There, he swept up the near-empty brandy bottle and tipped it to his lips.

"Stop it!" she ordered. She followed him, jerking the bottle away from behind. "You've had enough already. Talk to me, damn you."

"Damn *you!"* He yanked the bottle back, only to hurl it across the room. "I told you to get the hell out!"

"And I said no!"

"So help me God—"

"You'll do what?" She thrust her chin higher, deliberately taunting him. "You'll say what, Taylor? Tell me. *Tell me!"*

He flung the tumbler then, scowling as the crystal shattered into a Landseer original on the wall. She never considered him more the savage warrior—only Taylor looked about to make war on *her.*

Even as the thought seized her, he unleashed a raging, gut-deep snarl, spinning to add another dent in the wall. He cursed her again. He unfurled his fist long enough to twist fingers into the dark-blue drape and pull hard, hanging rings popping. He dragged the heavy material across the room behind him.

"Damn you, damn you," he continued the inebriated litany, "damn her. Ah God, damn her . . ."

Gwen turned as he chanted the curse five or six more times, changing the blame at that same point in the middle. Desperately, she wondered who this new "her" was . . .

Or perhaps her husband had just gone mad in one afternoon.

She stifled a sob at the paralyzing thought. *Dear God,* she prayed, *don't take him away from me now. Not now. Not like this.*

As if in answer, the seemingly dead log in the fireplace flared with a reserve of yellow flame. Gwen blinked in curiosity as the light danced over the Turkish rug—to illuminate a strange pile of papers collected there. At first, she just asked herself why Taylor would leave stacks of business records lying on the floor like that—

Then she spied the red satin ribbons binding the papers together.

Business correspondences did *not* come tied with red satin ribbons.

Gwen crossed the room, kneeled before the fire and slowly picked up a ribbon-tied packet.

As she lifted the pile, she noticed the faded edges to each page. Yet despite the letters' obvious age, they smelled as if they'd been dunked in expensive perfume just yesterday. Against her will, a deep feminine instinct stirred—in the pit of her stomach.

She willed her fingers to tug the ribbon free. Her throat wrenched in a knot before she finished unfolding the first thin sheet. She'd recognize the elegant feminine handwriting anywhere. The style had been ingrained to her memory since she'd first seen it on the back of Taylor's "lucky" calling card.

Constance Stafford had penned this letter.

My Darling Kit,

I miss you more than a flower misses the sun. I feel myself wilting without your kisses, withering without your body to nourish me . . . oh, darling, how can I bear it another day?

But bear it I must. Until this abysmal Orphan Society ball is over and done with at the end of the week, I must play the part of Taylor's dutiful countess—a role I accomplish so well only because the thought of you is my muse—

Gwendolen thrust the letter away. She couldn't read any further. Shock and rage churned a nauseating sea in her belly. Her lap still cradled the remainder of the packet; she flung it away as if the pages had coiled into poisonous vipers.

For a long moment, she stared at the scattered papers . . . then her stare widened, noticing the multitudes of other mounds across the floor, some inches thick. All of them reeked with that cloying perfume. Gwen remembered the scent well. It permeated the air of the downstairs gallery in Stafford House—the room she'd found Taylor in on that fateful morning, pouring out his heart to the woman he so desperately missed.

"Dear God." Furious tears leaked from her eyes, burned down her cheeks. She pressed fingers over her lips, struggling to stay the hot flood of disgust . . . She made the effort in vain.

"I believe you just read a chunk of the Kit phase." Taylor delivered the grim statement from the chair he'd slumped into at her right. Gwen turned to him, yearning to reach out to him—terrified to touch him. He still had the curtains in tow. He wiped a hand over his face, the strong brow, nose, and jaw covered in sweat, shadowed with fatigue.

"Th-the what?" she stammered back.

He closed his eyes as if to absorb the pain from his flinching features. "Lord Christopher Colcott, if I remember correctly. He and his mouse of a wife were frequent guests just after Danny was born. I assumed it was because they wanted inspiration to start their own family." He snorted in dark humor. "I assumed wrong, aye? It wasn't my *babe* who inspired the bastard at all."

"Taylor." She gave in to the longing, stretching a hand to him. "Taylor, I'm so—"

"Don't." With barely leashed violence, he shoved her away. "Don't." He snorted again, this time twisting his lips in grim irony. "To think I almost battered Helson to a pulp that night at the Moorford Ball, just for hinting at this. The man was right. He only states the bloody facts."

He rose then, dropping the drapes to scoop up a handful of more crumpled letters. "Kit grew tired of the game soon enough, though. He only lasted three months. Take a look at the American captain's letters. It was a 'serious' relationship with that one. A whole year."

"Merciful Father," she gasped.

"And he wasn't even the trash who got her killed."

"What!"

In response to her cry, Taylor threw another letter to her. This missive came scrawled in a strange, scratchy hand.

Constance, My Beauty,

It's been three days. Seventy-two hours of hell for me. I must see you. I know T. S. is speaking at his business club tonight. Make your excuses early and come to me. I've reserved the usual suite at the Savoy.

Don't disappoint me, my love. I need you.

Your Burning Beast

She swallowed back the scorch of bile before she read the most agonizing line aloud. "It's dated July 7, 1889," she rasped. "Nearly two years ago."

"Yes, it is." The words came low, taut, like a thunderstorm gathering force on the horizon. With the same strained tension, Taylor rose and stalked back to the window.

"The night she was murdered," Gwen softly stated.

"Imagine that."

"Then she was out on that street because—"

"—she went to meet her lover."

"Dear sweet God."

She looked to where the bare window framed him, his arms stretched out to grip the wall at either side, head dropping between his shoulders. Enduring a torment she could only begin to fathom.

"Goddamnit," he finally growled. "Goddamn her." His left fist thundered against the wall. "Goddamn *me.*" His right fist.

"No," Gwen protested, pushing to her feet. "You can't point the blame now. For heaven's sake, Taylor, not at yourself—"

"The hell I can't." His voice dropped to that hating snarl again. With each word, he slammed an opposite fist into the paneling. Left, right, left, right.

"I can point my blasted finger wherever I want to," he went on. "My finger has earned the bloody damn right. My moronic, fool-trusting, cuckolded finger can point wherever it damn well pleases!"

"Taylor—"

"Shut up." He gritted the order as blood oozed from the broken skin of his knuckles. He continued to pound.

"Taylor, dear God—"

"Shut up!" He grunted in pain and kept on hitting.

"No! You're hurting yourself!" She threw herself at his back, pulling on him with all the strength she had.

Taylor roared. He wrenched from her, breathing with the guttural pants of a rabid wolf, turning a glare on her aglow with wild yellow light. "Damn you! You have no right!"

By instinct more than rational thought, Gwen stepped back. But he came after her with a measured, predatory tread. "You have no right," he repeated with that same feral hatred. "Damn you, Connie, you *had no right.*"

The chill of the room seeped into Gwen's bones. "Taylor," she forced out, "I'm not Constance. Look at me. I'm *not* Constance."

"Danny. Your son, Connie—your son! If not for me, then couldn't you consider your own boy? Didn't you think of him before you went roaming the streets by yourself?"

The table and lamp at her back couldn't have picked a better moment to interfere. Gwen dodged around, positioning the furniture between them. "That was the past. Constance was the past, Taylor. Constance is dead. I'm Gwen!"

"You offered yourself to him like a common whore." The lamp flew from his fist; the table surrendered to his vicious kick. "You were so hot for that young stallion's rod, you got yourself killed like a ten-pence harlot!"

"Stop it!" Gwen shouted, racing toward the more solid barrier of the cherry-wood desk. "I'm not Constance. She's dead, Taylor—she's gone! Let it go! Let it—"

"No!" One moment she was three paces ahead of him, the next Taylor had become a flying wall, ramming full speed at her. He slammed her across the desk, scattering ledgers and pens and brass boxes as he pinned her atop the blotter.

She regained her equilibrium, only to blink up into his wolf's snarl, his fury-filled stare. She gulped, but the action brought a strange, terrifying awareness of her throat, within inches of his squeezing, lethal grip.

"You—died—for—lust," he finally grated. "You died—for nothing." Now breathing hard, he pressed his wet forehead to hers. A shudder claimed his whole body. "Ah, God . . . she died for nothing. The fight, the quest, the last two bloody years. It was all for *nothing.*"

"No." Gwen shook her head. She lifted her lips, pressing his in a soft but determined supplication. "No, it was part of growing. It was part of you and me. But now it's part of the past and we'll go on—"

"Stop it." He jerked away. "Stop it, damn you. It all doesn't come tied up in a perfumed bow like that. Lives can't be pasted back together, good as new."

"Yes, they can. You showed me they can! Taylor, *you* showed me. Look at me, Taylor. I'm Gwen. I'm your future. I'm your wife. And I . . ." She swallowed, gazing up at him through the haze of her tears, "I love you."

He snapped his stare back at her.

His features betrayed all the emotion of tempered steel.

"The hell you do."

He drove his mouth to hers, twisting cruelly, jerking her lips open to admit his tongue. Gwen yielded with whimpering abandon, giving him only warmth and softness and acceptance. When he pulled away, breathing even harder, she didn't release him from her gaze.

"I love you," she whispered again.

"Shut up."

He dismounted from the desk long enough to tear off her boots, shove up her skirts and jerk away her riding trousers, leaving her lower body naked to his hot and emotionless scrutiny. He ran a hand over the burgeoning swell between his legs as he raised one knee between her legs. He hiked up the second knee a moment later, spreading her wider.

"This," he told her as he opened his trousers and released himself into his hand, "is love, sweetheart. This is all there is."

Gwen watched him through a fog of feeling, her tears framing the sight of him stroking himself, growing harder and angrier. "That's not true," she whispered. "You know it isn't."

He shook his head. "This is all I know."

"It's not!" She squeezed her eyes shut.

"This is it." His weight pressed over her. "Raise your legs, wife. Take me now. Take my *love.*"

Hating herself for her ready reaction to his words, she did

his bidding. Gwen arched into him as he slid far inside her. He blasted a harsh moan against her ear. She wrapped her arms around him, taking his body as she also prayed to take his pain, yearning to heal him . . . needing to love him.

"I love you," she cried out again, willing their hearts to meld as easily as their bodies.

"There is no love." He thrusted harder. "There is only this."

"There *is* love—"

"No!"

"Yes!"

"No, damn you! No—"

The word broke off into gasping groans as he slammed a long, hot climax into her, body arching, head thrown back. When the tempest died, he remained that way for a frozen, interminable moment. Gwen almost raised a hand to see if he still breathed . . .

Until he fell forward with a primal, grieving shout, his body collapsing atop her as his throat erupted with violent sobs.

"It's all right," she told him, crying with him, still holding his body inside her. "It's all right now, my love."

He didn't negate her. He didn't swear at her. He didn't do anything but hold on tighter and pour his agony out into the crook of her shoulder. Gwen cradled his head there, urging him on . . . imploring to God that they'd weep enough of a flood to wash the ghost of Constance Stafford away forever.

Twenty-two

In some dark hour of that night, Taylor had finally slipped from her, stumbled to the sofa, and passed out into an exhausted slumber. Gwen rose after him, biting back the pain from joints which had lain crushed to a desk blotter for hours—yet thanking God for every bruise and crick. Her body willingly paid the price for the hope now sparking her heart . . . the desperate belief that at last they'd conquered the storms of the past. That now their future lay ahead with no more secrets or fears; a horizon of promise . . .

She had no idea that horizon hid a darker tempest than she ever imagined.

Three weeks went by—as Taylor's ice-hard wall of anger only seemed to grow. Barely a nick of a smile appeared in his battlements. Certainly not a sliver of warmth or a hairline crack of trust. He sealed himself deeper into the cold fortress every day, retreating farther into his bulwarks of misplaced bitterness.

Even on an especially warm July morning, that freezing front penetrated Gwen's slumber, forcing her to shiver awake. She clenched herself against the chill even as she tried, for the hundredth time, to fight the jolt of despair at looking over to Taylor's empty pillow.

Today, the cushion matched his unused side of the bed, too. But that observation didn't come unexpected. Over the last weeks, her husband spent most his evenings in long, silent hours behind the closed study door, bitterness and brandy his only companions.

Gwen had, of course, gone to him again. She still did, every evening. But now her appeals met only that maddening wall of bare civility. Her husband took time for a polite nod, perhaps an obligatory bow . . . nothing more. He certainly didn't take the time to look at her.

If he did, she wondered if Taylor would notice the changes in her . . . the subtle but monumental changes. She climbed out of bed now to stand before the mirror and make sure the transformation still showed: her hair and skin, gleaming with an extra "glow," her breasts, rounder and fuller, pushing at her nightgown's neckline, and her belly . . . skin stretching more taut over the precious swell every day . . .

The swell of Taylor's baby. Their baby. On his clandestine visit last week, Dr. Ramsey not only confirmed her intuition, but stunned her by estimating the babe was four, perhaps even five months progressed. The "cycles" she'd had, he further explained, were just spotting, normal in light of the stress she'd been through.

So it was real. Stafford House would receive a new life for Christmas.

She'd never been more happy.

She'd never been more agonized.

Nevertheless, as she trailed her fingers across her belly, she caressed reverently, already loving this child with a devotion past description. She wondered if the tiny being could feel her adoration yet. She wondered if the little heart beat in joy at her touch.

She wondered if the innocent soul ached with her confusion.

Beyond her control, her hands balled into fists. She pressed her lips together until they trembled. A sob escaped her anyway.

"I'm sorry," she rasped to the life inside her. "Little one, I'm so sorry."

The bedroom door creaked, startling her emotions into

check. Gwen sniffed hard and smoothed back her hair, hastening to put herself back together, but the damage had been done. She looked up to her reflection: a red-eyed, swollen-lipped mess.

She wanted to cry harder.

"Now, now, sweetie." Wendy's doting croon came from behind, followed by the clink of a morning tray. "Fighting back more of those expectant mama tears? Don't ye remember what the doctor told ye yesterday? Don't fight it. Let the changes happen."

Despite herself, Gwen laughed. The sensation felt oddly wonderful. She threw up surrendering hands. "I remember, I remember."

She turned as the kitchen mistress bobbed her capped head in satisfaction. "All right now," Wendy stated, bustling about to straighten the bed. "I've brought ye some tea, plain Earl Grey; what do ye fancy for a breakfast to go with it?"

"Breakfast?" She echoed the word in a moan more than a voice. She held up both hands again, this time in supplication. "No breakfast, Wendy. Not yet. Please—"

A strange tug at her abdomen forced her to punctuate the plea in a gasp. Gwen looked to Wendy, concluding the woman's startled eyes and gaping mouth mirrored her own. "Good heavens," she murmured, submitting to a little laugh. "I think our new Stafford just kicked for the first time."

"Truly?" Wendy giggled herself as Gwen guided her hand to the tingling spot. They fell into anticipating silence. Moments later, a tiny but distinct rap came at their fingertips. "My lady," the woman exclaimed, " 'tis wonderful!"

Gwen nodded through a renewed onset of tears. "It is, isn't it?"

Another silence stretched. But no joy marked this taut pause. The summer sun began to glimmer through the windows—directly onto the thundercloud of Wendy's features. "But it's not right, either," the woman growled. "Ye should be sharin' this moment with yer holy wedded husband, not the kitchen help."

"You're not the 'help,' " Gwen argued. "You're a godsend." She crossed and opened the armoire to search for one of the few gowns she hadn't started to bulge out of.

Wendy watched her search in knowing silence. "He'll see it himself before too long," the woman said solemnly.

"I know."

"What do you think he'll do if he finds out like that?"

"Wendy, please—"

"It's a question you'll have to answer, Countess."

"But I don't know the answer!"

She tried to press back the sob in her voice. She might as well have tried to untie the knot in her heart. She spun on Wendy, leveling a determined gaze as she declared, "I only know I won't announce something like this to the—the *thing* he's become."

Her friend's round features pursed in a frown. In response to Wendy's unspoken confusion, Gwen arrowed a stiff finger at the floor. "The man who passes out in that study each night is not my husband, Wendy. He's not Daniel's father. He's not even the man who sired this baby." She raised a tight fist to the middle of her stomach. "He's become Constance Stafford's legacy of hate. The trust she shattered . . . the knight she killed . . ."

Her voice faded beneath the despair of her words as she moved numbly to the window and looked out. Wharnclyffe's lake sparkled in the new day's sun. The sapphire waters supported fairy-tale swans. The fresh-cut lawns radiated lush green warmth; an endless cyan sky stretched above all the beauty.

Gwen turned her gaze east, past the stables and over the cobblestone bridge leading into the forest. And on that bridge, as she'd done so many times in the last three weeks, her imagination created Taylor from the feet up . . . legs braced in a proud warrior's stance, head held high, chest thrust into the wind—all encased in a vestment of blinding silver armor.

"But he's still a knight," she rasped to that image with a tremulous smile. "He's *my* knight."

She smiled wider then, the words a healing warmth on her tongue and her heart. "And he won't abandon his lady, Wendy." Confidence swelled her voice. "He'll be back—and I'll be there to tell him I believed he'd be." She turned and leaned against the sill, folding her arms confidently over her chest. "And then I'll tell him just what havoc his *lance* has wrought."

The words, she concluded, had become a lucky omen. Not only did one of her looser-fitting tea gowns—a luxury of sea-foam-green cashmere she thought she'd left back in London—magically appear in the back of her armoire, but Gwen's heart skipped as she descended the stairs to hear the amazingly lucid voice of her husband.

She stopped and listened for a long minute. Taylor discussed the care of Wharnclyffe's newest foal with the stable master, Seth. She smiled. The young man hung on her husband's every word, responding with a swift and worshipful "yes, my lord" and "certainly, my lord" following every statement. As the men crossed the front hall, she watched Seth's blond head nod eagerly, even noticed him trying to copy Taylor's confident stride.

But the lad stopped when he sighted her on the stairs. "My lady," he blurted. "Good morning. You are looking radiant this day, may I say. May I suggest?" he bumbled on, struggling to correct himself.

Gwen masked her laugh behind a warm smile. "Thank you, Seth," she answered smoothly.

Poise didn't come so easily when she pivoted to her husband. He'd thrown his wall of demeanor up again, stark and cold; apparently a snag of lint on his arm had become more interesting than her. "Taylor," she greeted, unable to erase an underline of question from the word. "Good morning to you, too, my lord."

He stared to the door as if seeking escape from a wart-covered hag. "Good morning, my lady."

Again emulating the employer he revered, Seth's features dropped to a seriously-miened scowl. "By your leave, my lord, I'll be seeing to those additions in the colt's diet now." At Taylor's nod, he dashed toward the stables by way of the kitchens—as rapidly as he could.

In the ensuing silence, Taylor checked his watch twice—and didn't look at Gwen once. "I have to go, too," he at last stated. He reached for the stand where his coat and hat hung readied.

"Taylor." Her tone no longer questioned. Blatant desperation took its place. She didn't care. "Taylor, we have to talk."

"I have a meeting with the overseer in ten minutes. And there's a problem with root rot in the forest. I'll be back late."

"Taylor, I'm—"

"Don't hold dinner."

"—Pregnant."

Her announcement echoed off the back of the slamming door.

She didn't feel him get in or out of bed that night. She supposed sobbing herself to sleep rendered her too exhausted to notice. Gwen moved through the next five days with distant attention, her mind centered more on the ceaseless litany of her heart and soul. *Please God, bring him back. Please God, don't let Constance win this time. Please God, not this time; not when there's so much to lose.*

And despite the growing desperation of her entreaties, she couldn't contain a gape of surprise when she rounded the corner into the dining room that Friday evening—to behold her husband awaiting her in spotless dinner attire.

Wordlessly, Taylor rose to guide her to her chair. As if taking a stage cue, Gwen stepped back. She couldn't help it. He looked her modern warrior truly come to life now, made of such perfect dark lines and flawless masculine grace that she thought herself dreaming . . . and if so, she didn't want a touch to wake her up.

"I—I've been dining with Danny lately." Her muddled mind refused to produce anything else.

"Danny was invited to a party at LaTerre Court."

Ah, reality once more. His polite but emotionless response stripped away the fantasy swiftly enough. Gwen blinked slowly, still assimilating the words beyond his aloof mien.

"Where his friend Johnny lives?" she replied. "I didn't know a thing about it."

"Because I made the consent for him." With the same cool authority of his voice, he scooped up her hand and guided her fingers beneath his forearm. But when he started for the table, Gwen refused to follow.

"I still didn't know a thing about it," she protested.

For the first time in nearly a month, their eyes met.

Her heart knew only wrenching disappointment in the moment. Gwen had expected . . . well, *something.* But absolutely nothing answered her gaze's fervent search. No determined copper fire. No probing amber light. Not even an angry black fleck or two.

Just one curiously cocked eyebrow over a flat and disinterested stare.

"I made the consent for my son," Taylor repeated. Like his stare, no challenge crackled the words. No fire. A strange, sad conclusion reverberated through her soul: none was intended. *I made the consent for* my *son.*

He'd issued her a command, simple and straight.

"So that's the way it is, then?" The words spilled from her in a rasp. "All the happiness we dug out of the mud of our lives, all the joy we built . . . is it just orders and obeyance now, Taylor?"

A nerve jumped in his jaw. Otherwise, she might as well have recited the rate of the Arctic ice flows to incite the reaction he gave.

"Stop it," he leveled without inflection.

"Answer me!" she persisted in a hiss. "Is this what you want, Taylor? This lie of etiquette and decorum?"

"Don't talk to me about lies." He jerked from her with sudden ferocity, whirling to grip a dinner chair with clenching, heaving muscles.

Gwen couldn't help a bitter laugh. "Oh, yes. I forgot. You're the expert on lies now. You've had enough time to justify that, haven't you, locked in that study, wallowing in yourself!"

"Wallowing in *what* self?" Oh, his eyes flared to life now. As he spun at her, Gwen stumbled back from the raging fire of his glare. "I have no *self* anymore, lady! Everything I was, everything I based my bloody existence on—"

"Is dead!" Gwen finished in a shriek. Her cry resonated off the tableful of crystal between them. She sucked in a shuddering breath, more for composure than survival.

"She's dead, Taylor," she choked again. "Yes, Constance lied to you. But Constance is *dead.* She's paid for her sins. Don't make *me* pay for them, too!"

Every muscle in her body ached with the effort to hold her tears. The baby shifted and kicked hard, seeming to sense her unrest. But she allowed only her fists the luxury of coiling in the shelter of her skirts, wishing Constance Stafford's soul would materialize just once, to receive the pounding delivery of her frustration and fury.

"Damn you," she winced into the brittle silence. "Damn you, Taylor Stafford. I'm Gwendolen. I'm your wife." *I'm the woman who carries your child this very moment; who wants to tell you so badly . . . wants you to see so badly. Can't you see me growing with your seed?*

"I'm Gwen," she repeated. "Don't you understand? I'm *not* Constance."

Their gazes confronted again. Again, Taylor betrayed nothing—just before stating, "And I'm not hungry."

He departed the room on noiseless boots. He didn't look back. The same way Gwen retreated to her sitting room . . . to share her silent tears with her unborn child.

* * *

"So will ye be comin', my lady?"

Camille twisted nervous fingers together as she asked the question the next morning, when Gwen sought the warmth of the kitchen to ease the dreary chill of her heart. She didn't regret her action. She'd entered in time to hear the pretty kitchen maid share joyous news, now spicing the air more potently than the fruit tarts in the oven.

"Do you really think I'd miss an occasion like your engagement party?" She laughed as she crossed the room to pull her friend into a tight embrace. "Congratulations, Cammy," she murmured as she did. "We're all so excited for you. Seth is a good man. He'll be a good husband, too."

"He's good, all right," another maid broke in with a distinctly feminine smirk. "If the way they're wrapped around each other every other minute is a sign!"

The round of bawdy laughter acted like a bellows on poor Cammy's cheeks. Nevertheless, the girl turned a joyous grin back to Gwen. "The party starts around six, at the boathouse. It won't be much, just a way of saying our thanks to all the kind people at Wharnclyffe—especially ye and the lordship." She looked down and shrugged shyly. "It truly means the world that ye want to come and wish us well."

At Camille's inclusion of Taylor, Gwen pressed her lips together against a grimace of discomfort. "Well, it means the world that you invited . . . us," she improvised. "But I think his lordship has . . . um . . . an important meeting tonight. He'll be upset to miss the fun. But you'd better save a seat for me!"

"I shall," Camille affirmed with a smile that indicated Gwen had pulled off a performance worthy of the Haymarket.

She dressed simply for the party, selecting a Roman-necked, drop-waisted gown in a muted spring rose—the color to lift her spirits, the style to hide her expanding figure. Gwen decided the results fair on the first count, a resounding success on the second.

Still, as she crossed the lawn to the boathouse, where space had been cleared and doors thrown open for the festivities, she felt about as gainly as one of the ducks waddling at the water's edge. She could only imagine what creature she'd compare herself to in five months.

But she promised God she'd feel as light as a butterfly if He returned Taylor to her side again.

As swiftly as the thought snuck up on her thoughts, Gwen cursed it. The increasing hopelessness of her wish attached more leaden weight to her steps.

She stopped in the darkness beneath a willow, leaning against the swayed trunk as a portrait of her husband swept her mind's eye . . . the portrait she now kept adamantly locked in her heart like a precious memory, for fear the image would soon become that.

But tonight, just for a moment, she pulled the picture out and looked. And yearned. She envisioned Taylor's eyes, alive with the brilliance of a thousand gold medallions . . . and his off-center grin, melting her heart with its white splendor. She sighed as she saw the crinkles at his temples, teased by the sensual chaos of his hair. She saw Taylor laughing, joking, just as the party-goers did ten yards away.

I miss him, her soul cried out. *Dear God, I miss him, that bastard.*

Just then, an eruption of masculine laughter broke into her grief. Or had her imagination made the sound real? Especially because the bellow sounded just like—

Gwen shook her head, denying the possibility. But when she compared the sound from the boathouse to the echoes in her head, to the reverberations of Taylor's laughter . . .

She pushed from the tree and hurried closer to the party, muttering a rapid prayer. And hoping. *Hoping,* as the laughter continued and pulled her with the power of a Pied Piper's tune.

Gwen stopped short at the boathouse's back door, just as that jubilant sound emanated from a beaming Seth Somersby. The groom-to-be shook hands and slapped shoulders with his friend, another Wharnclyffe stable hand, before erupting with that distinct chuckle once more.

The men tossed back swallows of their ale, but they might as well have thrown the cold liquid over her. Gwen dragged in a shaking breath, forcing herself to admit her delusion. She shook her head.

She didn't belong here. That much became clear. These people were happy. They had a reason to celebrate life. She wondered how she'd get through tomorrow.

She turned to walk back to the main house.

"My lady!"

A note of puzzlement tinted Seth's call. In an instant, Gwen found her path blocked by the horseman's strapping height and swarthy features. "My Lady Stafford, you weren't thinking of leaving before you joined us, were you?"

Gwen glanced to the lamplight-strewn earth. "Seth," she tried to explain, "I'm just not—I don't think—"

"No. I'm afraid I can't let you do any nasty *thinking* tonight. Cammy would never forgive me." He turned on a pleading grin. "You don't want to ruin a poor fellow's wedding night before he's even had it, do you?"

She felt a smile twitching her own lips. "That's not fair."

"But effective." Seth curled two confident fists to his hips—another stance borrowed from the employer he idolized.

"Stay for just one dance, Princess. Please?"

For the first time in weeks, the smile at her lips ached with its fullness. The joy in her heart rivaled the sun for glory. She turned to the handsome lad next to her and nodded a beaming yes to his request.

She and Seth entered to hugs and smiles which, in Gwen's opinion, glittered far brighter than any ballroom full of bracelets and tiaras. The simple dresses and unadorned suits of Wharnclyffe's comfortable community formed a more unforgettable tableau than a crowd of starched crinolines and stiff cravats. The simple five-man ensemble filled the room with sweeter melody than a twenty-member orchestra.

But she cherished the sight of the dance floor the most. She'd gladly forfeit waltzing on marble again for the delight of stepping onto this swept wooden expanse encased in its bower of roses, daisies, poppies, and gardenias. Swaths of pink, white, and yellow ribbons finished the romantic decorations.

"It's beautiful," she breathed. Her approval elicited proud grins from the crowd.

A voice at the back of the gathering piped, "Her ladyship is here and her ladyship is pleased. Now let's waltz!"

Exclamations of agreement layered each other. "Aye, a waltz!" "A waltz for Lady Stafford!" "Dance with us, m'lady!"

Gwen didn't argue. With a giggle so carefree the sound bordered on embarrassing, she let the sturdy arm she'd walked in on encircle her waist and whisk her into the familiar steps.

Her friends swirled next to her. A floral bouquet wafted above her. The summer night breeze warmed her. For minutes that she yearned would turn into hours, she forgot every tear she'd shed and prayer she'd whispered in the last weeks. The Gwen of two and a half years ago had returned, only more vivid . . . now, she didn't just reach for life, she grew with it.

The thought served as a vital reminder of her condition. Though she could have danced on, Gwen ordered Seth to let her leave the floor after three waltzes. He consented only after his future bride offered to couple him on the next three. Gwen threw a grateful look to Camille and promised Seth's quick return after he escorted her to a table where Wendy and the other kitchen maids saved a seat.

They'd taken no more than three steps off the floor when their smiles dwindled from their lips. Like the party was a music box and someone slammed the lid shut, the dancers stopped. The music sputtered into taut silence.

Gwen turned and looked up into the fury-filled face of her husband.

Twenty-three

She condemned her suddenly flaming cheeks, her stomach twisting like it hadn't since Aunt Maggie caught her reading *Wuthering Heights* when she was thirteen. Gwen jumped away from Seth, but instantly regretted the action; the assumption written across Taylor's face instantly worsened. His upper lip became a vicious curl. The skin over his jaw tightened to an accusing mask.

"Taylor," she managed to state gracefully. "What a sur—"

"My lord!" Seth stepped forward as he made the excited interjection, blind to Taylor's murderous glare. "This is indeed a surprise, and a very pleasant one. We were told you were unavailed tonight." The horseman extended a hand to his employer. "But I'm honored you fit our celebration in, sir. More honored than you'll—"

Taylor's fist cut into Seth's jaw. Camille's scream sliced the air. The youth's outstretched arm dropped across his falling torso. In speechless shock, Gwen watched Seth land at her feet, eyes already closed in unconsciousness.

"That's what you can do with your 'honor,' Somersby."

She heard her husband snarl the charge; yes, she even recognized the chest-deep resonance of his voice—but now, looking at this beast before her, Gwen remembered her allegation of ten days ago to Wendy, and knew, with an agonizing certainty, her words had been proven fact. This was *not* the man she'd married. This was no longer the man she'd fallen in love with, this mad creature leaning over the senseless youth like a wolf reveling over a shredded lamb.

Gwen struggled to keep standing. He might as well have driven those wolf's fangs into her heart. The wound stretched wider and uglier inside her, becoming too big, too painful—too much.

"For God's sake!" she cried, unable to stitch the injury shut this time. Six weeks of torture had taken their toll. Let the blood and the pain flow. "For God's sake, Taylor, we were only dancing!"

In reply, he only turned the curl of his lip into a slow, mocking smirk. "Mmmhmm," he growled. "And how many more 'numbers' were you planning until you had him 'waltzing' behind the gazebo, m'lady?"

For a moment, undiluted disgust tethered her to the spot. Then she jerked up her skirts, leaving the boathouse—and the amazed stares of their entire staff—in a humiliated rush.

She didn't stop until she stood at the lake's edge again. As she expected, Taylor's boots crunched in the leaves behind her. She whirled on him, still clutching her skirts in order to anchor her fragile composure.

"You are *sick,*" she spat. "Seth is betrothed to *Camille;* that's why we're all here. You'd know that if you forgot the past long enough to see the future!"

With one hard stride, he stepped next to her. He halted so close, she saw the veins of bloodshot exhaustion in his eyes. She felt the rigid tension permeating every inch of his body.

The other side of his mouth inched up now, deriding her. "The ring will go around his finger, sweetheart, not his cock."

Composure be damned. Gwen unlocked her hand and slapped him as hard as she could.

"Don't ever utter anything like that to me again," she whispered. Some deep instinct flattened her hand over her middle, as if protecting the innocence which lay beneath . . . perhaps the only untainted thing left in her life.

The gesture served a second purpose the next moment. Her

fingers pressed down her twist of nausea as Taylor tilted his face back to her, still grinning, still mocking her.

"Well," he sneered. "I see the second Countess Stafford has decided to follow in the footsteps of the first. How very touching."

"There's only eight pence in your pound, Taylor." Gwen stepped back, a black shroud descending over her heart, extinguishing the tiny flame of hope she'd managed to keep alive these last weeks. "Where have you gone, besides mad?" she rasped. "Where?"

He crossed his arms over his chest as the stubbled grimace of his jaw fell into place again. "Perhaps I'll answer if you told me where you and my stable master went Thursday morning."

"Thursday morning?" she stammered. *"What?"*

"Oh, Christ," he growled. "Spare me the confused pout. Do you think I didn't notice, *Countess?* Do you think I didn't see?" He gave a sardonic snort in the direction of the boathouse before he launched into a direct quoting of the youth's words in the front foyer that day: " 'My lady, you're looking radiant this morning.' " Then, glaring at her as he affected a breathy female pitch: " 'Oh, thank you, Seth. Let me expose my peachy bosom for you a little more.' "

"You bastard," she retorted. "You heartless, callous—"

"Ahhh. I see you're becoming quite proficient at the Countess Stafford dramatics, as well."

"I'm *not Constance,* damn you! Damn you! I don't love anyone but you. I've never been with anyone but you!"

"And I don't believe you."

He closed in on her again, stepping with a steady deliberation that, despite Gwen's hardest effort at control, sent a lump sliding visibly down her throat.

"With all respect, my lady," he snarled, "I suggest you get out of my sight."

Gwen swallowed again. But this time her throat burned with the constriction, her mouth filled with a foreign, tart taste.

"My Lord Stafford," she rasped back, never taking her eyes from his, "for the first time in a month, I think you're right."

The words of that last bitter exchange haunted her through the two days of packing her and Daniel up again, over the lonely train miles back to London . . . and through every empty hour of the next four months. The days grew colder, her body swelled bigger, and Gwen's heart mourned deeper and deeper for the husband she seemed to have lost forever. Sometimes when she struggled up from a chair, she pondered which burden she battled more: the babe in her belly or the leaden grief in her chest.

Now, on a grey afternoon in early November, Gwen blew a stray curl from her eyes and glowered across Stafford House's north sitting room at the caller who'd been watching her try to rise for five minutes. "You could help me up instead of standing there with that exasperating leer, Mr. Corstairs."

Bryan unfurled an innocent stare. "You told me you were fine. As a matter of fact, you told me not to take a step closer."

"That was before every trick Granna taught me for sitting up failed." She managed a self-deprecatory laugh as she finally succeeded at her task, albeit with the grace of an upended turtle.

The answering chuckle she expected never came. She turned to confront the troubled scowl beneath Bryan's bunched mustache. "Perhaps this visit should just be an indoor chat," he urged. "Perhaps I should set you right back down here and fetch the tea tray from the garden—"

"And I won't let you back in." She scooped up her cashmere shawl from the tasseled banquette. "I've been waiting for this walk all day. I almost had to pull down the parlor rapiers and duel Granna to get it."

"Still claiming she can do the job of three diplomaed midwives, is she?"

Gwen smiled as her friend secured the wrap around her

shoulders. "She means well. And she *has* been wonderful in instructing me about . . . everything." Her cheeks flared hot in memory of Granna's very detailed lectures of "preparation" for the big day. She shelved the explicit thoughts behind another rueful chuckle as she protested, "But she also thinks a lying in should be a literal *lying in.*"

"Ah, our Granna." Bryan swept the back of his hand to his forehead, turning the words into mirthful melodrama. " 'Yon tiger's heart, wrapped in a woman's hide.' "

Gwen speared him a reproving smile as they stepped out into the cool garden. "Witty but wicked, Mr. Corstairs. You ought to be sent to the corner to meditate your evil thoughts."

"Not I, fair maiden. Send Master Shakespeare. 'Tis he the cur who penned such words."

They walked a few steps down the gravel path before Gwen ventured in a tight murmur, "I only wish the police would find *their* cur." She hooked her hand under Bryan's proffered arm. "Were you successful getting in to Helson this morning? Did he say they had *any* new leads?"

"Yes, and no," Bryan responded to her queries in succession.

She released a disappointed sigh.

"I'm sorry, Gwennie." Her friend pressed his free hand over hers. "But after Lloyd proved his alibis and they were forced to release him, the trail broke off cold. And now that it's been almost six months since the Lancer acted last . . ." Bryan paused to take an uncomfortable inhalation.

"I know," Gwen filled in for him. She squeezed his hand to show she didn't blame the message on the messenger. "Now let me guess the next step. They're thinking about closing the file, hoping the beast has conveniently gone away."

"I'm . . . afraid so. The papers have started to hint the Lancer has gone the way of the Ripper. Some even speculate he *was* the Ripper. Either way, he's apparently gone. Perhaps dead. The press has given up. I think the people will soon follow."

"I think you're probably right." Gwen couldn't hold back another dejected sigh.

At that point, they arrived at the table Colleen had set with tea, scones, and assorted shortbreads. Gwen allowed Bryan to help her sink into a padded lawn chair and waited as he settled into the space opposite. But neither reached for the food or drink. Gwen sucked her lips together, commanding herself to blurt her next question . . . but innately terrified to do so.

Bryan's chuckle broke the silence. To her profound gratitude, he clearly read the question in her eyes already.

"Yes," he finally told her, "I managed to get to Wharnclyffe day before last."

Despite her girth, Gwen tensed and leaned forward. "And?"

"And . . ." a confirming nod, "Taylor let me in this time."

An anticipating gasp escaped her. "How did he look?" she fired. "What did he say? Did you ask him why he won't answer my letters? Why he won't even open them?"

"Whoa, whoa!" Bryan threw up pleading hands. He lowered them to the table, clamping fingers together into a strangely somber wad. Gwen's own knuckles curled around the chair's handles, forcing a stronghold against her heart's threatening flood of desperation.

"Gwennie, he—" The folded hands drew up into a steeple. "He told me he'd throw me out at the first utterance of yours or Constance's names. I complied. I thought you'd want to hear about him, no matter what."

She closed her eyes a long moment before nodding with a painful jerk. "Yes. You did the right thing." *He hadn't even wanted to hear her name. After all these months, the anger still had him blindsided.*

"Tell me about the visit," she managed a moment later. "How is he? How is the house? And Wendy in the kitchen? Camille and Seth, have they set their wedding date yet? What did he look like? Is he all right?"

"He's all right," her friend assured. "And he looked . . . well . . . *tired.*"

She sank back then, not knowing what to feel. Except the unending hopelessness which had turned the last five months into five centuries . . . and the rest of her life into one dark eon.

"So nothing's changed," she murmured. "Nothing at all. The seasons shift and the fashions vary, but he's not coming back like the spring thaw, is he, Bryan?"

"Gwennie . . ." Now Bryan's fingers reached for hers. His touch emulated his gently chastising tone. "Don't do this to yourself. Don't put yourself through this ordeal again."

"He'll keep returning the letters without even touching them," she went on. "And you know what?" With a harsh laugh, she reached into her pocket and produced another distinctive ivory envelope, the Stafford knot lovingly embedded in the sealing wax. "I'll keep writing them. I'll continue being such a *fool.*"

She drew in a ragged sigh. "I'll continue loving that lout so much it hurts."

"Gwen—"

She waved Bryan to silence. She pushed up from the table, motioning her wish to go back inside.

But before they started back up the path, she let the envelope drop from her fingers, forcing herself to watch its solitary slide across the table.

Taylor watched the envelope drop from his fingers and take a solitary slide across the table. He stared at the ivory vellum rectangle for a long moment—longer than he intended to—then caught himself with a muttered curse and diverted his attention back to his toast and bacon.

The letter glinted at the corner of his vision.

"Christ." He tossed a napkin over the carefully penned letters of his name . . . the script so like Gwendolen, steadfast to the point of stubbornness, yet feminine to the point of temptation. Agonizing temptation. God, he did miss her sweet, willing body . . .

He grumbled a more graphic obscenity. Devil take it, he didn't need this. Not when his head still pounded from the near coma he and Bryan had drunk themselves into night before last. Not when the brandy and ale had started to wear off, but the visions of her persisted. Not when Bryan's inebriated but damnably true ramblings still taunted the edges of his memory . . . hell, what was that Bryan kept babbling? One of those old Renaissance poets he fancied so much. . . .

" 'When my love swears that she is made of truth, I do believe her, though I know she lies.' "

"Shut up," he ordered to the remembrance of his friend entertaining the entire tavern as if the long oak bar was the Lyceum stage. "You always knew how to ruin a mate's morning, Bry."

Yet he sealed his own doom with the depressed words. His jab at Bryan didn't allude solely to this dreary November day, and he realized it. He aimed his curses at another dark-grey day, too. A dim morning where rain thundered on an orphanage's old lead roof . . . mist layered a window behind a face that created spring even in the midst of such gloom . . . a face alive with lush green eyes on blushing peach skin, and full rose lips, pursing in that adorable way at him . . .

"What do you want from me? I have nothing to say, nothing to remember . . .

"Did I remember anything? Did I remember it all? I'm so glad you're here, Taylor . . ."

"Stop it," he grated. "Stop it."

"I love you, Taylor. I'm your wife. I love you."

"No—"

"I'm not her, Taylor. I've never been with anyone else but you. I want only you."

"Liar." He slammed his fork against the china plate. "Liar! Damn you!"

He shoved the breakfast array aside in his fury to get at the envelope. He snatched the vellum up, clawed at the seal and yanked forth the contents—eight or nine pages filled with that goddamn beautiful script—and hurled them with a savage sweep of his arm.

The sheets fluttered down in taunting ambles around the path he rose and scorched into the carpet, pacing to rid himself of the weakness he thought long destroyed. Months, he told himself. It had been months. Blissful weeks full of uncomplicated peace. No more torture from any women or their lies . . . correct?

"Go away." He directed the dark mutter at one of the ivory sheets, now crinkled under his boot toe. He glared down at the curled script, his head throbbing, his body pulsing . . . his soul agonizing.

"Don't you understand?" he growled. "Then let me make it clear. Go away. Leave me in peace. Leave—me—alone."

Why didn't she understand? Why did she persist with this madness, when he'd made it clear he wanted no part of the absurd game anymore?

He released a gruff laugh. Yes, *game* was the appropriate term, wasn't it? The boundaries he'd learned so well, knew by heart by the age of ten, when fighting for his lady's honor was still an adventure with a wooden sword against Alistair the "dragon" in the garden. But later, they became the rules he'd depended on as they shoveled dirt into Mum's grave and he'd looked over the expanse of Wharnclyffe—the land and people under *his* earl's direction from then on—and knew true terror for the first time in his fifteen years of existence.

Yes, the rules had been there for him. Honor. Chivalry. Loyalty. The principles he lived by. The dogma he prayed to. The foundation of his life.

Sheer stupidity.

And yet her damnable letters came each week, begging him to come back and live for that lie.

"No, thank you," Taylor snarled to those silent, pleading papers around him. He jerked up from the chair with equal vehemence. "As a matter of fact," he added, "Go to hell, Countess Stafford."

He punctuated the last words by snatching each sheet up from the floor, until he'd collected the letter into a reckless wad in his right fist. With his left, he threw aside the fire screen and stirred the blaze into nice, letter-swallowing flames.

He glanced at the wrinkled sheets one last time. "I like what I'm living for now just fine, sweetheart," he murmured to them. "For once, I'm living for me."

He lowered the pages to the fire.

But something on the letter's final page jerked his attention. A small paragraph, different from Gwen's scrolling letters . . .

Granna's handwriting.

Curiously, he read her words.

His hand stopped. Then began to shake.

"Jesus," he grated. "Dear Jesus God."

I have never called a member of my family a jackass before, but I am doing it now. The shakily scrawled hand berated him for another three sentences before concluding with: *Gwendolen is having your babe in four weeks, Taylor. She could use your help. Get your bloody arse back to London.*

He yanked the letter back. Despite his wild shufflings, Taye couldn't get the pages in order. He ended up with page seven first, page one in the middle and concluding with page three, but he didn't care. No matter what the sequence, he drank in Gwen's words with the same explosion of joy and shock, elation, and mortification. His fury blasted away to meaningless dust.

And as that dust settled, the view of his life cleared for the first time in months. Before him, he realized, stretched the true vista of his future. It wasn't a safe enclosure of brick and mortar. It was a boundless and, yes, terrifying expanse, laid with roads he had yet to travel; full of unknown, possibly dangerous journeys to take. There would be obstacles. There would be pain.

But he wouldn't be alone.

The comprehension hit him like a second blast. *He wouldn't be alone.* Despite the hell he'd put her through, his princess had waited atop the ramparts of the castle for him, loving him so much she grew "with your beautiful child inside me," in her own curling, magnificent words. Taye set his imagination free to the vision of her now, full and ripe with his seed . . . their baby.

Their love.

"Gwen." He said her name for the first time in four months. The word resounded through him like an angel's chorus. "Gwendolen. Sweet Gwen. I've been such a goddamn idiot."

With that confession came the fear. His chest pounded with the sharp beats, every breath an effort to stay the portentous questions railing at him now: *If you've admitted you're a moron, what's to stop Gwen from realizing it? What if she already has? What if that rampart has become just too cold for her to wait on, without a shred of hope to cling to?*

"Wendy!" he bellowed, sprinting across the room. He repeated the call as he swept out the doors and up the stairs, three at a time.

"My lord?" The kitchen maid appeared with a wide gape over towel-wringing hands. "Is—is something wrong?"

He pivoted on the landing. "Only me, Wendy," he answered. "Only me."

The woman's hands halted in midtwist. "My lord?"

"Have Camille bring Seth to me," he yelled from the top. "Quickly!"

"Right away, my lord!" The cry echoed jubilant understanding through the foyer.

He found his valet nowhere in his dressing rooms. Strangely, he thanked God for the incident. Of all delays, propriety ranked as the most worthless today. Taye hauled out an overnight valise he secretly kept beneath the bed, jerked open his closet doors and began yanking shirts, ties, jackets, and trousers. To hell if they didn't coordinate.

"My lord?" Seth's address resonated with more bewilderment than Wendy's greeting. Behind the lad's flushed face, an equally winded Camille stood in the doorway, undoubtedly under orders to report back to the kitchen his lordship's latest turn of insanity.

The comprehension made him cock a stupid smile at both of them. "I never apologized for ruining your engagement party, did I?" He slapped Seth on the shoulder. "Guess I'll have to make it up to you with a bloody brawl of a bachelor party."

"My lord?" Camille said now, jaw dropping.

He moved to embrace the maid. "All right, you can come to the bloody brawl, too." She giggled as he smacked a sound kiss to her cheek. "Pull the phaeton out of the back if you would be so kind, Mr. Somersby," he requested. "I am in need of lightning-speed transportation as of ten minutes ago."

Seth's grin beamed enthusiastic understanding. "Hoping to catch the eleven o'clock train back to London, my lord?"

"Not hoping, lad." He waved Seth out, grabbed the valise and charged into the secondary dressing area.

Taylor stopped just an instant before opening an elaborate cedar box on top of the dresser. In one determined move, he pulled out the sole content inside and slipped it onto his left ring finger again. "Hang on, sweet Gwen," he whispered. "You won't be alone much longer."

Her curls and her eyes and her smile dominated his sights as he turned to shove some last items into the bag.

"My lord?"

He glanced up to Camille, still standing in the doorway with that wary posture about her. Yet as he looked, another giggle tempted the girl's features. "You're packing Mr. Corstair's garment, too." She motioned bashfully at the valise.

Taylor looked the same direction. "Well." He turned over the forest-green Ulster coat in his hand. "So I am. I suppose he left this here the other night."

"Actually . . . *you* did, m'lord."

He raised his brows in response to her expanding smile. "I suppose I borrowed it from him?"

"You were quite concerned about being cold when you and Mr. Corstairs returned from the tavern."

"Oh. I was?"

"Your exact words were: 'It's cold enough to piss icicles out there, Cammy my girl.' "

He looked back to the coat. Then to the maid again. "Then I guess I'd better check the pockets for icicles before I return it to Bryan, eh?"

Camille tittered. Taye held out the coat, wiggling his fingers in the pockets, sending her into throat-deep chuckles.

Then he paused. Along the lining of the inside pocket, his thumb traced over a strange shape. Thin. Light. Smooth. The feeling of luxury, most likely jewelry.

Taylor hunched a scowl of concern while he felt for a possible opening in the lining. He didn't remember Bryan cursing the loss of such a piece, but Bryan had an addiction-size closet full of clothes and accessories. He doubted the mishap had been noticed yet.

Ah, there it was. Taye momentarily grimaced. Devil take it, he could barely slip his pinky through the slit at the bottom of the pocket. And something else had also gotten caught in the opening . . .

He tugged hard, finally freeing a small scrap of material. Taye pulled out a wrinkled swath of dark-red silk. He frowned in puzzlement. The piece looked part of something else . . . perhaps a handkerchief destroyed while helping some comely lady in distress. At least that would be Bryan's story.

He dug back in to try for the jewelry. Still an arduous fit. Only purposeful manipulation or a tumble with quite a wild woman could have maneuvered the piece into the expensive lining. Taylor grinned in anticipation of the interrogation he'd launch at Bryan about his night with the alleged female banshee.

"What is it?" Camille finally subdued her giggles to ask.

"We'll find out," he grunted, "if I can get—my finger back."

With another oath and one more stubborn tug, he jerked free. His finger throbbed. The mysterious object ejected into the air. It hit the carpet with a muffled plop.

Taylor spotted a tiepin glinting atop the dark-blue Wilton. An elegant gold stem ended in a bulb of blood-red extravagance.

A ruby tiepin.

"What is it?" Camille wondered again.

"Don't touch it," Taylor ordered with a ferocity he instantly regretted. For Christ's sake, he raged at himself, a man was allowed to own a red handkerchief and a ruby tiepin without his closest friends jumping to conclusions.

"It's just a tiepin." He compelled gentleness into the words. He even shrugged his shoulders as he passed Camille, adding a casual, "You know, for all those boring men's activities, like bloody brawling bachelor parties."

He picked up the pin by its stem. As he did, the knob protecting the sharp end fell away and rolled off. Taylor peered across the Wilton's short pile for half a minute before giving up rescue efforts. Bryan could replace the part easy en—

His thoughts froze as he twirled the pin over, his gaze locking on the ruby head.

An ornate golden lion roared at him from the middle of the dark-red stone.

Just as Gwen had described in her hypnosis.

Taylor cursed the implication with every foul profanity he remembered, but the golden cat seemed to leap into his mind, overriding him with its roar.

In the midst of that terrifying din, more realizations suddenly joined the assault. Scenes from over the last year bombarded his memory, most vividly from just the other night in the village tavern, when Bryan threw one arm aloft and spouted Renaissance verse with all the "thee"s and "thou"s of—

Shakespeare himself.

Ah, God.

Taylor couldn't find air. The thick cotton of shock clouded his vision and coated his throat. He stared at his fingers on the gold stem of the pin, praying he'd blink and find it all a mistake, that he'd really picked up a sapphire instead. Wanting that roaring lion to become a tiger, an elephant—hell, an anteater—anything but the image embedded in the facets flashing the condemning crimson of hell.

But most of all, he wished he'd never moved his fingers again, sliding his grip up on the pin so the exposed point glistened clearly in his vision . . . the point stained with the brown tinge of aged blood.

The kind of point capable of etching a three-inch scar into perfect peach skin.

Taylor clenched from neck to stomach. Nausea burned his throat and stomach; he swallowed the bile down. He shook with his effort at control, a violent spasm centering in the pit of his gut.

"M'lord?" Camille's query came faint and broken, a strange jumble of syllables between the brutal waves of the spasms. "M'lord, what is it? What's wrong?"

"Seth!" he shouted, not wasting time to answer the maid. He barely saw her stunned expression fly by on his way to the window, shoving open the panels, shattering a pane in his horror-driven frenzy. "Seth! Leave the phaeton! Bring me Simba! Now!"

The youth dashed from the carriage house, steps uneven with incredulity. "The—the Thoroughbred you want me to ready for Ascot?"

"Do it."

Taylor whirled from the window and departed the dressing room in three steps. Behind, he left a gaping Camille next to his half-packed valise. He shoved the tiepin into the lining of his boot. He wanted the filthy thing exactly where he could get at it when he faced Bryan.

He corrected himself. When he faced the Lancer.

Christ and the saints. He'd become best bloody friends with the Lancer. The bastard who'd screwed his wife, then killed her.

He should have seen it. *He should have known.* He recalled Bryan's unbelievable openness and companionship in those grueling months when he'd had no one—when he was most desperate for a friend. Most desperate to trust someone.

He should have seen. But he hadn't. Now that filthy murderer walked, moved and breathed over a hundred miles away, completely welcomed by his home, his world—

His wife.

He slammed out of the house and tore down the drive to the stables. He stalked into the cool building as Seth tightened the last cinch around Simba's sleek girth. Without a word he mounted, focusing his rage on becoming one with the stallion as they raced to beat the train back to London.

Again Seth looked to him with eyes of understanding. "What else do you need?" the youth asked. No "my lord" finished the question this time. The offer came issued on the higher plane of friend to friend, not stable keeper to employer.

He honored Seth in return with his answer. "Keep my home well for me," he said. "And pray. Get down on your knees, Seth, and pray to God I'm not too late."

Twenty-four

She wasn't late, Gwen realized with a sigh of relief, stepping down from the carriage Bryan had sent for her as Big Ben gonged the seven o'clock dinner hour from the opposite side of St. James's Park.

Before she mounted the steps, the townhouse door opened. She smiled in pleasant surprise at the sight of Bryan himself, presenting an unusual but dashing image in a formal black cutaway evening jacket, velvet waistcoat, and velvet-piped pants.

"You look wonderful," he announced in a tone that warmed her despite the windy nip of the night.

"I think those are my words," she returned, casting a sardonic glance down her protruding front. Her simple dark-blue visiting gown peeked from beneath her heavy flannel cloak. "I feel more like the lost whale run aground on your beach for the night."

"And I feel like the lucky sailor who's found the magic mermaid." He wrapped an arm around her waist to help her climb the half dozen brick steps.

Gwen chuckled as they made slow, steady progress. "My goodness. Such poeticism, and not a 'dost not' or 'prithee' in the line. Are you losing your touch, Mr. Corstairs?"

An expression crossed his face she'd only seen once before. Gwen remembered the same odd tilt of his mustache and the knowing aversion of his gaze from the night he'd taken her home after the agonizing day of Danny's disappearance.

The observation both puzzled and comforted her. It seemed that in the midst of her most empty times—especially the last few weeks—Bryan saw a special something in her, a strength even she didn't know she had.

"Perhaps I'm saving the 'prithees' for a more perfect moment," he answered her, with an equal air of mystery.

But Gwen had no chance to ponder the statement. The next moment, he ushered her through the door and into air redolent with a smell that pushed aside everything but warm familiarity.

"Honeyed game hen." She nearly wept the words, breathing deep of the sweet and juicy aroma. But she laughed as she turned once more to her friend, now leaning against the dining-room doorframe with the confidence of a gambler holding a royal flush. "You scoundrel." She waved an accusing finger at Bryan. "You remembered my favorite dish."

He smiled. Her pleasure clearly pleased him. "Now aren't you glad my dinner invitation wouldn't take no for an answer?"

"Yes." She nodded emphatically, and meant it. "Let the gossips talk!" she added, waving a carefree arm in the air. "They couldn't possibly chatter worse about the scandalous Staffords than they already have."

"So I was right?"

She tilted Bryan a reluctant half-smile. "Yes. I give up; you were right; this was just what I needed."

She smiled wider as she looked into the happy summer blue of his gaze. "But not because of the food," she stressed. "Because of the thought behind it. Because of your friendship. Your caring. All your kind words . . ." She hesitated, blinking back more silly tears. "For calling me a mermaid when I look like Moby Dick."

Her imagery made them both crack awkward laughs. "Come on, Moby," Bryan mumbled past another abnormality for him—a bashful flush. "Your plankton awaits."

If just the smell of the dinner made the evening feel like her birthday, the presentation turned Gwen into Victoria at the jubilee. She stood in the doorway for a full minute before

Bryan persuaded her to sit, gaping at the table set with glistening crystal, china, and silver beneath elegant candelabra. Tureen-size vases surrounded the scene, brimming with fresh tulips, roses, chrysanthemums, and even exotic birds of paradise and island hibiscus.

"You're batty!" she laughed at her friend. "I don't deserve all this."

As he lowered to the opposite chair, Bryan leveled that cryptic stare at her again. "You're beginning to sound like your husband," he replied softly. "Convicting you of another woman's guilt. You deserve all this and more, Gwennie."

The remark ushered a blush over her own face. Gwen plunged her gaze to her lap. "Lord, I'm famished." She feigned ease she suddenly couldn't be farther from feeling. "Eating for two, all that sort of tripe."

The hens arrived and her mouth watered, but every bite of the meal lost its flavor to the awareness of Bryan's continued study upon her. He stared steadily, trenchantly, an unnerving departure from the card who usually distracted her with melodrama and outrageous jokes. Nevertheless, she succeeded in keeping her food down, then pretending a satisfied sigh as she looked across the table again.

She blinked at an empty space. No Bryan. Not even Bryan's chair remained behind the barely touched plate.

"Don't you want any more?" His murmur came just inches from her ear.

Her missing heartbeat erupted as an astonished cry. Despite her weight, Gwen started in her chair at Bryan's sudden proximity, a hand's space away. His armchair pressed against hers; his gaze loomed close and piercing, like blue ice chips strewn through her veins.

"Dear God. Bryan, you scared us both to death." She splayed an explaining hand to her stomach, where the little Stafford made a sound kick in agreement. She winced and asked him tightly, "What in the world are you about, sliding around the room like an alley cat?"

He answered with a slow, smooth smile, giving Gwen the impression he hadn't even listened to her. "Eating for two, remember?" he merely said, heaping more spiced beets and a second hen on her plate.

Again, Gwen disguised her anxiety with a laugh from the opposite end of her emotional pool. "No, thank you," she protested as he reached for the julienned carrots. "Really, Bryan. I'm full. I'm bloated. I truly am a whale now."

Before she finished the words, his hand slashed out to cover hers. He seized her fingers with a ferocity that made her gasp, yanking her knuckles against his chest. Through his waistcoat, Gwen felt his heartbeat thrumming like a train piston, pumping hard and fast.

"Stop it!" he charged in that same eerie, low tone. "You're not a whale. Damn it, Gwendolen, you're beautiful." To her further shock, he pressed his lips to her knuckles, then her wrist. "You're so beautiful, it hurts to look at you sometimes."

"Bryan," she managed to stammer—to plea?—her pulse now hammering. The baby didn't help, pummeling a request to learn the waltz early. "Bryan, that's very sweet, but—Bryan, let my hand go. You're holding too tight."

But his grip constricted harder, his gaze cutting sharper. Another laugh erupted with the harshness of a winter wind. As the sound buffeted her, Gwen swallowed the bile of confused fear. He looked like her best friend, spoke the voice of her best friend—but she wondered if those wild Bible stories weren't just ancient Roman fare, and that some runaway demon hadn't moved in to Bryan Corstairs's body.

"Bryan, please." She waged another unsuccessful attempt to pull free. "You're hurting me."

He laughed again. "Yes," he murmured, nodding fervently, "yes, the pain. It hurts, doesn't it? Oh, Gwennie, you *do* understand how I hurt. I always knew you did. I always knew."

He crushed another kiss to her hand, then pulled her palm to his cheek, next to the wide, chilling gaze which beheld her.

So lucid, Gwen thought. How could he appear so lucid, speak so clearly, yet—

"You're so lovely," he proclaimed.

Now raw fear lightninged down her spine. Gwen tried to break free again. Bryan held fast. His lips parted beneath his mustache. He licked those glossy, hungry surfaces. His breath came faster as he leaned closer. "And yet your beauty isn't empty," he whispered. Closer. Closer. "You understand me. You do. My Gwennie, my Gwennie."

He crushed his lips against hers.

With the assault of sharp mustache and desperate tongue, sheer terror replaced her fear.

"Bryan!" Gwen breathed hard as she clawed him back, using the same fingers to backhand his tobaccoed taste away from her lips. The baby emulated her inner turmoil, pounding hard now.

"I don't know what you're thinking," she gasped in pain and panic, "but stop thinking it; stop it now! Things haven't been right between Taylor and me, but he's still my husband and *that* is that! Your—your flirtation is certainly flattering, but—"

His explosion of laughter even stilled the baby. On first instinct, Gwen wanted to join him; here was the boisterous Bryan again, her friend who could cajole the Pope to join a party. But a moment's more observation exposed an angry, almost mocking edge to the outburst.

And he still didn't let her hand free.

"Gwennie," he chuckled, shaking his head, "is that what you think this is? Just a little 'flirtation'?"

She had no answer for him. Instead, Gwen searched his face, waiting for—praying for—the playful quirk of those expressive eyebrows, the distinctive scrunch of that mustache to tell her the game was up, that the time had come to applaud his most amazing performance to date.

Not a breeze of mirth ruffled his features.

Bryan drove another tide of dread through her as he leaned

close again, his gaze unblinking. "Gwendolen Victoria," he stated solemnly, "you are not just a 'flirtation' to me. You are my angel. My life. Gwennie . . ." his voice fell yet lower. "Don't you know I love you?"

The baby didn't just kick then. The hellion flipped a full somersault—learning the maneuver from Gwen's shocked senses.

"Bryan," she stammered, "you can't love me. Not like that. I'm Taylor's wife—"

"Taylor!" His voice detonated as his gaze did, the light-blue ice igniting into pure blue fire. "Taylor, the monster who hasn't spoken to you for half a year?"

"Four months—"

"Shut up! Taylor doesn't know you're alive! He returns all your beautiful letters—he doesn't even acknowledge your existence!" A tortured whimper vibrated past the lips he caressed to her inner wrist. "The most perfect woman this city has ever known, and that bastard squanders you away like a whore. Christ! He could have found what he was looking for by throwing a random dart at the social register!"

Gwen schooled her body to perfect stillness now. She silently implored the baby to do the same. Dear God, it all started to make perfect, horrible sense. Bryan's quirks tonight weren't funny *quirks* at all. They were signs. Signs of a desire long gone unrequited . . . a fury long gone unsatiated. Two passions restrained too long and now ready to snap, rending a man's mind in two.

"You don't mean that," she said slowly—still acutely aware of his unrelenting grip. "Bryan, most of those women are your friends. They're good ladies who care about—"

"Care?" he raged. "You dare say those bitches *care* about anything or anyone but themselves?" He tossed his head back, roaring in angry laughter at his joke.

"Let me show you all the *caring* those people have given me, Countess." He lurched up from his chair, dragging her with him. He pulled her to an oak hutch at the side of the room, and jerked open a drawer. Inside lay piles of yellowed newspaper clippings, English and French and American, dated from six to seven years ago. All the pieces touted the talent of an astounding new stage actor . . .

"Brian Leeds," Gwendolen read from a page, speaking the name in a breath of awe. She fingered a pencil sketch of the handsome young performer in costume for *Hamlet.* "Good Lord, I was only fourteen when I first saw him on stage. I had a mad thing for him, as all my friends did. I cried when he died in that shipwreck . . ."

But the word tapered to a shocked stop in her throat as comprehension blazed through her mind. Gwen snapped a stare at the man next to her.

"Heavenly Father," she gasped. "You're him, aren't you? Bryan, *you're—* "

"The 'most magnificent talent on three continents.' " He quoted the article she held. "And so very pleased to meet you." He dipped a short, sardonic bow.

"But—" She shook her head, trying to put together mismatching puzzle pieces. "But why?"

"Why not?" he countered with a harsh smile. "That's the question I asked myself when dukes and robber barons and even Victoria herself started asking to meet me. Yes, when all the invitations came 'round backstage, with pleas to join their parties and balls and teas." He waved his arm toward the window facing the street. "So I went to their tailors and their jewelers, and I went to their bloody balls. I dressed like them. I even began to talk like them."

"But you weren't them," she said softly. For the first time, for a moment, Gwen didn't fight his grasp. She heard the ache in his voice, and she understood it. She understood all too well. Conventional torture was a merciful alternative to the soul-deep wounds those ballrooms and salons inflicted.

"No," Bryan agreed, "I was *not* them." His grip tightened on her again, harder than before. "They made that quite clear the day I called on Lord Anthony Ashton, hat in hand, declaring my love for his 'exquisite' daughter, Daphne."

A heavy pause ticked by. Gwen finally supplied, "You . . . offered for her hand."

Bryan nodded. "I offered for her hand. And, to my dimwitted surprise, old Tony barely forced out his refusal before making sure I knew which way was out. Thinking back on it, I still wonder how he stomached having a filthy actor soil his Persian carpet for *that* long."

"What about Daphne?" Gwen asked in a pained whisper. "I took riding lessons with her. She was so headstrong, following her own will instead of Lord Ashton's, anyway. Didn't she protest the decision?"

It was *not* the right question to ask. She reached the conclusion when Bryan slammed the drawer shut with a deafening bang.

"Daphne watched dear Papa throw me out without blinking a pretty eyelash. When I looked back at the mansion one last time, she was smiling." His mustache jerked, denoting Bryan's hard lock of teeth once more. "She was glad to be rid of me." He dropped his head, sandy hair falling over his squeezed eyes. In a bare rasp, he finished, "I wanted to kill myself."

Gwen quietly filled in the next chapter of his story. "So you did."

Bryan nodded again. But this time, the movement glided with the slow ease of assured triumph. He lifted his head, smiling once more. "I gave my 'farewell' performance of *Othello* in New York before embarking on the 'voyage' which destroyed Brian Leeds forever. I spent the next year in Cornwall, at the most generous behest of Lady Rothmore, one of my staunchest admirers. With Claudia's help, I created and purchased every last trapping that became the past and present of Bryan Corstairs."

His features darkened then, and he softly clucked his tongue. "Such a shame, though . . . how dear Claudia passed away so suddenly after that year."

"Passed . . . away?" Gwen asked, struggling to excuse her underlines of trepidation to the melodramatic mind of an expectant mother.

Bryan's slow, confident smile did not make her task easy. "Heart failure," he replied. "Or so they say.

"Anyhow, when I arrived back in London, I secured an invitation to Daphne Ashton's engagement party. I followed the guest of honor to the patio when she went to get some air."

His smile grew wider as his voice lilted higher, as if conveying a child's bedtime tale. "I walked right up to her, and told her how beautiful she was. She didn't recognize me from the Prince of Wales. Can you believe that? I suppose my talent was better than anyone imagined."

He chuckled once, very softly, before murmuring, "Daphne made it so blasted easy to kill her."

Gwen felt the color drain from her face and plummet to her toes. An insane urge tempted her to laugh with him. But her lips could only stutter, "That—that's not funny, Bryan."

His casual shrug jarred her composure harder. "You're right, I suppose. Except for the part about how frantically old Tony covered the scandal. I would have dearly liked to see dear Daphne's name slurred all over the front pages. She was a special slut, you know. My first."

"Your . . . your *what?"* Gwen only managed a rasp as volume to the words. She welcomed the pounding thunder of her heartbeat in her ears, the distracting kick of the babe once more—anything to free her mind from the suspicions her logic hinted at now. The shocking, petrifying, *impossible* suspicions . . .

But Bryan gave her such a beaming smile and such a proud nod that even the pain in her belly didn't override the agony in her heart—and she realized what an absurd word *impossible* could be.

"You see, all the records list Emily Roarke as my official first." Bryan expounded as if he discussed nothing more than a successful business venture. "But I wish that wasn't so—"

"Emily Roarke." Gwen repeated the name in a gasp. "But—but she was the first of the Lancer's—"

Then her throat denied her any further air. She choked, drowning in a sea of nausea and disbelief and inundating horror.

"N-n-no!" she cried, shoving at Bryan with all the force her cumbersome form allowed. "No, it can't be, oh God, it can't be!"

"Hush, my heart." His murmur brushed her, soothed her, contradicting his tightening grip. His breath rasped hot and rough at her ear as his hand moved up her arm, to anchor her against him. "Just hush and listen and understand."

"Understand? You filthy, lying—you *murderer!* Oh, God. Oh, *God.* My best friend. I called you my best friend! You're him! You were him all along!"

"But don't you see?" He smiled serenely; Gwen swung away from the sight, certain she'd lose her dinner. "Oh, Gwennie," he chided, "certainly you understand. You can see that's the way it was meant to be. I wandered the streets at night, driven by my hate, vowing not to stop until I'd ridded London of every last bitch like Daphne. And they all made it so easy, cowering like I was some kind of freak, just like their papas told them to. In their parlors or in those alleys, their attitudes were no different. They hated me, and I hated them."

He stroked an iron-hard finger under her chin then, forcing her gaze back to him. With every inch his adoring smile curled up, the bile surged higher in her throat.

"But you, Gwennie," he murmured as if giving new words to a hallowed prayer, "oh, you were so wonderful and different. You looked me straight in the face, even as I towered over you in that alley, ready to take your life. You were so gorgeous, so proud and defiant and brave . . . so unlike the others. I ripped off your dress because I was going to take you with my body instead, and never let go—"

"Don't!" She struggled frantically against him. "Stop it! Please, Bryan!"

"But you fought back and you escaped," he went on, oblivious to her pleas. "And that's when I knew, someday, I had to have you. You would be my own beautiful angel. And now you are."

"No, I'm not!" She clawed at the hands which held her so effortlessly. "I'm Mrs.—Taylor—Stafford. I'm married to Taylor!"

"I said to hell with Taylor."

With each viciously seethed word, his fingers taloned deeper into her shoulders. He dipped his sweating face lower over hers. He stopped when their noses touched and his slick lips nearly slided against hers again.

"But . . . but he's your friend, too." Gwen pushed the imploring whisper past clenched teeth, trying to move her mouth as little as possible.

He raised his face to laugh at her, deeply, mockingly. "Friend?" he snorted. "Taylor Stafford is not my friend, heart. The man was just vulnerable enough and stupid enough to trust me with the secrets of his ridiculous 'quest' for the Lancer. And then when you jumped on his bandwagon of ideals and chivalry . . ." He emitted another derisive chuckle. "Well, as a favorite playwright of mine once penned, 'Here comes a pair of very strange beasts, which in all tongues are called fools.' "

At the final blow of Shakespeare's line, Gwen shut her eyes and gulped against her pain. "An act," she grated. "It was all an act. You were just giving the greatest performance of your life, weren't you? Pretending to be my ally, my friend—"

"When all I wanted to be was your love," he finished instead. He pressed close again, filling her sights, making her ill. "Please Gwennie, you've got to understand. I did it all for you, my heart."

"I'm *not* your heart! I'm not your anything, Bryan. I belong to Taylor!"

"No. No." He smoothed back the errant curls from her face. "Not anymore. You're mine now."

"I am Taylor's. I have given him my heart, my love—"

"No!"

"I am going to have his child!"

"Devil's spawn. I'll kill it, too."

"Bryan, I'm his wife!"

"You are nothing to him!" He dug shaking fingers into her skull, forcing her to look at him now, into his raw and raging stare. "You are everything to me!"

The first devastating spasm coincided with his last shout. Gwen's mouth fell open as she finally found a power strong enough to help escape his hold: pain. Sharp and sudden. Straight through her abdomen.

She pushed away and stumbled back, feeling as though she rode a spear to her chair, where she dropped, struggling for breath. The moment she plummeted to the cushion, warm, sticky fluid drenched her petticoats and thighs.

"Oh," she gasped in stunned comprehension. "Oh, no. Bryan, my water's broken. I'm going to have this baby—soon. Tonight!"

To her wide-eyed horror, the announcement only spurred another loud, delirious laugh. "Good! Perfectly excellent, my heart! We'll be rid of the wretched little beast that much quicker. Then I'll work on making you forget Taylor Stafford and the blight he's been on your life, forever!"

He paced the carpet in front of her while continuing an excited, mumbling monologue of his plans, whooshing past the candles so his shadow gyrated a frenzied dance on the brocade wallpaper. By sheer force of will, Gwen lurched forward and stopped him by coiling her hand into the velvet trim of his coat.

"Listen to me, Bryan—*please.* I've got to get to a doctor, now!"

"No." He waved distractedly, as if she were no more than a street waif begging him for candy. "No, that won't do. You're mine now. Nobody else must know that. Especially a hospital full of people, staring and asking questions . . ."

"Bryan, for God's sake!" But Gwen's hand slipped as she fell back with another contraction. "The baby's early! It could die!"

"Splendid." Not a pause of hesitation preceded the answer.

"By the good Lord," she panted, blinking back frightened tears. "You're serious!"

He only paced faster. The candle flames bobbed higher. His shadow danced wilder.

On pure, desperate instinct, Gwen bolted to the window and flung it open.

"Help!" her scream sliced the serene night on Saint James's Square. "Dear God, somebody help! He's going to kill my—"

A gush of air replaced the next word. Bryan hooked an elbow around her neck and hauled her back inside. The room whirled as he flung her against the wall. But before Gwen reestablished her equilibrium, an enraged roar filled her ears. Bryan's sweating, red-eyed face filled her vision.

"Don't you *ever* try anything like that again." His growl trembled as violently as his fist against the wall . . . as his other hand wrapped around her throat. "You will ask me whenever you so much as step out to the necessary!"

Again the pain came to Gwen's aid at the perfect instant. As another contraction ripped through her, she rechanneled the agonizing force, shoving him off her, then plunging to the table for support.

But not for long. She heard Bryan curse, then scramble for her again. *Dear God Dear God* she prayed, scrambling around the dinner array, hoping to use at least the barrier of the dishes and candles as a weapon.

Weapon. The word collided in her mind with the sight of the crystal and china before her. She curled a hand around a Waterford goblet and didn't wait to hurl it at the head of the monster stalking her.

Bryan bellowed in pain. "Jesus! You bitch! Get over here! You will mind me, damn you!"

Gwen threw a plate and backed farther away. This time,

Bryan dodged the assault, erupting like a malevolent hurricane—directionless, uncaring of the havoc he left behind.

He hurled his chair aside and kicked hers over. The spirits cart went crashing the same direction, bottles of brandy, wine, and cognac shattering across the floor. He grabbed the flowers from their vase and snapped them in half, stomping over their fragile petals.

"Get over here!" Again a seething command.

Despite her body's overwhelming entreaty to crumple up into a ball and ride the contraction on incessant screams, Gwen raised the other goblet she'd taken with her. "I—belong—with—Taylor."

"You belong with me!"

"I won't ever belong with a murderer."

"I love you!"

"I hate you!"

Bryan's lips curled back on a raging, guttural outcry—just before he swept his body across the table, dragging everything atop the linen cloth with him. The flawless array tumbled into a chaos on the floor.

Including all eight tapers in the candelabra.

Twenty-five

Before Gwen could gasp in terror, the candles ignited the tassels on the drapes. In another half-minute, flames devoured all three layers of velvet, gossamer, and marquisette covering the windows. The room flared to demonic orange life. Oxygen and heat hissed toward the ceiling, torching the painted deer and elk prancing on the frieze—and illuminating the contorted features of the man bearing down on her.

"Now come here." The words curled from Bryan's mouth as black smoke twisted on the air behind him, a monster's gnarl blinded to all but possession and lust.

"Bryan." Gwen slid against the wall, groping away from him and the flames, not sure which terrified her more. "Bryan, stop this insanity. We have to get out of here!"

"We're not going anywhere, heart."

She didn't doubt he meant it. She looked into his eyes, but no longer saw even the remnants of a man in the glazed white-blue surfaces. Bryan had gone, lost to a madness where fire didn't consume the wall behind him, where reality didn't exist and life didn't matter, including his own.

The only reality he knew was her.

The conclusion brought everything but comfort. For in that same moment of revelation, another realization seized her:

She'd only save her baby by stepping into that existence with him.

Gwendolen pressed her lips together, summoning every ounce of courage from every corner of her soul. Even then she only managed a small step forward, but she lifted her chin and formed her mouth to the words of a clear, if not convincing, declaration. "All right, Bryan. I'll stay with you. I'll be with you."

For a moment, his features blanked, utterly unreadable. Then he released a disbelieving laugh. "You—you will?"

She forced her head to jerk a nod as the flames consumed both sides of the window. *Dear God, didn't anyone outside see what was happening?*

"Oh, Gwennie." He rushed to her, eyes alight and arms outstretched. "You've made me more happy than you'll ever know."

What am I going to do? He's coming closer, and if he grabs me again he'll never let go and—God, the pain! The baby—my baby—will die!

Her eyes swept the room, praying to God for inspiration as she feigned girlish shyness at Bryan's advance. Yet at every turn, it seemed she only made it in time to watch the fire destroy her possible weapons. With every second, the searing storm crackled closer to the double doors which opened to the main hall—and freedom.

She backed further, against the kitchen door. The flames roared higher, the heat creeping along the walls toward her. Her eyes widened. If not for the destructive force of the blaze, she'd call the sight mesmerizing. Even as a shudder possessed her, those yellow-orange fingers seemed to crook at her, as if beckoning to her.

And for a strange, insane moment, Gwen heeded that call.

Her gaze followed the flames' patterns along the walls and floors until they pointed exactly where their appetite desired to feast next. She nearly cried out in elation when she received their message, swiftly figuring their destination.

The inferno feasted on the overturned spirits cart, favoring the pools of Bryan's favorite brandy. The potent liquor trickled over the cart's side, becoming estuary to a dark river across the carpet.

The river Bryan stood directly over now.

No spare moment lent itself for the luxury of decision. As the fire licked across the floor, up the brandy river, Gwen stepped forward to Bryan and succumbed to his ravenous kiss.

She almost gagged on his thrusting tongue before his confused growl broke them apart. Moving by raw instinct, she shoved away, then pushed back through the swinging kitchen door.

"Aagghh!" she heard Bryan bellow. "You bitch! You *bitch!*"

"Heavenly Father," she rasped. She whirled and darted a frantic glance around the kitchen. In wrenching dismay, she remembered Bryan bade the cook retire after the meal was prepared; every utensil was either hung neatly or stored properly.

Including the butcher knives.

She dashed to the first bank of drawers bordering the room. Gwen tore them open two at a time, finding silverware and cookie cutters and dish towels—but not a knife beyond a butter spreader.

She shrieked as the kitchen door slammed in.

Bryan stood in the portal, breathing like a dragon bearing down on a sacrificial virgin. Soot marred the waistcoat over his heaving chest. Sweat poured down his face.

Fire climbed up his right leg.

Gwen didn't know which struck her harder—the shock or the next contraction. "Oh, my God." She clutched her abdomen. "Oh, my God. Bryan, do something! You're on fi—"

"Shut up! You dare try to whimper an apology now, you silly slut? You're just like the rest. I'll make you pay. I swear to God, I'll make you pay."

His words came twisted by the pain certainly searing up his side. But then, Gwen realized, he probably couldn't delineate the pain in his body from the pain in his soul anymore.

"Bryan," she pleaded. "I'm sorry. I never meant— I'm so sorry."

"No. It's too late. Too late for your sobs and your sorries!"

Her horrified wail echoed in her ears as he shuffled closer, raising burning claws of hands—aimed at her throat. His eyes reflected the flames leaping off his jacket, the irises now pure, haunting iridescence, locked unblinking on her.

But her cry trickled to a choke when his own lips twisted up in a sad grin, like a porcelain Harlequin clown, just before he lunged one more leaden step at her—

Then plummeted to the floor in a burst of sparks and stench.

Gwen watched him for an eternal, horrified moment. Then she crumpled next to him in a moaning sob, sent there by the impact of her next contraction and the sight of the fire swallowing the kitchen—as well as whatever remained of the being she'd called friend.

She dragged the back of a hand across her face, attempting to clear her vision. The soot on her hands only worsened the stinging haze. Another contraction stabbed her—so close; they were coming so close now—forcing her to lie back on the surprisingly cool floor of the townhouse's back hall. She rode out the wave of pain with the short, harsh breaths Granna had taught her.

And immediately afterward, she screamed. She screamed with the pain and the fear, the sorrow and the shock, the desperation and the anticipation . . .

But most of all, she screamed for a miracle.

She screamed for Taylor.

Nothing, Taylor swore, nothing in his thirty-one years had prepared him for the raw terror slamming through his chest now. No fear came close to the dread which began in his own front hall, when he'd barged into his home bellowing for Gwen—only to be told she had finally accepted Mr. Corstairs's "kind invitation to dinner . . ."

Dinner. She was having dinner, *tonight,* with Bryan.

Bloody Christ.

He pressed the bay stallion beneath him into a more furious

gallop down Piccadilly. Gwen would be safely home dining with him, his mind condemned his soul—if he'd listened. If he hadn't let his petty, *stupid* arrogance get in the way, assigning the whole world responsibility for licking the Earl of Stafford's wounds. If he'd acted like a *true* earl; if he'd recognized *nobleman* as only the fancy way of saying *humble man.*

But it was too late for regrets. Taye only hoped it wasn't too late for Gwen to forgive him.

Yet as he and the bay careened onto Ermyn Street, still a block from Bryan's townhouse, billows of black smoke and snarling orange light scorched that hope into sickening horror. Taye knew, with unnerving but unmistakable surety, the flames licked at the address he'd once considered a second home.

"No." The word fell out a disbelieving mumble. Then like a heat bubble coming to boil, *"No!"*

He didn't have to kick the horse. The bay acted as if one with him, racing faster, hoofbeats clacking the staccato rhythm of his repeated prayer: *Please let her be alive, please let her be alive, please let her be alive.*

They bounded onto Saint James's Place, directly into a crowd gawking at the drama of the fire. As startled shrieks and curses erupted, Taylor searched the common. He combed the crowded walkways, trying to see past the shifting light and smoky shadows. He shouted her name, desperately envisioning her mussed curls and love-filled face emerging from the sea of curious gapes peering at him now.

She didn't appear.

"Sweet God." He had to transfer his worst fears to truth now. He jerked his sights to the blazing building.

As he watched, the blaze blackened the last few feet of a side wall and licked its way to the roof.

Sweet God. Sweet God. Gwen.

He didn't remember sliding from the saddle or sprinting across the lawn. He hardly recalled the hands lashing him back or the voices shouting him away. Taylor wrenched off the first and ignored the latter. A man's face appeared in his path; he dispelled the jabbering nuisance with one punch and kept striding toward the inferno.

As he bounded up the townhome's steps, he jerked off his coat. Taye wrapped the garment over his head. He twisted his shoulder into the suffocating heat, bracing to smash back the door.

An unignorable hand jerked him back. As Taylor found himself thrown back against the handrail, an enraged bellow blended with the fire's roar. "God blast you, Stafford! What the bloody hell do you think you're doing?"

He spun to square off against Helson, nose to nose, the detective's face as crimson as the sky above them. "For a while, I thought you'd recognized the disrespectful ass you were and stopped trying to do *my* job," the policeman snarled, "but it seems—"

"But it seems, you bastard, I *did* do your job."

Disrespectful? Oh, yes. But did he give a damn by now? The answer didn't matter. All that mattered was time—and what he'd lost of it.

Taylor took the most direct route to recover the seconds. He leaned down to the tiepin still firmly embedded in his boot. An angry jerk pulled the gleaming piece loose; he slammed the ruby head into Helson's palm.

"Merry Christmas," he sneered. "As you'll recall, this was one of the Lancer's tools of choice. We can prove that now, if you haven't let the corroborating witness already die in there."

He took the policeman's stunned stare as ample permission to kick in the door and dive into the dense black smoke.

"Gwen!" he bellowed, instantly fighting his soot-stung eyes and heat-filled lungs. "Gwendolen, I'm here! Answer me!"

Only heat thrummed and sparks popped in answer. Dread curled through his blood just as grey vapors snaked through the air. Taylor tamped down the useless emotion, schooling himself once again to the steeled, focused state of mind he'd lived with in those first months of hunting the Lancer.

Think, think. Think, Stafford, think.

She'd come for dinner. That would have placed her and Bryan in the dining room—at the back of the house, to the left from the wedge where the case clock still surprisingly ticked beneath its blackened hull and broken glass.

He stalked that direction. His feet sloshed on the carpet, now drenched by the firemen's effort. By the time he breached the gap which once held the Pompeiian-style doors to the dining room, he breathed hard from running doorway to doorway. He didn't know how else to disperse the growing terror at the sight of each scorched room.

He assessed the blackened remnants of the dining room. Fire or no, the overturned table and splay of the chairs told of a struggle. If there had been, he thought with sudden and racing hope, maybe Gwen had escaped. Maybe she'd resisted Bryan, overpowered him somehow—

And maybe she hadn't.

"Damn." He drove his boot into the burned table. "God *damn!*"

He hurled a charcoaled vase into the blistered wall before whirling fire made it impossible to stand still. Mindlessly, he shoved through the door to the kitchen.

Taylor strode through the burnt shell of a room, ramming charred drawers shut, clenching back the urge to tear the ruined cabinet doors off their hinges and hurl them against the wall.

"Gwendolen!" He threw back his head in shaking agony. "No way, Gwendolen! You're not letting me off this easy! I have some things to say to you. You're going to let me grovel them properly at your feet if it's the last thing I do! Do you hear me? Gwendolen!"

He hurled both fists to the air, his soul cursing—and praying—to whatever powers listened in this night's deathly, smoky sky. "Answer me, damn you!"

He circled the dank grey room again, pacing; stalking harder and harder so he wouldn't hear the ominous reply of burning timbers if he stopped.

"No," he growled, booting the pantry door. *"No."* A tight

punch to the cutting board. *"No."* Another kick, sending a tattered chair flying. *"No-no-no-no!"*

The anguish came rapidly, uncontrollably, a physical explosion so violent, Taylor wondered why he wasn't writhing on the floor while looking up at his guts splayed out on the ceiling, dripping his drained lifeblood. But he continued to yell, if only in punctuation of the blows he dealt to everything in that room, over and over, pouring out his hate . . . pouring out his love.

He didn't heed the scream when it first came. *Only your imagination,* his mind counseled. *Only your brain beginning to go insane. Welcome it. Welcome it.*

But the second scream used his name. "Taylor! Taylor, here! I'm in the back hall!"

He stopped punching. He lifted his head. Slowly. Tentatively. "Gwen?"

"Taylor!" she shrieked. *"Come now!"*

He sprinted across the kitchen and yanked back the door to the servants' hall.

He nearly tripped over a charred lump in his path. Taye kicked the black heap, rolling it over—

And identified the half-melted face of Bryan Corstairs.

"Taylor!"

He leapt over Bryan; raced down the hall. Only now he had a problem. The first ten feet beyond the door had been doused of flames, but farther down the passage, flames still curled and collided with each other. The sparse hallway had been abandoned in favor of efforts to save the opulent front and upper rooms.

From the other side of the blaze, Gwendolen screamed again.

At the same moment, Helson caught up to Taylor. The policeman's face belied the same grim quandary knotting Taye's gut.

"Donovan! Whitterbury!" the inspector commanded back

toward the kitchen, "We've got a woman trapped down this back hall! This blaze has to be put out. Now!"

"Now is too late," Taylor snapped.

He didn't stop to allow Helson's contradiction again. In a swift arc, he swung his coat around his head once more. He took one more deep breath and shouted, "I'm on my way, Princess!"

Instant heat engulfed him, consuming and intense. Taylor ignored the searing pressure, concentrating on his feet, aiming one boot in front of the other through the fiery tunnel. Through the layers of camel hair coat and roaring fire, he heard Gwen's cry again. He doubled his pace. She sounded hurt . . .

And if she was, he swore, he'd contract the most expensive Gypsy in the country, séance Bryan back from hell, and kill the bastard all over again.

"Taylor!"

"I'm here!" he told her on his triumphant burst into the small back room.

Then for a long instant, he could say no more. Christ, she was more lovely than he'd remembered. Lying there on the small maid's bed, the swell of their child straining against her sweat-sopped dress, the sight of her exploded his world at the same time she fitted everything back into place.

She emitted a shaky version of that achingly familiar half-sob, half-laugh. "Oh, God, you really *are* here! I prayed and prayed; for so long, Taylor, I prayed you'd come— Oh— *ohhhh!"*

Only the strength borne of pure fear propelled him to her side. In strange and helpless horror, he watched as she writhed into the mattress, features contorting in pain, fists gripping the coverlet until the material nearly ripped.

"What is it?" he heard himself grate. He saw his hand attempt awkward touches at her shoulder, her damp cheek, as if she were a glass figurine he'd shatter if he squeezed too hard. "Ah, God. What did he do to you, Princess? What did Bryan do to you?"

"Bryan!" Her echo rasped with the lilt of remembrance. "Bryan. He's—he's the Lancer—"

"I know."

"He's dead!"

"We know." Assured she really wouldn't break, he stroked the wet curls off her face and gently kneaded her shoulders, unsure what else to do or say.

Her approving smile sent ecstasy to his toes. "Taylor," she whispered, in pure and joyful welcome. He smiled back and leaned over to kiss her.

She shrieked in his face instead.

"What is it?" he demanded. "For God's sake, Gwen, what's happening?"

Surprisingly, she laughed then. "Your babe." She guided his hand to her stomach. "Your babe is coming, Taylor."

"What?" He jerked back, unnerved that she laughed again. "You—you're—*now?*"

"Soon."

His heart crashed against his ribs. "No!" He needed more time. He'd only found out about the babe this morning. He was going to be a father again . . . Jesus, this took getting used to. He needed more time!

But like a fool, he'd squandered that time.

Gwen smiled as she lay back again. "This child is a Stafford," she said. "He's not taking no for an answer."

Taye gaped at her for a second more. How she could lie there so calm and serene while the world burned down around them seized him in nothing short of amazement.

Then he realized why.

She trusted him. Even after bearing the disgusting brunt of his misplaced fury—after he damn near raped her, labeled her an adultress, banished her from his sight and ignored her existence for half a year—she trusted him with not only herself, but the new life they'd soon bring into the world.

The gift went far beyond the forgiveness he barely expected. It stunned him. Humbled him.

It drove him into action.

"Helson!" Taye shouted, bounding for the door. To his relief, the flames only met him with half their intensity. The fire crew worked swiftly.

Yet that only solved a portion of his challenge. When he eyed Helson's platypus nose through the smoke, he waved and bellowed again. "I need a medical stretcher and a ready coach!" he commanded. "And a midwife!"

"A *what?*"

But Gwen's next contraction canceled the chance to explain. Taye fell back to her side, letting her crunch agonized fingers around his again. With a grimace, he watched her neck strain and her jaw clench, longing to take any of her pain into his own gut.

Two more contractions crashed, then ebbed. Taye glared at the doorway, now sweating as profusely as his wife. Ah, God, his lovely, burgeoning, *agonized* wife . . .

Where the hell was that stretcher?

Helson and the fire crew broke through as another contraction died away. "It's about bloody time," Taylor snapped, though not recognizing his voice, pitched beyond normal with fear and concern. "Is the coach waiting?" Helson nodded curtly. "Good. Advise the driver we're bound for Wilton Crescent—as fast as his horses can be lathered."

But a half hour later, those horses strained at bits that weren't about to go anywhere. Taylor paced the cobblestones of Ermyn Street, his steps taking turns with every agitated curse he knew. In front of the coach lay a wall of two smashed wagons and a crunched dray. The conveyances' inebriated drivers slid on spilled milk, fruit, and newspapers while slinging slurred arguments about who caused the fiasco.

Yet *that* accident showed more promise of clearing than the fire wagon which trundled up behind them fifteen minutes ago, and promptly snapped an axle.

They were trapped.

And Gwendolen screamed out to him, louder than before.

Taylor raced back to the coach. He climbed in to the sight of his wife now lying prone on the seat, head thrown back, gritting in agony. He fell to the carriage floor next to her, grabbing her hand. "It'll just be a while longer, princess," he soothed. The words sounded stupid, inept, useless.

"I'm . . . afraid . . . not," Gwen panted.

Despite the sweat pouring down his face, a chill gripped him from head to toe. "What do you mean?" Taye slowly asked.

His wife beamed that astounding smile again. But only for a moment. "I mean your baby wants to see his father, my lord. *Now.*"

"Wh-what?" he blurted.

"He's coming now, Taylor—and I'm going to need your help."

"My help? No—Gwen—"

"Yes!"

He fell back on his heels. Taylor felt her relentless hold on his hand, heard the raw torture in her voice, but the sensations seemed unreal, a concept his mind couldn't—or wouldn't—comprehend.

This was *not* how things were supposed to happen.

Yet as quickly as he formed the judgment, he shook his head in shame of it. What was he so terrified of? He'd helped at least a dozen champion Thoroughbreds make their way into the world. He'd watched a hundred more Wharnclyffe lambs, puppies, and kittens birthed on fields, in barns—even the kitchen floor.

None of them were Gwen. None of them were his beautiful wife in such wrenching agony. None of them were his own seed and blood, so precious, so dependent on him for their new life.

So dependent on him.

"I can't!" he growled, twisting away. "Damn it, I can't be responsible—"

"You *are* responsible!" Gwen yelled, writhing with another contraction. She lifted her legs now, pulling him back.

"If I fail—Gwen, if I fail you again—"

"You won't!" She shook her head against the cushion. "And you never have. You've—you've given me—the greatest triumph of all."

"All this pain?" he countered sardonically.

She shook her head again. "Your love," she panted with a laugh.

Taylor shifted closer of his own volition now. Crouching there with her, awash in the light of her eyes and the love in her smile, he didn't feel like the Earl of Stafford anymore. He felt like the bloody King of Spain.

"And I do love you," he told her.

"Then help me bring your love to life!"

At that, he set to work. With quick, deft movements, Taylor removed her underdrawers and pushed her skirts to her waist. Amazingly, he found himself flashing her a flirtatious smile. "Your body is the most lovely thing I've seen in months, m'lady."

Another contraction cut off her answering laugh. Taylor gripped her thighs, helping her ride the spasm, coaxing her to breathe while he gently opened her to him. Like the gathering breakers of a storm, another contraction crashed nearly on top of the first. Now Gwen's scream cut off at its crescendo, her face contorting in silent, unspeakable pain.

"Stay with me, Gwen," he prodded. "We can't do this without each other, remember?"

"Bloody hell," came the exhausted retort.

"You're beautiful." He meant every murmured syllable as he positioned himself between her legs, now impatient to see every wondrous detail of this new life they'd created.

"And you're insane." She plummeted back against the seat. "I'm so hot, Taylor. I must look so wretched. I *feel* so wretched."

"You look incredible."

He bellowed the words extra loud over her next scream. He watched, spellbound, as the gap between her thighs widened even further. "Yes," he shouted. "Keep it up, love!"

"Taylor—" Gwen's chest pumped hard and fast. Her legs trembled against his hands. "Taylor, I can't take it any longer."

"Yes you can." He seconded the command with his constricting grip. "Just a little bit more, princess. You can feel it, can't you? You're almost there." He squeezed her thighs harder. "And you're so bloody beautiful."

"Bloody, maybe," she snapped. "Ohhh— Oh God, noooo!"

"Almost . . . there," he encouraged.

"I can't!"

"You can!"

"Damn you to hell!"

He laughed—less at her spitfire's language than at the exquisite vision before his eyes. He reached down and touched the top of the little crimson head in shaking wonder.

"Ah, God. Gwen . . ." His mouth worked, but no word in the three languages he knew formed adequate description for this moment, these feelings, this miracle. "Gwen. Our child . . ."

"He's here?" An unbelieving sob. "Taylor, really?"

"The head." He stared at the flawless ears, nose, mouth, and eyes that slid smoothly into his hand. "I've got the head. I need just one more push, sweet. Come on! One—more—push!"

Her long, agonized cry drowned his last word, undulating in time to the convulsions of every muscle she possessed. Her thighs trembled against his hands; her fists beat at the squabs.

Her body gave up the tiny, red-streaked form of their perfect baby girl.

"She's breathtaking." Taylor gaped at the unbelievable beauty cradled in his hands.

Gwen struggled up on her elbows with a wan smile. "She?"

"Well, at least you got that part right," came a wonderfully familiar bark from the opening doorway.

For once, Taye welcomed Granna's fierce frown down to the deepest recesses of his heart. And for once, he gladly relinquished control of a situation into her fussing hands.

"Thank the good Lord I decided to tutor your wife about these proceedings," she growled while taking his daughter from him. She delivered a firm, wail-inducing slap to the lass's posterior. "I see my advice served her well, in light of your more than conspicuous absence for the last four months, my lord."

"Granna," Gwen chided in a weary murmur.

Taylor pressed silencing fingers to her lips. "I deserve it." He gazed into the depths of her eyes. The green softness there reminded him of new life now more than ever. "As a matter of fact, I deserve much more."

"Taylor, stop it. You were just—"

"A total ass."

She only joined her smile to his in answer. Taye leaned and brushed her lips with his, closing his eyes as he savored the feel of her again, the all-woman scent of her again . . . the life-giving sensation of loving her as he always had, wholly and completely and forever.

"Thank you for never giving up on me," he finally whispered against her mouth.

He felt her smile again. "I'm a Stafford now," she explained matter-of-factly. "I won't take no for an answer."

He chuckled and shook his head. Then, leaning up to take in all of her radiant features once more, "What do you say we take our daughter home now, Countess Stafford?"

She emulated his amazed expression. "A little girl," Gwen said in wonder. "That hellion kicked me every night like a champion boxer in the making."

"She's a Stafford," he countered—then laughed as she chorused with him, "won't take no for an answer!"

Epilogue

The big oak bed creaked this Christmas Day as Taylor cinched the knot on her blindfold one last time. Gwen began to giggle, but the sensuous press of his lips on hers turned the sound into a needing moan. She leaned back against the headboard, knowing his form so well she didn't need her sight. She pulled him down with her, molding his body to hers.

"Mmmm," she sighed when they dragged apart minutes later. "Whatever new game you have up your sleeve, my Lord Stafford, you'd better show me now. The children will be awake soon."

"Yes." She sensed him nodding reluctantly. "They will, won't they?"

She let loose the rest of her giggle. "So show me this new version of blindman's buff . . ." By the time she finished the sentence, her tone became an anticipating purr. But Taylor's sharp departure from her arms and off the bed induced a scowl of confusion.

At his incessant tug on her hand, she frowned deeper. "Up," he ordered. "We have to go downstairs to play."

Gwen didn't budge. "Taylor!" she protested, shocked at the maidenly blush she felt on her cheeks. "The children—"

"Can play, too, if they want."

Now she detected the edge of sarcasm in his tone. She smiled. "What are you up to?" She wagged her free index finger.

She imagined all kinds of warrior's expressions to go along

with his measured sigh. The effect was very stimulating, trying to guess which darkly irresistible expression he wore.

"The question, my Lady Stafford, is not what *I'm* up to," he growled . . . and suddenly, she realized he took well advantage of her blind-folded condition, shifting close and sweeping her up into his arms. She shrieked but he didn't seem to listen. She kicked but he didn't seem to care.

"Now, now," he chided her, kneeing open their bedroom door, then striding out into the cool morning air of Stafford House's north hall, "we don't want to wake the children, remember?"

"I think that's exactly your plan, you rat." But she laughed more than stated the words, accepting her fate as Taylor carried her down the main stairs.

As they progressed across the foyer, Gwen found herself thankful for her temporary lack of vision. Because of it, she had the chance to notice with her inner sight many little and precious things about their home this special morning: the majestic scent of the pine boughs they'd brought back from Wharnclyffe to deck Stafford House's halls, the distinctive tastes of apple cider and hot cocoa lingering on the air from last night's festivities . . . and the warmth and strength of this man who held her, playfully humming *God Rest Ye Merry Gentlemen* into her ear.

When Taylor stopped and set her down, she went willingly, a little excitedly. She felt a girl of six again in her bare feet and her lace-collared nightgown, awaiting Santa and the magic he brought with the dawn.

Taylor slowly removed her blindfold.

Her excited heartbeat stopped and her smile lowered into a puzzled frown.

They stood in the downstairs hall, in front of the door to the room dominated by Constance's portrait. The room she'd walked into that fateful morning, so many months ago, and discovered Taylor kneeling in prayer, confessing how he'd—

She shook her head, cutting off the memory. "What are

we—" She looked up at him, unveiling the full force of her hurt. "This isn't funny."

"No, it's not," Taylor concurred. He stepped to her and cupped her shoulders, dipping his mouth to hers in a tender caress. "I'm never joking when I say I love you," he whispered.

She pressed her lips together at the sincere words, nodding her trust. She signaled him to open the door.

With a dazzling smile, he did.

With speechless wonder, she gasped.

Not an inch of dark walls or haunting portraits remained. Instead, the blinding white of the snow outside bordered the room. She gazed at the breathtaking view through gleaming glass panels, their tops joining in a soaring atrium over their heads. The canvases of the gallery now came as artfully swirled plots of redolent earth, freshly "painted" with every flower she could imagine. Crimson roses blended with milky lilies. Fiery birds of paradise brushed demure African violets. A corner had been set aside for wild daisies, mums, and larkspur. A miniature hothouse bloomed with tulips and orchids.

"Oh," she breathed. "Oh, *Taylor.*"

She stepped forward, brushing petals with her fingertips, inhaling the heady mixture of soil and blooms with greedy delight. She kept blinking, certain that each time she did, this unbelievable Eden would be gone and they'd be standing there staring at each other in their fig leaves.

Instead, her husband walked toward her, looking tousled, rakish, and magnificent in his silk robe and seldom-used bed pants. He reached and lifted the tips of her fingers in his.

"It's a symbol of the new start you've given me," he told her. "And how serious I am about thanking you for it."

Gwen glanced down. "But Constance—"

"Will hold a place in my memory for the gift she gave me in Danny. I've had her portrait rehung in a place of honor over the Sapphire Bedroom." His fingers traveled beneath her chin, where he tilted her gaze up to see his soft smile. "But my life is yours now, Gwen. And my heart . . ."

He finished *that* sentence by kissing her again, wetly and thoroughly.

"Merry Christmas," he finally murmured against her mouth. "Now the Lady Stafford can play in the garden any time of year she wishes."

She pulled back and gave him a misty smile. "As long as the Lord Stafford can come play, too."

"Well . . ." he slipped his grip to her bottom, growling seductively into her ear, "as long as he can come . . ."

"I love you, Taylor," she sighed as he nuzzled her neck.

"And I love you."

"And I love you, too!" Danny's dark head and toothless grin nudged them apart; he squeezed them each by a leg as Taylor mussed his hair. All three of them looked up as Veronica Racine Stafford's lusty cry for her breakfast joined the family repartee.

And they laughed, holding each other tight as the first rays of a new dawn sparkled down through the glass dome.

Dear Friends,

Hello once more from California! And first of all, please accept my deepest thanks for all your kind words about my first novel for Pinnacle Books, *Trade Winds.* Wow, I never knew there were so many people in this universe who shared my love of the Caribbean . . . but what a wonderful surprise to discover such a fact! Thank you!

I do so hope you've liked Gwendolen and Taylor's story equally well. I thank you for trusting me enough to "make the jump" all the way from the 18th century Caribbean to the gilded world of Victorian London. I have to admit that on a personal level, the leap was rather easy. This period, this city and especially the Victorian people themselves are endlessly fascinating to me. Just think: barely hidden beneath those waistcoats, cravats, bustles and corsets laid incredibly sensual, loving and passionate natures. The contrast was too exciting to ignore!

Atop this germ of an idea, I received my conflict from a surprisingly modern source: a news story I saw about a woman who had been assaulted in much the same way Gwendolen was, but who couldn't get anyone to believe her story. She had, as they are fond of saying, "asked for it." After seething about that for a good hour or two, I knew, in my own small way, I'd right the wrong by naming my character Gwen and healing her with the love of a man like Taylor Stafford.

Love heals all. It's a decidedly different theme than the concept behind my *Trade Winds* crazies, but I felt it just as profoundly, and hope you did, as well. And while we now leave

Gwen, Taylor and the kids to enjoy their holiday celebrations, I have some great news for you: I'm not done with Victorian England yet—and I'm *very* excited about it!

As a matter of fact, my next book for Pinnacle goes beyond the "special" category for me. Writers have a saying about some books being "books of the heart." Well, *Redemption* is a book of my *soul,* something proven vividly every wrenching and precious moment I spent writing it. I still don't know where this story came from, or how it happened, only that writing it was a gift; a treasure I shall cherish for quite a long time.

Denise has kindly allowed me to give you a peek . . . so I hope you like what you see, and will return for the rest of the story in January 1977! Until then, please *do* keep in touch:

P.O. Box 10059, #338
Newport Beach, CA 92658

Best Always!
Anne Cartier

One

Marcus found her. At last, after a bloody hour of pacing the catwalks and searching the chaos of sets, costumes, curtains, animals and humanity below, he found her.

Now that he had, he didn't let her out of his sight. She joined the mayhem by way of the green room door, flanked by two other actresses who shared her confident look—the result of a successful preliminary rehearsal. Marcus didn't blink as he watched their bustled and beflounced forms trek across Drury Lane's stage. He didn't blink—and he didn't breathe.

He felt the heat surge through his senses, centering behind his temples—as he expected it would, as he hoped it wouldn't. Slow yet intense, the fire momentarily scorched away his vision, heralding the need and pain wracking him. As if he needed a reminder.

The resulting glow in his eyes would give him away like a lightning flare if she tilted her gaze an inch toward him, but Marcus didn't care. He stood there, as paralyzed as he'd been last night and the two months of nights before that, and watched her. And watched her.

And he remembered why he'd given up on this insanity called feeling three hundred years ago.

Loneliness was hell.

People weren't supposed to feel lonely with a hundred other people around. Gabriela Rozina ordered her mind to accept that fact as she stopped at the center of Drury's stage, directly in the midst of preparations for the show's first all-cast rehearsal.

Yet as scenery whizzed by, stagehands shouted, the ballet girls giggled and Act Two's flock of lambs bleated away to await their cue, an uncontrollable, irrational emptiness surrounded her . . . an aloneness so complete, she might as well have stood on that wooden plane in solitary blackness.

Circling to face the rows of unoccupied seats—the "house," as management neatly classified it—didn't ease her ache. And that, Gaby commiserated, tied her most confusing knot. For the last two months, this sight hadn't given her insides even a quiver, where once a glimpse of Drury's magnificence set off butterflies of joyous anticipation.

Yes, for two strange, sad months . . . ever since that crucial afternoon when she'd gone to Buckingham Palace. She'd stood in the rain with a hundred other actors and actresses, sharing their silent pleas for the arrival of the notices signed by Victoria's own hand. . . .

The queen answered their supplications. At four o'clock that day, the word became official: the Prince's Grand Theatre Troupe would be transformed from ambition to reality within a year. The finest works of English theatre would be rehearsed, then taken to every corner of the globe welcoming them—performed only by a meticulously-selected company gleaned from the finest stages throughout the British Isles.

Imagine it, Gabriela had gasped along with the hopeful faces around her. A royally-sanctioned company, cheered by crowded houses across the globe. . . .

It wasn't just the opportunity of a lifetime.

It was the chance to call the whole world *family.*

It was the fulfillment of Gabriela's dreams. The end to her emptiness. And more.

Her heartbeat thrummed double tempo as she simply thought about the Prince's Troupe again. But hastily, Gaby ordered the rhythm under control. She could *not* fall into the trap of deluding herself. Shattered expectations were no longer her specialty. Yet she'd never aimed her hopes at such a spectacular goal . . . could she earn the rank as one of Her Majesty's "meticulously-selected" few? She didn't have all the experience. She didn't have all the credits.

But she had all the passion. And she had every ounce of the precious dream—in her soul, where it mattered.

Somehow, Augustus Harris had seen that. Yes, *the* Augustus Harris, London's youngest and most innovative producer . . . so, at nineteen years old, she'd landed here, beneath the gas lights of London's most famous theatre, rehearsing the first part "Augustus Druriolanus" himself cast her to.

There were times—many times—when Gabriela still couldn't believe her blessing. As Augustus's new discovery, she'd catapulted from "nothing" to "promising" inside of three months. *She* still felt the same, but a few daring journalists even began their raves in this week's papers, extolling Augustus's "fresh and exciting flower in the dying London theatre garden."

So why, at now of all times, did she feel like a sapped daisy, ready to be pressed and forgotten in a book? Why did this gawky loneliness return each night to shred the crumb of confidence in her soul?

Even at the age of seven, when only a chipped chapel bench comprised her stage and a dozen other orphans her audience, the anticipation of performing had stirred music through her blood. Each "show" orchestrated her heart in a chorus of fulfillment. She'd ached with the need to pour out her soul before a crowd, then accept it back brimming with their laughter, tears and applause. Could there be any sweeter ecstasy on earth, any greater way to quell the emptiness which had yawned so deep and black since the day a five year-old Gabriela had dropped tear-soaked daisies atop the fresh graves of her parents?

Just like the emptiness clinging to her soul now.

She tried to concentrate on warming up. While humming a

series of vocal exercises, Gabriela read through her script again, taking note of pages with the underlines denoting her dialogue or prompts.

In truth, she labored unnecessarily. She'd memorized the scenes weeks ago. Augustus had, of course, reserved the female leads of the next three productions for the French diva gracing Drury with an extended visit, but the parts he assigned Gabriela were a far cry from chorus girl. From the first rehearsal on, Gaby vowed to prove herself worthy of the honor.

Now she fervently prayed she could satisfy that commitment.

"Ready for first cue?" a throaty voice asked at her shoulder.

Gabriela turned to meet the confident smile curling Donna's lush lips. Her roommate's name stood proxy for the actress's full stage title—"Donna, as in *Prima* Donna," she constantly reminded the tabloid writers—and Gabriela didn't think she knew a person who filled the flamboyant requirements of the persona more.

"I'll never be ready," Gaby tried to banter back, her nerves racing faster as Act One's ballroom backdrop unfurled from the flys over the stage.

"Oh, dove," her friend drawled, "none of us is ever ready. But, Luuud," Donna amended, her leaping eyebrows directing Gaby's sights to a figure approaching down the right aisle, "at least you've got *that* on your side."

A bevy of squeals from the ballet coincided with Donna's appreciation of the top-hatted, leather-gloved blade striding closer on his patent leather boots. Yet unlike her swooning castmates, Gabriela's tension climbed with every step those boots took. The sight of Alfonso Renard transformed her empty stomach into an acidic churn of dread.

Why, she lamented, tonight of all nights, did the man have to appear at a rehearsal he had nothing to do with? Why did he have to dissolve what poise she *had* garnered by forcing her to battle his lascivious paws? For being, in his own words, one of the city's "most up-and-coming producers," the lecher had an astounding amount of free time to take advantage of Augustus's hospitality—and actresses.

"Oh, he's good," Donna crooned, eyeing Renard's "bashful" wave at the dancers. "Modest, but manly. Sort of . . . Lancelot crossed with a bit o' the Black Irish."

Gabriela said nothing during another round of giggles and sighs. "Black, you said?" she finally snorted. *"There's* an apt description of his heart at last."

She emphasized the sentiment by jerking her script open and burying her face so far between the pages, the text blurred. If the ballet wanted the viper's attention, let them have it.

Her heart sagged when she heard Renard stride right by the dancers. Her spirit plummeted to her toes when the rustle of his coat ceased at the edge of the stage . . . directly in front of her.

"Miss Rozina?" came that distinct, slick-as-oil voice. "Don't tell me you weren't even going to say hello."

Was it her imagination, or did Renard's line act like a prompt for silence throughout the building? When she heard the ballet captain's gossipy whispers even from across stage, Gaby knew the infuriating answer to that.

Slowly, she lowered the script and forced herself to meet the black, rapacious stare waiting at the stage's edge. "Good evening, Mr. Renard." She managed the reply only by locking her back teeth.

A mock scowl fell across Renard's sharp features. "Come, come. It's just Alfonso, remember?"

She gripped her script tighter, certain her knuckles had turned as white as the paper. "Alfonso."

His satisfied grin replaced the frown. The ballet loosed another collective sigh. Gabriela struggled to take a decent breath of air. It wasn't easy, especially when he reached beneath his overcoat to produce an eye-popping bouquet of red tulips and roses.

Then even the blasted lambs fell into silence.

"I've brought you a gift," her visitor murmured into the expectant pause.

Gabriela released a long, heavy breath. The man's smirk didn't falter.

"Mr. Renard—"

"Alfonso."

"Stop it!" He hadn't crossed the line of her patience. He'd demolished it. Finally willing to brave the titters from the orchestra, Gaby stomped down the stage's temporary steps and hissed, "I have made it perfectly clear that I will not accept your gifts!"

Renard only responded with a perfectly remorseless shrug. "Oh, little Gaby. I apologized for the pearls, did I not?"

"After I threw them in your face."

The man had the grace to color. "That's water in another tide. Now, these blooms . . . think nothing of them but what they mean—"

"Another lure into your bed?"

He chuckled. "You're witty today, dear. They are but a tiny reminder of my admiration. A fleeting token of my wishes—"

"I don't want them."

"For your good luck."

Gabriela's snag of breath preceded everyone else's by just seconds. *Devil take him.* He'd done it now, and his impeccable, cocky grin showed it. To wish a performer "good luck" anywhere near the theatre, let alone three steps from the bloody stage, boded certain failure to the performer.

To undo the damage, for the entire cast's sake, she'd have to take his wretched flowers. And the knowing kiss he trailed on the back of her hand when she reached for them. And the possessive, almost brutal rake of his eyes over her body as she turned the blooms over to a stage boy.

"There, now." He leaned and whispered it into her ear as the final dagger in the ordeal. "That wasn't so bad, was it?"

Gabriela willed herself to breathe, though it meant suffering Renard's opulent cologne. For only then did she gain the strength to reply in a voice dripping with acid-laced honey: "If you must know, sir, it was as pleasant as letting a maggot kiss me. And if you dare try such an underhanded stunt on me again, I promise I'll dispense of your roses, and their thorns, in an area much further south of your pretty face."

She only made one mistake with the proclamation: firing the words so near him. Alfonso coiled a furious hand around her arm before Gaby could step away. But even if the man ripped her arm out of its socket, she willed her gaze to remain steady, her posture proud.

"You used to welcome my face," he finally growled.

"And you used to be a kind and considerate friend."

"Friend?" He spat and laughed the word at once. His endlessly black glare bore into her, teeming with the force of his acrimony. "You little fool, Gabriela. Don't you know me yet? I have no need for *friends*. I'm not a milksop who wastes my money or manners on enterprises that won't pay me well in the end. That's why I'm going to be bigger than your precious Augustus some day. I'll produce the biggest plays London has known, with the biggest ticket take, as well."

"That's splendid." Though her throat quivered with the effort, the retort flowed with a cool disdain even Victoria would applaud. "I do, however, apologize that I won't be in London to see this conquest."

Gaby should have expected his answering tremor of fury. And the bruise he twisted tighter into her arm. Nevertheless, she notched her chin yet higher, clenching back the outcry clawing in her throat.

Then, strangely, Renard laughed—a low, mocking snort. "The lady won't be here," he repeated. "I see. So we're still entertaining our pipe dream of stardom with the Prince's Grand Theatre Troupe, are we?"

It was the one slur she couldn't deflect with a shield of composure. The one barb able to penetrate her soul and deflate it into a mass of raw vulnerability. "What do you know of dreams?" Gaby rasped. "What do you know of beliefs or hope?"

Renard laughed again. The sound ripped Gabriela deeper than any audition dismissal she'd ever been dealt.

"I only know that most dreams don't come true," he sneered. "So why you pine away to join that company, royally sanctioned or not, is beyond me."

"And it is beyond me why every performer, producer and stagehand in town is *not* vying to win a place with the Prince's Troupe." Gaby couldn't help it. Her limbs gave up their battle against Renard as her mind's eye succumbed to the glorious vision . . . the adventures and images she'd dreamed so many times, she often wondered if she'd been born with them.

"Don't you see?" she implored then. "Don't you realize the feat they plan to accomplish? Only the finest English works will be showcased, from Shakespeare and Marlowe to opera and musicals. And the entire world will be waiting . . . the entire world will remember the performers who take these works to them. It's a chance to inspire thousands, perhaps millions across the globe."

"But you can be an inspiration right where you are."

Renard's soft protest blew into her ear again. "You inspire *me,*" he continued in a coarse murmur. "Can't you think of it, dear Gaby, even now? My brilliant scripts and staging, complimenting your hot-blooded Italian delivery—"

"My hot *what?*" She shoved from him with a stiff lurch. Something akin to nausea quirked her stomach. "Wh-what does my blood have to do with anything?"

The man actually tossed another chuckle at her. "You little vixen," Renard teased. "As if you didn't know. Gabriela, you'll seduce all of England on my stage . . . all that Italian passion, inspired by the private lessons you'll receive in my arms. We'll be unstoppable together. Just think of it!"

But Gabriela thought of nothing but the bile roaring up her throat, the wild need to find a hot bath and scorch away the shame his words encrusted over her. She yearned to flush back the outrage and hate she thought she'd tucked away into one rarely-visited cubicle of memory. . . .

Aye, that's right; her seventh birthday tomorrow, Parson Reeves. That will make two years she's been here at the orphanage with us. Such a delightful child. What's that? Oh aye, you be right again, that does make it harder to discourage her dreams. And she always dresses so pretty when the families come, looking to adopt. But it's that tainted blood of hers, Parson. It's so . . . obvious. That thick Italian hair. Those eerie Italian eyes. The girl can see straight to my soul with those eyes. I'm certain of it. It's too bad. Just too bad.

Gabriela gained her freedom from Renard's talons with one desperate, despising shove. Then she ran. She ran from the loneliness and the fear, and she didn't stop.

❁ ❁ ❁